THE
HARMONY
PARASITE

THE HARMONY PARASITE

GREGORY D. LITTLE

Cursed Dragon Ship
PUBLISHING

To Mom. For all the obvious reasons, of course, all the things for which I can never thank you enough. But also because when I watched the Rankin/Bass animated adaptation of The Hobbit and asked if there really was more to the story the way Gandalf said, you said, "well, actually," reached for your battered old copies of The Lord of the Rings, and read them to me.

CHAPTER 1

THE BAR of ice-cold stone jabbing into the small of her back stimulated Giana Novak's awareness enough to awaken her. She opened heavy eyelids and exhaled a breath it felt like she'd been holding forever. It emerged as a puff of warm fog, the perfect illustration of her second sensation: the air around her was as freezer cold as the stone. She lay in some kind of tunnel of ice and stone, and even that was hard to make out in the fitful glow of LEDs that flickered off as much as on.

As she rose on limbs that ached and shook at the same time, her eyes adjusted to the dim light enough to see the awful truth around her. She was not *technically* alone in this tunnel, but every other person with her was dead.

Memory flooded back. Giana stepping through the Bridge portal, flush with triumph at her successful flight from her dying Host. They had done their task well, her kind, rotting the ageless creature from the inside out. The universe would be spared any more of its stultifying influence. And though their mandate had not included surviving the Host's death, surely doing more good was better than doing less?

1

In an everchanging universe, stability equaled death. But her kind were the death of stability, and Giana would be their herald.

The bodies sprawled around her were not of her doing. She remembered stepping through that portal onto an arcing span of light. Then there had been a savage, wrenching pull, and she'd retained consciousness only long enough to witness herself become a thing of faceted light, one surrounded by several others, all hurtling through the darkness together, leaving many others behind and passing those already on the Bridge ahead of them.

Deeper darkness had descended, and she had woken here.

She performed a quick count. Four bodies. And she thought it had been four others dragged along that span with her. Apparently she had been the only survivor. Surely this was not how Bridge travel was supposed to function? From what she knew, Earth had built the Bridges to serve as means to colonize worlds. A colony with 80 percent fatality rates before even arriving did not seem viable.

The bodies had begun to hypermutate. It was a peculiar kind of motion that one could easily mistake for renewed life if they didn't know any better. Although all appeared human, Giana counted three Coldgardener natives and one revenant. It was possible to tell the difference by the form the hypermutations took. Each creature was frantically trying to revert to its true form, so the revenant corpses produced a mishmash of human-looking bones and organs, while the natives had bone spear-legs erupting and milky white eyes sprouting everywhere.

None of her kind. Her kind didn't suffer hypermutation. Her kind *were* hypermutation.

She reached out subconsciously, searching for more like her within her range of sensing, which itself was as vast as a world. That meant she should have been able to sense more. But there was nothing. A void of emptiness she hadn't known since being that other Giana, and that version of herself hadn't known how alone she'd been.

The cold began to bite into her more sharply. She needed to find some kind of shelter. It would not do to make it so far only to die from hypothermia. Perhaps that was what had happened to these four.

The lights. She could follow the lights. They would lead her somewhere. She was in some sort of cave system, and since the floor had a very distinct slope, heading up seemed a better idea than heading down. She took heart as the lights in the tunnel brightened, grew steadier. That was how it seemed at first. But the whooshing noise, a rush of churned air, clued her in that something else was going on. The light was getting brighter, but directionally.

Behind her.

She whirled on protesting limbs, staring down the descending tunnel in time to see a tiny shape flit around the nearest bend. Backlit against the rising glow, it looked like a broad, black arrowhead with feathered edges, but far from being rigid. It bent and twisted as it moved, as though it could push off the air itself to stay aloft.

Some instinct made Giana freeze as the tunnel abruptly filled with the swirling creatures, and behind them, growing ever closer, rose the light, beautiful and terrible all at once. The feathered arrowheads swarmed around the bodies, blanketing them in churning motion that eclipsed even their twitches of hypermutation. With the help of the light shining ever brighter, she could see that the churning shapes did not hover in the air, as she'd thought. Each sprouted from the end of a filament so fine, it would have been invisible if not for the light it reflected.

As though each of the creatures was a single leaf at the end of an infinitely attenuated vine.

But, interesting as the exact method of their movement might be, Giana was far more concerned about the cluster of creatures that detached from the rest and approached her. They swirled all around her as she tried to hold perfectly still, hoping that it was the motion of the hypermutation which attracted them and that if she could just remain motionless enough . . .

A quartet of the things settled in front of her face, twisting and looping—not to hold their position in the air, as she'd thought, but for reasons unknown—as they hovered like the points of a trapezoid. Their gyrating shapes were like independently moving eyes staring into her, staring through her, and for the first time since she'd made her final transformation, Giana Novak felt something like real fear.

Beyond the twisting leaves, the light grew and grew, setting the cadence for her mounting dread until, suddenly, it peaked and began to recede. The swarm of creatures fled as the radiance did, dragged back along their retreating filaments, flooding back down the tunnel. The four observing Giana were the last to go, and from them she felt an unsettling reluctance to leave.

It took several moments of shocked stillness for her to realize that the swarm had taken the bodies with them. In truth, Giana had no idea how long she'd been standing there in an empty tunnel, dumbfounded. On Coldgarden, she had been the master of all circumstances, a holder of all knowledge. Here, she knew nothing. She *was* nothing.

That had to change.

"I beg your pardon, miss," a voice said behind her. "But are you quite all right?" Giana whirled again, fists clenched at her sides, ready to revert to her true form, stunned she hadn't already done so. The voice was accented, German or something similar, according to her badly fragmented knowledge of human history and culture. The man, though, was like no one and nothing she'd ever encountered.

By her estimation, he stood well over two meters tall, and though he was wrapped in clothing which looked very warm, he seemed oddly proportioned to her, too thin and long of limb. But what stood out most were the places where there should have been skin but wasn't. He wore no gloves because his hands were fleshless metallic frames. In place of eyes, he had two synthetic lenses that pivoted like eyes would but glinted too large in the flickering lights. And the top of his bald head was completely covered—or perhaps replaced—with what looked like some kind of metal and plastic plating protecting electronics.

For what was presumably the first actual human being Giana had ever met, he certainly wasn't what she'd expected.

"Ma'am? Can you hear me?" That politeness, that deference. Even with so much of him replaced, his still-human mouth spoke with a kind of reverence. One directed at Giana.

Best not to ruin the one advantage she might have.

"I heard you," she said. Keeping her voice authoritative was some effort, but she managed. That was good, because she certainly couldn't overawe him with her knowledge. He hadn't mentioned the light or the creatures at all. Either he'd arrived too late—perhaps they'd been leaving because of him—or he knew what they were and was not interested in them. Giana found the latter very hard to believe, but this was not her world. Best to keep things simple for now. "I wonder if you could point me to the nearest shelter. I seem to have taken a wrong turn."

Both those lenses of his flicked downward as one, then back up. It seemed very much like a blink reflex, as though her answer had surprised him. *Good. Keep him on his back foot.*

"I'm looking for someone down here," she said. "Several some-ones. Perhaps you can help me find them."

"I confess, I don't think I've ever been more surprised than I was when I turned the corner and saw you standing there," he said. "I don't believe I've ever seen an Equatorian down this deep into Shady-side. But finding missing people is what I do. If your loved ones are missing down here, I won't rest until I've found them."

Giana smiled.

CHAPTER 2

THE BAR STOOD in the most extreme outskirt of Sunnyside, just east of the solar fields under a Stone Dome that had either partially collapsed long ago or only ever been partially intact. *Last Call,* the dive was named, and Squad Lieutenant Ansley Reid had to give the owner credit for the layering of jokes there.

"Quite the view," Sergeant Hastings said as she emerged from a tunnel to the habitat, and though she said the same thing every time they wound up here, she was not wrong.

The textured, curving stone above ended abruptly, terminating in a jagged edge. Working to transform the outcropping back into a proper dome, one capable of holding an atmosphere, Anaranjadan authorities had closed off the space with latticework of composite glass and gleaming struts. This formed a massive bay window of sorts, through which the baleful orange light of their planet's star eternally poured in. Not direct light, of course—the rocky landscape beyond saw to that. And what light did make it through was still partially obscured by the ever-present dust in the air.

But even indirect light was enough to heat a space to lethal levels on this world. Transparent though the window appeared in the visible spectrum, it was doing plenty of work to cut down on both heat and radiation, otherwise the space the window enclosed would be literally unbearable.

Other Stone Dome areas, such as those a bit closer to the population center, had carefully maintained forcefields as a backup to the enclosing stone walls and ceiling that doubled as projections of an ideal blue sky. But the further toward the edge of colonial civilization one went, the cheaper the solutions tended to be. That the solar fields beyond Last Call were critical to maintaining the colony seemed to matter not at all. More to the point, the people who worked them didn't seem to mind the neglect they received from the population centers in return.

This was, Ansley reflected, one of the joys of Harmony.

Despite the remoteness from, well, *anywhere* of note, Last Call was one of the few places in the colony where a person could get a view of the real Anaranjado, specifically the surface world where humans couldn't survive unprotected. So, even beyond the workers who frequented it, he'd never seen the bar anything but busy. If Ansley were being blackmailed into setting up a bar at the ass-end of nowhere, he supposed there would be worse locations to work with.

The building itself was old—probably original colonial prefab—and natural shelter or not, it looked one errant breath from falling away to dust indistinguishable from that coating every surface of the rocky desert crevice the dome enclosed. Once upon a time, such an obvious shithole—unusual view or not—would have sent Ansley calling for his family security detail to be doubled on the spot. But five months into his six-month detail with the Anaranjadan Colonial Militia had softened his stance toward shitholes, provided they served potent enough alcohol.

"Don't suppose you're considering calling duty hours early, sir?" Sergeant Hastings loaded the question with the same gusto she used to slot a power pack into her sidearm. She gave him an equally loaded look.

"I can probably be convinced, Sergeant." Ansley's answering grin was lopsided and, he knew, about one centimeter from being the open invitation she was so keen on.

Regulations or no regulations, his squad-sergeant wasn't shy. In this case, she just wanted a few drinks, but she'd been putting the full-court press on getting into his jumpsuit since the moment he'd been assigned the leadership role in the squad. And when he'd confronted her about it, she hadn't bothered trying to hide it.

And he *was* enjoying the chase. He hadn't given her what she was after, not yet. Caving too quickly would be no fun, after all. But he made it plenty clear he encouraged her pursuit, implying heavily that eventually he would let himself get caught.

Only one month to go in his detail now. She must be getting pretty desperate. He enjoyed that thought as he eyed her, playing out his consideration of shirking duty for booze. Giving in was what he wanted to do, sure. Hastings probably saw it as a double win, if not triple. Clock out early, get wasted, and get off.

Of course, he had no idea what percentage organic she was. The only people on the colony of Anaranjado who even approached baseline human—a few fanatic luddites squirreled away in outskirt Stone Dome settlements aside—were the wealthiest of the wealthy, those who could afford to fully climate control their self-contained environments.

For everyone else, there was cybernetic enhancement, up to and including full-on organ and limb replacement. Honestly, the sky was the limit, legally speaking, except for tampering with the brain.

It meant that every person he met out here in the "real" world was a bespoke combination of flesh and machine, and you could never tell just how much something like alcohol would affect them. Not to mention how it could affect other things. Ansley was not picky and had taken lovers of all sorts, but he did prefer it when women were natural where it counted most.

Which might have factored into Hastings's sudden eagerness to knock back a few with him. Get him drunker than she could be and the chase might end considerably earlier. And he might be convinced. She was smart and funny and not bad to look at, even with the dehydration-resistant scales in place of her skin. Quite a bit taller than him, too, which he liked. Of course, that went for nearly everyone who wasn't baseline. Tall and slender made for a higher surface area to volume ratio, better heat dissipation.

To hell with it. He'd never been afraid to toss the dice and see where the evening led him. And it wasn't as though they were knocking off *that* early.

"All right," Ansley said, pitching his voice to be heard by the entire unit. "I think we've patrolled enough for one day. Squad, you are officially off-duty."

Whoops and cheers from most of them. All but Hastings. Her eyes flashed with undisguised eagerness. He loved how up-front she was. Her brain probably wouldn't even let her consider being otherwise.

God bless Harmony.

"I'm buying the first round," Hastings said, her grin widening as if she could read his thoughts, but only the parts she'd want to hear.

"Who am I to argue?" Technically, his first priority ought to be to report into Command. Portable comms units struggled this far out, but that hadn't really been the reason he'd failed to check in. And as it had been two standard weeks since his last comms connection with HQ, a full week longer than was required by regs, he doubted that excuse would fly anyway. Someone there—someone very high-ranking who shared his last name, almost certainly—was bound to be getting antsy by now.

But Ansley Reid really hated checking in. It always made him feel like he was back on his nursemaid's metaphorical apron strings, a woman who was terrified that a single screw-up would see her banished to just this kind of outskirt settlement. Which seemed a silly thing to worry about when his parents could barely be bothered to acknowledge his existence. As the only building here, the bar would have a comm unit of its own. He could always link up with it after he sobered up. Maybe by now there would be some update on all those rumors of a communication from one of the other human colonies.

Fuck it. He was this long overdue on checking in. What was a little bit longer? Maybe he'd have had a little fun with Hastings by the time he bit the bullet.

Ansley and Hastings brought up the rear of the loose knot of Anaranjadan Colonial Militia making their way toward the bar's inviting shade. Ansley only hoped the owner had taken his strong hint from their previous visit to bring the climate control up to a tolerable standard. *I'd be nice to only be sweltering for a change.* Even in his protective uniform, Ansley felt constantly on the verge of heatstroke this far from the Meridian Cities. It was almost enough to make him want to trade in his normal skin for an upgrade.

Almost.

He was openly admiring Hastings's swaying hips without fear of being called out on it when something odd happened. He caught a flash of light in his peripheral vision, a momentary brilliance so overwhelming to his eyes, even at the edge, that it almost seemed to make a noise. He caught a sudden, acrid whiff of ozone on a puff of breeze from the normally stagnant air.

The light faded as Ansley, and the rest of his squad, turned to see what had happened.

That was when they saw it. Within the deepest part of the rock wall's shadow, a dark mass had appeared, one Ansley was quite certain hadn't been there a moment before. It was so bathed in gloom cast by the blinding glare through the bay window, he couldn't begin to guess at a color beyond *dark*.

But he forgot all about such mundane questions when the shape moved, undulating in a way that resembled a creature shaking itself as though dazed. Though that seemed like hopeless anthropomorphizing, since Ansley could see no proper head on that body, elongated but fat, like an overfed leech.

It writhed drunkenly out into the light as though every tiny movement was agony, and he could finally say it was a very dark green studded with what looked like two rows of eyes alternating milky white and obsidian black. Then it opened a mouth at its near end and disgorged a torrent of green, steaming fluid onto the rocks around itself. Like it was sick and had to vomit.

Ansley had only those two brief movements to process that the thing was *alive* when it unsheathed six limbs of articulated bone with scythe-blade tips. It twitched its mouth-end in their direction, seemingly noticing them for the first time. Ansley couldn't take his eyes off the thing, which was bad because a series of identical flashes took place nearby the creature. After another, stronger breeze carried that stink over the squad and he'd blinked the afterimages from his vision, now the single creature had been joined by four more identical ones.

"Hostiles! Hostiles! Hostiles!" Sergeant Hastings screamed, falling immediately back into her role, barking formation orders. Ansley should have been calling out those orders, but he could only bring himself to stare. They were alive, some kind of animal.

No animals lived on Anaranjado.

He kept thinking this, locked in a loop of denial as the monstrosities moved as one, scuttling toward them with horrifying speed, their great, toothless mouths lolling open as if in anticipation.

Then the entire squad was screaming.

CHAPTER 3

THE HEAT HIT Stefani like a full-armed slap as she collapsed, shaking, from the great corridor of nothingness onto hard, hot, dusty ground. Only now did she recall what had happened to bring her to this point. Somewhere in between stepping onto the Bridge span in dying Coldgarden and being deposited wherever this was, awareness of her circumstances had been driven from her mind.

The reintegration of those memories, recent though they were, was the second slap.

Ella. In a panic, Stefani unslung the carrier she only just remembered she was wearing. Ella stared back at her, curiously silent despite all the disruption. But her eyes were bright and clear beneath her tangle of apricot hair, and at meeting Stefani's gaze, she smiled tentatively.

The flush growing in her cheeks was tentative, too, but it seemed to be spreading. Whether this was heat or illness, Stefani couldn't say.

I've got to find Giana. She promised to take care of Ella's illness. It had been a punch to the gut, Giana's revelation that Ella had been infected by Gene Sequencing, infected by whatever thinking disease

Giana herself represented. A punch to the gut that Stefani had not allowed herself to feel properly before this moment.

"Mama," Ella said in a whisper, as though she knew something Stefani did not. The thought sent a chill through Stefani despite the sweltering air. Holding Ella tightly and protectively, Stefani finally stood and took in her surroundings properly.

She had stepped out—or materialized or whatever she'd done—in a narrow space between what appeared to be the walls of two buildings. One foot was planted squarely on a set of paving squares of various sizes, which haphazardly petered out into the orange, sandy stone her other foot stood upon. The alley, if that was the proper term for it, terminated at a smoothly curving wall of that same stone at about ten meters further on. She could see no source for the oppressive heat. The entire space, as near as she could tell, was enclosed in stone, and the domed ceiling was set with some kind of lights that looked to mimic sunlight but didn't project heat themselves.

The heat was the product of the air itself. It was like being in a furnace.

Marri. Karl. But scan the same tight space three times though she might, none of those who had stepped onto the Bridge span with her were anywhere in sight now.

Stefani had a paralyzing moment of fear that only she and Ella had made it across safely when she heard the first cries from beyond her alley. They piled upon her disorientation, layering fear upon fear. She was here, alone but for her vulnerable and defenseless child, and she was not much more capable of defending herself than Ella.

Except that wasn't true.

I am not Stefani Palmieri.

At least, she wasn't *just* Stefani Palmieri. There was another presence in her, the vaguer, more violent presence of the first man she'd absorbed. He wasn't someone she wanted to call upon often, but under threat, he might be just the ticket. She could feel him now, a nettling surge of irritation reacting to the grating calls of fear filtering into the alley.

More important was the fact that she was a creature who had absorbed those two people. "People" really. They had only thought they were human, after all. She was the real deal. As real a deal as remained anyway. The revenants weren't human any longer, but their ancestors had been.

And a revenant, even one shorn of its armor and bulk as Stefani was, could do a whole lot more damage than a human.

Steeled in this fashion, she returned Ella's carrier to her back and left her alley, determined to find the source of the noise.

It did not take long.

The alley opened onto a kind of market square, and the market square was packed with life forms of all kinds.

There was no other way to think about it. Her ancestors had not been able to distinguish true-blue human from Coldgarden's native mimics, but their revenant descendants could. A sizable portion of the people caroming around the square—specifically those who were not dressed for the punishing heat—were those very native mimics who had tricked themselves into believing they were human almost a century ago.

Reassuringly, Stefani did see a few of her own—other revenants who had reclaimed their humanity, or as close as was possible anyway. With Karl and Marri missing, they needed to be her first stop, though she did not immediately know which faction of her people they belonged to.

She could hope that such things had ceased to matter.

And though Stefani saw no sign of Giana, whatever cancer or virus or fungal analog she represented, there were a number of her kind present, looking just as human to the untrained eye as anyone else. One man even had the uniform of a lancer on, though it was hard to discern past the glowing white gelatin that Stefani's eyes saw past the false human face.

What drew Stefani's eye more than any of those groups, though, was the bulk of those present in the square. They wore nearly identical bodysuits which looked tailor-made to protect them from the baking heat of this place.

They were something Stefani had never seen before, something she had longed to see her entire life. And just like every other group present, she could tell the difference.

They were humans. Real humans.

Instead of joy, she felt an overwhelming shame. Not until that moment had she realized how much she held onto the idea that her kind were the last of humanity, a dying ember, yes, but an ember still aglow with stubborn heat.

Now here she was, face to face with *real* humanity, and she saw at last the lumbering monster that she was. If these people could see her form, her true form, they would recoil from her.

Not that they weren't doing that already. Most were scattering for dwellings or shops or any shelter they could manage. A few were wailing and pointing, seemingly locked in a prison of their own terror. More than a few of the new arrivals looked around with terror too, and Stefani could hardly blame them. She'd had some idea of what they had been fleeing from when they'd poured across the Bridge span, and she could still scarcely wrap her mind around it.

What must a person who had merely been going about their evening when they were suddenly seized upon an inexplicable urge to gather in Heart Ward, an urge forced upon them by an entity of unimaginable scale and power? How many had managed to resist the call and were now dead for it?

Whether due to the death of the planet-being they had left behind or the simple physical distance that now stretched between them and their "father," as Marri seemed to think of that cosmic creature, the spell had well and truly broken. The people of Coldgarden were shaking themselves as though to fight off a sudden bout of vertigo. Coming out of whatever trance the cosmic creature had put them under.

Soon, very soon, a general panic was going to begin, if not outright violence. Stefani had no idea which of the many factions present would initiate that violence, but she was certain they were teetering on the edge of an abyss.

If Iaz, either the pre- or post-death Iaz, had been present, Stefani would have looked to her. Despite the fact that both iterations of the woman had been unstable and dangerous by the end, Stefani's urge to huddle near the familiar was so strong, she would still have deferred to a woman who so naturally commanded authority.

But she saw no sign of Iaz. No sign of Ali.

Karl. Marri. No one. No Giana, who had yet to cure Ella of the child's ailment as promised.

I'm all she has, Stefani thought, steeling herself. *I'm all any of these people have.* She was still a magistrate. A name, maybe even a face, they would recognize.

"Everyone, listen to me!" Her voice rang out, cutting across the general, rising din of the market square. People frantically spinning, looking for familiar faces or landmarks, perhaps, turned to regard her. "I need you to remain calm!"

"What happened?"

"Where are we?"

The two shouted questions came so quick, one after the other, they almost seemed part of the same cry.

"Our world was coming apart around us," Stefani called back. "If we had stayed, we would have died. We took the only way out we had. This world is a human colony." She'd almost said "another" human colony, but that was a can of worms best left both unopened and stuffed as far back in the shed as possible for now. Then she began to lie flagrantly. "There is room for us all here. But right now, we need to find shelter from the heat."

"My family! They were right beside me! They aren't here now!"

This prompted more such cries, and Stefani felt a twist of agonized sympathy. But she was not done lying.

"Your family is safe. We couldn't all arrive at the same point; there were too many of us. You'll be reunited soon." At least she could hope the words were true. "But right now, we have to see to our own safety!" She was already eyeballing a large structure at the end of the open area that seemed like a communal gathering place of some sort. It looked large enough to hold them all, as long as too many more didn't show up.

There are too few of us. The thought exploded in her mind. *Where are the rest?* But she couldn't focus. Her head was throbbing. Ella had started to wail behind her. The heat was oppressive. Now that she'd had a better look at the dome covering this town, she saw that the dome's underside sported a strange, repeating pattern, like wedge-shaped feathers. It must be an artifact of whatever tool had been used to excavate the space. But regardless of the roof over all their heads, whatever sun lay beyond that stone must be a real beast, because it turned the space into more of an oven than a haven.

The crowd still looked half-asleep where they weren't panicking.

"Please," Stefani pleaded, trying to rouse them to action. *Be specific. Tell them where to go.* "Right now we *have* to go to—"

Someone screamed. Others joined the chorus. There were shouts of "hypermutation!" Stefani struggled to find the source of the dismay, but the crowd obliged her by falling away from it in a rush.

It was not hypermutation. It was worse.

A thick, flattened worm of a body, green-black and glistening despite the heat, two meters long, unfurled a set of six bony, scythe-like limbs upon which it hoisted itself from the baking ground. One of the Coldgarden natives had, through some unprecedented combination of stressors, remembered what they really were.

And they did not seem happy about it.

CHAPTER 4

SPIRALING lines of color unraveled into glowing filaments, the latter fading, and Karl Yonnel became an entity aware of himself once again. A moment ago—or had it been a thousand years?—Karl had been standing in the center of Coldgarden at night, the city going insane around him as the very world came apart. The very first things he was aware of in this new place beyond himself were a heat and light unlike any he had ever experienced slapping him in the face like a near-miss from a lance discharge.

The second thing he was aware of was mad chaos assaulting his senses from every direction at once.

The glare and the transition from night to whatever the Bridge had been to blinding light made it almost impossible to see, but his aging eyes did eventually adjust. All around him, people reacted to the jolt of arrival at wherever this place was.

The milling masses grew by the second as people simply puffed impossibly into existence in brilliant flares of light, displacing and knocking to the ground any who were already occupying the space. They stood upon a bright metal pad of some kind, which did not help the heat or light situation. Karl thought he could feel his skin crisping like vat-grown meat on the griddle.

"Stefani!" Karl called out. "Marri!" It was difficult to make himself heard over the growing din. Not only were others crying out for their own loved ones, general grunts of effort or cries of rage grew in volume with each passing moment.

Karl called out again. When he got no answer, the heat baking his brain took up his focus. *Shelter. Got to find shelter.* There was, however, no shelter that he could see. Despite the crowds, Karl had always been taller than average. He saw no buildings at ground level that could provide protection from the relentless, pounding sun. Worse, the bright metal they stood upon reflected the heat radiating down from above right back up at them.

There were, however, curved stripes of shade upon the ground like the arcs of a circle. Karl risked a look up. He couldn't manage more than a blinking glimpse, but, backlit against the ferocious orange glare of a star that had to be about to swallow the planet he stood upon whole, he could make out the same concentric bullseye of rings. They hovered in the air, with the widest of the rings hanging lowest and each consecutive ring rising from there, until the entire apparatus outlined a dome in space. And beyond them stood an actual dome, transparent latticework of metal and glass, the trusses too thin to provide any additional shade from the punishing orange light streaming in.

Even having to cut its way through air which looked choked with dust beyond the dome's exterior, the light felt like a physical pressure upon him, baking his brain and muddying his thoughts. But Karl recognized the bullseye shapes. He had just stepped through an identical apparatus back on his own world. This apparently was the other end of the Bridge's span. He wondered in a heat-addled moment if he left the confines of that dome then stepped back onto the pad and within its boundaries once again, would he be sent back to his dying world? Would he step out into cool, merciful darkness and a planet yawning open onto hellfire?

The heat of this greenhouse chamber was such that this was

almost a comforting thought. But somehow, he knew this had been a one-way trip.

More importantly, the hovering rings provided what little shade there was to be had, and the new arrivals were starting to figure that out. As more and more appeared and the space filled up, the struggle to claim a modicum of shade escalated in intensity. Violence was only a matter of time, and it was anyone's guess if it would erupt before mass heat stroke.

The monstrous sun was partially obscured by both the omnipresent dust and the horizon, but Karl had no idea if it was rising or setting. If the former, they might all die in this hothouse shortly, having traveled across the galaxy only to buy themselves very little time. Karl couldn't imagine what high noon on this world was like. He decided to hope it was setting, that the shade would only grow. But regardless of the time of day, there was nothing for it but to try to find a place for himself in the shade.

The bark of pain in his hip as he moved did more to ground him, to convince him this was really happening, than anything else his senses told him. Some of the people were in a catatonic stupor, as if the transition between worlds had broken something deep inside them. Despite the horrific glare, they stared wide-eyed at nothing. Others moved, but in a shuffling daze.

This made perfect sense, of course. Karl was among the few who had actually known what using the Bridge entailed. The overwhelming majority of the population had been led to the reassembled technology in a kind of trance by the planetary-scale being responsible for all of their existences, a last effort to save some part of itself before dying and dooming all life remaining on the planet.

Feeling a sudden flood of empathy, Karl stopped at the first dazed person he encountered. He took the man by the shoulders, shaking him lightly when he couldn't get those staring eyes to focus.

"Come on, man! We can't stay out here. We'll fry." The man didn't respond in any way, except to resist being pulled out of the rough loop he was walking in. The one thing he seemed absolutely intent on avoiding was staying alive. With a heavy heart, Karl abandoned him.

He tried twice more, the second time attempting and failing to pull a woman up from where she huddled in the baking light. On his third attempt, on one of the pacing people, the woman actually met his eyes.

Then her face unzipped itself into a gelatinous mass of white, glowing goo which extended toward him like a clam emerging from its shell. In sudden fear and disgust, Karl shoved her to the side. Much to his surprise, she went with little resistance, keeling over as the rest of her body dissolved into goo, which sizzled and popped like fat wherever it made contact with the broiling metal of the pad.

It struggled to rise, but the heat of the pad fused its strange flesh to the metal. It went so far as to sacrifice parts of itself to escape, but it was too late. The dying sounds that emerged from the creature—one of Giana's disease-people—were far enough removed from human that Karl felt a stab of gratitude toward an otherwise uncaring universe. Monster or not, he did not want to hear that agony emanating in a human voice.

He stopped trying to help the helpless after that, much as it pained him. Maybe all of the dazed were just disease-monsters or revenants. He could tell himself that at least.

His attempts at humanitarianism had cost him. The edge of the nearest shadow was a teeming mass of people fighting for space. Paradoxically, those on the outermost edge of that wall of people seemed in less distress than those a row or two in, who not only didn't have shade but also had body heat coming at them from all sides.

This time the screams sounded all too human.

Karl found he couldn't bring himself to add to the suffering in a fight that wouldn't get him the shelter he needed in any event. His ruined hip would see to that. Everyone who still retained their volition was waking up to their peril and making for those few stripes of shade. Many shoved those less responsive individuals out of their way.

It really sank in then that he didn't have long to live.

A voice rang out across the open space of the Bridge pad, amplified almost to the point of pain. "Do not move! All of you, raise your hands and place them on your head."

Karl spun to see the speaker. He was able to easily, partly because of his height but mostly due to theirs. A dozen of them waded inward from the dome's edge through the sea of people. Each of the new arrivals stood over two meters tall by his estimation, and they were dressed all in black that shone in places, which seemed insane for the heat. But in the intensity of the glare, it was difficult to make out more. Beyond the freakish height, they at least sounded like and were basically shaped like humans, so Karl supposed that was something.

"Do as he says!" Karl's words left him before he consciously realized he was going to speak. The order went out in his best lance commander voice, pitched as a command he expected to be followed with no hesitation.

Despite the circumstances, it felt good.

Of course, these weren't soldiers; they were a bunch of panicky civilians coming out of a kind of trance, along with a handful of assorted monsters. Neither group was tremendously likely to heed him, and he'd be lucky if one percent of the people fighting for shade were lancers.

"Nighttime protocol!" the same voice cried out, and abruptly, there was darkness.

The heat didn't vanish—there was still the metal pad beneath them with all its remembered sunlight radiating back up at Karl—but it diminished so much he felt a wash of relief. Despite this, the screaming was only growing in intensity. But Karl could barely hear it. As though his body had been waiting for that tiny reprieve, he felt a different kind of darkness wash up and over him, and he knew no more.

CHAPTER 5

THE SOUNDS of rising chaos around Stefani faded to a ringing in her ears. *No. No, not now.* But the world did not heed her denial, however vehement. Faced with a native gone feral and the threat that posed, Stefani's vision tunneled as she felt herself recede into her own mind. From the other side of that tunnel, a new presence appeared, stepping forward.

"No," she said aloud, as though this carried more force with reality than the thought did. "No." She kept repeating it, a new mantra, a way to keep the evil at bay. But fairly quickly, her words were no longer spoken aloud. They existed in her mind only, her denial having come full circle.

And Trevor Volkes took over.

He stretched, luxuriantly, truly feeling the limits of this new body for the first time. Palmieri's delusion regarding her true nature had been like the door of a vault, keeping him locked inside the prison of her denial, unable to escape except in brief, emotional outbursts. All in all, it felt good to move real limbs again, even if they did belong to a woman half the size and weight he was accustomed to. He had to remind himself that this was deceptive, that he was far stronger, even in this feminine cast, than he felt.

Still, the ache between his shoulder blades was real enough. Palmieri's brat riding him like a mule. He considered just unslinging the pack and leaving her here, but even in thinking it, he felt the bundle of resolve that was Palmieri strengthening, kindling her rage into a blaze powerful enough to reassert control. And so he backed off that idea before she could build too much momentum. He prided himself on knowing which fights to pick and which to avoid.

Mostly, he did.

Despite this, as Archon Teodori's onetime top enforcer, he'd been regarded as little more than a rabid dog in his first life, and based on Palmieri's fear and hatred of him, her determination to keep him locked away in a tiny corner of their amalgamated mind, that remained true in this strange afterlife he occupied as well. But now she was going to learn just how lucky she was to have him around.

Because a reputation as a rabid dog could be useful, particularly when no one expected you to be coldly analytical in the run-up to explosive violence. It was his analytical utility more than his propensity for violence or even his loyalty which had earned him enough trust to be told Coldgarden's darkest secrets. This despite the fact that he wasn't a member of Gene Sequencing or an elected official in the ruling cabal of city leadership. That reputation was also why so many people had died by his hand with looks of utter shock on their faces. Trevor never seemed to give them what they expected before he killed them.

His analysis of this particular circumstance, meanwhile, was brutally simple. He was dealing with a Coldgarden native reverted to its true form. In the handful of times he'd dealt with situations like this—each one a Gene Sequencing fuck-up of epic proportions as some experiment went awry—several factors had always been true.

Firstly, the creature was more than capable of overpowering and killing even a group of humans. Had Trevor still been a revenant in the full of his power, armor and all, it would have been an even fight, but that was no longer the case. That bitch Palmieri—and the other revenants like her—had given up the greater portion of their fighting strength to better pretend to be human.

He hoped it had been worth the exchange.

The second factor was therefore of the utmost importance. Every single time Trevor had seen something like this happen, the resulting feral native had not been in peak fighting form, but rather confused, frightened, and trapped in a kind of waking nightmare as to the truth of their circumstances.

It made them so much easier to kill, but by his estimation, he had only a few seconds to make use of that advantage before raw instinct took over.

"Grab it!" he barked to the general crowd. "Now, before it can get its bearings!" He had little hope of help here, but he had an alternate plan already locked and loaded.

As he expected, not a single Coldgardener moved to obey his edict. They were too frightened and too practiced with the notion of what could happen if they sustained even a minor injury. Too smart, in other words.

But the residents of this new world, much to Trevor's shock, obeyed both readily and en masse. Those who hadn't already fled for shelter, wearing their identical protective suits that made them look like they'd been stamped out of an assembly line, swarmed the many-legged worm. Moving as though sharing a single, tactical mind, they gripped its bony legs by their bases and spread them wide, lifting the creature from the ground. It thrashed, and several went down with cries of pain, one a bloody death rattle. But more swarmed into the holes this opened.

"That's it," Trevor said. "Hoist it up. Show me its belly." That was where the blow had to be struck.

The Gene Sequencing types had obsessed over the superficial similarities between natives and revenants, but those began and ended with the legs, really. Both had six of them. Mostly, that was true. Revenants didn't tend to hold the same shape for long, but they averaged somewhere around six in Trevor's experience. More important than number was utility. Both sets of legs terminated in blades razor-sharp enough to rip to shreds just about anything they wanted. The difference was that revenant legs were covered in the same chitin carapace as the rest of them, while a native's legs were something like naked bone with toughened sinew almost as hard to damage.

But it wasn't the legs he was interested in. The natives had a weakness revenants did not. Their hide was not hard chitin but tough and leathery. Very resistant to damage but not entirely so.

Trevor hated it when random citizens made the leap back to their true form, and he was honest with himself about why. He had spent years trying to make the same transformation himself, ever since the secret had been revealed to him. That very night had been his first attempt, but it had been an utter failure, and he had never gotten one iota closer.

But for this, he didn't need to be like the thing he was about to end. There were much easier ways, discovered through the harshest lessons possible.

Back on Coldgarden, there had been a weapon designed specifically for this. Here, he would have to make do. But thankfully, despite this form having shed so much of its power in making the transformation to a human that could trick anyone looking, he had enough ability to remake his form to get the job done.

He strode up to the twisting, thrashing creature, which looked more as though it was fighting itself than attempting to harm anyone.

"Hold it still," he said. He despised hearing his command delivered in such a high, feminine voice, but authority was more about tone than pitch.

In truth, the belly was no more vulnerable, on average, than any other place on the creature's body. The combination of thick hide and dense musculature made breaking through nearly impossible for any hand-carried weapon beyond a lance. They'd had some success with fire in the lab as well, but that had its own practical limitations.

And of course, this method did too. But as long as he had useful idiots willing to be maimed and die to hold it still, Trevor could make it work. He found the spot easily enough. It was the same on all of them, a place where two slabs of muscle overlapped in such a way that left a curving seam just beneath the hide. Any kind of straight hit would have no effect, but a blade bent into an arc just so could slide through that seam and puncture something deep and vital within the creature. Trevor didn't know what and didn't care.

He strode up fearlessly to the struggling creature, held upright and splayed by the volunteer army, and placed Stefani Palmieri's hand upon the spot. He thought it best not to let the colonists of this world see exactly what he was doing, lest uncomfortable questions be asked. Pressing his palm firmly against that dark, rubbery hide, he willed the bones within to reshape themselves into a curved, stabbing blade of just the right proportions.

With a grimace, his blade of hardened bone punched through the leathery hide and found the groove between muscles, following it all the way up. With an alloy blade, he would have been limited to what had been fabricated, but here, he simply kept feeding more of himself into the creature's depths until it began to shudder so hard it nearly shook free of its captors.

They looked to have found their fear at last, but as he had not retreated, neither did they. Trevor withdrew the blade fully, re-knitting his own bones before removing his hand and stepping out of range of any death throes.

The great worm gave one final, spasmodic twitch, then slumped to the ground in a tangled heap of limbs, something viscous and awful oozing out of the hole Trevor had left. The stench was abominable.

That had been as satisfying as he'd remembered, and how curious it was to feel the physical pleasure of watching the creature die ripple through the body of a woman rather than a man. Perhaps he could get used to this form after all. It would be even better when he killed a human, he'd wager. A real, live human, technically his first.

He was not the monster he allowed everyone to think him. Despite the pleasure he felt at watching a life snuffed out, he had never killed anyone just for that. Always the killing had been necessary—or ordered—and the associated reward just that, a treat for a job well done. Though come to think of it, now that he was back in control, he might make an exception for one person.

Marri, the little brat who had caused him to be killed in the first place. Her he would kill at the first opportunity just because the whelp had it coming.

He felt Stefani's rage rise up too late to resist it, and abruptly it was all around him, scouring him like burning whips. She stuffed him back in his same corner of their shared mind, crammed down even deeper than before.

That was all right, he told himself. He'd broken free once before.

He'd have the chance to do it again.

CHAPTER 6

STEFANI SHUDDERED with barely contained rage as she reclaimed control of herself. Trevor Volkes she banished to the furthest corner of herself. If she could have torn parts of her mind up and piled them like debris across the door she locked him behind, she would have.

That had never happened before. She could not allow it to happen again. And she would *never* let him touch Marri. Provided she could find Marri. And Karl. And Giana. She had to fight off a wave of despair.

"How did you kill that awful thing?" One of the people who had obeyed Volkes's command ran up to Stefani, tears in her eyes. "What was that awful thing?"

"It looked like a person, then changed!" Several people took up this shout. By their accents and clothes, they were all natives of this world. This was bad. It was never going to be possible to keep the secret of Coldgarden's various life forms forever, but Stefani could have hoped for more than a few minutes.

Fully in command of herself once more, she backed away from the dead Coldgardener out of long instinct. The hypermutation would begin soon, and she didn't want to be close enough for it to spread. She was not alone. A wide, empty ring was forming around the creature. The locals who had been holding it up dropped it, taking their cue from their visitors that this creature, dead as it was, should not be lingered near.

A hopefully safe distance away, Stefani took fresh stock of the situation and did not like what she found. Despite the lack of direct sunlight, the baking heat of this enclosed space was already stifling. She wondered how the locals managed. It had to be something to do with their form-hugging suits, some sort of embedded cooling system.

"What the hell kind of hypermutation was that?" This from an obvious Coldgardener. "That didn't look random at all! And look, it's stopped. It's just laying there."

The irritatingly insightful person was right. The slumped form of the Coldgardener bone-worm lay utterly still in death, a concept foreign to anyone from that world. Giana had described hypermutation as an unconscious attempt by the sufferer to return to their true form. Now that this creature had done so, that need was apparently gone. Like it had found a perverse kind of peace in its final moments.

But Stefani could not share that peace. Some note in the speaker's voice made her hackles rise. This wasn't just someone giving vent to their random fears. They were actively thinking through the situation.

A series of screams erupted suddenly from the same general direction of the latest speaker. Most were incoherent cries of terror, but Stefani caught a pair of clearly spoken words, even over Ella screaming in her ear.

"Another one!"

Whether the first speaker had "remembered" or some other person nearby had, it hardly mattered. Because amid exponential cries of fear, Stefani was faced with a terrifying realization. While transformed Coldgardener natives might not hypermutate, their tendency to remember what they were might spread with just as much ferocity and with a far more lethal outcome.

The crowd scattered suddenly as no fewer than four more of the natives burst forth, their slavering, toothless jaws dribbling acid that popped and smoked as it hit the stony ground. The creatures spun rapidly in place as though in coordinated dance. They ignored most of those people nearby. One made a series of lunges toward a cluster of the locals to this world. It would surge forward, pause, then surge again, as though it couldn't quite decide what to do with these strange creatures.

On the third such lunge, it didn't stop. Apparently, it was going to assume the worst and treat them as a threat.

"Run!" Stefani shouted to the black-clad locals when they looked too dazed to respond to the impending violence. It was a mistake. One of the other three Coldgardener monsters halted in its spin to point directly at her.

And it had no trouble identifying Stefani, a revenant, as a threat it should be killing.

Stefani suited her own words, turning and diving into the crowd, determined to put as many people, of whatever flavor they were, between her and the charging bone-worm. All thought of their well-being fled her mind. This was about getting Ella to safety. She barreled toward a knot of people too close to slip between, lowering her shoulder. But instead of bowling through them, she all but bounced off to cries of pain and indignation and, very shortly, terror as those ahead saw what followed her.

The crowd pressed too close around her for her to understand why they couldn't give way. Stefani spun to face her pursuer, preparing to transform to her revenant form. She had given up too much of that form to be a match for one of the bone-worms, but it was fixated on her, and for the sake of her daughter, she had to try. She half-expected Trevor to try and fight his way back into control, but apparently he was only interested in killing things that couldn't fight back.

But before she could make that shift into black-and-gold, oily agility and power and catch the charge of the enraged creature, the air around it rippled in a way that struck Stefani as profoundly unnatural. Abruptly the creature was in a heap, its disparate parts shattered, torn, or cut with unnaturally clean lines from one another. It went from charging in bloody-minded fury one instant to a piled heap of gore burping out trapped gases the next.

Stefani let out a breath at the same instant a voice rang out across the space, godlike in its volume.

"Everyone stay where you are! I will have absolute stillness under this dome, or by the Good Doctor's grace, I will do the same thing to each and every one of you that does not belong on this world." The voice resonated through the air, amplified by some means Stefani could not see. "My name is Colonel Almeida of the Anaranjadan Colonial Militia. By order of Commandant Reid, we are hereby taking command of this settlement. I repeat. Everybody, stop where you are. Do not move."

There was a smattering of cheers. Stefani felt the same way, despite being almost as afraid of whatever had happened to the bone-worm. Thankfully, she summoned enough self-control to avoid actually making a noise. She had no idea if what was happening now was a good thing or a bad thing for her going forward, but at least Ella was safe for another moment.

People her hind brain identified as soldiers fanned out from gaps in the crowd, forcing themselves through in some cases. They were tall, far more so than the residents of this town, each easily two meters or more by Stefani's reckoning. Their uniforms were form-hugging bodysuits over some kind of scaled armor underneath. The scaling even continued up over their faces somehow. It must have been some kind of advanced protective sleeve they wore under the uniform. They carried sidearms that looked strange, but much too small to be powerful enough to turn the bone-worm inside out.

Stefani kept waiting for one of the other three to attack, or for more Coldgardeners to transform into bone-worms or revenants or disease-monsters. But apart from the soldiers moving to occupy the space, an unnatural stillness had descended upon the domed enclosure, and fragile as it seemed, it held.

"We are currently securing the exits as well as emergency life support equipment, and we will presently be separating you into two groups," the colonel continued, her words crisp, firmly under her control. "Those of you who live here will be placed into one group on the westward side of the clearing. New arrivals, you will be placed into a second group on the eastward side. My people intend you no harm. We ask that you cooperate fully with any orders given to you by ACM personnel, and we will get along just fine. But if anyone attempts any kind of hostile action, I will be absolutely merciless in protecting the people of Anaranjado. That needs to be very clear in your minds."

As people began to move, Stefani saw the reason behind the sudden peacefulness in the stillness. The other three bone-worms had been given the same treatment as the one hunting Stefani had. She wondered if the soldiers had hit all four at once somehow. She thought about how close she'd been to transforming and wondered what would have happened if she had. Likely she'd be in a heap of dismembered parts.

And Ella with her.

The splitting up took some time because the soldiers approached the action very methodically and carefully. Wise, under the circumstances. This Almeida knew her business. Stefani, meanwhile, tried to distract herself from the heat and worry over how Ella would respond to it by watching everything that was going on around her, hoping to glean as much information as she could.

When her turn came, Stefani goggled. One of the two soldiers who came to collect her and Ella was the largest man she'd ever seen. She thought he must be the better part of three meters in height. Though he would have been a big man in any circumstance, barrel-chested and with shoulders more than a meter across, most of his added height came from oddly proportioned limbs. Both his legs and arms were longer than average human legs and arms. As he drew close, she could easily see why.

They were machine, not flesh, with a reflective black sheen. This man had replaced entire limbs with mechanical copies. The scales covered his entire face, going from coarse to fine along his musculature, which allowed him to make movements as subtle as facial expressions.

The scales weren't worn. They were some kind of replacement for skin.

"My name is Staff Sergeant Horváth, and this is Private Ballinger. You will come with us please." He had a clipped accent Stefani didn't recognize, but considering how far up she had to crane her neck to look him in the eye as he spoke, she instantly obeyed. She couldn't tear her eyes away from him, in fact, some atavistic part of herself registering him as a threat within easy grabbing reach.

Her unwillingness to look away was the only reason she had any warning. They were passing another knot of people, Horváth's gaze directed elsewhere, when a man with a vacant expression began fiercely glowing.

Oh no. That was all she could manage. Stefani was paralyzed by the understanding of what was about to happen. Horváth was an enormous person, but Ballinger was much closer to normal height, and he was too slow to recognize the threat. The disease-monster dropped the top half of its disguise, became a pair of human legs supporting too many limbs with too many joints, all splaying outward. The joints snapped closed as one, engulfing Ballinger's entire left side.

His scream ripped the air, setting Ella and several other children off. Horváth whirled, knocking over half a dozen people in the process, to behold what was happening. That same part that had whispered to Stefani she would be the prey if Horváth chose to be the predator set her scooting out of the way.

"Billy! Billy!" Horváth's voice was like anguished thunder as he ripped and tore at the disease-creature consuming his squad mate, trying to pull them free so Ballinger could get away. But for all Horváth's prodigious strength, the over-jointed limbs bunched and thrust themselves outward, sending Horváth sprawling, bowling over still more refugees. Ballinger's eyes were already glazing over as the substance of the creature oozed its way around and up his neck, like a throat climbing its food by the act of swallowing it.

Worst of all, as it closed over the crown of Ballinger's head, the white gelatinous substance of the creature's body began to shrink as though to fit itself around the contours of his head, and with frightening speed, Ballinger's face reappeared. But it was no longer screaming. Instead, it looked at peace. Almost beatific. That lasted all of a few seconds before the entire mass went instantly black as oil, collapsing into a sludgy puddle of goo and loose mechanical parts.

Then it was Horváth's turn to scream. "Billy! No!" He rose, whirling, but this time people had possessed enough sense to give him space. "Where are you? Which ones of you? I will kill you all!" His voice was full of rage, but tears also.

A general panic began brewing until booted feet approached.

"Subdue him!" That was Almeida over the loudspeaker again. The soldiers looked uneasy, but they obeyed orders, darting in with their wands. Horváth roared and twitched with every jab.

"Monsters, all of them! Attack them, not me. They aren't human!" His rage seemed to have no limits. But at last, his limbs shut down on him, and he lay there in the dust and dirt, thrashing, trying to drag their dead weight. The tears leaking from his eyes and mucus from his nose as he sobbed told Stefani that at least his innards were still made of flesh.

"Final warning!" Almeida's voice crashed like a falling mountain. "I have my orders, but I will exterminate every last one of you refugees if any more of my people are attacked." Her voice shook with the same anger Horváth held, but it was better controlled.

A little better.

Pulling Ella from her carrier to try and comfort her back into quiescence, Stefani shivered, hoping against hope that no more of the mindless disease-creatures—whom she didn't believe capable of acting in rational self-preservation—numbered among the crowd.

Hoping that no more of the bone-worms remembered what they were.

CHAPTER 7

IN THE CHILLY confines of her unlikely rescuer's subterranean dwelling, Giana waited with barely constrained impatience. Again.

Jürgen Fennec, the strange machine-man who had arrived just as the even stranger swarm of creatures had departed on another of his "canvassing operations," as he called them. This involved, as near as Giana could tell, him ascending to the parts of these tunnels that actually still contained inhabitants beside himself and asking questions on her behalf. He had embarked on the first of his trips immediately after getting her settled. Today marked the second straight day of such investigations.

Always assuming he wasn't just lying to her to make her stay put. She wasn't physically afraid of him, but he did hold all the power in terms of his knowledge of this world.

He had made no mention of the strange creature—creatures?— she'd encountered upon arriving, and she had not felt secure enough in the lie of her identity to ask and risk his suspicion. She still was unsure if he'd even caught a glimpse of the things.

Giana instead had tasked him with looking for any sign of Stefani, Karl, or even Marri. Really, news of any Coldgardener would do, but given that Mr. Fennec believed Giana to belong to some class of people to which he owed extreme deference, Giana did not want to advertise that she was actually from another world.

So she had made her closest acquaintances out to be missing family members. She'd gathered from his flummoxed reaction that this was not a very plausible story, but if she was as wealthy and powerful as he seemed to think, perhaps that bought her some expectation of eccentricity.

In any event, it had bought her a little time.

His quarters were little more than a prefabricated, multi-lobed yurt designed to blunt the worst of the cold in the caverns and tunnels outside. To say he lived a spartan life was to grossly understate matters. With a single, hard-cushioned couch, a coffee table that was essentially a polymer plank on stunted legs, and a single stand-lamp, Giana felt she could be forgiven for assuming that she was about to be subjected to a police interrogation. She had not been admitted to his personal rooms in the structure, but given her impression that he only had enough furnishings to not be completely off-putting to potential clients, she wondered if he even used a bed.

Given the amount of him that was machine, perhaps he simply plugged himself into a wall outlet. And even if he wasn't mostly machine, he was an actual human, not one of the several varieties of pretend-human that had come over from Coldgarden. There was nothing of that world in him, so she would not be able to turn him.

Not yet.

She longed to search his rooms regardless, and not only to satisfy her curiosity. What she lacked now was any kind of control over her fate, and what she needed to reassert that control was information. But he seemed a secretive and mistrustful person. Why live all the way down here, where he had to ascend several levels even to interact with other people, otherwise? This fact, and the fact that he'd nonetheless been willing to leave her alone here, meant he likely had ways of keeping an eye on his home remotely.

And she couldn't afford to lose his trust just—

Something interrupted her train of thought. It was like a whisper, but one with the power to knock her flat.

She had been reaching out constantly since her arrival. In the same way she'd been able to communicate with the portion of her kind which had infected the Host's brain to make it spare her rather than condemn her back on Coldgarden, she could form mental links with other things like her. The larger the mass, or the more direct a lineage to herself, the easier that process was, though it was taxing even when successful.

So far, it had emphatically *not* been successful.

But now, the whisper. It was faint. Far away. But not far at the scale of light years, which would have been impossible. One of her kind—they had no name for themselves, a fact which proved annoying when trying to think of one's people in the context of human language—had crossed the span of the Bridge and arrived on planet.

Relief crashed over Giana to a frankly unseemly degree. Until that moment, she hadn't been aware how frightened she was that she —improbable as it seemed—might be the only one who had made it across the Bridge alive. In some respects, it would have made her work here easier. A lone infiltrator instead of a mob arriving like a surging tide.

She didn't like how human that emotion felt. Still, others were arriving. She'd waste no time making use of that fact.

Giana closed her eyes, trying to get a sense of direction. Far enough up to indicate the surface, but not the surface directly above her. There was a considerable lateral component to the direction as well. Mr. Fennec had referenced something about relying on the planet's internal heat to avoid freezing. But he had also gone up—his choice of word—to find people to question. Which suggested Giana was deeper below the planet's surface than most, if not all, people on this world. She had no idea how far Mr. Fennec ventured on these jaunts of his. Perhaps as far as this connection she felt now.

She burned with curiosity, with *need,* to see what each was seeing.

After a few more flutters of that whispering contact, Giana found, to her surprise, that she recognized the source. She had met a pair of lancers at a ward checkpoint on Coldgarden's last night. They had already been turned by her more feral cousins by the time she'd arrived. Sparing them from a half-life of insane hunger that was likely as tortuous to them as it was useless to her, she had imposed herself upon them, trying to force them back into a semblance of order.

The man had been too far gone and had died horribly. But the woman had survived and gone forth to turn more.

This presence Giana now sensed was her.

Giana held her breath as she considered. She had transformed this woman directly. That meant taking it further, even from this great distance, was possible. But did she dare? It would be far, far more taxing than simply holding a link between them. But she needed information, and she needed it now, while others were still arriving on this world and there was the potential for chaos within which she could most effectively operate.

That was it, then. Her decision made. She steeled herself for the coming discomfort and reached out to the woman as she once had before. But this time, she carried the full violent intent of the infinite mutability her kind was capable of.

CHAPTER 8

ANSLEY'S dim recollection of the squad's map had been correct after all. The town of Ashrock appeared around the connecting canyon's last bend. Despite the permanent dryness of the air, he could have wept with relief.

But he was pretty sure he didn't have any moisture left in his body for useless things like tears.

He plowed forward, increasing his plodding gait to the fastest lurch he could muster. Even in sight of salvation, he knew if he stopped to rest now, he wouldn't get back up again. He'd just bake to the rocks like a spare bit of food that escaped the pan directly onto the stove-top burner.

To take his mind off all the pain he was in, he turned it toward dealing with the problem he could no longer put off: getting his story straight. There was nothing he could have done, of course. The creatures had been remarkably efficient in their attack, each one separately going after each of his squad mates. His shock had caused him to lag behind. This, and the fact that not enough creatures had materialized to take on the entire squad at once, had been what saved him in the end.

That and Hastings's ferocious refusal to die quietly. She had been howling Ansley's name at the end, her voice at last cut off by the gurgle of drowning in creature acid. Ansley had fought down vomit at that sound, at the acrid stink of melted flesh mingling with scorched electronics. The same flesh he'd been so eager to see more of just seconds before. Whether she'd been begging for help or imploring him to escape, he would never know.

But he couldn't think about that. He couldn't think about the fate of the bar either. Some deeply ingrained instinct had told Ansley that was the next place the creatures would go after tearing his squad mates apart. So he had run back into the tunnel he'd come from. And he'd kept running. But now his running was done, at least for a time. And as long as he played his cards right, he would not have to run anymore.

It wouldn't look good, the commanding officer of an ACM patrol squad also being the only member of that squad who survived an attack upon that squad by unknown entities. Though he knew his father could and would shield him from any real fallout, Ansley Reid had just been handed a very concrete lesson about the limits of wealth and status as protection against physical harm. He was not safely ensconced in Meridian Equatoria behind the walls of one of his father's habitat compounds and guarded by his father's very well compensated security detail. He was at the Sunnyside frontier, and here, there apparently be monsters.

Regardless of his inability to do anything to save his people, the hardscrabble folk who lived out here wouldn't take kindly to the truth. If he went and blurted, "I'm the only one who survived because I ran as soon as I realized they were all dying," well . . . Harmony might protect him, or it might do the opposite. One of the things he'd learned during this detail was just how oddly it behaved sometimes, particularly this far from the cities.

Warning. You're here to warn them. Get them focused on the threat behind you, not the specifics of your story. It should be easy enough. Hell, it might even be the correct way to prioritize matters.

He could use something else to focus on himself. Any moment he wasn't considering how long he had until dehydration claimed him was filled with flashes of memory of the creatures' bone-scythe-limbs removing arms and legs and heads. Gouts of blood and coolant everywhere.

Or, most frequently, his tormented mind would call up high-definition images of Hastings's head melting in a projectile torrent of acidic bile the creature had vomited into her face.

To look at the scorecard, you'd think Ansley's squad hadn't attempted to defend themselves at all, but they'd gotten dozens of shots off by his fractured recollection. And Ansley wasn't even certain they'd hurt the things. They had shrugged off the voltage of the squad's weapons like static cling.

Ansley strode into the settlement facing no barrier, no guard. Its totally enclosed nature existed to ward off the settlement's historic enemy: the burning face of Naranja forever consuming the unseen horizon.

He was trying to work out how he was going to convince the settlement of what had happened—Equatorians could provoke odd reactions among the general public, he'd found, not just the expected deference—when he noticed something off about the settlement that surprised him now that he was out of the connecting corridor and into the area under the Stone Dome proper. Ashrock was large, far more sprawling than most sunward settlements he'd visited on his patrol tour. But even given this, there were an awful lot of people moving about the streets, way too many people.

And none of them looked like he expected them to look.

It wasn't just that they were un-augmented, baseline humans—though that was a large part of it. This far from the wealthiest portions of the Meridian Cities, very few people looked like that unless you stumbled into one of the fanatic settlements, of which Ashrock did not number.

But it went further. None of them were wearing anything that remotely qualified as protective gear rated for this level of heat. The colonists had arrived to find the Stone Dome chambers already in existence. They cut the impact of Naranja's rays from "rapidly lethal" down to merely "extremely inadvisable" for a baseline human. Since there had been a race of intelligent beings on this world before humans had arrived, that perhaps stood to reason. The human colonists—his ancestors—had been forced to adapt themselves to suit their environment.

Among this group of people, though, Ansley saw more than a few faces already showing signs of heat stress. There would be heatstroke and death before much longer if they didn't get inside.

It was enough to shake him out of his trauma-induced fugue, enough to make him realize just how deep into that fugue he'd been.

What the fuck is going on here?

Ansley had joined the ACM for a tour of duty because it had been the fastest way to earn a berth on the *Ultima Thule* and, ultimately, a way off this rock. Some sort of public service, however cursory, was the stated requirement, even if just on paper. Ansley had plenty of friends who had bribed their own way onto the paper and thus the colony ship, but Ansley's father was a very by-the-book sort of person considering he was wealthy enough to buy his own book with its own set of rules.

The fact that he ran the ACM obviously didn't help.

But the sight of so many people so close to expiring from the baking heat of the enclosed space fanned the tiny ember of duty Ansley must still have felt deep within himself. He raised his voice, speaking before he'd really thought what he was going to say.

"Attention citizens! I'm Squad-Lieutenant Ansley Reid of the Anaranjadan Colonial Militia. State your business for being out in the heat and your reason for having no protective gear."

The people must already be deep into thermal distress, because those that reacted to his voice at all turned to look at him as if in a daze.

"Where are we?" an older woman called out. Her face was beet-red with the heat. This burst the dam. The cries came from everywhere, directed at everyone and no one.

"How did we get here?"

"What happened?"

"Why can't I remember?"

"Gods below, is this a dream? I thought I was dreaming!"

They rose to a din, a wall of unintelligible noise. He stood there in helpless alarm, thinking they must be far worse off than he'd assumed. Then it clicked, sudden understanding like the full, unimpeded force of Naranja's rays upon his mind.

Those rumors he'd been hearing the last time he reported in. They had to do with the Bridge, another colony making contact. Now there were strangers here, and not just people, but alien monsters.

Holy shit. It happened. These people are from another world. Traveling so far without a ship was insane to contemplate, but it fit nothing else he could think of. And it was, after all, how the colonies had originally been founded.

The rising din of the crowd drove him from his stunned thoughts. Then one voice cut through all the rest, hooked Ansley's ears and his attention.

"People! I need you to be calm."

Ansley sought her out, this commanding presence of a woman. He caught a flash of coppery hair poking up above the rest of the crowd. She'd found something to stand on, the better to project her voice. At first, despite the accent and the patrician lack of scales, Ansley mistook her for a member of the ACM. She wore some kind of uniform that definitely skewed military. A second glance told him it was no ACM uniform he'd ever seen, but the impression had already been set, in his mind and elsewhere.

He loved a bossy woman in uniform. Plus, her words had the immediate effect of calming the din somewhat.

"I know it's frightening, what's happened to us," the soldier-woman said, continuing to weave her spell over the tumultuous masses. "But we will not make it if we don't pull together and help each other!"

"We can help," another woman, this one with a local accent, said into the settling quiet. "We don't know who you are and where you came from, but you are human, just like us. We don't have much to offer, but what kind of people would we be if we turned you away to be dried up by the heat?" Now it was her turn to raise her voice. "Good people of Ashrock, no more hiding in your homes. These people need our help."

Ansley had learned during his five months of outskirts-patrolling that Harmony took strange paths in different settlements, sometimes paths that wandered far afield of the intended we-are-all-one-big-happy-species sentiment the creature was supposed to awaken in people. Yet doors all around the settlement chamber's stony walls began to hiss open. Tentative faces peered out, definitely frightened, but willing to engage.

"Please," the local woman said to the strangers in her midst. "Come out of the heat and into the conditioned spaces. All else is dear enough that we will have to be careful to ration it out, but cool air we have in abundance."

Ansley took advantage of the sudden focus on the local to thread his way through the crowd and up to the soldier-woman, the one who had so arrested the crowd when they were at their most rowdy.

He was surprised to find she was actually dark-haired, that shining flash of red having been some trick of the dome's reddish, embedded lights when she'd been standing on her impromptu stage.

"Squad-Lieutenant Ansley Reid of the Anaranjadan Colonial Militia," he said again, sticking out his hand to her for a shake. "And who, may I ask, is the leader of this invasion force?" He meant it as a flirtatious joke, but the truth was he still had no idea who these people were or where they'd come from. But the idea that this was a mere instance of coincidental timing with the creatures that had wiped out his squad was too much to credit.

Indeed, there was a part of him that wanted nothing more than to shake her down for any information she had on the alien monsters. But another part of him wanted to simply pretend none of that was happening and keep flirting with the pretty lady.

"Lance Corporal Giana Novak," she said. "Of the Coldgarden Lancer Corps."

"Coldgarden?" he asked, newly suspicious.

"New Calgary, you'd know it as," she said with a shrug. "Names evolve over time, I suppose." he asked,

New Calgary. His amazement of a few moments earlier crashing back down upon him full-force. He knew the name New Calgary from his historical studies. He whistled for effect. "If any of my Diaspora Studies class is still rattling around in my head, that's quite the hike from here." As though any human colony wasn't.

"You seem surprised to see us. I wasn't sure if you'd received warning that we were on our way. I'm given to understand we did call ahead," she said, raising a quizzical eyebrow as if to suggest this was somehow *his* fault.

"Communication is difficult this far from the population centers," he said by way of deflection. "Maybe you can enlighten me where my leadership has failed to." He almost added "over dinner" but took hold of himself instead. Flirting was nice and all, and the colonial charter in theory required members of different Earth colonies to render aid when in need, but these people still owed their unsuspecting hosts an explanation of what they were doing here. "I hate to be awkward," he began.

"But you'd like to know how we got here and why," she finished for him. Not a question. He liked her more and more with each passing second. She had large, beguiling eyes and an equally beguiling figure, at least as far as he could make out as she shifted from foot to foot, the uniform clinging in various fetching places.

"Look, I don't mean to come off suspicious," he said, giving in to his libido with a self-effacing grin. "There are just these regulations. You're in the military. You must know how it is."

"I am," she said. "And I do. And I wish I had a good answer for you, but all I can tell you is that the eggheads had been playing with the Bridge for days. Then there were a bunch of earthquakes fit to end the world. The Bridge came to life, opened a portal to who-knows-where—here, I guess—and the order came to evacuate the colony. Everyone through." She shrugged matter-of-factly. "And here we are. It's been an eventful hour."

"Only an hour?" Ansley asked, surprised enough that he blurted out what he should have kept to himself. Those creatures had appeared a full day ago. Either this group of refugees had been here longer than this Giana was claiming—hard to believe, since it would be so easy to cross-check—or the arrivals were happening somewhat displaced in time. Still, it might explain why there'd been no warning on this side in a way that didn't make it Ansley Reid's fault.

Still, she made no mention of the alien monster or any others like it. So he had difficulty believing she was being totally upfront with him.

"Now that you're here," she said, and the coyness of her tone snapped his focus back out of his head and onto her. "Are you in charge?"

"I guess I am," he said, raising an eyebrow at her in turn. "ACM would certainly have jurisdiction during a crisis of this sort. But I could use a liaison to help me coordinate with your people. So I'm going to have to ask you to stick close while we sort through this mess."

"It's a heavy burden of responsibility," she said with a mocking half-smile. "But I will rise to the challenge."

And so the two of them set about trying to carve order out of chaos.

CHAPTER 9

JÜRGEN FENNEC WAITED until he was certain he was unobserved to pass through the well-hidden door down into his tunnels. This required leaving the main thoroughfare of the lowest habitat levels and negotiating the various barricades that had been installed to deny the curious access to the now-forbidden parts of Shadyside. An easy enough thing to manage, since Jürgen had been the one to subvert them in the first place. It was an action he could perform by rote, and just as well because today his mind was driven by twin obsessions: namely, his two clients. Though perhaps "would-be clients" was a more accurate term.

Having *any* new clients was rare enough these days, ever since his official warnings about the Cult's activities had driven the Equatoria-ordered closure of the lower tunnels, where he still resided. Rarer still was his feeling of ineptitude, for he was going to have to disappoint Ms. Novak for a second straight day when he arrived home with no leads having emerged.

Anyone looking at his situation from outside would have called him mad for helping a woman who hadn't paid him a cent yet. But Jürgen knew his own mind well enough to understand his patience about getting paid in this particular case, however dire his personal financial straits.

Besides, Giana Novak was an Equatorian. Her kind were notoriously stingy—but even more notoriously wealthy. Even absent that, the novelty of her presence alone had been enough to intrigue him into offering to help. If one of the colony's de facto royalty had ever left the rarefied air of their hermetically sealed habitat on the planet's surface to descend to these stygian depths, Jürgen had never heard of it. And he would have heard of it.

When he'd found her wandering the forbidden passageways two days ago, disoriented and looking for help, everything about her had screamed that she didn't belong. Wearing nothing more than a thin jumpsuit, her clothing had been punishingly inadequate for frigid tunnels which regularly alternated between rock and water-ice. But what marked her as one of the colony's upper crust was that she sported not a whisper of body modification that he could see. Almost every person on this world had augmented themselves with cybernetics or full-on prostheses to better tolerate this infernal world's extremes. The most notable of the holdouts to this habit were members of that uppermost of the upper crust, and even they often adopted cosmetic alterations.

And if she was coyly deflecting his talk of rates, just being in the good graces of someone with Equatorian clout could get him set up for life. Jürgen had more reason to know this than most. More importantly, it could bring enough visibility and power to bear on the Cult to wipe it out once and for all. No more wall-them-off-and-hope-for-the-best mentality. That way lay disaster.

Besides, Ms. Novak was down here looking for lost family members. Jürgen, more than perhaps anyone else on this entire blighted rock, could sympathize with that particular plight.

He walked the winding path, striped white and black with ice and rock and fitful lighting, back to his domicile without thought, passing by the usual array of abandoned buildings back from before the ban on living here had come down. There was just Jürgen now.

Just Jürgen and the Cult. It had been a difficult decision, defying the will of Meridian Equatoria, but someone had needed to keep an eye on the Cultists and their scheming. Simply walling them up wouldn't deal with the problem.

Jürgen possessed no biometrics the lock to his combination home and office would recognize. He had tried a DNA scrape once, but it took far too long to confirm his identity with the equipment he was able to afford. So he had reprogrammed the lock to read the particular energy signature of a tiny trickle off his personal power cell.

The door interlocks disengaged, and the structure's miniature airlock opened itself to him. The airlock was more for heat than for pressure. Given his current house guest was in no way equipped to deal with the cold, it was all the more important.

Once fully inside, Jürgen did not hesitate. It was not in his nature to hold back on bad news. He could vaguely remember a time when the opposite had been true. Perhaps it was one small matter he could thank the Cult's tampering for.

But he was not given the chance to speak. As commanding and icily confident as she had been almost from the moment he'd met her, his new client paused from pacing like a caged animal to round on Jürgen. Her face was as animated as he'd yet seen. She almost looked feverish.

"One of them is here," Ms. Novak said. "And I know where."

CHAPTER 10

With a single step, Marri Palmieri left the city and world of her birth, passed through a portal into nothingness and onto an arcing span of light. She had less than a heartbeat of time to feel awe at the shifting rays of blue-white luminance when she felt a tug across her entire being and was yanked bodily forward by some unseen force.

She tumbled, flailing for purchase where there was none. She watched her hands pass through shifting beams of light without interrupting them, as though the light was the solid thing and her flesh the insubstantial. In a building panic, she watched her hands become long bone claws before shifting back to the hands of a thirteen-year-old human girl. None of it made any difference. She was the prisoner of this rail of light, and she could no more influence it than she could change direction mid-jump.

With each tumbling pass, she caught glimpses of other entities. People, really, but in this place between places, they looked like cascading flows of geometric shapes, each one growing instantaneously out of the straight edges of its predecessor to form a new facet, each new growth accompanied by a sound almost too low to hear. Except sometimes those facets had faces. She saw Giana. She saw Karl.

She saw Stefani.

There were others, too. A male cop, face still twisted up into a snarl of injured pride and rage even though he looked half-asleep. A female lancer, red-haired and vacant-eyed above her uniform and armor. A child Marri didn't recognize but who could have been one of her Mice in another life. Other faces, all ones she didn't know. All the other people who had stepped through onto the Bridge at around the same time she had. All of them borne away from their dying world to somewhere else, some other planet entirely.

The unknown of it was almost enough to make Marri forget to feel afraid of the insanity going on around her right now. Then a portion of each turn allowed her to look out beyond the beam of light she was chained to, out into infinite darkness lacking even stars, and she stopped being afraid of the beam of light and began to see it more as the fragile haven it was.

It was the only order in an otherwise featureless void. That was, until an angry orange glow arose from somewhere further ahead of them. This new light brightened moment by moment, and Marri recognized it as what she'd seen through the Bridge portal before stepping through. Only then it had seemed as imminent as sunlight when she stood just inside a building's front door. And as the light shone upon Marri more and more brightly, she felt something else too: a rising heat.

She had just made her peace with the impossibility of everything around her, achieved something in the neighborhood of calm as their apparent destination came into view, when she felt a silent ripple pass through her formless body. The beam quaked all along its length.

Quaked and shattered.

It split into first dozens, then hundreds of smaller beams, each of which splayed out in different directions like unraveling twine. Marri had just enough time to see the chain of shapes that was Giana suddenly leap forward along one of those few strands still nearby. She moved as though she'd punched an accelerator nobody else possessed. But Marri had no time to contemplate her own much slower pace before being wrenched violently down another path. It felt more like a sharp angle than a gentle curve, and though she lacked form, she could apparently still feel pain.

Something's wrong. She had no proof of this, just gut instinct. But that had seldom led her wrong in the past.

The orange light and its accompanying warmth faded, as did the greater mass of the splitting beam. Only a small handful of those strands of light still hung in Marri's proximity, and they were no longer close enough to make out faces of those that rode them. In place of brightness and warmth came a deeper darkness and a prickling cold that grew to sear almost as much as heat would have.

She heard the voices before anything. Strange, electronic voices, raised in argument. Almost shouting. They started off distant but grew louder and more distinct moment by moment. Each possessed a strange distortion to her ears.

"If you have called this meeting for no other purpose than to challenge my authority over this order, Lukas, I fear you have wasted everyone's time."

"A rich claim, coming from you, Mathieu. You have dragged us kicking and screaming down the wrong path for years now. No more, I say. You can pile as many of the same exact failures up as high as you like, but you will never reach success."

"Such impudence! Did the Prophet not entrust me with this order's continued leadership before—"

"The Prophet did not comment on our leadership structure one way or another, which is very different than endorsing you," Lukas said. "And the Prophet is gone in any—by the untainted mind!"

The cold was so all-encompassing Marri didn't even realize her journey had ended until she opened her eyes. She was no longer riding that beam of light through infinite dark but crouched in a place, a room of some kind, huddled around herself desperately for warmth. This room was pleasantly if dimly lit, but calling it dark compared to the place she had just passed through was laughable. She could make out the shapes of people seated around her in a loose circle.

Or rather, seated around the large, stone table she had apparently materialized atop the center of.

There were several gasps of shock, and now, in the room with them, Marri could identify that strange distortion as an electronic sound. Like a person heard gasping over an intercom speaker—not their real voice, but a projection. Then one of those not-voices actually spoke.

"Are my optics malfunctioning? Or did a young Equatorian girl just appear in front of us? Is anyone else seeing this?" It was the voice of Lukas.

"I see her," said another voice, Mathieu. "I think it's safe to say we all do."

"It's just as he said would happen," said a third voice, the deepest and most resonant of all. "'In our moment of greatest doubt,' he said. And lo, the Prophet spoke true."

Voices sprang from all directions, as though they'd been predators lying in wait. First they were murmurs, but they quickly grew more heated. Marri tried to follow them, but even though she could understand most of the words, their accent was strange. Some words even sounded like a different language. The combination turned everything into a jumble in her head.

Her eyes finally adjusted—apparently the formless Marri that traveled between worlds didn't possess night sight—and she tried to really take in her surroundings. The stone table she crouched atop was bitterly cold. Just removing her hand from it was a relief. Whatever it was, it seemed to pull all the heat from her body wherever it touched.

The figures surrounding the table were strange in more than just their voices. Each wore a set of hooded robes. The color of each robe varied with the figure. They were similar only in their cut and their faded, tattered quality. Some of the figures wore their hoods raised, but for the few that didn't, Marri got a clear look at their faces.

Or what would have been faces had they been people.

She stared, not at skin or eyes or smiling teeth. Even snarling teeth might have been a comfort. Instead, they were metal with huge lenses for eyes and crudely articulated mouths. No two were alike, but none were more than a child's drawing of a human face.

"Child," said Mathieu. It came from one of the hoods, too dark to see into. "Please, do not be afraid. We will not hurt you. We've been waiting for you."

Nope. Marri didn't like that, however kindly the man sounded.

"Stay away!" she said, trying to rise, partially falling, then succeeding on her second attempt. Her legs were like jelly, like they hadn't existed until thirty seconds ago.

Maybe they hadn't.

"I want to get out of here!" She fought to keep her voice from breaking. She would not cry. She was not a child anymore! "Where is Stefani Palmieri? Where is Karl Yonnel? Giana Novak?"

Some of the hoods regarded each other in poses of confusion. The gestures looked so human Marri could almost forget what must be in those hoods.

"We do not know of whom you speak, Child," said Mathieu. "But if they are fellow travelers, I'm sure they will arrive in due course."

"How do I get out of here? You have to let me go!"

The man—if he was a man—rose slowly to his feet but made no move to approach.

"No one will try to keep you here," he said. "You have my word."

"Mathieu?" one of the others said, his voice far more uncertain.

"She will come to us when she is ready and not before," Mathieu said harshly. "Child," he said to Marri. "The door behind you will take you out of our hermitage. Follow the hallway straight and you will come to the exit. But there is nothing out there for you. If you wish to wait for your friends, you can do so here in a place of safe—"

"Leaving now," Marri said. She had no way of knowing if he was actually directing her to the exit, of course. But she had to try something. And he sounded like too much of an old coot like Karl to be so deceptive on the fly.

The door opened at her approach, which saved her trying to find the release.

The hallway beyond was long and straight, as the robo-man had said it would be. Marri was halfway down its length when the door at the far end was wrenched open. A figure stepped in from beyond.

Trap! The hallway erupted into strobing red LEDs and a blaring siren.

"Are you Marri Palmieri?" the figure called at her, his own voice nearly as distorted as the robo-men Marri had left in her wake. Though his sounded winded, as though he'd run all the way here in a hurry.

"Yes," she answered automatically, too stunned to lie convincingly.

"Come with me."

CHAPTER 11

REVELING in the hot water sluicing deliciously down the skin of her back, Caroline du Vernay shrieked at an unexpected chime echoing around her shower walls. *A message. Just a message*, she told her racing heart. It was not a common experience, not while she was thusly indisposed, in any event.

Startlement quickly gave way to annoyance. The reason it was not common was she had restricted messages in here as much as they could be restricted. Only the most dire or important were permitted past the filters. She could have trusted such tasking to her staff, but filters couldn't be finagled or prevailed upon the way ordinary people could. The shower was her sacred space, ironic since the use of so much water on such an arid world had to count as some kind of sin. Either her message filters had failed, or the colony must be collapsing around her.

For the sake of whoever had sent it, she prayed it was the latter.

Her seldom-used shower wall screen informed her that the message was text only, not video, so she went ahead and opened it.

Leeeen. It's happening, right when I said it would. Almost to the hour! Get your ass up here. P.S. You owe me ten mil. Don't think I'll let you welch.

The message was unsigned, but she didn't need a name to know who had sent it. Only one of her acquaintances—she would never stoop to call Niklaus a friend—would address her like that.

And only one had browbeaten her into betting him when the off-worlders would arrive.

Don't be mad at him just because you were stupid enough to accept the bet.

She sighed. Ten million. If this really was happening, she needed to get to the meeting room as soon as possible, but her reputation amongst her peers was battered enough without Niklaus crowing to everyone what a deadbeat she was. Besides, she thought she had that much easy to hand.

⋈

Caroline arrived still in a huff over the interruption of her morning. Why everyone—even colonists from another world!—seemed so hell-bent on disrupting her routines all the time, she would never know. Her arcology's central meeting room was nearly full when she arrived, which only added to her annoyance. She kept her head down and moved quickly toward her customary seat, but knowing her luck, the first person to notice her would be—

"Leeeeeen!" Niklaus called out through hands cupped around his mouth. "Care-oh-leeeeen!" Caroline ground her teeth behind her close-lipped, pasted-on smile. Niklaus *still* loved to mock the way she'd asked that her name be pronounced in the French fashion, but the only thing more annoying than his mockery was the intensification that came when he knew he was getting to her.

Caroline often reflected what a shame it was that the Equatorian class was exempted from being airlocked onto the planet's deadly surface.

Ignoring her tormentor, she kept her gaze focused on the west side of the 360-degree windows as she made her way to her seat. The windows started where the wall ended—just above head height.

Westward, they opened onto the artificially altered view of their parent star Naranja, the looming, orange sun dominating a wisp-thin atmosphere a muted shade of that same orange. But thanks to the constant efforts of the distant Scenic View Station projecting its image alteration fields high and wide, Caroline looked instead upon a sky that perfectly mimicked Earth's. So they were told, anyway. It was all glorious, azure blue with Naranja replaced by Sol, a burning white ball the proper and decent distance away.

Not at all like this hellhole.

Had Scenic View Station not been functioning, they couldn't have held this meeting here. Everyone present would be in the process of going blind and irradiated to lethal levels by now.

"Leen doesn't like to acknowledge me when she knows I've got something on her," Niklaus said in a faux whisper to his immediate neighbor, Xian Ginevra.

"Personally, I think it speaks poorly of the girl that she'd *ever* acknowledge you," Xian said as Caroline finally sat, fighting back a laugh. The woman was just as prickly to everyone—and this comment was hardly a praise of Caroline's character—but when Xian's guns were turned elsewhere, it was usually worth a chuckle.

"Careful, Xian," Niklaus said, his attitude flash-freezing on the spot. "When you have an attitude like yours, you can't afford to make any mistakes."

"Now that we're all here," said a voice from the far end of the table. "I'd like to get started, if that suits. I have an upcoming arraignment to research."

The comment in and of itself was notable. Halford Heller was as legendary as judges ever got. That stood to reason—the entire legal system of Anaranjado was his sandbox, after all—but so far as Caroline knew, he didn't often personally hear cases these days. They had to really interest him.

Alone amongst the attendees, not just here, but across all of the Equatorian arcologies, Heller resembled one of the other, poorer citizens of Anaranjado. Nearly every Equatorian had declined to alter their own bodies to accommodate the harsh planet. It instantly marked their status during the rare times when they left the arcologies and mingled amongst the ordinary citizenry. It set the Equatorians apart, proved that they alone had the resources to survive on this world without *needing* to modify or mutilate their bodies.

There were always *some* tweaks, of course. Even the body-purist zealots who lived at the colony outskirts consented to the replacement of faulty joints and organs and certain upgrades to handle the brutal climate their tidally locked world gifted them with. And most people had a basic data interface feeding curated info streams directly into their awareness, though thanks to the organic requirements of Harmony, that was as far as technologic tinkering with the brain was permitted. Posture though they might for the sake of status, no one in this room was wholly organic.

But of her social class, only Heller, so far as Caroline knew, had gone completely in the opposite direction. Perhaps that was why he was so popular with the masses. The people's judge. He was fully encased in scales, rather than the usual fashionable smattering. His synthetic eyes, as expressive as any person's, glowed a blue too luminous for eyes produced by nature. And if his body was the result of the cybernetic bleeding edge buttressed by vast personal wealth, his mind—though every bit as much meat as the rest of them—was as sharp as any on the planet.

The chatter around the table quieted with Heller's suggestion, as it normally did. Niklaus spoke next, meaning that it was him—or one of the underlings in his technological sandbox, anyway—that had detected whatever had precipitated this meeting.

"Perimeter sensors both at the old Bridge site and in surrounding environments have detected at least seven span openings just in the past two hours. There are some strange readings at other locations as well, places where sensors aren't calibrated for Bridge-type energy readings. Solar interference means we're still waiting for disparate networks to catch up with their reports as well. But given those limitations and the fact that we've already confirmed three arrival points, what we're seeing is consistent with there being more."

"I thought that overzealous xenolinguist reported just a single communication from a single colony," Xian said. "Are you saying we're being *invaded* in some coordinated action or attack by multiple colonies at once?"

"Not what I'm saying at all," Niklaus said. "Even the energy signatures we've positively identified seem off. I'm rapidly transitioning from 'educated guessing' to 'bullshitting out of my ass' here, but I think something scattered the span. Split the incoming beam so that it's not opening a single portal in one location but a number of much smaller portals across different areas on our end. Which means—"

"Scattered the span?" Xian interrupted with an audible scoff. "Is that even possible?"

Niklaus shrugged, unfazed. "If I'm right, then yes, because it's happening." He sounded so much more confident and competent now that he was not shit-talking Caroline or Xian, as though he forgot to be an asshole when his mind was engaged elsewhere. The dichotomy just made her hate him even more.

"Which means the numbers we're seeing now—in the hundreds, I'm guessing, are likely only a portion of what we'll ultimately see. If my people are right, scattering like this would be not just across space, but across time. You might have a million people stepping onto the Bridge's far end at roughly the same time and they might arrive here over hours, days, weeks even. I'm talking aside from the real-time two-week delay we predicted after the test message came through." He flashed Caroline an insolent grin. "And by *we*, I mean *I*. When you think about it, it makes my winning the bet even more amazing."

Fortunately, he would never let Caroline get too far down the path of forgetting what kind of person he really was.

"So they're here." This was Margaret Polliard, a deceptively motherly woman who had her hands in the health care sector of the colonial economy, a very lucrative enterprise on a planet so thoroughly committed to killing its inhabitants. She and Caroline's sandboxes crossed over frequently. "What are they doing?"

"Well, that's where things get weird," Niklaus said, his smile betraying his perverse love of delivering shocking news.

"I think I can speak best to that, young man." This was Wellington Reid, the self-styled commandant—so the person who paid the salaries—of the Anaranjadan Colonial Militia. Anaranjado had no formal military, so they were, in effect, mercenaries with a state-tolerated monopoly on violence. But she would never say that to Reid, whose tone was as stiff as his ramrod-straight posture, the only person here to adopt a military bearing.

"The colonists arriving at the Bridge site, where the bulk of our response force was concentrated, were taken into protective custody without serious incident," Reid said. "That being the case, there were several oddities, which my staff on-site are investigating further. More information on that when I can confirm it."

Caroline felt the frustrated curiosity ripple through the room. It mirrored her own. But Wellington Reid didn't like speculating aloud, at least, not outside his inner circle of close advisers, none of which were present. Prodding him to do so when he didn't want to would be counterproductive.

That normally wouldn't have stopped Equatorians from trying, but there was a very strong unwritten rule among them. Whether in this arcology or one of the others—who were undoubtedly meeting now and discussing this same issue from alternate perspectives—people stayed in their own sandboxes. Caroline didn't tell Reid how to run the ACM, and Reid didn't tell Caroline how to handle matters with Harmony.

"Two other reported incidents of arrivals in populated areas were far more violent in their reports. There are certainly casualties. How many, and on which side, are very confused, even for war reports. But I authorized the deployment of an experimental technology based upon the Bridge time-space distortion fields, and that appears to have averted at least one full-scale disaster as it was beginning."

Niklaus looked up sharply at that. "I didn't give you access to that tech for weaponization purposes."

"Then it's a good thing you didn't outright forbid it, now isn't it? Or I'd be bound by our polite little rules of interaction we've so daintily drawn between our respective fiefdoms, and we might collectively be in a world of shit right now."

Shocked silence greeted him. Wellington Reid was many things, but a man of profane outbursts was not one of them. He seemed not to notice the response to his mini tirade.

"My early reports are clear enough on one thing. There is something wrong with these colonists. Make no mistake. Either that or there are impostors among them who aren't human at all. Whichever it is, I am strongly considering harsher actions and moving my people to a much higher level of caution—at the barest minimum—when dealing with any of them."

Then his entire manner grew stiffer, if that were even possible.

"There is also one outskirt ACM patrol that should have reported in but has yet to." He turned to Niklaus, acting as if his previous outburst had never happened. "I would very much like to cross-reference my incident reports with your sensor readings to determine if their failure to call in might be the result of yet another incursion."

Normally, Caroline would have given a request like this even money at best. Less, after the stinging rebuke Reid had just delivered to Niklaus. The commandant could ask, but Niklaus might just say no. But there was an intensity to the older man's gaze that shook Caroline a bit, and she saw Niklaus register it as well. This was something personal to the commandant. She recalled that his son was currently serving in the ACM and wondered if that were related.

"I'll have the report sent to you," Niklaus said without argument, and the sudden tension in the room lessened. It was always such when a jurisdictional conflict between them was averted. Each of them had the power and resources to inflict real harm on the others should they desire, even if the means of that harm differed wildly. So it was always a relief when someone was willing to back down.

"Thank you," Reid said mildly. "I'll be sure to forward the report to you on the experimental technology's performance. I'm told something in it burned out after a single use. My on-site commander had to bluff her way through the rest of the confrontation."

Niklaus scowled and looked as though he very much wanted to respond to this. But he held his tongue, and Reid's eyes went back to scanning his personal tablet as he continued, taking in some data stream the rest of them weren't privy to. "On top of what I've already mentioned, we are receiving additional reports virtually minute-to-minute. The situation is very fluid in a way that troubles me greatly."

"What is the status of the ship?" As ever when Heller spoke, Caroline had to fight against jumping in surprise like she had back in her shower. It wasn't just that Heller seldom spoke in these meetings. The man had an unnatural stillness about him. Maybe it was all those synthetic parts lacking the organic need to fidget.

"Exactly where I told you it would be when this group asked me so nicely to accelerate two weeks ago," Xian said sourly. The *Ultima Thule* was in her personal sandbox, her company being the only one with the construction expertise to build something as vast and complex as an interstellar colony ship. "Which is to say 'not finished.'"

"Yes, I recall your admonitions. But can it safely transit to the target world?" Heller pressed, his mouth tightening a little at the corners.

"With regard to structure, propulsion, and life support, yes," Xian said, the words sounding dragged out of her by hooks. "At least, in theory. But the cargo sections are incomplete. We'd lack the resources to sustain a full complement. And the ship's governing mind is practically an Alzheimer's patient. It would require months, if not years, to work out all the quirks there."

Caroline almost interjected. The ship's mind was her purview, after all, and she didn't appreciate it being disparaged, but Xian was essentially correct in her analysis. AI was forbidden on Anaranjado, as was only logical and prudent. Any purely synthetic intellect would have offered a way around Harmony's control.

And while that stricture did not apply to Equatorians—nothing was explicitly forbidden to Equatorians—it meant they lacked any kind of practical expertise in the subject. Not an ideal foundation upon which to place the weight of an entire colony ship—including all their lives. As a result, they had gone a different direction, and *grown* an organic brain especially suited to the purpose, using all the experience working with Harmony had taught them. And the brain had its own version of the organism, of course.

But though it had achieved consciousness and was as developed as a human mind in many ways, it was still very much a work in progress.

"If anything went wrong that the ship-brain couldn't address—" Xian continued.

"I believe I have a solution for that," Heller said cryptically. Caroline blinked, because it was her sandbox, and she very much did not. "Regardless, I think we need to prepare for the worst-case scenario and assume that a quick escape from this world might shortly be in order. For those of us with the appropriate credentials, at least."

"There's also the issue of the lottery process for who gets to be on the crew," Xian said. She was flailing now. Generally, when Heller took a stance against an opinion you held, it meant you had lost the argument, whether you'd had a chance to advance your own position yet or not. Xian knew this as well as anyone, but she was a stubborn woman. "We haven't even begun the process of selecting from among the populace—"

"My solution will work for that as well," Heller said. By the clipped nature of his voice, it was an obvious solution, at least to him. He declined to elaborate, but likely he was saving that solution for Xian's ears alone. Instead, he turned his cybernetic gaze upon Caroline, and she found herself sitting up straighter without consciously meaning to.

"What of your situation?"

Our situation, she wanted to correct him. This concerned them all. But in a very real way, it was all on her, and she didn't know of any way to squirm out of that fact short of recovering Subject Rho. Harmony was her sandbox, however much she had inherited it from her father.

She had lost the program's most prized asset on her watch.

"I'm fairly certain the Cult has Subject Rho," she said. Her people had spared nothing in their interrogation of the one suspect they'd managed to apprehend.

"How certain?" Heller's voice was never anything but gentle, but his disappointment in her was profound, as vast as the unfiltered sun in their sky.

"Certain enough," she said. She turned to Reid. "I may need assets to get him back."

"We're a mite busy at the moment, in case you weren't listening," Reid said with a tight smile.

Definitely his son, Caroline thought. The man's whole world was shrinking down to that one fact before their very eyes.

"I'm sure an enterprising young woman with your 'connections' in that part of the world must know someone who can look into this matter for you," Reid went on.

My connections. He meant her past romantic relationship with a non-Equatorian. Fucking them was fine. She'd wager at least half the people at this meeting had done it. It was, after all, one of the most delicious of taboos. Feelings were the problem. Her dalliance was years in the past now, but it was a stain she would never live down. If she hadn't inherited everything to do with Harmony research and thus gained ultimate responsibility for the glue that held the colony together, Caroline knew she'd have been cast out long before.

All that meant it was a bitter pill to swallow indeed that her best option for finding Subject Rho was the very man she'd had her unfortunate dalliance with.

"I have an option or two worth investigating," she said, refusing to elaborate further. In truth, she had already reached out to Jürgen once, priming the pump so to speak, while being careful not to reveal *who* was reaching out to him.

"Please do," Heller said. Caroline hoped he would let the matter lie at that, and to her relief, he obliged, turning back to Xian as though Caroline's portion of the matter was settled. "If a radical element really has taken Subject Rho, that only amplifies the urgency of your preparations."

A radical element. Said as though Meridian Equatoria were not responsible for that very element's formation.

Xian looked mutinous, but she managed to bite back any retorts she might have been considering.

"And Caroline," Heller said. Shit. She wasn't off the hook after all. His pronunciation of her name was as flawless as ever. Disappointed in her or not, he at least afforded her a respect few of her peers did. But that just made it worse. "It's only my opinion, of course," he said. "But it seems to me that Subject Rho has become more liability than asset to us at this point."

"We need him to—"

"I understand that the work he allows us to do is important," Heller said gently. "But if an anomaly like him happened once, it will happen again. And I can't help but note the timing. Just as you were arguing in favor of expanding his use-case, as it were—an argument firmly rejected by your peers as unsound, I might add—this happens. Quite the coincidence, that."

"You can't think I had anything to do with this?" Caroline had trouble getting the words out around her shock and fear. It wasn't fair. Heller acted like her proposal's rejection had been universal, but he had spearheaded it. There was no way to be certain what the others really thought in that instance.

All she had argued was that since Harmony provided them so many indirect benefits with keeping the populace in line, why couldn't it benefit the Equatorians directly if they adopted it themselves?

Heller had *not* liked that.

"That's not what I'm saying at all." His tone was placating. "But this should underscore the dangers of such suggestions. The people need Harmony to tame the barbarism and rebelliousness inherent to their temperaments. We suffer no such afflictions. Our positions in society prove this. They must be controlled for their own good. For us to be controlled in the same way, even if it conferred benefits upon us, would be an abomination against the natural order."

"I just—"

"Just promise me you'll consider how much harm Subject Rho could do—maybe *is doing*—in the wrong hands. Consider whether your odds will be better at removing Subject Rho from the equation instead of recovering him."

Caroline had to fight the urge to argue further. It would do more harm than good.

"I will," she said, and Heller smiled as he nodded in thanks. Still, the disappointment on his face lingered, and it withered her. It had seemed so foolish to her, so backward, the Equatorian refusal to make use of the very organism which made their society run so smoothly. Smoothly on paper, anyway.

Why not use it to improve their own cognition or emotional resilience or *anything* their brains did sub-optimally? Why deny themselves the truth of the superiority they already believed themselves to possess?

Perhaps if she hadn't hired the wrong person to investigate those very matters, the concept might still be something her peers would countenance.

Instead, she had put their entire class, their entire way of life, at risk.

She was barely aware of the meeting breaking up around her. Much as the idea pained her, she had to get back in touch with Jürgen. She rose to go and do that only to nearly collide with Niklaus, smiling his very best shit-eating grin.

"Pay up," he said simply, proffering a hand.

With a noise of disgust, Caroline reached into her purse and withdrew the secure cash chit. The whole of the ten million was on it. She'd considered bringing many, *many* chits of smaller denominations just to be a prick about it, but ultimately that would have been more trouble than it was worth.

She pushed it into his hand and kept right on pushing, turning the whole thing into a gesture shoving him aside as she swept from the meeting room, ignoring his mocking laughter as it followed her.

CHAPTER 12

"MY NAME IS JÜRGEN FENNEC," the man said as he bodily dragged Marri down the corridor the robed man had indicated was the exit. "Your family has hired me to find you." Given the way he towered over her, easily the tallest man she'd ever seen, it was difficult to get a good look at him. His coat was high-collared. It reminded Marri of Father, the Strange Man, only without the hat.

"My family? You mean Stefani?" Marri kindled with hope. "Karl?"

"No," Jürgen Fennec said brusquely. His accent was strange, blunt and so confident it almost sounded aggressive. Marri had only ever heard similar accents in passing back in Coldgarden. "Giana Novak."

Marri almost balked. Giana was the last of her group she wanted to see. A distant last. But thinking about it, anyone she knew would be preferable to a bunch of weird, hooded strangers who kept creepily calling her "child."

Still, Marri had literally just arrived. It begged the question of how Giana had gotten here quickly enough to hire someone to find the others. She recalled seeing Giana rocket ahead.

"Where are the others?"

"I do not know," Jürgen said. He hesitated slightly before admitting. "You are the first I have found. I will continue looking however. You may rest assured."

"Do we have to move so fast?" Marri's shoulder was starting to ache. "I don't think they're following us."

"Yet," Jürgen said. "They argue ceaselessly, but you can never presume to know who will come out on top." He did bring them to a halt, but it was because they'd reached what looked like a heavy outer door, probably the one he'd entered from. From a pocket of the coat, Jürgen withdrew a device and plugged it into a slot by the door, which clunked open.

"I don't know which is more worrisome," Jürgen said. "The fear that next time I try this door it will be hardened against me, or wondering why they never bother?" But Jürgen frowned at the door readout. "Interesting. I speak too soon. They have blocked me from a deeper portion of the complex. I wonder . . . But that is a question for later." Marri thought it was one of those times when a person was just talking to themselves, so she didn't answer.

They exited into tunnels of bare rock and ice. Marri had only thought the meeting room she'd arrived in was cold. This was frigid beyond imagining. Her teeth began chattering instantly. Yet the further away they got from the door, the more Jürgen seemed to relax.

"What relation is Giana to you?" he asked after one particularly awkward stretch of silence. "You two do not look alike."

Sister? Mother? Appearance aside, neither made much sense due to the particular age difference between them. Marri wondered if "creepy aunt" was a valid answer.

She split the difference. "She's more of an unofficial aunt." It was hard to get the words out between chatters.

"Ah. Like your godmother?"

Marri had no idea what a godmother was. "Exactly."

They walked on in silence for a time, Marri trying to scrub her hands along her arms to generate a little warmth through friction.

"I've been wondering ever since meeting Ms. Novak," Jürgen

said, breaking the silence. He no longer sounded blunt and bluff, but like he was dying of curiosity while trying not to show it, a failed attempt at being cagey. "How did you and your family come to be down here?"

He's tried to get this out of Giana and gotten nowhere. He's hoping a kid will be more likely to let something slip. Unfortunately for him, Marri had quite a bit of experience verbally squirming out of a suspicious adult's crosshairs.

"Well, it wasn't my idea." True enough. It had been Father who had commanded they all flee the planet for their lives. "I'm only a kid. I just do what the grown-ups tell me." Also not a lie. If a planet-sized alien being who might as well be a god wasn't a grown-up, no one was.

And if her misleading statements led Jürgen to suspect this was all Giana's fault, Marri was fine with that, since it technically was.

Apparently her evasions had worked because Jürgen lapsed back into silence, allowing Marri to focus on not dying for the remainder of the walk.

At last they stood before a much smaller building, albeit one that possessed a round hatch very much like the one the robed robo-men had installed as their front door. Jürgen plugged something on his wrist into a socket on the door shaped for the purpose, and it rotated itself aside. Almost immediately beyond was another door, almost identical, but Marri could only spare attention for the blast of blissfully warm air which greeted them only to rush out into the smothering chill of the tunnel beyond.

"Step inside and we can begin to warm you up," Jürgen said, his words clipped and efficient. Marri obeyed if only because she lacked the will to resist at this point. The door slid shut after Jürgen joined her, and a fresh blast of hot air flooded the tiny chamber. Then the inner door opened into a small but cozy space with a figure huddled in blankets on a couch along the back wall.

"There you are."

Marri knew the voice before she realized the blanket-swathed figure was the woman—or "woman"—speaking. Giana's head emerged from the blanket bundle's apex, her skin paler than usual, her eyes sunken looking.

She looked as though she'd spent several nights in a row lying wide awake.

Neither Giana nor Marri had ever liked the other, and that was before Giana had been revealed to be some sort of walking disease-monster. Or maybe, before she'd *become* some sort of walking disease-monster. Marri still wasn't entirely clear on that score. It didn't really matter. However many versions of Giana she had or hadn't dealt with, she'd hated them all.

"Thank goodness Jürgen found me!" Marri said. "It was so scary out there." She wasn't sure if she was overselling it or not. Giana looked annoyed and trying to hide it so probably.

"You must be exhausted," said the woman who personified the word. "Let's get you warm and rested, and then you can tell us all about what happened." There was a tightness to her words, probably too subtle to pick up on unless you knew her.

We need to get our stories straight, is what Marri heard in that tone. Giana might not look good, but her thinking was still sharp at least.

And she was right. Marri didn't really want to be found out in some complicated lie, even if it would annoy Giana. The thought of it was stressful, exhausting. And then, all of a sudden, it became over-whelming. It felt like a weight was pressing down on Marri's chest, a weight which grew with every breath.

"I could really use a bathroom," Marri said. It was the first excuse to extricate herself from both their presences she could think of.

"On the left," Jürgen said simply. Marri ran for the door he'd indi-cated before Giana could gainsay her. All of a sudden, for reasons she couldn't explain, she had to be alone. It felt like a joke or a prank that had become real.

The bathroom was the most normal thing Marri had seen since arriving on this strange world. It could have easily been mistaken for any bathroom in any low-rent place in Coldgarden. Without thinking why, Marri turned on the sink as high as it would go and stared at her reflection. She'd meant it to be just a glance, but then found she couldn't break her own gaze. It was like being trapped forever by yourself, a pair of plaintive brown eyes like hooks in her soul.

And then, out of nowhere, she began to cry.

CHAPTER 13

MARRI EMERGED from the bathroom an hour later, red-faced and puffy-eyed. She was utterly humiliated. Despite the running water, there was no way they'd missed her wracking sobs. And even if they hadn't, the proof of it would be all over her face.

She hadn't cried like that since her mother died, and that was a time she thought about as little as possible.

"It's been a hard few days," Giana said. She sounded entirely sincere for once.

"Yep." Marri croaked the word, not daring to say more.

"There's no shame in having to let it out."

Marri continued to say nothing, but she spared Giana a murderous glare.

"How long were you with the Cult?" Jürgen either didn't notice the tension in the air or had just decided it wasn't going to stop him getting his answers.

Having had no chance to form a shared story with Giana, Marri opened her mouth to answer then let her eyes well up and shook her head as if she just . . . couldn't. It made her want to throw up, but it was safer than trying to improvise. It was also kind of scary that she could put herself on the verge of crying again so quickly.

Giana stepped in. "She vanished two days ago, the day before you found me. But I already told you that. Not long after we arrived here, we got separated." That subtle glare was back. Marri's breakdown had given them no time to plan. Marri was just going to have to improvise.

A cult, Jürgen had called the robo-men. And he hadn't bothered to mask the hatred in his tone.

"They kidnapped me," Marri blurted. "Just after we arrived. I went wandering down an alley alone, just trying to see what I could see, and suddenly everything went dark. I woke up just a little bit before you found me."

As lies went, she had told worse, but also much better. Being unconscious for several days seemed unlikely, but at least it would spare her having to provide details of her "captivity."

Jürgen was frowning. It was hard to read his expression with him wearing those goggles, but he seemed to be in thought. Perhaps he wasn't sure how much to say. Marri certainly understood that feeling.

"Do you have any new injuries?" he asked. "Any pain you didn't have before, as if someone cut you or performed some kind of medical procedure on you?"

"No," Marri said, newly disturbed.

"That is well. Still, better to be safe than sorry. It would not be appropriate to ask to examine you, but I would encourage you to please have Ms. Novak look you over when you have more privacy, just to be certain."

"All right." Marri wasn't sure what else to say. It was hard to keep her focus on the lying when she was goggling at Giana's statement, which Jürgen had not contradicted. Marri had been on this world less than three hours by her estimation. Now here was Giana, saying she'd arrived more than a *day* ago?

How was that possible? They'd left Coldgarden at the same time.

As if reading her mind, Giana flashed an I'll-explain-it-to-you-later look.

"But forgive me," Jürgen pressed Giana. "You still haven't

explained what precisely you are doing down here. Surely you realize how unusual this is, for someone of your station, not to mention an entire *family*—with a child, no less—choosing to come here."

While Marri was trying to figure out just who the hell Jürgen thought they were, Giana was all over it. "Your instincts are correct. We aren't here by choice. We were compelled here by circumstance."

"Perhaps at some point you will trust the detective you've hired enough to explain the entire story. I would be far more effective at helping you if you did so, and it would not be the first kidnapping I've investigated and resolved satisfactorily." He indicated Marri with a not-so-subtle gesture. "In the meantime," he said, turning to Marri, "we must speak of the Cult, and why you must be watchful, and never again go anywhere near their lair."

I didn't go there by choice, she almost said, but this was one of those adult moments where they were going to have their say no matter what you said back.

"Yes, tell us about this cult," Giana said. Marri knew her expression. Ravenous curiosity. She was trying to learn everything she could about this world. Even though it was obviously the smart move, Marri mistrusted the impulse when it came from Giana. "We do not receive much news of such things from Meridian Equatoria."

Jürgen shook his head, frowning deeply. "It is difficult to imagine such a gap of experience, especially since I have lodged formal complaints with them directly. But I have always heard stories of how insular you can be up there. So I will speak as if you know nothing, even if I can't believe you have truly never heard of them. They represent a sect of radical body-modifiers, intent on utterly eliminating biology from humanity, in effect, of removing humanity from themselves. Or themselves from humanity."

That explained all their robot-ness. Marri wondered how much of them was still . . . She couldn't think of another term but *meat*.

"Why?" Giana asked.

"They believe that which makes us great, makes us one people striving against the universe, is actually a set of shackles binding us, holding us back." He lowered his hood then, and Marri restrained herself from letting out a little breath of surprise.

"I am more familiar with their methods than almost anyone alive," he said.

His head was completely bald, except that wasn't really the right term, because it wasn't skin up there, it was a glinting, striated metal in the shape of a skullcap. He removed his goggles next, and for a moment Marri thought he wore a second set underneath.

Then she realized she was seeing his eyes. Or the machines that had replaced his eyes.

Artificial lenses glinted in the cold light of the ceiling LEDs. They shifted, and Marri heard a little whirring as servo motors rotated his electromechanical eyes inside metal sockets.

"This was their handiwork, I take it?"

"Correct, Ms. Novak. I made the tragic mistake of going to them during a confusing time in my life. It took my parents dying, freezing to death down here in the tunnels looking for me, before I awoke to their madness and made my escape. So you see why I was so anxious to help you, despite no talk of compensation."

"You needn't worry, Mr. Fennec. I promise you will be more than adequately paid." Giana's empty promise seemed to satisfy the man, and he went on.

"The Cult seeks to not be human by their own admission. As this is their stated goal, I need express no concern over their well-being. Humans look after our own. All others are rivals at best, enemies at worst. Had I the legal authority to do so, I would exterminate every last Cultist, or at least get them declared Defective and imprisoned or banished from the world to the orbitals or beyond. Anaranjado would be better off without them."

Anaranjado. It had the sound of a place name, perhaps even a world name. Marri filed it away. But it was the rest of what Jürgen said that truly had an impact. Marri wondered if Giana felt the same chill she felt at these words. It was so bone-deep, she thought even Jürgen should have felt it.

Humans look after our own. All others are rivals at best, enemies at worst.

"But you must both be exhausted," Jürgen said with his normal abruptness. "Ms. Novak has been using the bedroom and I the couch here in the office since her arrival, but I'm afraid I have only the one bed, and it is not big enough for two. However, there is a spare cot I can make up, though I'm afraid it would not fit in the bedroom. Working out of my home as I do, it behooves me to make my office the most impressive part of this place," he added as a kind of apology.

"We can take the couch and cot here in the office," Giana said. "It's not fair of us to put you out of your own room any longer."

A beat. "If you're certain?"

"Yes, quite certain."

"Very well. I will see to it," Jürgen said.

CHAPTER 14

JÜRGEN SPENT the next little while routing his work matters to his bedroom terminal. Unfortunately for his Equatorian guests, this meant that any privacy they might wish for their reunion would have to wait. Once he was done, he was all set to give them that time alone when Marri approached him.

"I'm hungry," she announced without ceremony.

"I'm sorry for her bluntness," Ms. Novak said. "But I could also do with a meal."

Jürgen couldn't blink anymore, but that was the impulse he felt.

"I showed you where the nutrition bricks are stored, yes?"

"I'm afraid I ate through all of those by the end of the day yesterday," Ms. Novak said. "In all the excitement of locating Marri, I forgot to tell you."

Jürgen did not eat a lot himself—not enough of him was biological to need to eat much, and he had several implants which could store glucose and protein long-term, reducing that need even further.

Still, for his all-organic houseguests, this obviously wouldn't do. His calculations for how much even a single baseline human would consume in a day had obviously been wildly mistaken.

"I do not cook," he said. He also had no ingredients to cook, so it had been something of a pointless statement. He did have a small emergency stash. It was against his nature to dip into that in what, to him, did not qualify as an emergency. He could go back up to the habitat levels to replenish his normal-use stockpile, but he was quite tired. This was mostly in his head—quite literally, since most of his components didn't get tired, but his brain still needed rest. "But I do have another stash of bricks."

He could replenish this just as easily as his normal stockpile, after all.

Ms. Novak had consumed the bricks without complaint, but Marri, upon being handed one, was not so delicate in her feelings, at least as they showed on her face. Still, she maintained a minimum of politeness verbally, even as she grimaced with each bite. Giana slipped away to bed soon after. She looked, if Jürgen was any judge, significantly worse than yesterday. It was strange. Aside from her disorientation, she had seemed in perfect health when he'd found her, and she had not been out long enough to suffer from the effects of exposure, which were hardly delayed in any event.

"Please let me know if you need anything," Jürgen said as Marri rose some ten minutes later to join her. As the door between kitchen and office slid shut behind the girl, Jürgen could already hear the deep, rhythmic breathing of Ms. Novak asleep.

CHAPTER 15

THE NEXT TIME Karl saw light, it was not orange and angry, but cool and blue tinged. The sun wasn't here. That meant he must no longer be outdoors.

His eyes snapped open—or tried to. He rubbed at them as though to force them to do what he commanded.

"Relax, Mr. Yonnel, everything's all right," said an oddly accented voice. It had an artificial quality, as though it was coming through some kind of speaker.

"—am I?" The first word had come out a garbled mess, but he'd meant it to be "where." He found to blink sleep from his eyes.

"You're in a medical facility, Mr. Yonnel. This is the human colony of Anaranjado, and you traveled across a Bridge to get here. Do you remember that?"

"Yes," he croaked. "Medical facility?"

"Yes," the voice said again. This is the Sunnyside Central Medical Center. I assure you, you are quite safe here. Outside the Meridian Cities themselves, no medical facility on this planet is larger or better equipped. May I ask if you are comfortable? Do you require any adjustment in the room temperature?"

At last, he managed to bring the light into swimming focus, only to see an older woman with a pasted-on smile looking down on him from behind the plastic faceplate of some kind of hazard suit which covered her entire body. The glare of the lights and the shadowing effects of the helmet made it difficult to make out her features.

He found he was lying down, his top half partially elevated. *Hospital bed.* His clothing had been changed as well. The street clothes he'd left Coldgarden wearing were gone. He now sported a slate-gray body suit of a substance he would almost compare to flow-matter if that hadn't been such a ridiculous assumption. No one could afford to dress hospital patients in material so expensive and difficult to produce. He tried to think back on how he had gotten here, or at least to those frenzied last moments of consciousness, but the sudden imposition of suffocating darkness and the screaming from all directions left his memory a soup.

"Very comfortable," he answered belatedly, trying to sound nonthreatening. "Which is a bit of a surprise, if I'm honest. I thought it would be a lot hotter basically everywhere based on how things were when I arrived."

"Yes, I can understand your confusion. This world was chosen as a colony settlement because it was believed conditions were much more suitable for human habitation than they turned out to be. But the important point is that most of our Sunnyside facilities and settle-ments are safely underground. That doesn't include the Bridge site, where you arrived. But it most definitely includes this hospital. This site was chosen because the cavern is especially large and deep, and we are sitting at the bottom of it with a great deal of shaded, empty space over our heads before you even reach the surface rock. We prefer our hospitals to be cold. It helps stifle infection. Now, are you in any kind of discomfort, Mr. Yonnel?"

"No," Karl said. "Other than the etiquette kind where you know my name and I don't know yours. How do you know my name?"

In answer, she held up Karl's handheld. "We recovered this. I trust you recognize it?"

Karl nodded, hoping nothing too difficult to explain remained on the device, since they seem to have gained access to it.

"Good," she said. "I hope you'll forgive the invasion of your privacy. We were trying to determine whether you had any allergies to medications or other medical needs we should be aware of. It does not have much in the way of usable information, but it did indicate your name, at least."

That made sense. Handhelds were fairly dumb devices once they were cut off from their home network, which now lay in ruins some massive number of light-years away from wherever Karl was now.

"If you are up for it, Mr. Yonnel, I'm hoping you can answer some questions. They are of a somewhat urgent matter, I'm afraid. You and your fellow refugees have all suffered a terrible shock, so I can give you some time, but not as much as I'd like."

"I don't mind answering your questions," he said, hoping it would prove to be the truth. "But I would like to know who you are." Might as well begin at the beginning. It might give him a chance to summon up whatever remained of his lancer self-discipline.

"My name is Dr. Helena Cardiff," the woman said. "I am part of the emergency medical response team detailed to the medical facility nearest the Bridge site by my government when it became clear that a crossing event was indeed impending. We did have some warning, thankfully, because of your colony's test message approximately two weeks ago. Otherwise, I suspect things would have been far more chaotic, though that's hard to imagine."

Two weeks? Karl hadn't been aware Stefani had been that far along before they'd even broken up. But then, she hadn't exactly been herself then. Or at any time since they'd begun dating. It didn't track with what he'd known of the project, though. It seemed more likely that the Bridge distorted time in some way. It distorted space readily enough, and the two were related, he knew from some distant memory of physics class.

But those kinds of thoughts were not the path toward calm. Karl tried to assess Dr. Cardiff instead. The woman had a brisk, no-nonsense demeanor that immediately put him in the mind frame of thinking of her as a colleague. Which led to his next question.

"Are you . . . military?" He'd been going to say *a lancer*, but of course that particular organization had been a quirk of Coldgarden.

She paused for a considering moment before replying. "I'm a major in the Anaranjadan Colonial Militia," she said, seeming to re-appraise him on the fly. "Are you military as well, then? Your ID didn't indicate as much."

"Ex-military," he said, deciding to spare her his jargon.

"You must excuse me," she said. "Would it be more courteous to address you by your rank?"

"No, no," he said, fighting down a wince. "Just Karl is fine."

"Very well, Mr. Yonnel. And is your service where you got that injury to your hip?"

Karl barked a laugh despite knowing it would hurt. "Something like that." He froze in surprise. The laugh hadn't hurt. In fact, he found he couldn't feel his injured hip at all. The shock of it cleared the last of the cobwebs from his mind.

His confusion must have been plain on his face.

"We've corrected the injury," Dr. Cardiff said. "It was a simple enough procedure. You were lucky. Doubly lucky."

"How so?"

"I said I had questions, Mr. Yonnel. Are you ready to get into that portion of things?" Her words and tone promised an imminent change in her demeanor. Karl had never been a cop, but he suddenly felt he was staring at one.

"I'm guessing I know what you are going to ask, considering that haz suit you're sporting."

Despite the helmet making it difficult to tell for certain, he thought she smiled thinly at the remark. At the very least, she seemed to take it for his assent. "You are lucky, Mr. Yonnel, because you were among the first we took in for medical evaluation and, as the ultimate result of that evaluation, the procedure to correct your hip. Had we waited on either of those, they would be on indefinite hold. Medical procedures of any kind on your fellow refugees have been halted because of several *incidents*."

If they were lucky, all she was talking about was hypermutation.

"And you were doubly lucky because based on our initial observations—and unbeknownst to us when we began your procedure— you stood a decent chance of being a victim of one of these incidents yourself." A thread of nerves wormed through her voice. If she'd been the one to operate on him, she must only now be aware of the danger she'd been in.

Except, of course, if everything the great being at the center of Coldgarden's planet had told them was true, the people of this world would be in no danger. Not from hypermutation contagion effects, at any rate.

"How many have we lost?" he asked.

"Seventeen so far, most in a seeming cluster. But you are getting ahead of my questions for you, and I prefer to keep such things tidy."

"May I ask why you are asking me? The way you are talking, it doesn't sound as though you've talked to anyone else."

"Ah, yes. The overwhelming majority of your fellow colonists displayed significant levels of confusion, agitation, and in some cases, hostility." The pause before the last word was brief, but Karl was pretty sure it had been there. "As a result, we have sedated everyone recovered from the Bridge site—nonviolently and non-invasively, I assure you."

She had neatly identified that worry, then, which meant they were already putting some things together.

"It was easier to get some under than others," she went on, "but for the time being, particularly during this period observation, I think it is best for all parties. You were identified by the forward team as being someone attempting to calm the chaos. In fact, my squad lead bet me that you had a military background based on how you behaved, so it seems I owe him a drink. Regardless, it makes as much sense to speak with you first as anyone. Satisfactory?"

"Yes," Karl said, though he could still wish she'd picked anyone else. Particularly someone more gifted in lying than he.

"Very good. For starters, Mr. Yonnel, what can you tell me about the affliction that seems to only strike and kill your people when they take injury?"

"Before I answer, I need to know if my loved ones are safe," Karl said. He wasn't sure why he was using vital medical information as a bargaining chip, but it was also the only one he had, and in case he couldn't convince Dr. Cardiff he posed no threat, this might be his only chance. "I crossed the Bridge with three others. Four, if you count the baby." He considered describing each of them, but if they'd pulled his ID so easily, maybe names would be best. "Stefani, Marri, and Ella Palmieri." He paused, but even if he didn't much care about Giana, she might have more information. "And Giana Novak."

"These are your family? Your people?" It was an oddly phrased question, but it was the warmest she'd sounded since Karl had woken, so he made no attempt to hedge or qualify his response.

"Yes," he said simply.

"I will of course ask after them, Mr. Yonnel." She bent to some kind of console and, struggling because of the massive gloves she wore, tapped out a series of commands or inputs or something directly into the glowing screen. She confirmed spelling in a couple of cases with him, then completed her query and turned back.

"Now while we wait for word, I really must insist you answer my questions. The safety of both my colony and your fellow refugees depends on it."

Karl decided to assume that this was her making good on her promise to search for the others. He also felt safe in assuming he couldn't stall any longer, so he wracked his brain. He needed to appropriately convey the risk to Coldgardeners while convincing Dr. Cardiff that her people—Anaranjadans she had said?—should not be at risk while *also* making sure she still took care, in case he had everything wrong.

While not also revealing the truth of the people of Coldgarden and getting the lot of them cast out into the withering sun to desiccate like slugs.

"That's a long story," he said.

"We are currently barred from performing any medical procedures on your people, Mr. Yonnel," Dr. Cardiff said. "Or even allowing them to wake. It will remain this way until we get answers to my superiors' complete satisfaction. So I've got time, but many of them may not."

Karl blew out his cheeks. Where to begin? There was a chance, particularly if he was the only one they were talking to, of at least buying some time.

"It's called hypermutation," he said. "Anytime anyone from my colony gets sick or takes an injury, it's a threat to our lives. And you should know that this can have an amplification effect. If one person starts to hypermutate, others nearby can, even if they were perfectly fine a few seconds before. That's probably what happened with that cluster of casualties you described. But," he added as she stiffened, "to the best of my knowledge, hypermutation should only affect people who were born on my world."

Giana, or whatever Giana had become, would have been better at this. Or Marri. Or Stefani. Karl had always found it easy enough to prevaricate or even outright lie if he was ordered to by a superior. It was much harder when he had no one to point to but himself. Still, he thought he could manage if he kept it to true statements, even if they were misleading.

"The bottom line is it's not so much a disease as a quirk of the biology of that planet that found its way into us over the generations," he finished. That was true on several levels.

"And what evidence do you have that it can't spread to *my* people?"

The planet-sized creature whose immune system I and most of the city descended from told me. At least I think it did. Nothing about that conversation seemed real to him even now, despite still being so fresh in his mind.

"Well, I know we've studied it extensively. I mean, obviously. I'm not an expert." She would quickly sniff out the lie if he pretended to be. "But everything I've heard from the biggest experts we have is that if you weren't born on that world, you wouldn't be susceptible."

"Our people who had significant exposure before we were aware of the threat, myself included, are currently under quarantine," Cardiff said leadenly. "So I suppose we'll see for ourselves soon enough." She fixed him with her gaze. "And is that the reason your people fled your colony to come here? To get away from the environmental effects causing this . . . hypermutation?"

Karl almost leaped on this perfect, gift-wrapped explanation for their arrival. But something in him told him to pause and think. Maybe more of Iazmaena Delgassi's paranoia had rubbed off on him than he realized.

Or maybe it was Dr. Cardiff's eyes. Now that his eyesight had adjusted to the ambient lighting and he really looked at them, they didn't look normal, those eyes. Opalescent, almost seeming to emit a faint glow, they looked technological. And finally getting a look at her face, what he'd taken to be some sort of body sleeve that came up to wrap around her chin and the starts of her cheeks now looked to be more grafted-on than worn.

If everything he'd seen the past few days was to be believed, Karl wasn't a human in the slightest. But this woman, he now thought, wasn't entirely human herself.

So he changed what he'd been going to say.

"No. Hypermutation is a daily hazard, but we've learned to live with it—more or less. What we were running from was the creatures."

Because, even without that little pause she'd almost slipped past him, it seemed impossible that there had been no incidents of *that* kind.

"Creatures," she said with zero inflection.

"Yes. Our colony was overrun with them at the time the Bridge was opened. It's too much to hope none of them made the crossing along with the populace."

"Describe these creatures to me."

Careful now, old man.

"There are three kinds," he said. This was a risk, but a calculated one. He thought it best to omit as little as possible, and he knew every kind of creature on Coldgarden had been present there at the end. "One is easiest to describe as a giant insect. Larger than a person. Black exoskeleton with a colorful sheen. Mean disposition. We called them revenants, and it was my job to protect the city from them once upon a time."

"I see," Cardiff said. "And the other two?"

Careful. Careful.

"One like a white, glowing mass with limbs like centipedes—"

"Excuse me?"

"Too many joints," Karl clarified. "They look like gelatin, like you might squash them if you step on them, but that's not the case at all. And they move like lightning when they want to." He had seen as much when the Arjun-creature had attempted to assassinate the Iazmaena-revenant. Gods below, she was probably on-planet too, stirring up who knew what kind of trouble.

"I see. And the third?"

This he was most reluctant to detail, because their numbers included Marri and, he assumed, himself as well.

"Like a thick worm or a leech, but with six sharp, bony legs."

"Six legs? Another insect creature?"

"I don't think there's any relation," Karl said carefully. "Aside from both creatures' sets of legs being strong and sharp enough to kill."

"I see. Quite the menagerie," Dr. Cardiff said. "I will of course need as much detail as you can give me on all three life forms, but which would you say poses the greatest immediate threat?"

Karl willed his forehead not to sweat. "The revenants," he said. Old habits died hard. "The latter two are newer," he said. "We've lived with the specter of the revenants for a century, but these others . . . we know less about them. We haven't even settled on a name for them."

"Since you say you've lived with these *revenants* for so long, would you say it's reasonable to assume the appearance of these other two creatures is what finally convinced you to flee?"

"They certainly didn't help."

"Yet you say we should be more worried about these revenants. Why?"

Shit. He'd been trying to guide her thoughts away from the natives, away from *him* and all the people like him, and he'd put his foot in it.

"More as a matter of pragmatism," he said. "I think you are more likely to run into the revenants. There were more of them in the city when we made the crossing." And now he was flat-out lying.

"I see. And are there any other aspects to these creatures we should be aware of?"

Now Karl was sure of what his gut was telling him. He was being tested. They already knew more than they were letting on, and they were seeing how honest he would be.

"Yes. These creatures can change their shape."

"To suit their environment, you mean? Some kind of morphological response to new stimuli?"

Karl had no idea what that last part meant, but he got the gist. "Yes," he said, thinking of the revenants adjusting their number of limbs to suit the circumstances. "But also more substantially. They can take the shape of people, even, in extreme cases."

A beat.

"I see. And when you say they, which do you mean?"

Now was the moment. Did he try to deceive her here, shift most of the suspicion of infiltrators onto the revenants? But if they went searching for one kind of false human, how likely were they to miss all the other false humans?

When it came down to it, had any of them had any right to come to this place, to bring their fucked-up plague of an ecosystem to this unsuspecting colony? Karl himself was not a human, but that newfound knowledge didn't erase the fact that he'd spent his entire adult life safeguarding what he believed to be humans from revenants. It wasn't a loyalty he could just switch off.

"All three sets of creatures," Karl said. He couldn't deny them that info, that warning. But, to his shame, he also couldn't confess everything. Not when it might lead to harming his loved ones. Wherever they were. "All of them can appear to be human to varying degrees of complexity and under the right circumstances." He thought for a second longer, then decided to forestall the obvious question. "And before you ask, no, we've never worked out a good way to detect infiltrators amongst us. It's why we've never been able to free ourselves from them."

She regarded him for several long moments. "Thank you for your forthrightness, Mr. Yonnel. It makes it easier to trust you when you are up front about what you know. I can certainly understand why you'd want to flee that place, but I'm sure you can understand the dilemma your little exodus has put us in here."

He'd guessed correctly. They'd known at least some of what he'd told them already. The bit about looking like humans, certainly. Now she trusted him, at least a little.

But where his judgment about her had been right, hers regarding him was wrong.

"I can definitely understand, doctor. All I can say is that if we'd had another option, we'd have taken it."

"Yes, well, while we work out a means to locate these infiltrators and confirm that hypermutation is not a threat, you will, of course, remain here as part of your recovery. Though I'm pleased to say that it should be a swift one. I'm a bit surprised to see a colony as old as yours has no appreciable use of bionics, cybernetics, or the like. But Harmony takes some strange paths, lord knows."

Karl blinked. Even more than the earlier one about morphologies, he had no idea what that sentence meant.

"Regardless, I think you will be pleasantly surprised at your new hip. I'll let you rest for now, but we'll be along to test your movement range before too long. And my superiors will undoubtedly have more questions. Until then, you are safe here." She turned to go.

"Please, doc," Karl said. "You'll let me know if you get word of my people, won't you?"

Her smile this time seemed more genuine than the previous ones had. "Of course. Oh, and before I forget. What was your colony name? If I look up your Harmony failure rate specifics in the archive, it may help with both your people's treatment and a side project of mine."

"I'm sorry," Karl said, "but you have me at a loss. Harmony? I don't know what that is."

Cardiff blinked, seemed to teeter off balance without actually moving, then recovered herself. "My apologies for any confusion. Just the colony name will do for now."

But her tone had lost some of its warmth.

Karl had to think. If she was referring to old records, *Coldgarden* would have no meaning for her, but the automated distress call had given the colony its original name.

"Calgary," he said, reasonably confident in an answer for once. But she frowned again, turning back to the console and tapping away.

"New Calgary, you mean?" she asked with a direct look.

"Oh, yes, of course," Karl said. "People get lazy and just drop the *New* a lot of the time."

"And does the name 'Coldgarden' mean anything to you?"

Karl's mouth went dry, and he had to work moisture back into it.

"I ask because that name was prominent in the distress signal we received prior to your arrival."

The distress signal. Karl hadn't been aware that was what had been transmitted.

"I wasn't aware you'd heard the distress signal," he said in full honesty. "You were talking about historical archives, so I went with the name I thought you'd recognize."

"Of course. Thank you for being so considerate," Dr. Cardiff said, but the words had a performative sound to them now. "You rest up, Mr. Yonnel. I'll be back to check on you soon."

She turned and exited for real this time, leaving Karl alone with his worries that he had profoundly misplayed his hand.

CHAPTER 16

JÜRGEN WOKE to a beeping signal on his home terminal that indicated a meeting request. He'd have preferred to check on his guests before getting to work, but he saw this call was from the other fish he was trying to land, and he didn't want to anger anyone prickly.

He accepted the call as he sat down in front of his terminal screen. The display recognized his arrival and came to life, displaying a figure backlit sharply enough to reduce them to a silhouette.

"Mr. Fennec," said a voice with heavy electronic alteration and a thick French accent. This was them, then. Presented gender was impossible to discern through so much distortion, but the altered voice was the same as the first time they had made contact. "I hope I haven't woken you."

"I apologize if you had to wait," Jürgen said to his client-to-be. Or perhaps his client-to-be's representative. He had no name nor any other identifying information. The initial contact had made it clear they desired discretion, and Jürgen made it a policy not to ask until it was a necessity.

"It's quite all right, Mr. Fennec. I serve at the pleasure of my clients, the same as you. People such as us do not always have the luxury of determining our schedules."

"I appreciate you being so agreeable," Jürgen said.

"And I appreciate your continued discretion with this matter." So he was indeed dealing with an intermediary. That implied a desire for secrecy every bit as much as the pains to hide the caller's identity. "Now then, I'm afraid there is still some debate about exactly how much information my clients are willing to share."

"The name of the missing will be sufficient to get me started." Jürgen tried to conceal his impatience. Yet another mysterious client withholding information.

"I'm afraid it won't. You see, this individual has some . . . unique medical needs that must be taken into account if and when you locate them successfully."

Impatience flared to irritation. "Forgive me, but if the person requires some kind of urgent medical intervention, that is all the more reason to cease this delay, formally hire me, and provide me with the relevant details."

Though he could not see the person's face, Jürgen Fennec could read the sudden tension in their shoulders. He decided that a little extra push was needed.

"I know how difficult it can be," he said. "We all seek the maximum amount of societal benefit from our actions, but how to choose between the welfare of the weak and the command of the powerful?"

The shoulders relaxed.

"You are as your reputation paints you, Mr. Fennec. I am relieved, I must admit." Jürgen wasn't aware he *had* a reputation with the kind of person this representative must answer to. The accent reminded him, not for the first time, of Caroline, though her accent had just been a whisper compared to this, and she hadn't contacted him since just before he'd taken up with the Cult.

"I do my best to run a transparent and honest business," Jürgen said, unsure how else to reply. "And I try to cater as best as I'm able to each individual client's needs. But please understand that it is a business. I can't keep the lights on with innuendos."

"Thank you for understanding, friend," the person said, as if picking out only the part they'd wanted to hear. "It is, alas, not an easy choice for my clients to make. Which results the greater good: rescue or sacrifice?"

Sacrifice. Jürgen's stomach plummeted. He kept his voice concerned, but only mildly so. No need to telegraph his desperation unless it became advantageous to do so. "Do you mean to say they are considering canceling the job entirely, then? Even before it begins?"

"That is not on the table at this time," the person said. "My clients are united in their desire for you to find the victim. The difference of opinion is between saving him or killing him."

Jürgen's mouth went dry.

"I am not—"

"Please understand that I am not supposed to be telling you any of this until a decision has been reached. But due to the extended nature of the arguments, I became concerned you might think the job was canceled."

"My friend, you must know that I am not a hitman." Jürgen could not totally purge the shaking from his voice.

"Not even if the kidnappers are part of the Cult my records say you hate so much?"

The world around him fell away for a brief time.

"Obviously, for such a dangerous assignment"—the person now sounded like they were talking around things forbidden—"you can expect to receive a formal Equatorian Dispensation to commit lethal violence in the pursuit of our shared goal. But I need to be clear that this Dispensation has not been granted yet."

This was it. This was his chance to end the Cult in a way that broke none of his oaths to himself and his colony. He could rid Anaranjado of its most dire threat in one fell swoop.

This confirmed that his clients-to-be were Equatorians, and even if no payment changed hands, a Dispensation of that sort was worth any amount of money. It was priceless. And therefore, desperate to land the hook lest this mother-of-all trophy fish get away, Jürgen Fennec pressed every advantage he could think of.

And it was absolutely worth the price of killing one innocent man. If it even came to that.

"Friend, I will level with you. If there is an urgent and complex medical need in play, it is *absolutely imperative* that we find this person as soon as possible. If they were taken against their will, the odds their captors are familiar enough with their needs to properly administer to them are, to be blunt, frighteningly small. I understand you are beholden to your clients, and they have yet to render a decision, but if you wait much longer, that decision will be made for them."

"We have reason to believe that the Cult is well-equipped to take care of this man," the representative said.

The part of their hermitage I was barred from earlier. That had to be why. At least it told him where to look when the Dispensation at last came through. *Two cases of missing persons, both separately involving Equatorians.* That beggared belief. Unless, of course, the two sets of clients were in fact related to one another.

In which case, Jürgen might already have a leg up on this mystery.

"You will hear from us soon, I promise." The representative seemed concerned by Jürgen's sudden lapse into silence.

"Of course." There was nothing to be gained by squeezing the poor person further. Not yet. But he could leave them with a hook, something to prove his prowess, even if it was really just dumb luck. "But I may have already solved part of this mystery."

"Oh?"

"Have any of your clients, or perhaps their families, perhaps taken matters into their own hands and come looking for the victim in question themselves?"

"I . . . haven't heard any such thing." The surprise sounded genuine. "What would make you ask this?"

"I've recently pulled two people, a young woman and an even

younger woman, out of a spot of trouble down here. They have . . . the look of your part of the world, if you take my meaning."

The handler did. "Mr. Fennec, I can assure you that if anyone *else* from 'my part of the world' had gone missing, now of all times, the uproar would be beyond imagining." There was a pause, as though he'd suddenly thought of something. "You say they simply turned up unexpectedly?"

"Yes," said Jürgen, fully expecting more information to be forthcoming imminently.

"In just the last day or so?"

"Yes," Jürgen said, now feeling as though he was the one behind the proverbial eight-ball.

"You may want to check the news, Mr. Fennec. I can't be certain, and this might just be the paranoia that is rapidly becoming so popular nearer the surface, but I suspect it might be quite relevant to you."

CHAPTER 17

THE CALL LEFT JÜRGEN AGITATED.

On the one hand, he'd been unwilling to employ real force against the Cult without some sort of official sanction. Turning on your fellow colonists was beyond taboo, even when violence was not involved, and whatever his feelings on the subject, nobody had determined that the Cult had fallen out of that category.

But now that such authorization was pending, perhaps his warnings had not gone unheeded after all. Once the giddy thrill of this realization had faded, however, it left a curiously empty feeling in its wake. Daydreaming about wiping out the Cult that had taken so much from him was all well and good when it was just that—a fantasy. Facing the reality of it meant the greatest test yet of the moral code he held himself to.

The code that the Cult had forced him to create.

The implications piling up in his mind weighed heavily, so he decided to take a trip up a level into the populated areas. News. The handler had said something about his new guests and the news.

Jürgen knocked on the door to his office in case either was not decent.

"I need to step out for a moment and go up into the populated areas. Do not leave the premises while I am gone, please." Realizing belatedly that this made *him* sound like a kidnapper, he hastened to add: "If you require a trip out, we can arrange that later, once I return. But it is not safe for you to wander these tunnels alone."

That ought to be sufficient. Surely, given Marri's kidnapping, they both realized the danger was real and would honor his request. Just in case, though, he stopped briefly by his spare coats hung up near the entrance to his home.

His guests discomfited him, all the more so now because of the handler's freighted implications when discussing them. It would not do to avoid taking *any* precautions.

The trip to the upper levels—which everyone else on the planet would call the lower levels—was not a long one. Jürgen was careful to time his bypassing of the barricades blocking access into the lower tunnels to when he would not be noticed. Going up was as second-nature as going down, and he was able to quickly assess his surroundings.

The arrivals of first Ms. Novak and then Marri had thrown off his usual routine. He had just been up here looking for leads on Marri and the others Giana had tasked him to find. But leads for local goings-on were precisely the opposite of keeping tabs on the news of the surface world above. Consequently, he had failed to keep his ear to the ground with regard to current events.

Now that he was focused more on the latter, he was able to really internalize the strange atmosphere he'd unconsciously noted earlier. There was a nervous energy to the people he could see. Everyone moved faster, their shoulders hunched.

This was odd. Anaranjado would never be called a safe place, but Cult aside, most of the hazards were environmental in nature.

Harmony saw to that.

Today, though, Jürgen watched their eyes swiveling as though seeking out some new threat they'd had no time to accustom themselves to. Wasting no more time in pointless speculation, he walked to the nearest public charging station. His power cell was running low enough that his bio-mechanical feedback filters were starting to translate the lack into a feeling of physical hunger to press him into addressing the matter.

He didn't like things to get that far, but the public chargers were quite cheap, fed as they were from the infinite sunlight of Sunnyside. He still had to eat actual food periodically—which was not cheap at all—but the almost-free energy went a long way, and so much of him had been replaced with synthetics during his time with the Cult that his biological needs were low.

Most importantly, though, this set of charging stations came with a convenient data feed that provided a steady news drip.

He stepped into the alcove, accepting both ports when the requests to connect came through. Power began to flow into him as information streamed into his eye data port. It was like reading at hyper-speed but with less data loss.

He nearly jolted himself out of his connections in shock as the headlines bombarded him.

Potential Alien Communication Confirmed, Aliens Arrive on Anaranjado.

Human Colony Evacuated. Refugees Arrive in Force.

First Bridge Activity Since Colony Founding.

Clashes at Arrival Sites Spark Armed Conflict Concerns.

Jürgen recalled the news item regarding the potential communication with another human colony from a couple of weeks back, buried deep in the feeds though it had been. But matters had clearly accelerated dramatically since he'd last checked. He dug down past the headlines.

The arraignment of the xenolinguist responsible for the unauthorized response to the off-world communication attempt has been expedited, says an unnamed official with knowledge of the case.

A stupid thing for that linguist to do, if the charges were true. Anaranjado had its share of hard and fast rules, but few were more severely enforced than the ban against any engaging with beings from off-world. The injunction was more directed at the various alien species that populated this sector of space, but it took little imagination to guess that some xenophobic, isolationist policymaker would extend it to humans from other Earth colony worlds.

Jürgen scrolled on, digging into the fringier side of information providers. These were more known for paranoia than for accuracy, but that didn't always make them wrong. The unity of Harmony had more positives than negatives, but an unwillingness to put leadership to hard questions was definitely one of the latter.

In one of these sources, known especially for all things xenophobic, he found the bleeding edge of the rumor mill hard at work.

Government officials refuse to comment on rumors regarding newly arrived colonists who pose as humans but are not.

That seemed a step beyond improbable, but Jürgen filed it away anyway. He kept scrolling.

Government officials strenuously denied that the launch schedule for the Ultima Thule *has been accelerated as a result of the arrival. "The colony ship has been a top priority since construction was approved, and it continues to be a top priority. Nothing about the recent news has changed that priority in either direction," the official statement read.*

It was not difficult to guess what his contact had been hinting at. It left him with a question of which was less likely: the notion that two separate groups of Equatorians had taken a strong interest in the Cult in the last week, or that his new guests weren't Equatorian at all but from another world entirely?

At last Jürgen reached the true dregs, slop not worth polluting his mind with. Things about monsters hiding amongst the refugees, murderous creatures with otherworldly powers of disguise. Harmony had changed many things about the human race, but fear of the unknown had not been one of them.

Still, he felt a great deal more informed than he had an hour ago. And somehow, he didn't even feel the slightest surprise when one of the listening devices he'd planted before he left his home pinged him that something interesting was happening there.

CHAPTER 18

MARRI WAITED until Jürgen had fully left the building before she went over and shook Giana, who opened bleary eyes at the disruption.

"You've slept enough. Are you going to explain how—"

Giana's vision cleared with frightening speed, and she held up a warning finger. Her large eyes, sunken even deeper into dark hollows, roved the room in an ostentatious manner.

She thinks he's got the room wired to monitor us. It seemed odd to Marri to bug your own office, unless he'd only set it up since Giana had arrived. But, though she wanted to disagree with the woman just on principle, that old familiar suspicion and mistrust, honed from years of living on the streets, made it a little too easy to believe that she might be right.

Marri scrambled to think of an innocent-seeming question to pivot toward.

"What's wrong with you?" she asked. "You look sick."

"It was a tiring journey." That Giana was responding meant she too thought this question was safe. "I'll recover fully soon, I'm sure."

Marri wasn't so sure. She'd arrived feeling perfectly fine, or however much that was possible after having jumped across light-years of space in a few moments. Clearly, Giana's journey had been much more trying. Marri had no idea why that would be, and no safe way to just ask directly either.

"You went on ahead of the others," Marri said carefully. "I remember seeing you . . . leave early."

Giana's eyes had returned from their wandering around the room to fix Marri with a stare that was a little too intense for the girl's liking, as though Giana wanted to constantly remind her to guard her tongue. But she did answer.

"As our host said, I've been here a few days." She gave the tiniest little shrug. *I don't know how,* that shrug said. Still, Marri wondered if it explained the woman's ailment.

What if we all get sick if we stay here that long? It was not a pleasant thought, but there was also nothing she could do about it, so Marri pushed it aside.

"I wonder if that means Karl and Stefani got delayed in getting here." Jürgen had mentioned he was looking for them as well, so Marri judged that safe to mention.

"Or it's possible they didn't hear about our change of plans and went somewhere else entirely," Giana said. She was speaking as much with her eyes as with her mouth. Marri had never noticed how expressive they could be, but she found she could read quite a bit of what the woman wasn't saying aloud. "In fact, I think that's a likely guess."

This isn't where we were meant to appear, those eyes seemed to say. In other words, it might be Marri and Giana that were the weird ones, while everyone else arrived as planned elsewhere on this world. This thought was more comforting.

"I think I'd like to take a nap while Jürgen is out," Giana said.

"You just woke up," Marri said, indignant. But Giana lay back down. Her eyes drifted closed, and for a nonplussed moment, Marri thought she was already asleep. Then Giana's eyes snapped open, fixed once again on Marri, their intensity making clear what was actually happening here.

"Don't get into too much trouble while I'm asleep." Her tone was light, almost playful, but the eyes told a different story. *See what you can find out about the area without dying while Jürgen is gone.* And more than that. *This is me trusting you to get something important done.* Then Giana's eyes closed again, and her breathing evened out almost immediately. If this was a pretend nap, it was a convincing one.

It didn't matter. Jürgen Fennec had told them not to leave, but Giana surely burned with the same curiosity Marri did. And it was a lot less suspicious and more believable for a thirteen year old to sneak out while her "godmother" was asleep than it would be for Giana to scout around, particularly if she really was ill.

As if to punctuate the thought, Marri felt a sudden, scrabbling *need* to be out of this place exploring. This was, after all, an entirely new planet. She had no way of knowing if the entire thing was underground tunnels like what she'd seen, but the fact that they reminded her so much of Underguts back home, albeit a very *cold* Underguts, did appeal to her.

Jürgen had worn layers of coats when he'd rescued Marri from the cultists, but the tiny front room of his home, between the outer door and the inner, had a pair of coats hanging on hooks, so perhaps where he'd gone off to wasn't as cold as where the cultists had lived.

Marri grabbed the smaller of the two, putting it on. It was made of an unfamiliar, slick material she'd never seen and didn't seem like it should be very warm, but almost immediately she felt overheated in the climate-controlled space of Jürgen's home. The coat was still too big for her, but the strange material seemed to cling where it should. So it didn't hang off her so much as bunch up in places.

She wondered if the outer door's lock would work both ways and, if it did, what she might be able to do about it with her handheld. But it opened easily enough from this side once she'd remembered to close the inner door.

The chill of the tunnels settled upon her, and suddenly her too-hot coat seemed a touch inadequate. The branching tunnel that ended at Jürgen's house led back to a crossing path. The left way angled up and the right path was more leveled off, though Marri recalled from their trip back that it quickly split off into numerous directions. She'd come out here intending on going whichever direction she'd felt Jürgen *hadn't* gone, the better to avoid getting caught. But given that she was already a little chilly, she thought heading up might make more sense. She'd just have to risk it.

Marri had wanted a straight shot. Even though this would greatly increase her chances of getting caught by a returning Jürgen, she hoped the fact that it led to more populated areas also minimized her chances of getting lost. This wasn't Underguts. She didn't have it memorized. But she was quickly disappointed in her hopes. Additional tunnels connected to it, arriving from haphazard directions and following no obvious pattern she could see.

Still, she thought she'd be okay if she just kept heading up.

Moving was as good a way to stay warm as any, so she set out at as brisk a pace as she dared, straining her ears for any signs that someone might be sneaking up on her. At least it was well-lit enough to see. In fact, the embedded lights called her attention again to the strange pattern etched into the tunnel walls. Whether stone or ice, the pattern held true across every surface, transforming them from perfect smoothness into something that looked a lot more like interlocking wedges with jagged edges.

It must have something to do with whatever digging equipment had been used to carve out the tunnels, but considering how uniform it was along every surface she could see, Marri found it strange that the little interlocking shapes were so *irregular* the closer she looked. Instead of a piece of rigid machinery relentlessly boring through rock and ice, it looked more as though each tiny gouge in the material had been hand-placed, leading to differences in spacing and places where the pattern stuttered.

She was walking more slowly now, engrossed in the pattern, trying to see if she could make any sense of it, when a bare hand fell upon the bunched shoulder of her coat.

Stupid Mouse! She had let her fascination get the better of her wariness. Someone had crept up behind her completely undetected. She could hope for Jürgen, but he had to be ahead of her still. She whirled, partly to break the grip, partly to see what she was dealing with.

It was Iazmaena Delgassi.

CHAPTER 19

DR. CARDIFF'S promised return visit took far longer than he'd expected, and without being explicitly told not to, Karl decided he was going to try to test out his new hip on his own. Reassuring himself that he would stop the moment he felt any significant pain, he swung his legs from the mattress and out over the side of the bed. All the while, he braced for a jolt of agony that never came.

Thus encouraged, he placed his good right side down first, allowing it to bear most of his weight. Then he slowly attempted to share the load by bringing his left foot down alongside his right.

He found himself, much to his surprise, standing upright with no discomfort. Not *less* discomfort. As far as he could recall, his left hip now felt better than it had even before his injury eight months ago. In fact, his uninjured right hip was now the sorer of the two, and that was just the expected wear and tear of arthritis and age.

Probably just lingering anesthetic. Some kind of local pain blocker. It was possible he was doing himself real damage just by attempting this. But somehow, he didn't think so.

Of course, standing was one thing. Walking was another. So Karl attempted to walk. Attempted and succeeded. He paced the length of the small room and back again, feeling only the dull aches of joints worn by age. The remembered spikes of agony that had literally dogged his steps since that encounter with Iazmaena Delgassi in the archon's office were just that: memories.

Almost afraid that it would break some spell and return him to his hobbled disability, Karl fingered his bodysuit, looking for a way to open it and examine the area. Much to his shock, it pulled apart with relative ease along a previously invisible seam. He was so startled he let it go, feeling as though he'd been caught doing something inappropriate. The material sealed itself back together on the instant, leaving no blemish.

Self-healing. It is flowmatter. It even formed completely enclosing footwear, including arch support, something his battered old feet could appreciate. Tentatively, he peeled away a swath again and took a look at his hip. Or rather, what he could see of his hip, because even beneath the layer of suit, the entire thing, centering on the site where he'd taken the wound, was encased in some sort of black, segmented material that looked a lot like synthetic scales. They merged with his skin so flawlessly that they didn't even leave a raised area in the bodysuit.

It was disconcerting enough that he almost wished he hadn't looked. The way the little bits of room lighting that slipped in past the shade of the gown to glint off the scales reminded him entirely of the sheen of revenant carapace.

Easy, old man. Focus on the fact that you can walk normally again. As shameful a thought as it was, everything that had transpired over the past few days almost felt worth it to him for this simple fact.

He was just wondering if the scales were a kind of advanced bandaging that would eventually be removed—surely that had to be the case—when the door to the room hissed open, and Dr. Cardiff stepped back in along with two orderlies. All three wore bodysuits not that different from Karl's own. No more haz suits. Maybe she'd believed his claims about hypermutation, at least. Surely that had to be a good thing.

"Up and about, I see?" she said briskly then *tsked.* "You should have waited until someone was present to make sure you didn't face-plant, but from the looks of things, the surgery was as successful as we'd hoped it would be. How do you feel?"

"Doc, it's nothing short of a miracle! I didn't have access to the best care back on our colony for, well, for reasons not worth going into. But even that would have paled in comparison to what you all have done here. My hip feels like its back in its twenties. Thank you."

"I'm glad to hear it," Cardiff said. She didn't sound glad, though. As with the end of their previous talk, her tone didn't match her words.

Karl's ebullience faded some. He found his gaze drawn to the orderlies flanking her just beyond the doorway. At first, he took the men for being very dark-skinned, but then he realized, as he saw the light play off them, that their bare arms and faces sported similar black, shiny scales to those now encasing his hip. Without the haz suit complicating his view, he took a closer look at what he'd thought was a body sleeve that came up just past Dr. Cardiff's chin. But he could now see it lay *underneath* the flowmatter body-suit she wore currently. She, too, was partially encased in these scales.

He tore his gaze away, not wanting to be caught staring. As though staring might be the catalyst that transitioned this encounter to its next phase—whatever that next phase was.

"So what's next on my recovery checklist, doc?" Karl asked, willing himself to remain calm. It was a strange place full of strange technologies and customs. He told himself it was normal to feel a sense of discomfort, even menace, when so much change had been forced upon him so fast.

"I've been going over your answers to my questions from earlier. Cross-checking them against our own observations." It was an odd, roundabout way to answer coming from a doctor, and it did nothing to ease Karl's anxieties. "Tell me again about the failure rate of the Harmony present in your colony."

When he didn't answer right away, she elaborated. "I want to be able to link what, if any, impact this 'hypermutation' phenomenon you described has had on the organism."

Karl thought her words held the barest hint of pleading. *Tell me what I want to hear. Make me believe you.*

The trouble with that was he'd already told her he didn't know what Harmony was. She made it sound as though she was pretending she hadn't heard that and was giving him a clean-slate do-over. It was not lost on Karl that this time other witnesses were present.

Large, surly looking ones.

Fighting a powerful urge to somehow go along with what she was saying despite having no idea in the slightest how to do that, Karl grimaced as he responded.

"I'm sorry to disappoint you, doc, but I don't have the foggiest idea what you're talking about."

"Yes," she said with a heavy sigh. "A few of the other early surgery candidates have wakened as well, and none of them know either. I was hoping you might be the exception because . . . well, it doesn't matter why. I'm marking you down as part of our test, Mr. Yonnel, which is about to begin. These conditions are less than ideal, but—"

"I don't understand," Karl cut in. "Test? What are you talking about?"

"All human society functions successfully because of Harmony." Cardiff's tone had shifted. She sounded as though she read from a prepared script now, one she had memorized long ago. "And *only* because of Harmony. That goes doubly for Anaranjado. On a diffi-cult world with minimal resources remaining to it, societal accord is absolutely crucial to avert the collapse of order and resulting loss of life."

Judging by her change in expression, the script had ended, and Cardiff began speaking with her own words again.

"We, of course, wish to extend what hospitality we can to you and your refugees. But we can't do so until we are satisfied that you will abide by the same values we hold dear, or near enough as makes no difference. Not a single New Calgarian we have interviewed in this facility has had any idea about Harmony, what it is, and what it means. That correlates with our historical records referencing your colony, which indicate New Calgary was founded in part explicitly to *resist* the uptake of Harmony across the human species." She made this sound like the deepest possible betrayal. "These two data points agreeing so readily are extremely troubling. Hence, our test."

Karl's mounting alarm must have registered on his face because she switched tack. "Has there been any sort of massive disruption to your societal archives back on your world? Any large-scale loss of knowledge?"

"Yes!" Karl said, eager to be able to give her an answer she wanted for once. "We even called it the Loss. An almost total wiping out of records from before that point." He hesitated, but ultimately felt he had to keep propping up the old lie he'd already relayed to her. "It happened with the coming of the revenants a century ago."

"I see," she said, and a spark of excitement had entered her eyes. Karl thought it almost looked like hope. "By the Good Doctor's grace, there is still some hope then."

"Hope?" Karl had no idea what the Good Doctor's grace was, but if *the Good Doctor* was anything like *the gods below* on his world, he wasn't sure he wanted to find out.

"That our records about your colony are wrong. That your collective forgetfulness is just a horrible accident. That the strain somehow evolved to propagate without direct human intervention. All these assumptions could explain it, but we must also be realistic. It would be exceedingly unlikely for even one of those assumptions to be true, much less all three."

"Can we at least postpone the test while you do more investigation?" Karl said, gaze flicking to the orderlies.

"I'm afraid not," Cardiff said. "The test is the most expedient way to answer our outstanding questions. But you don't have to worry. There's very little risk to you with this test. Provided you are all properly implanted and have simply suffered some collective memory loss about Harmony, nothing will happen. If, on the other hand, you *aren't* implanted, this will rectify that."

"Now hold on," Karl said. "What do you mean when you say I have to be *implanted?*"

"The organism is harmless, I assure you."

"Then why didn't you say there's *no* risk?"

"In truth, I would say that if it weren't for this hypermutation phenomenon. But even given that unlikely event, that would not be the fault of the organism. It merely facilitates a more collective-minded mode of thinking and feeling, essential in all situations where large numbers of humans are expected to cooperate toward a greater end."

"Be that as it may, I'm not terribly interested in adopting some universal mind frame your colony invented without any say-so in the matter." Karl backed up as he spoke until he found himself planted against the wall opposite the door. He was as far as possible from both the threat and escape. So, a mixed bag.

Cardiff frowned consideringly.

"You'll have to forgive me. I've never once in my life encountered someone who didn't know about Harmony, so it is difficult to abandon what I consider to be common knowledge and talk in basic enough terms. I should clarify that the organism is not an invention of this colony, as you seem to think. Harmony was first adopted on Earth, some time before the founding of the colonies. A human being without Harmony in this day and age is, quite simply, an oxymoron."

"Except maybe not my colony, you said." Karl couldn't help it. The blanket assumption had put his back up. *She's right, though. I'm not human. None of us are, really.* But also, that wasn't the point she thought she was making, and she was dead wrong about that.

Dr. Cardiff gestured for the two orderlies to approach, and Karl had a sudden, sinking feeling. It sank further as she produced a syringe with a very long, very fine needle.

"If you are from the colony of New Calgary, as you say, and you are indeed human, as you say, then this will have absolutely no effect on you." Her words had a *this is my final offer* feel to them. "Your already established organism will reject the presence of the new nymph, and you won't notice a thing. If you are human and don't have one, it will be an unpleasant few days, but you will likewise almost certainly be fine and far better off in the long run."

Despite rolling through the options like a waiter announcing the daily specials, Dr. Cardiff's frosty tone of disappointment indicated she had a strong suspicion which dish Karl was planning to order.

"And if you are *not* human, and we inject you with this organism custom-tailored to human biology, then it's very difficult to guess what will happen. I suppose that depends largely upon which of the creature categories you described to me you belong to. Now," she said, approaching, "please hold very still. The easiest method of delivering the organism to an adult is via the tear duct, but for obvious reasons, you really don't want me to miss. I can only hope you've been honest with us, with *me*, Mr. Yonnel."

CHAPTER 20

"DON'T BE AFRAID!" Iazmaena exclaimed in that particular way dangerous people talked that made Marri very afraid. "I'm not going to hurt you."

"That would be a change from last time," Marri said, narrowing her eyes. "Which was, what, two days ago?" Less, technically.

"That was before I wound up here in this frozen hell all alone," Iazmaena said. Despite her words, she wore no coat, but she didn't seem to be suffering overly much. Noticing Marri's look, she must have put two and two together because she added, "Revenants tolerate the cold surprisingly well, turns out."

"So we were enemies until you needed help, you mean," Marri said, proceeding to the heart of the matter. "And now you have no revenant friends to do your dirty work for you?"

"Wherever they ended up, it isn't here." Iazmaena spoke as though she were completely unaware of the sarcasm in Marri's tone. "But you're wrong to dismiss me. I can help you."

"And why should I trust you to do that?"

"You used to trust me just fine—"

"Oh, please," Marri said. "You aren't the real Iazmaena."

"I know Stefani has been over this with you," Iazmaena said. "I *am* her. I'm just some other stuff too."

"So was it that other stuff that tried to kill us, or was it *her*? We all wanted the same thing by that point. You didn't have to attack us!"

"You're right," Iazmaena said. She raised placating hands. "You're absolutely right. I didn't have to attack you. But I was very angry. Stefani's delays had ruined half my plans! That city and the people in it should have suffered—"

"Our planet was coming apart!" Marri said, exasperated. "Anyone who didn't make it to the Bridge and get over to this world is dead."

"And they deserved so much worse for what they did," Iazmaena said darkly. Then she visibly got a handle on her emotions. "But that's over now. It didn't happen the way I wanted it to, but it's over." She looked to Marri. "I would like a fresh start with you. And as a sign of my good faith, I will show you the entrance to the upper tunnels, which you are about to miss by going the wrong direction."

⚬

For all her big talk, Iazmaena seemed as unsure of the door's location as Marri was, and it took her several dead ends and missed turns before she found the correct tunnel which wound its way upward. Less random and organic feeling than the other tunnels, it led them up a steep, spiraling path that terminated in a door: black, featureless metal surrounded by a thin halo of gleaming light.

Marri steeled herself as she approached. She hated having no idea what she would find on the other side. She'd been unaware until maybe this very moment how much she relied on her knowledge of Coldgarden, all its streets and alleys and dark corners, for her sense of comfort. Everything about this world was strange, but worse yet, it was *unfamiliar*.

The door seemed determined to prove the point by steadfastly refusing to open at her approach.

"There's a trick to it," Iazmaena said. She was smiling a strange little smile. "Otherwise, how could your half-robot friend get out? See if you can figure it out."

Marri was not in the mood for games, but glare though she did, Iazmaena said nothing more, merely watched her. And she did have a point about Jürgen. So Marri began looking around. She closely examined the stone into which the door was set. Jürgen was tall, so if there was some kind of release, it could be too high to reach, but there was no sense in not checking—

There it was: a crease in the stone that would vanish the moment you got more than half a meter away, almost as if it was some kind of technological trick.

"How did you find this?" Marri asked, reaching for the handle concealed within.

"I waited and watched," Iazmaena said. "If you find a door, sooner or later someone will go through it."

The seals on the door popped open, and a crack appeared down the center. Marri had been expecting them to open fully, but the release had been a mechanical rather than an electronic one. Less chance of failure, but it meant you had to either squeeze through the crack or push the doors further open yourself.

"Why didn't you go through it yourself?"

Instead of answering, and for all her talk of tolerating the cold, Iazmaena rushed up to the opening, basking for a moment in the rush of warm air that poured through. Her haggard face glowed warmly with it. She turned with what appeared to be genuine thanks to Marri. There was light also. Marri saw for the first time how haggard the woman looked. Not sick, like Giana, but as though she'd had a rough time.

"When did you arrive?" she asked.

Iazmaena again ignored the question. "Are you coming?" she asked instead, staring at Marri expectantly.

"Are you going to answer any of my questions? Why are you acting so strange?"

Iazmaena rolled her eyes. "I arrived two days ago. Up here." She gestured around her, the open door still separating them. From Iazmaena's side, Marri could hear achingly familiar sounds. The sounds of a city.

Suddenly there was a click, and the door began slowly closing. It must be on some kind of timer. Marri felt a scrambling need to go through, even though they could just open it again, but Iazmaena, for once, wasn't done talking. "I *did* go through the door myself, but the other way. Last night. But I got stuck because I didn't know where the release was and, as you can see, it closes after a few seconds regardless of which side you open it from."

Marri darted through the narrowing opening, Iazmaena close on her heels.

"I wandered around a little bit and ultimately took shelter nearby the door and waited for someone to use it," Iazmaena said conversationally. "A little while ago that half-robot man did. So that's how I knew how to work it. But I'd seen his place in my wandering and wanted to get a look at it while he wasn't around. Then I found you before I could get there. Satisfied?"

"I'm not sure how satisfying it is to have you answering questions only after the answers become obvious, but I guess."

"Then shall we go exploring, you and I?"

Marri hesitated. On the one hand, Giana had sent her to find out information about this place. Going to where the actual people other than weird cultists and weird Jürgen lived seemed like a good way to do that. On the other hand, this open-ended invitation to wander unfamiliar subterranean streets also seemed like an excellent way to take Marri someplace Giana wouldn't know she'd gone and have something really horrible happen to her.

Her suspicion was apparently plain on her face, because Iazmaena returned an impatient look. "Stay if you want to," she said. "If I get bored, I might drop back through to see how you are doing all alone back down in the depths."

"I'm not alone," Marri said defensively, immediately regretting it. "Giana is here too."

"Oh, well if *Giana* is here," Iazmaena said mockingly, "you've got absolutely nothing to worry about."

"She's saved my life before," Marri said, still sounding defensive to her own ears. She flashed back to the attack from the creature that had been Archon Graysteel, the burning stripes of pain she'd left on Marri's back, how Giana had stepped in to prevent Marri from turning into something similar.

"And gotten you to trust her, apparently," Iazmaena said. "Makes one wonder if that was the point of the exercise all along."

"I don't trust her!" Marri said.

"Then are you coming?" Iazmaena asked. "Or are you going to keep being childish? If it makes you feel better, you can wait as long as you like to follow me. Then you'll be out of grabbing range or whatever childish thing you're worried about."

That word, *childish*, was like a brand to Marri's side. She had never gotten to be a proper child. She was certainly not going to be accused of it like it was a bad thing.

And she was not going to let the false Iazmaena Delgassi trick her by pricking her pride.

"You go on ahead," she said. "I'll see you when I see you."

Iazmaena held up her hands in mock surrender. "Fine by me. If I was really concerned for your safety, I would tell you that's a terrible idea. But as you so enjoy pointing out, I'm not the 'real' Iazmaena, so do whatever you want. Bye, kid."

And with that, she turned and strode away. Marri peered after her as she climbed a ramp to what appeared to be street level, vaulting over a partial blockage of debris, but she vanished from Marri's eyeline more quickly after that. Marri marked the direction she'd gone in any event, resolving to go another.

Then someone was stepping back over the debris pile and moving briskly down the ramp. Not Iazmaena. Too tall.

It was Jürgen.

Marri had half turned to run before she realized the door was shut.

"Not so fast, young miss," Jürgen said, gripping her shoulder. "We have a great deal to discuss."

CHAPTER 21

FOR KARL YONNEL, it was the strangest moment in a life full of strange moments. Dr. Cardiff advanced on him, syringe in hand, trying to gage if he meant to cooperate or not, her two hulking orderlies forming a phalanx close behind. But all the most interesting things were going on in Karl's mind and body.

Abruptly, he was moving, surging forward with uncanny speed even as the world around him slowed down. But as his body moved with more power and purpose than it ever had, even in the prime of his youth, his mind fell away, back and down and down and down into endless darkness. The world slowed further, further, grinding down until time itself practically stopped.

Then everything snapped back into place, as though a collapsing building had reversed itself into a whole structure again. Only it was a different structure than it had been when the collapse had begun.

Karl, still hurtling through the air, thinking at normal speed as the world crawled through molasses, stared out now through vision like nothing he'd ever experienced before. Everything seemed distorted, but with particular points of interest in sharper focus and relief than he'd thought possible. The two orderlies. Dr. Cardiff's free hand, balled into a fist. The tip of the needle. He was aware of all of them equally, could somehow split his regard to cover all of them at once.

One of the orderlies shoved Dr. Cardiff out of the way, lunging past her, each of them moving as though trapped in drying amber. Karl brought his arm up to guard, though the idea that he could stop anything the large man wanted to do was laughable. But that was before he watched his arm, now a segmented, bony claw nearly as long as he was tall, rake itself across the man's chest.

Flowmatter cloth parted, and the claw struck sparks off the black scales beneath, but the bladed tip still managed to find the minute gaps between two rows, prying them up and tearing into flesh beneath. The man roared in pain, but something in Karl told him it was not a mortal wound, not even one that would really slow the brute down.

Get out of the room. It was more instinct than words, and it sounded like a great idea in theory. The problem was both orderlies were still between him and the door. Even the one he'd wounded remained upright and, as a bonus, now looked very angry.

As though merely thinking about the problem could summon the solution, Karl opened his mouth wide and gave in to a sudden churning in his guts. Vile, smoking green liquid spewed forth, dousing both orderlies from waist to head. What had been the sharp intakes of pained breathing and scowls of rage morphed into cries of utter agony and looks of bewildered terror.

It was easy to butt his way past their crumpling forms after that. He moved, trying to think as little as possible, trying to surrender to the instinct that had gotten him past that, his first hurdle to escape. But the surge of speed he'd experienced as he charged his attackers failed him once he reached a long hallway and needed to cover distance quickly. Something was wrong with him, some hitch in the movement of these long-forgotten limbs.

He'd burst through the flowmatter bodysuit when he'd trans-formed, and now it was wrapped tight around his right foreclaw. But it wasn't this which fouled his movement. The problem came from further back. He tried to look at his left hip, which he gaged to be the source of the discomfort. But to his dismay, his body didn't want to move that way anymore. He couldn't turn to look at himself because he could only turn with his whole body. But the answer came to him like the flashing lights of the newly blazing alarms strobing the hallway.

They fixed my hip. They had fixed his hip for his *human* form. Now that he had transformed into his true form—and this was the moment he truly grasped that for the first time—the fix was still in place, but it was not meant for his biology any longer. He could move at his full, terrifying speed in short bursts, but not over longer distances.

The cruel irony was not lost on him.

Resolving that there was no going back to beg Cardiff's forgiveness now, he still had to try to make good on the escape he'd begun. So he began stutter-stepping his way down the right branch, the shorter portion of the hallway, hoping it would lead to some exit or at least to a place where he could keep any fighting to close quarters.

His distorted, multi-focus vision shifted, and he became aware that part of the wall was opening to his left—a door he hadn't noticed. A woman in a uniform that looked like security burst out. She was all covered over in scales like the orderlies had been, the ones on her face fine enough to allow for more complex expressions. Karl was thus able to register her shock and fear when she laid eyes on him.

She clawed at something slung around her hip—*weapon!*—then drew an object that she leveled at him like a gun even though it was like no gun he'd ever seen. She pulled the trigger and Karl tingled all over, but much to his shock, did not feel injured in the slightest. More to the point, the shock he felt was mirrored on her face.

Then the world lurched around him, sending him caroming off the nearest wall. For a moment, he thought he'd been hit by some delayed response, but the security guard went staggering as well. When Karl had recovered enough to right himself, he saw the walls, the ceiling, even the floor riven with cracks. As if someone had rung the building like a summoning gong, more doors opened ahead of Karl. Three in total, each with one security personnel poking their heads out. At the first sight of Karl, two of them ducked back in, shutting the door behind them. Maybe it was fear, or maybe they didn't have anything. The third, however, looked as though he was considering rushing Karl when the building lurched again, harder this time.

This time, part of the ceiling collapsed.

Karl surged forward as fast as he was able, weaving through debris as it fell, sidestepping the lunging man so committed to apprehending Karl that he risked being crushed. Karl avoided both, and the man avoided being crushed. But instead of launching himself into another attack, and instead of Karl trying to get away, they both hung there, frozen in equivalent shock.

The ceiling of the hallway, as well as numerous adjoining rooms, was gone, collapsed or blown free. Dr. Cardiff hadn't lied about where they were. Karl looked up now into a darkness representing not the night sky, but a solid cavern ceiling. He could tell because even with his strange new vision, the pinpricks of light, which would have been stars had they been on the surface, were too regularly spaced and patterned to be anything but artificially placed there.

But it was the other set of lights that most commanded his focus. At first they put Karl in mind of one of the Lancer Corps flyers back in Coldgarden. But even if the size and sound of its motors were about right, the configuration of running lights was wrong. There was one thing Karl was instantly sure of, though: this flyer, or more accurately whoever was flying it, was responsible for part of the roof collapsing. After all, those flyers back in Coldgarden had been armed as well.

Someone was attacking a hospital. That was bad enough. That it was the hospital where all the Coldgardener refugees were located told him what was really going on here. He didn't even need the voice projecting from the flyer's loudspeaker, but he got it anyway. It was deep, guttural, and full of rage.

"Attention, invading vermin. You will surrender now, without condition, or you will be eradicated! All hospital personnel, you will turn over every refugee and present yourselves for inspection. Any attempt to escape or aid in the escape of a refugee, and especially any attempt to transform will be met with immediate and overwhelming lethal force."

Scuttling sideways to avoid the spotlights of the flyer as they probed the wound it had made, Karl reeled inside his new form. Nothing in Dr. Cardiff's demeanor, even at her most menacing, had been anything approaching this. He'd seen lancers crack before under the strain of dealing with revenants. He'd watched an archon buckle under mounting paranoia. Anyone talking like that and in control of weaponry had to be taken with the utmost seriousness. It all added up to one conclusion. Even more so than a few minutes ago, Karl needed to be anywhere but here as rapidly as possible.

But he hesitated. *Stefani. Marri.* If they were here, if Cardiff had been concealing them from him, to leave would be to abandon them to her tender mercies, hers or those of the pilot. Even if they weren't here, Karl was abandoning countless more of his own people.

As if to make his decision for him, a siren began blatting throughout the hallway in both directions.

"Code Red!" a mechanistic voice declared. "Code Red! Dangerous patient escaped."

Inside his mind, Karl winced. No chance of doing anything but escape now. He had to hope against hope that his loved ones were elsewhere and that someone could talk this maniac down in the meantime. The alarm ceased briefly, and suddenly it was Dr. Cardiff's voice over the same loudspeaker.

"All ACM personnel, this is Major Cardiff. This facility is under attack by a rogue element of the ACM. I have just received authorization from Commandant Reid. You are to disregard the escaped patient alert until the rogue element has been neutralized."

Apparently her voice was loud enough to reach the ears of the flyer, because suddenly the pilot's voice was blaring right back.

"Belay her orders! She has likely been compromised already. Any of them can transform at any time. They are trying to replace us. I have seen it!" The flyer pivoted away from the hole in the ceiling, discharged several volleys of whatever weaponry it was packing toward another part of the building, as though the pilot thought lethal force was mere punctuation.

How many did he just kill as an exclamation mark?

"Attention, unidentified pilot!" Cardiff said. "This is your only warning! Disengage your unsanctioned action now or you will be fired upon—"

In answer, the flier spun in a circle, its weapon firing in coughing bursts all the while. The entire building shook this time, as though it were on the edge of collapse.

Karl realized with a start that his erstwhile hallway attacker had vanished. He needed to do the same.

"Negative," roared the pilot. "Orders or not, our mandate is clear. We protect the people of this world, our people, from all threats. There is only one way to eliminate this threat. All ACM personnel, stand down or be counted amongst our enemy!"

Karl had two options. One was to try to negotiate the hallways of a large building he didn't know and might shortly become impossible to navigate. The other was to leap to the roof and at least have a straight shot to some kind of safety.

His "fixed" hip nearly fouled his jump, but he managed to put five of his six scrabbling limbs upon a portion of roof solid enough to support him, hauling himself the rest of the way. With his peculiar configuration of eyes, it was difficult to judge long distances, so he picked a direction and ran as fast as he could.

Apart from air exchangers and access ports, the roof was at least relatively clear, though the further he ran, the more impact craters he encountered. He had no idea what he was looking for, but the flyer had gotten in somehow, which he hoped meant he could get out.

Behind him, the flyer whirred as it circled, occasionally firing at the building, but whether it was some combination of his dark coloring and the dim light in the space or just dumb luck, none of those shots fell near Karl. He was not being targeted. At least not yet.

As he neared the closest edge of the building, the cavern wall looming close just beyond, Karl began to hear other weapons being discharged. Smaller than the ones the flyer packed though they might be, someone was at least fighting back.

Our second day here and we've already started a civil war. It honestly sounded about right, considering Coldgarden's track record, but there was more bleakness than humor to the thought. The bleakness intensified as he maneuvered himself to direct his gaze back to his own level. He could see no break in the cavern wall, at least not here. There must be a way out, but clearly it lay elsewhere.

Nothing to do but follow the edge of the building until he found that point.

"I see you, creature!" The voice gave him less than a second's warning before part of the cavern wall shattered, spraying shards of rock everywhere, pelting Karl's thick hide. But no direct hits yet.

Seeing no reason to abandon the fastest way he could think of to find the way out and every reason to get a fucking move on, Karl scuttled along the building's edge as fast as he could. More impacts struck near him, on the ceiling, the cavern wall. Everywhere, it seemed, but him.

"Not me, you fucking idiots! Your enemy is over there!"

Karl risked a look. However many ACM personnel were stationed at the hospital, they appeared to have taken advantage of the distraction Karl had provided to mount their own assault on the flyer. Karl watched as smoke emerged from one of the sideboard motors. Unbalanced, the craft began a slow rotation. Whomever the pilot was, he responded to this imminent catastrophe by squeezing down the trigger and shredding the roof of the hospital in an ever-widening arc.

Karl only realized the extent of the damage when the portion of the roof he was standing on shuddered and collapsed.

He found himself in a room littered with newly made debris.

Several screams ripped the air, a shadow lunged at him, an arm swinging something which gleamed metallic in ruined, flickering lights. Karl acted without thinking. He acted without meaning to, falling back on instincts far older than himself. He vomited more of his caustic bile onto the attacker, and the screaming abruptly redoubled despite one of the voices falling silent.

He got a look at the melting form of his attacker then. It was a doctor, just a man in surgical clothes slashing at him with some kind of scalpel or similar. He died in the worst possible way as Karl watched, stricken. The other two people in the room, nurses, scrambled out the nearest door.

Get out of this place before you kill anyone else. Afraid of what he might do without meaning to, Karl followed the retreating nurses. He had little experience in hospitals, but he thought it likely he should follow the arrows pointing out the operating rooms in reverse. More impacts shook the building, and then a truly large one sent more cracks through the walls.

Just keep running.

At last, Karl burst through into what looked like a building lobby. If he'd thought the screams were bad before, they were nothing compared to now. Karl didn't give himself time to care how many people he left traumatized in his wake. He burst through the front doors and, exulting, found himself in a stone tunnel leading directly away from the building at an upward angle.

Freedom. Such as it was, anyway.

CHAPTER 22

"WELL," Giana said two hours later. "That's something, anyway."

Surveying their combined work, Ansley could only agree. The town of Ashrock had opened itself up to the refugees with a rapidity and totality that Ansley could scarcely credit. Even seeing it with his own eyes, it was hard to believe. People's food and water stores were being gathered and tallied in preparation for being divvied up while they awaited relief from the capital. Town elders were surveying homes, determining how much sleeping space each could be expected to offer.

Ansley had broken away from the hubbub as soon as he'd located Ashrock's comms array. Wireless comms were difficult with the colony being overwhelmingly underground and with their parent star, Naranja, pouring out so much interfering radiation, so each settlement had its own hardwire comms unit, usually centrally located.

As discreetly as possible, Ansley had contacted Militia Command, both to report the loss of his squad and to request help for Ashrock. He'd been told in no uncertain terms that all the ACM's available assets were otherwise tied up. Assuming his squad hadn't encountered the only alien monsters on the planet, that tracked with the first part of his report. Still, it was surprising and a little ominous that he, being the commandant's son, didn't receive a higher slot on the priority list.

So long as things remained peaceful in Ashrock, Command had told him, he could not expect relief before morning at the earliest. Looking around now at the sheer number of people they had to house, it was definitely going to be a rougher sleep cycle than he was used to, even in the officers' barracks. But Ansley thought they'd be able to keep everyone fed, watered, and sheltered until help arrived with relief supplies and transport to the Meridian Cities.

Then, they would cease to be Ansley Reid's problem.

Still, he found himself hoping that at least *one* of the refugees might hang around after the others had left.

"Hello?" Giana said, waving a hand in front of his face. "Anaranjado, this is New Calgary calling. Do you read?"

"Sorry," he said. "I guess I was staring off into space." Truth be told, until she'd spoken, he'd been assuming that was what Giana had been doing as well. He'd noticed she had a habit of staring off into space at times. In his mind, they'd just been sharing a companionable silence.

"It's all right." She had a nice laugh. "A long day. Speaking of which, does the day ever end here? I know we're underground, but I keep waiting for things to cool off."

"Not on this side of the planet," he said. "We're too close to our parent star. Tidally locked. The same side of the planet always faces the sun. I've read that's how Earth's moon was too. It's why it's so delightfully hot here and so fantastically cold on the far side."

"What a paradise we've come to."

"Yes indeed. But we do at least get darkness on a regular basis. The habitat lights will start dimming soon to let everyone know it's time to sleep. But tell me about your world." He decided to soft-pedal this. He didn't want her to think she was being interrogated.

"A lot greener and wetter," she admitted. "We had real days and nights, and air you could breathe outside of sealed habitats."

"A big change," he said. "One you are taking extremely well, if I'm being honest."

"Suspiciously well, one might even say?"

"Suspicious is too strong a term," he said. "Curiously well, let's say."

"Let's just say it wasn't exactly a paradise either. The decor was nicer, but I'm guessing you don't have the same wildlife problem we did."

"I think I ran into a group of your wildlife problems," Ansley said. He did not add what it had done.

Giana sighed. "I wish I could say I was surprised any of them made it through, but I doubt they're the only ones." She looked at him with gravity. "They are nasty pieces of work, and they have a habit of turning up where you least expect. But we didn't choose where the Bridge from Earth sent our ancestors." She pulled her gaze away, glancing once again at the closed landscape around them, the unnatural dome of stone that served as this settlement's sky. "Same as you, I expect."

Now a companionable silence did descend. Ansley let the mental exhaustion of the day settle over him. Beside him, Giana yawned.

"I think it's about time to check on where they have me bedding down for the, er, 'night.'"

"We call them sleep cycles here."

"That's a mouthful to say."

"True," Ansley admitted. "But it feels like less of a tease."

"And here I thought you were a man who might enjoy a good tease."

"If you like, I can pull strings to make sure we get assigned to the same building."

"Thanks, but no," she said with a laugh. "I think that might be a bit too crowded for my taste."

Ansley frowned. "No more crowded than any other building."

"I know," she said. "But at least if you aren't there, it won't feel like a wasted opportunity."

And before he could think of a reply to that, she was off, presumably hunting down the town elders.

Just get to tomorrow, he told himself. *After that, who knows what might happen?* At the very least, it was something to think about beyond the past two days.

Ansley woke from a quite-crowded-but-not-in-a-fun-way shallow sleep to the sound of screams coming from outside.

He rose like a shot, elbowing the people on either side of him and stepping on two more in his quest to find the front door. The home had well-installed blackout shades, so even the habitat's emergency lighting was nonexistent. It almost felt like a real, sunless night. The kind a better planet might have.

As he had predicted, every single home in Ashrock was like this, packed to the gills with New Calgarian refugees. Suspecting that the close quarters might give rise to some tensions during the sleep cycle, Ansley had not removed his uniform prior to bedding down—no point since Giana was in another building entirely—so he opened the door as soon as he'd managed to tiptoe-leap his way there around sleeping forms.

A large number of groans arose from those unaccustomed to sleeping in the oppressive heat. Ansley didn't pay them any mind. He was too busy stepping out of the home and into a nightmare.

A number of people, both locals and refugees by their clothing, were being menaced by some kind of creature. It should have been hard to see in the sleep-cycle lighting, but it produced a radiance all its own. And by that baleful glow, Ansley saw it was nothing like the bone-legged worm monsters which had targeted his squads. With the thought came the memories he'd tried so desperately to seal away. But he forced his vision to un-tunnel and his mind back into the present.

This creature was more amorphous, a shining mass of what

looked like white gelatin but far firmer and stronger, sprouting all over with over-articulated limbs of too many joints. It seemed to have spilled out from one of the other, equally overstuffed homes, herding the occupants out with it.

The few Anaranjadans in the group, despite never having seen this kind of thing before, were much quicker to run. Or maybe the creature was less interested in them. As Ansley watched, the creature struck, lashing out one limb each at three of the refugees.

Far from running like their lives depended on it, they almost seemed mesmerized by the monstrosity before them. Only one broke free of their apparent hypnosis fast enough to scoot out of reach. Of the other two, one was impaled, speared through the gut and hoisted high so that the man's screaming form slid down the limb toward the glowing main mass of the formless creature, his own gushing blood lubricating the motion.

The side of the creature's main mass opened a seam all along its length as its prey approached. The piercing limb suddenly seemed more like a tongue. It dragged the man hungrily into the new mouth yawning open to envelop him. Once it had done so, the mouth sealed itself shut, the man trapped inside. Ansley saw the glowing mass bulge where the man tried to push his way free and thought he might be sick.

The other victim's fate was, if anything, even more awful to behold. Instead of an impaling spear, this limb struck like a ball of glue. All of one arm, half of a leg, and most of the woman's torso were engulfed with the first strike. But the sticky mass was not content to merely pull her in to be devoured. It slithered along her in every direction, and when it oozed its way over her screaming face, Ansley had an unobstructed view as it poured itself into her ears and nose and mouth and eyes. Her screaming died on a gurgling choke, but Ansley knew a part of him would never stop hearing it.

It was then that Giana appeared and all but collided with him.

"We have to go," she said. "Now!"

"What are you talking about? We have to help them!"

"There's no saving them!" Her voice was plaintive. "Not once it's started."

As though the town were listening, the alarm started up. It had only one purpose: sound an evacuation.

"You haven't been honest with me," he growled at her.

"I know," she said. "I'll explain everything. But right now, we have to go. I am being absolutely honest when I tell you that, if we stay, we die."

Ansley hung there, torn. He knew what his duty was, what his squad would have expected of him. There could be no question there. But he also knew they were dead. He also knew he was not a soldier, not really. He was a rich scion of Equatoria fulfilling the minimum requirement of social service to earn a berth on the only ship leaving this planet, a life plan which suddenly seemed far more appealing than it had a few days ago.

"We have to go!" Giana said again.

"All right," he said. "Follow me, before anyone notices we're leaving."

⋈

"You're no soldier," he told her once they'd run long enough and fast enough to outpace any who might be following.

"I could say the same about you," she said. She placed a hand on his arm, and he turned to look at her. Their strides didn't break, maintaining their brisk walk. "No true soldier would have left all those people." Her tone expertly drew the sting from the words.

"Why don't you tell me exactly what the hell we just saw back there?" Ansley said, keeping his voice firm to distract himself from the firmness taking shape elsewhere. *You are angry with this woman, not aroused by her.* He didn't believe his own thoughts though. "And don't try to tell me that was the first time you'd seen something like that."

"I admitted as much, didn't I?" That much was true, at least.

She'd used that knowledge to convince him not to stay. "But you're right. I didn't lie to you, but I wasn't totally honest either. There really were a bunch of earthquakes fit to end the world, but they weren't the only reason to want to leave that nightmare world. We'd have left a long time ago if the secrets of the Bridge hadn't been lost until recently."

"So you colonized a world full of alien monsters?"

She thought about it and nodded. "In essence, yes."

"More than one kind of monster, too, right? That glowing one wasn't the only kind I've seen."

"Really?" she asked. "Which of the others?"

"Fuck me, you mean there's more than one other kind?"

"Three kinds total, counting the one we just saw," she said. "And, maybe later." Her smile was roguish.

"You can smile like that, talk like that after what we just ran from? What we just did?" But he was smiling too.

"What better time?" she asked. "I told you. I already pegged you as a smart person, not a heroic one. I'm the same, trust me. Think of it this way. How can anyone warn your leadership about the threat if no one gets out alive?"

This justification, so close to what he'd told himself following the deaths of the rest of his squad, sent chills through him despite the omnipresent heat. And he *had* warned his command about the thing that had killed his squad. He would do the same here.

"They only know about the one kind of monster so far, since that was all I knew to tell them." He couldn't quite pull all the accusation from his tone, but it didn't seem to faze her. "And since you asked, it was like a worm, only with legs made of bone. Very dark green, almost black."

"Yes, them," she said. "They're no more or less nasty than the other two, just a different flavor of awful."

"Where did that white one come from?"

"It must have been disguised as one of the refugees."

Ansley's stomach dropped. "I'm sorry, what? They can *disguise* themselves as human?"

"Fairly well," she said. "Though they would never pass if you started questioning them one on one. In a big crowd though, it's much easier for them to go unnoticed."

"And again, you thought this wasn't worth mentioning?"

"Be honest. Would you have helped us if I'd told you?"

He decided he would be honest. "No. Well, maybe *you*."

"We did our best to screen who got to cross the Bridge," Giana said. "But in the end, it was too chaotic. I'm sure we missed some. Hopefully not too many of the white ones, since they can convert people into more of themselves. The others, though, they can still disguise themselves, but they at least mostly just like to kill."

Ansley's mind was whirling. "What kind of hell-world did they dump you on? And how have you survived all this time?"

"Two very long stories," she said. "But you'll have to get me pretty drunk to go through all the details."

That sounded just fine to Ansley. There was something about this one. Perhaps it was that she looked like she came from Equatoria —all the New Calgarians did—but had the forthrightness of a soldier.

"We need to find another comms unit capable of reaching the capital," he said. His attempts to distract himself from his burgeoning arousal were not going well. "Militia Command will need to be informed of this additional information ASAP."

"Don't worry," she said. "I'll support whatever version of the story you want to tell. We're in this together, you and I."

"I bet you say that to all the self-serving fake soldiers," he said.

"Oh no. Trust me, I'm very selective."

Forcing his mind away from daydreams of what he could expect once they found a modicum of safety, Ansley turned his attention back to their path. He needed to make sure they made no wrong turns, and his canyon path navigator had died some ways back.

CHAPTER 23

JÜRGEN ENTERED his home with the girl in tow. She had clammed up completely on their way back down, refusing to answer any of his questions. Picking her up by the scruff of her stolen coat, he deposited her on the couch in his office beside Ms. Novak, who looked at least as concerned as she did ill.

"I asked you not to leave while I was out," he said to them both. He shifted to focus on Giana. "I found her up in the habitat levels, preparing to wander off who knows where."

"I'm sorry for not watching her more carefully. I was taking a nap." And indeed, Giana looked as though their sudden arrival had roused her from sleep. "I'm sure you know how children her age can be. I hope no harm was done."

He thought he caught a quickly stifled glare from the girl to the woman, but Marri sounded contrite enough when it was her turn to talk. "I only wanted to see more of the area. I'm sorry."

Jürgen Fennec wasn't buying it, though. Not after what he'd heard.

"What would you say if I told you both that I know you are not from this world? That you arrived recently via Bridge technology from another world entirely. A doomed world."

Both of them stared at him flatly.

"Before I left for the habitat levels, I placed one listening device in each of the two coats I left behind. Just in case one or both of you decided to go exploring against my instructions."

Marri suddenly looked very hunted, and well she should.

"I have no idea who you were talking to," Jürgen said to the girl. "I only heard your half of the conversation. But it was enough to put you two together with the news I just learned about up in the habitat levels."

Still, that he'd missed half the conversation was irritating. Between hiding the device deep inside the coat and the difficulty of wireless underground communications, Marri's voice had been so garbled he'd barely been able to make it out. He hadn't heard her conversational partner at all. Possibly the girl had been speaking on some kind of communication device of her own.

"We're from New Calgary," Giana said before Jürgen could ask the question. "We're sorry to have misled you, but we had to leave that world under duress, as you heard. We couldn't know how our arrival would be taken. And we weren't even supposed to arrive in this part of the world at all. Marri must have run into one of the others. Surely we can't be the only two down here."

"If there are others down here, I will find them," Jürgen said. Easy enough to spot them now that he knew to look for Equatorians where they didn't belong. "And I do understand why you might be reluctant to confide in me. If everyone from your world is as baseline as you two, seeing people like me must come as something of a shock."

Giana's smile was a touch embarrassed. "I mean, maybe a little. But now that we're safe to ask, if you'd be willing to tell us something of this world, it might curb certain people's curiosities." She inclined her head sideways at Marri, earning a covert glare.

Jürgen thought about it. Certainly sharing public information could not be considered dangerous, even with off-worlders. The prohibitions against dealing with aliens were strict indeed, but these were not aliens. They were humans. Being from another colony didn't change that fact.

"Very well," he said. "I believe that can be arranged."

He leaned over his desk and called up its holoprojector. It was a far cry from state of the art, but it would be sufficient.

The planet, color-coded a more-or-less accurate orange, appeared as a stationary ball of light. "Anaranjado," he said, gesturing at the world. "The world we are on now." Then the image zoomed out to show the orange star Naranja. "Naranja, this solar system's star. K-type."

"Seems really close," Marri said. Her eyes had lost their suspicious cast and widened at the display.

"Punishingly close," Jürgen said. "The images are not to scale, but we are more than close enough, I promise you. Anaranjado has been in this orbit, and correspondingly, this climate, for as long as humans have colonized it. It's commonly accepted that the algorithms which selected it as a potential colony world back on Earth were operating on obsolete observation data."

"Meaning it was in a better orbit previously," Giana said. Her interest appeared as sharp as Marri's, if more restrained.

"Most assuredly," Jürgen said. "We know this for multiple reasons. First, the geology of the surface, as well as subsurface and Shadyside deposits of water-ice such as those you see in these tunnels, make it clear that liquid water once flowed abundantly, something that is no longer the case on either side due to the tidal-locking of the planet to the star and subsequent temperature extremes."

"What's big enough to shift the orbit of a planet this size so late after its formation?" Giana asked. "Some sort of impact? Larger planets migrating?"

"Nothing so mundane, I'm afraid," Jürgen said. At his gesture, the holoimage zoomed back in on the planet, this time populating it with semi accurate surface detail. This brought into focus the massive rift running along one of the planet's meridians and the three rectangular shapes emerging from that rift, evenly spaced with respect to one another. The southernmost of these megastructures was slagged mostly to ruins. "In fact, at some point in this world's past, it was host to another intelligent species. We know very little about them, but we can surmise a great deal from these structures and their original purpose. At some point, this world's prior inhabitants tried to shrink the planet's orbital radius with the end goal of seeing it swallowed by the parent star."

"What does that mean?" Marri sounded like she was trying to decide whether to be outraged or not.

"The structures are engines," Jürgen said. "Engines capable of gradually bleeding off the planet's orbital speed until it would be consumed."

"But why would the people who lived here do that to their home?"

"We have no way of knowing," Jürgen said. "All we do know is that the attempt failed due to the failure of the mechanisms below the surface." He pointed at the melting damage on the southernmost engine. "That damage is most obvious here. However this happened, the world was spared, though clearly, not without great cost. Naranja boiled most of the atmosphere away. Life on the surface became quite impossible, and even elsewhere, native lifeforms larger than microbes are more rumor and supposition than fact."

"How do you all survive if nothing else can?" Marri asked.

"There are controlled spaces where some food can be cultivated. It must be carefully rationed, however. And to limit the number of calories required, most turn to other means of energy consumption and conversion." Jürgen took the opportunity to indicate his own cybernetic components. "One thing this world does not lack is solar energy, after all. But your question brings up another mystery. When the original human colonists arrived, they found a world with potential sites for habitats dug below the surface, all empty but all with survivable temperature conditions, if barely. But given that this was a world that had a breathable atmosphere once upon a time, such facilities made no sense. It has led to some . . . odd rumors, to say the lea—"

"So if your people barely eat, and there's still barely enough food to go around, what are we going to eat?" Marri sounded more worried than curious now. As if on cue, her stomach growled.

"You are fortunate this is a Harmony world," Jürgen said. "There were always rumors that a few of the colonies were not, that they'd rejected Harmony." He freighted the words with import. "But here, we help our own." The sneer came unbidden. "Most of us, at least."

Marri looked on the point of asking something, but Giana forestalled her.

"You're thinking of the Cult? They've rejected Harmony then?"

Beside her, Marri frowned, as though in disapproval of this grim news.

"Yes." He realized he hadn't been explicit earlier. "That's what I meant when I said they'd rejected humanity. You can't have humanity without Harmony." The statement would never stop hurting, but he lashed himself with it every chance he got. "They want to kill the organisms entirely, rip them from our heads, wipe them out!" His voice was ragged by the end.

And in me, they succeeded, or close enough as makes no difference. It was a secret he didn't want anyone to know, least of all himself. But it was also the reason he would fight the Cult to his dying day, at least as much as he was permitted.

Giana's eyes widened in shock. "It's difficult to imagine what such a drastic change would mean."

"I know exactly what it would mean," Jürgen said. "It would mean a return to the old ways. Division and discord, greed and self-serving action dominating everyone's behavior. The Cult view the organisms as a prison for our minds, but the rest of humanity understands the truth. Their presence in our brains frees us to be our best selves."

And if I don't recover that man from them, who knows what

they'll do? This reaffirmation of his other case, his mission, steeled him for what he had to do next.

"Forgive my passions," he said. "They go beyond even my personal feelings. I've just been hired for a case that could have ramifications on just this topic if I don't bring it to a successful close soon."

"It has to do with Harmony? And the Cult?"

"Yes," he said with reluctance. "The Cultists have kidnapped someone of extreme importance to the leaders of Anaranjado. It is critical that I remove this person from the Cult's control. All my efforts must be devoted toward that end." He stopped himself before he gave away too much. Best to get on with this before that could happen. "Which is why you have to go."

"Go?" Marri cut in. "What do you mean?"

"I took Ms. Novak in when I believed her to be a client and, quite frankly, a rich one capable of paying me back for whatever expenses I incurred while she stayed here. However, you are no longer clients, but refugees who have landed on my doorstep. I do not hold your false pretenses against you, but that doesn't mean I can afford to let you remain."

"We can still be clients. We still need help to find the others," Marri said.

"And you can pay me in what precisely? No, I'm afraid even if that were so, I now need to focus on my primary task. It is far more important."

"But where are we supposed to go?"

"You may resume your exploration of the habitat levels at your leisure. I will no longer stop you. I have just explained to you our history on this world to better orient you. I will take you to someone I know who can help you get started. This much, I can do. But no more. To be completely honest, I often struggle supporting just myself. I can't manage two more individuals, both of whom require actual food on a daily basis to survive."

Marri leaned forward in a manner Jürgen almost thought of as predatory. It was odd enough—and unsettling enough—that he found himself leaning back, as silly as that was. The girl was less than half his height, but still she seemed on the verge of rushing at him.

Giana's hand stopped her. She didn't touch the girl but barred her path with one arm.

"That's no way to treat our host," Giana said. She stood and approached Jürgen slowly. "I understand why you are doing this," she said, "and what it's costing you."

Had he possessed human eyes, tears would have sprung to them at such undeserved understanding from her. Because of course it was not costing him the way it would have had his Harmony symbiont still been properly integrated in his mind. The pain came from knowing that he should have felt crushing guilt and didn't.

"I will pack you what supplies I can spare," he said, abruptly flustered. The guilt came then, but it was a muted, pathetic thing. Perhaps, had his Harmony symbiont been functioning, he'd have continued to house and feed them, and ultimately would have died. That sort of thing had been known to happen. But without it guiding his actions, showing him the moral path, there was just his imagination to go by. And reliance on imagination and a kind of honor system faltered quickly when he had no choice but to abandon it.

And he truly did have no choice, even if he wasn't being entirely honest about why. But he still had to try and do his best. To act as if he was still part of the greater tribe of humankind. That included his guests. "Ms. Novak," he said, turning to face Giana. "I would have a word alone, if you would."

"Of course," Giana said. Jürgen looked to Marri, expecting the girl to go, but Marri stared stubbornly back. After a moment, Giana rose, obviously in some discomfort. Feeling unaccustomed pangs of empathy, Jürgen gestured her to the front of his home. Marri made to follow.

"Stay, Marri," Giana said firmly.

The girl looked like she was about to swallow her tongue, but she obeyed. Meanwhile, Jürgen helped wrap Giana up in as many spare coats as he had and led her outside.

"What was so urgent you had to speak with me alone?" Giana said.

"I wanted you to know the real reason I must do this. There are extensive records leading up to the diaspora from Earth. I know your colony rejected Harmony."

"If you say so," Giana said, her voice muffled by the layers of synthetic fabrics draping her. "If that's the case, we rejected it so thoroughly, I'm afraid, that I'm still not entirely certain what it is or how it works."

"What's important is that an existence without Harmony is the overriding goal of the Cult. It is all they dream about. Twice they have tried to achieve that with locally acquired test subjects, and twice they have failed." Jürgen steeled himself. This was difficult, but it was important he conveyed to her the seriousness of the threat. "I was the first of those attempts, and their alterations of me were so profound, they cut off my Harmony symbiont from the rest of my brain. It survives still, but it can no longer influence my behavior."

"That sounds profoundly invasive," Giana said. "And quite difficult for you."

"It was and is," Jürgen said, feeling a rush of gratitude for the show of empathy. "I am forced to act as best I can as though it still influences me, guess at how society would want me to behave at any given moment. But I am getting sidetracked. I believe the Cult is attempting to do something wholly different, something I am determined to stop. But if they were to realize that a large number of humans who do not possess the organism have arrived on this world, and that one of them was actually *in their lair* the other day, I do not think it would take much for them to pivot to their old attempts, or to try both in parallel. Either way, it would be very bad for both of you, but the girl in particular."

"Why Marri more so?"

"Three reasons. She is young, she is nearby, and they are already aware she exists. And, if you'll forgive me this fourth reason, she is seemingly healthy compared to you. Both her youth and her health would be a boon to them. Her proximity makes her an easier target than someone who arrived elsewhere."

"And you aren't saying this to both of us because you don't trust her not to run off and do whatever she wants."

"Precisely."

"Thank you for that," Giana said.

CHAPTER 24

"WHAT DID HE SAY?" Marri demanded.

"To watch you carefully," Giana said, a glint of amusement in her bloodshot eye. "He doesn't trust you to be smart regarding your own safety."

Marri tamped down her disgust. Just another adult assuming she was some helpless child. It even transcended worlds.

"I'm sorry," Marri said, turning her disgust upon herself. She hated apologizing to anyone, most especially Giana, but she felt she had no choice. "I let him catch me. Let him listen in on me."

"He would have found out eventually," Giana said. "You only did what I asked of you. It's just accelerated the inevitable." Her words were calm, but she looked terrible. It amplified Marri's guilt over her spilling of their secret. She waited for Giana to ask her who she'd been talking to in the caves, but strangely, the woman didn't. She must really be feeling bad to miss such an obvious question. It was a relief, but it also made Marri worry.

She's not a woman, and you don't have to feel bad for her. Still, she couldn't forget how Father had charged her with Giana's safety. *Safe crossing of the Bridge, he said. That's over now. You owe her nothing.*

Yet it felt like a lie.

"Hopefully Mr. Fennec's contact will be able to offer us a place to stay while we are looking for the others," Giana said.

"Shouldn't we go where other Coldgardeners are? They'll have food there. If most of us showed up other places, they might be better set up to handle us there."

"No," Giana said. "Here is where we need to be. What's happening down here is important. Jürgen is attempting to handle it alone. If he means to take on the Cult, he's going to need our help whether he realizes it or not."

Marri blinked. Of all the things Giana was, willing to help without getting something out of it was not one of them. Marri fixed the woman with her most skeptical look. Sometimes words were not as effective as simple expressions.

Giana locked eyes in return, her stare implacable despite her obvious illness, and Marri felt a wave of exhaustion wash over her. She'd never minded locking horns with Giana before, but for some reason, just the thought of battling over every little thing made her want to curl up and sleep.

Marri broke the stare first.

"Something you'd like to say?" Giana asked, her voice strangely soft in her victory over their little battle of wills.

"I want to know what you're really up to, but you'll never tell me," Marri said.

"And I want to understand this world, and what our place in it might be. Right now, that means staying in this area. But I will need your help. If you want to view it as making up for your mistake earlier, that's fine. If you prefer to focus on how I see you as someone who has real skills they can contribute, not a child to be coddled, also fine. Whatever works best for you."

"So long as I do what you want, you mean. What help can we be to Jürgen?" Marri asked.

"I'd think that would be obvious. Unless you've already forgotten how to do it."

Marri blinked in surprise. She held up her hand, letting her fingers fuse and morph into a curved bone claw as a little show of defiance.

"Good," Giana said, smiling. "Very good."

CHAPTER 25

IT WAS NOTORIOUSLY difficult to find a single time when an entire arcology's worth of Equatorian leadership could physically be in the same room together. This went doubly for short-notice, emergency meetings. So their next meeting to discuss what was coming to be called the New Calgarian Incursion took place with each of the attendees calling in remotely and otherwise going about their evenings.

Caroline was careful about selecting her filter prior to logging on. She wished to make it look as though she was still at her office as opposed to her study. She'd rotated the room to face the night side of the planet so the view wouldn't be as false. The view of the stars always calmed her. She also kept the healthy glass of wine she'd poured herself well off camera.

Niklaus was the first into the meeting room, of course, with Caroline the second. That made it virtually impossible to avoid speaking with him.

"Leeeeeen," he said in his most grating voice. "Do you know why we are calling a meeting when I'm supposed to be convincing the Bletchley twins to—"

"I have no idea," she said quickly, desperate to blot out his next words. "Polliard indicated urgent, so here I am."

"Working late, I see?" There was a smirk on Niklaus's face Caroline didn't like. As though he saw right through her filter's deception. Given his access to information technology, possibly he did. He was in his office as well, or at least appeared to be. Based on what he'd said about the twins, his view was likely as false as hers.

On the other hand, he might just be fucking with her.

She was spared from answering by the appearance on her monitor of a pair of windows containing Margaret Polliard and Wellington Reid. They appeared seemingly already engaged in conversation, as though they'd had a meeting before the meeting. It was a heated discussion, but Caroline didn't catch much before Reid clamped his mouth shut, apparently realizing they were no longer alone.

"Go ahead, Wellington," Margaret said, a small smile of triumph on her face. She must have been the one that brought them into the shared meeting space, then. "Tell them what you only wanted to tell me."

Reid's face flushed red with obvious anger. "Since you are so insistent on involving everyone, I'll keep my peace until and unless the others show up. Two can play at your childish games, Margaret."

"The one threatening to take his toys and go home if he can't have his way is the childish one, Wellington," Polliard said. "But since I do so loathe repeating myself, I'm content to wait."

Caroline normally would have kept her own peace, but half a glass of wine had loosened her tongue some.

"Can someone please tell me what is going on? I'm very busy, and—"

"Addressing our wayward experimental subject issue, I trust," Heller said, popping into a new window. He too was in his office, and though he was clearly reviewing some kind of documentation on a separate tablet, he was studiously careful not to let the contents of that tablet screen come into view of the camera. In another window, Xian Ginevra appeared, close on Heller's heels. Caroline didn't know why she thought so, but she had the sense those two had been meeting as well.

They were all here now. They could have gotten started, but everyone was deferring to Heller's question such that Caroline felt compelled to answer.

"I'm waiting on feedback from the other arcologies," she said. "This is an incident that affects us all. We should all have a say in how we approach its resolution."

"Admirably democratic of you," Heller said. But despite the praise, the disappointment in his voice was once again evident. "But it is high time you take charge of your sandbox, the way your father would have. I know you were put in charge years earlier than you planned, but no one knows this subject and its issues better than you do. Deep down, you know what has to be done. Stop waiting for someone to tell you to do it, and just do it."

Trying not to visibly wither, Caroline had to resist the urge to grab for her wine glass. The best she could manage was a wordless nod, but she at least maintained eye contact.

"Good. Now that's settled, *again*," Heller said, "I'm hearing rumors that I may have yet another high-profile criminal case dumped on my lap imminently. Care to elaborate, Commandant Reid?"

A spasm of something like rage passed across Reid's face—the man had still not regained his equilibrium after Margaret had ambushed him into this meeting. "We've had an incident."

"A bloody fucking disaster is what it is!" Margaret rode over him. "And I mean that literally." If Reid's anger was surprising, mild-mannered Margaret's obvious rage stunned Caroline. "One of the cybernetically enhanced apes he calls a professional soldiering force stole a flier and practically leveled the only hospital in Sunnyside. The loss of assets is catastrophic, the cost to rebuild astronomical."

"*Leveled* would be an exaggeration," Reid protested. "But the incident was both dire and troubling."

"More than troubling, I'd say, Wellington." For his part, Heller didn't appear surprised by the revelation in the slightest, which, judging by the faces of the others just now finding out, singled him out. "Are we to take this to mean that the rumors flying around are, in fact, confirmed? That these visitors from another world include some kind of alien 'monsters' who can appear human? Or are you merely employing the most delusional psychopaths on the planet and inadequately constraining them?"

"There have been more than enough incidents, from anecdotes to recorded events to sworn statements by medical personnel, to prove that we are indeed dealing with some percentage of alien infiltrators with these refugees." Reid sounded as though every word were being beaten out of him.

"What percentage are we talking about here?" Xian made most of the things she said sound like accusations, so for this question to stand out was saying something.

"It's funny you should bring that up." Margaret's voice dripped with sarcasm. "My people were in the process of determining that—"

"*Our* people," Reid interjected. "We have joint assets on site."

"Those that survive, yes," Margaret responded. "Any hope of a scientific understanding of what we're facing, one involving a statistically significant population of the refugees, has been dashed by one of your lunatics."

"The man is in custody!" Reid snapped. "Dietrick Horváth will see justice for what he did. Our good friend Heller will surely see to that."

"Justice can't un-kill my assets, dear," Margaret said. Caroline had never heard her so condescending. "And it certainly can't unfuck what's already been thoroughly fucked in terms of information, either."

"Aw, shit," Niklaus said, giving voice to Caroline's own thoughts. "Grandma Maggie is on the warpath today."

Margaret ignored the comment, probably to Niklaus's good fortune.

"Now all our off-world patients, who were nice and under control before, are scattered to hell and gone. We've got some of them still. But a majority we've lost, either to death or escape." Her voice rose as she spoke. Caroline goggled. The woman wasn't even at the apex of her tirade yet. "And that's to say nothing of the collective years of experience lost as your man tried to kill every human being he could find just in case a few of them were aliens!"

"It's been more than a few if even half the reports I've seen are true—"

"Half that hospital was our own people, Wellington!"

"I am working right now to ensure we recapture as many of the escapees as we can," Wellington pushed on. "And we're going to reassemble you a *statistically significant* group of the refugees so that your experiments—"

"If you really think you can put this vase back together, Wellington, you are even more stupid than I took you for—"

"Enough." Heller's voice cutting over Margaret was calm, but it commanded silence and received it from everyone on the call. "Enough out of you two. And enough for me. Ginevra, it is time to move forward with the *Ultima Thule*. We are leaving."

"Just like that?" Xian's incredulity could have encompassed the galaxy. "We abandon this world we've been at such pains to tame and control?"

"This was always the plan," Heller said sternly. "Ever since we detected the likely world and you conceived of the ship. All we are doing is moving up the timetable. If you've yet to make peace with that inevitable outcome, Ginevra, now is the time to do so. If there's even a chance our control over the colony is at risk, it is imperative we launch the mission intended to hedge our bets on long-term viability."

"The others—"

"We have a threat of an unknown magnitude whose numbers continue to grow hour by hour. And our first, best chance to understand that threat is now lost to us. The others," he said with a certainty that could level mountains, "will see reason."

"I haven't lost this fight yet!" Reid insisted. "We haven't even mounted a truly organized campaign to root out the monsters from the refugees, and—"

"Have you had word from your son?" Heller cut in.

"I—yes." In his window on her screen, Reid looked both chagrined and relieved. "Yes, he checked in at Ashrock, one of the outlying settlements. His squad was attacked by these creatures. He was the only survivor. We haven't had the assets to spare to retrieve him, but the situation there was stable at last check, and he's due to check in again with his superior shortly." His tone said he would be monitoring that situation himself.

"I'm glad he's safe," Heller said gently before pivoting back to his original point. "But Wellington, if you truly want the ACM to be of service, then I suggest you use them to evacuate as many of the outlying areas as possible. Have the people pack up their food and escort them to the Meridian Cities. One thing that seems clear based on what we've seen is that be they human or alien, these New Calgarians have no reliance on cybernetic augments or replacements. That means they have to eat and drink. If we deprive them of as much easy food and water—be it nutrient blocks or humans—as we can, it will slow down their advance and keep our people safe at the same time. Then your ACM can form a cordon around the Meridian Cities and have that much smaller of an area to defend while we make ready to launch."

That was, Caroline reflected, a pretty good idea. Judge though he might be, Heller's command of tactics seemed sound to her. Either Reid agreed with her, or he wasn't willing to continue to push back against Heller because he simply nodded.

"Yes," he said. "Yes, I see the sense in that."

"Good," Heller said. "We will issue an evacuation order for those settlements, then. Everyone is to pack up as much food and water as they can, spare power cells, et cetera, and leave the rest behind."

"I suggest we set some sort of time limit," Reid said. "That way ACM units will have a chance to assist in the evacuation, but no one will hold themselves up waiting for help that isn't coming."

"Yes, good," Heller agreed. "Which brings us to the matter of ship prep. As of this moment, each of you is sworn to the strictest of secrecy about the accelerated timetable for our departure. With all that's going on, we risk a general panic if we let slip that we are jumping ship, as it were. Tell absolutely no one. Not a soul."

"We have to tell our staff, surely," Caroline cut in. "They'll be packing our belongings, after all. And they're coming with us, of course. Hard to keep that a secret."

"No," Heller said simply. "The need to leave quickly and quietly has changed that. No staff. The only crew we are bringing are those we can exert absolute control over."

"Of course we can *control* them," Caroline said, not wanting to hear what he was saying. "Harmony—"

"I'm talking about *absolute* control, Caroline," Heller said. He let his words sink in. Margaret was the first to get there.

"Defectives," she said. "You're talking about the population of Defectives operating Scenic View Station."

"Precisely," Heller said. "We don't have to tell Defectives where to go because they only go where we send them. They can't tell anyone because they won't know what's going on."

But. But my people. Caroline wanted to object, but no one else was doing so. And she had already ruffled feathers enough her last meeting. Besides, on some level, she knew Heller was right.

"That will be the ACM's other task, Reid," Heller said. "And we might as well pull in as many of the trams to the Meridian Cities as possible. No sense giving the enemy any easy means of movement." He continued issuing orders then. It was not a thing he did often, which by itself marked this out as a momentous occasion. But not one of them thought to contradict him. And in some respects, it was a comfort.

Now Caroline had the guidance she only now realized she'd desperately craved. Nothing that happened from here on out with her own set of instructions would be solely on her shoulders.

CHAPTER 26

"I APOLOGIZE you aren't seeing our little slice of heaven at its best," Ansley said to Giana as they walked. Since their flight from Ashrock, they'd passed no fewer than three tram call stations.

The tram network connected the outlying settlements and significantly speeded up travel time between them. Even the ACM used them for their patrols. But each time he'd tried to call one to help them on their way, he'd received the same message:

LOCKED OUT DUE TO SPECIAL ORDER.

That sounded like some kind of state of emergency had been declared. Ansley hadn't heard any such. But then, he was also down a comms person.

"A little walking never hurt anyone," Giana said teasingly. Still, she looked sweaty and generally miserable, even if she was trying to put a good face on it.

Moving between outskirt towns on foot was a slow process sometimes—as Ansley was discovering—with hours between habitats. Whatever intelligence had constructed the network of hollow chambers and connecting tunnels had apparently given no thought to

158

human walking speed. Unfortunately, this gave Ansley a lot of time to think.

After the disasters with his squad and then at Ashrock, after Giana's revelations about the nature of the monsters the New Calgarians had brought with them, Ansley had expected pandemonium at every settlement along the path toward the Meridian Cities. He'd expected fear, paranoia, accusations. Neighbor turning against neighbor. Of course, with Harmony in play, the worst of those human tendencies to shrink the circle of *us* would be held back. It was so hard to remember that sometimes, considering his own circles.

But still, he'd expected something beyond ringing, eerie silence. Yet the next settlement he and Giana walked into stood entirely abandoned.

Ansley had spent months patrolling these pisspot little Stone-Dome towns as part of his tour of duty. Even on a planet as harsh and unforgiving as Anaranjado, such settlements, dirt-poor and struggling though they may be, had a certain vitality to them. It was something he only realized now, when he beheld a town that clearly lacked this quality.

"Why do you look so unhappy?" Giana said, giving his shoulder a teasing punch. She pointed at the dust. "Look, you can still make out the footprints everywhere. They must have gotten word of the threat and made for somewhere more defensible."

Ansley studied the tracks. "It looks like the ACM's been here, as well," he said, placing his own boot in a similarly sized track to show they matched outlines. "Maybe they got the people out."

"Exactly. This is good news."

"Good news?" He was genuinely perplexed. Giana looked at him with sudden indulgence, as if only just realizing he were a bit slow and would need things explained to him.

"It means word about the threat is spreading," she said.

"I need to find the town's comms unit. I'm past due to check in, and they need to know what happened in Ashrock since I last reported in."

She blinked as though this was the opposite of what she'd wanted to hear. "Do you have your story straight on that?"

He didn't, but he began spinning one out on the fly.

"I made contact with you, and I considered the intel you could provide more valuable than the safety of the town," he said.

"And is that intel worth the lives of everyone in that town?"

"We don't know that it came to that."

"But you don't know that it didn't, either, so you should assume the worst."

"This is a world of collective self-sacrifice. Harmony sees to that."

"You don't seem very self-sacrificial."

Careful, now, Ans. He had to watch what he said lest he give away too much.

"There's a natural level of flexibility, particularly when it comes to responsibility and leadership positions." He decided to turn it around on her, partly to put her on the defensive and partly because he was genuinely curious. "Surely you've seen the same phenomenon on your world."

She regarded him with an unreadable expression, her face totally blank. But it was gone so fast, replaced with a mischievous grin, that he half-thought he'd imagined it. "Don't mind me. I just enjoy giving a hard time to people I think are cute," she said with a wink. And before he could react to *that*, she'd grown serious and solemn. "I'll help you find the comm unit. We can search twice as fast if we split up."

"No need," he said. "Regulation states they always have to be stored in a central structure." He glanced around. "There." He indicated the largest building, a dome half again as tall as the others. "That'll be the town hall."

He jogged over, Giana keeping close. Unfortunately, his fears were realized as the door failed to open at his approach. As a public building, it shouldn't have been locked to anyone, but clearly the ACM had activated safeguards—probably for the first time ever—against potential intrusion when they'd left.

"Stay here and keep watch," he said. "I'm going to go looking for an override." Someone in the town, one of the elders, would have one. He just had to hope they'd forgotten to take it with them.

✶

Ansley didn't make it far into his search before it became clear this was no slapdash evacuation, however hastily it had been arranged. The first five buildings he tried, all those closest to the town hall and therefore most likely to house the elders, were sealed up tight. He went around to the back of each, spending ten painstaking minutes shuffling slowly through the narrow gap between buildings and the habitat's stone wall, just to make sure there were no back entrances to any of the structures that someone had forgotten about.

Defeated on all fronts, Ansley was looping back around to the front, beginning to think they'd have to find a way to break past the locked town hall, when Giana called out to him.

"Ansley! I got it open."

He ran the rest of the way in a kind of shock, arriving to find it was true. She stood there, the door open wide enough to admit a person. "What? How?"

"Someone didn't clean it very well," she said. "I think it wasn't actually locked. Sand or grit were just fouling up the mechanism. I managed to blow enough of it out for the machinery to take over."

Ansley examined the now-ajar door, perplexed. He'd been certain it was locked. Now that he took a closer look, though, he saw his error. There was the slightest bit of damage to the locking mechanism, a warping of the metal, as though it had sustained a hit of significant force before the town had emptied out. An accident in the panicked evacuation, maybe.

"You just have to glance at it for more than half a second next time before giving up," she teased.

You've gotten too little sleep, he told himself. *And too much trauma.* That likely had more to do with it. Regardless, they were in now.

"This way," he said. "All these town hall buildings are laid out the same." The comms unit was always in the back, a straight shot from the entrance, yet well past the point where any normal citizen might stumble upon it and start fiddling, ruining the settings. Still, the pictograms on walls and floor labeling different sections of the buildings made it obvious enough where to find it.

His heart sank the moment they arrived at the room though. The front face of the unit was partially caved in, as if someone had swung a massive, blunt instrument at it in a fit of rage.

Maybe that was why they hadn't bothered to fix the door lock. The ACM might have ensured no potential enemy could make use of the comms unit to gain any intelligence advantage on Militia movements.

"That doesn't look good," Giana said, jogging up beside him. "I'm guessing by the way you look, it's not going to work?"

"As you said, best not to give up after half a second." Ansley tried to inject some hope into his voice, but as he tried the standard activation sequence, the console didn't respond at all. Based on the lack of a readout, it wasn't even transmitting a standby signal.

That, at least, might get noticed.

"Well," he said. "I'm not going to say this can't be fixed. But I certainly don't know how to fix it." *And my tech specialist was carved up like a roast.* He tried to banish that image from his mind. Doing so required him to physically shake his head as though clearing it of mental cobwebs.

Giana regarded him seriously.

"I'm guessing this isn't the kind of thing you want to hear right now," she said. "But you aren't going to be able to reach your command from here. Probably not even before the next . . . sleep cycle has passed. You said the next town is even further than this one was on foot, right?"

"Yes," Ansley said, feeling the weight of this truth settle over him.

"You're exhausted. Mentally even more than physically. I can see it. And frankly, so am I. We need to recover a bit before we press on."

Ansley thought about the slaughter they'd left behind—twice, in his case. How powerless he was to stop any of it alone. *You already updated Command once. You are doing your best.* Surely they knew all the relevant information by now. Giana said there were thousands upon thousands of refugees, which means they must have appeared in dozens of places.

"You're right," he said at last.

She smiled encouragingly. "See? Smart."

"But every building I tried was locked up tight. And they can't all have been mistakes on my part."

"We'll just have to camp out here then," she said. And, taking her in, he saw how much less flushed she looked now that she was in a structure with proper climate control.

"Makes sense," he said. "And I'm guessing you are probably as hungry as I am. So I think the first order of business should be to find some supplies."

"A man after my own heart," she said, her smile broad and mysterious.

CHAPTER 27

THE COLONY of Anaranjado appeared to consist of a series of dome-shaped caves carved out of sandstone. Returned now to his human form so he walk comfortably, Karl had re-dressed himself in his flow-matter jumpsuit. Once freed from its death grip around his foreclaw, it had gamely reassembled itself around him.

Karl quickly learned that each chamber was linked by doors and narrow, claustrophobic interior canyons or tunnels serving as hall-ways. At a certain point, he came upon a light rail system and began to follow it, having had no better thoughts about which direction to pick. He found the rail linked most of the doors and chambers and hallways as well, though Karl saw no sort of vehicle that would ride on said rail.

This was a pity, since it meant he was forced to cover the distance on foot. Despite this, he had yet to tire. He was certain this planet had slightly lower gravity than Coldgarden. Either that or they had done more work on him than just his hip.

Oh well. It wasn't like any driver of said vehicles was likely to let him aboard for a ride. Not once they got a close look at him and saw he looked nothing like an Anaranjadan native.

Whatever vehicles were intended to use the rail system, they couldn't be all that big. The width of the doorways and the canyon hallways wouldn't have allowed something even as big as a Coldgarden tram.

Aside from this discovery, he also learned quickly which sorts of doors he was searching for and which to not bother investigating. Whoever had laid out the design for this networked labyrinth of eerily perfect, hollow domes of rock, they had not bothered to link every door via rail system.

The rail-linked doors were all of one type. On approach, an amber LED would light up for a few moments, followed by a shift to green, and the door would open to admit him. Beyond lay another domed cavern or canyon tunnel much like whatever he was leaving behind. What the door was checking for, he didn't know, but he never encountered one that rejected him until he deviated from the rail.

It happened in a sudden fit of anxiety that he was missing an easy and obvious path of escape. This led him to attempt to pass through one of the circular side doors. Those doors all looked more robust, and they were also a lot less frequent. The one Karl chose to approach was set at the end of a spur branching off from a canyon tunnel at something close to a right angle.

Walking up to this door produced a decidedly different reaction than the rail-linked doors.

At first, everything was very familiar. As Karl tentatively approached, the circle door shone an amber light identical to the others. Only this time, it did not automatically shift to green and grant him passage. Instead, a transparent panel in front of a palm pad set off to the door's right side slid away, and the pad extended on some unseen servo, proffering itself to be pressed. Karl might have done so had he not heard the locks slamming home on the rail-linked doors—both the one he'd intended to take before thinking to try this side passage and the one he'd entered from.

Fearing that he'd blocked himself in, that this was some kind of trap he'd blundered into, Karl backed away hastily. Absent his proximity, the amber light went out. The palm pad retracted, the transparent pane sliding back in place in front of it.

Most importantly, the straightaway doors over the rails unlocked themselves.

Once he'd calmed down enough to think—and hastened through the next door to a new corridor with no side exits—Karl considered what he'd seen. The straightaway doors opened upon his mere approach. The side doors required some kind of additional input, essentially asking *are you sure?* Then, while you were thinking about it, the straightaway doors locked themselves down.

It almost seemed like an airlock.

So far, every place he'd been since arriving here had been inside. He'd only gotten one look out, through the transparent dome partially enclosing the Bridge site. What he'd seen told the story of a world far more hostile—at least in terms of climate—than the one he'd come from.

Now he wondered if it even harbored a breathable atmosphere. Could it be that the straightaway doors were checking to ensure there was atmosphere beyond before that amber light clicked over to green? Could it be the side door he'd very nearly opened led out onto the unprotected surface?

It was far from a comforting thought, the notion that with a single misstep in a world he didn't understand, he'd be dead.

The door at the end of this latest canyon tunnel opened and exposed Karl to a wash of punishing orange light and brutal heat— heat which went well beyond the baseline stifling warmth he was trying to acclimate to and made him recall the Bridge site's glass dome. His sense memory was accurate. He stepped out into another area walled in stone but domed this time in trussed glass, just like the Bridge area he'd arrived in, only much smaller. Along one section of stone wall lay an array of lockers that looked like they might store protective equipment.

And growing in the orange light of that swollen sun were an array of cacti of varying types arranged in carefully cultivated rows of planter boxes.

"A greenhouse," he said to no one, wiping sweat he could not afford to lose from his brow. Despite the heat, he felt a small measure of comfort. This was the first place he'd been on this entire planet that made it feel like normal people might live here somewhere.

But his relief, thin as it was, evaporated entirely as a rumbling hum rose in his ears. He quickly identified the source: the rail which neatly bisected the rows of planted cacti was vibrating, as though something was traveling along it. The sound was growing louder.

And it was coming from behind him.

Visions of a tram packed with militia soldiers sent to hunt him down now that they wouldn't have to shoot inside their own complex filled his head. He looked around himself in rising alarm. There was nowhere to hide. Even the lockers weren't big enough to hide his frame.

The lockers.

He ran to check them. They opened without requiring any special access, and he found they contained tools and protective gear, as he'd suspected, and bottles of water, the mere sight of which reminded him of how dry his throat was.

Guzzling down a bottle as fast as he could without choking, Karl examined the suit. It would cover his whole body, and while the visor was transparent, he thought the glare from the sunlight pouring in would probably help disguise his face.

So that was his choice. Try to outrun the approaching vehicle—whose vibrations were growing quite obvious now—and hope he found a better place to hide or don the suit and hide himself in plain sight.

He grabbed the suit, putting it on as fast as he could. Grabbing a random assortment of tools, he jogged awkwardly over to the far side of the chamber and busied himself pretending to prune a cactus. It was no accident he chose the cactus best positioned to hide him from obvious view.

The door to the chamber through which he'd entered opened, and at first Karl thought his worst fears had come to pass. The tram which entered had open-top cars, which gave him an easy view in, and he saw an array of militia soldiers bristling with weapons. They looked far from pristine, as though they'd recently seen action. He saw the anger and resentment stewing on those soldier's faces, and his heart sank. If the Coldgardeners were fighting them in some concerted way, they were even less likely to view him as someone worth bringing in alive.

Then Karl got a better look, and he realized that it wasn't what he'd feared.

It was so much worse.

The soldiers—none of whom so much as glanced his way, Karl noted with relief—were not alone in the tram. They were not even the most numerous people. As the cars stretched longer and longer, the front of the tram exiting the greenhouse chamber before the back end had even appeared, Karl saw not dozens, but hundreds of Coldgarden refugees, all looking as battered as the soldiers, if not more so.

But more important than any of that, he saw Stefani, with Ella clutched tight in her arms.

Not a single person had done more than glance Karl's way, but he nearly rushed the tram then. Only the knowledge that this would draw the eye—and likely the fire—of every soldier lining the trams kept him still.

Be smart, old man. Follow them. See where they're going. Then you can rescue them.

CHAPTER 28

DURING THEIR SEARCH of the building, it became quickly apparent to Ansley that however hurried the town's evacuation may have been, it had been very thorough in terms of removing everything consumable from the premises. His half of the building yielded nothing beyond a few emergency water pouches which had slipped behind a cabinet. He returned to the lobby with a stomach growling all the more for having been denied.

"I have good news, and I have better news," Giana announced as she entered. "Good," she said, holding up a pair of ration bricks still in their foil wrappers. "Better." With her other hand, she brandished a half-consumed bottle of brown liquor.

"Where in the world did you find the booze?" Ansley asked. Hungry as he was, he felt the craving for that even more strongly. The last few days had honed quite the edge in him, and now, at last, he was presented with something to dull it.

"Taped to the underside of a desk," Giana said, her smile one of wicked delight. "Someone—one Mayor's Aide Richard Alastair to be specific—apparently needed a little something extra to get through their day." She reached Ansley and handed him the bottle, then set to tearing open the ration pouches.

"The ACM must have cleared out this building themselves. No one with a need bad enough to conceal a bottle at work would have left it behind willingly." Alcohol came dearly on Anaranjado. Any food product not necessary for survival did.

Over the course of five minutes, they ate their respective ration bricks. Over the course of the next hour, they drank their way through half the bottle's remaining contents. Giana's slightly unfocused gaze kept drifting to the lobby viewscreen. Connected to some external monitoring stations, it displayed the unchangingly sere landscape outside the Stone Dome.

"I understand why and all, it's really weird that the sun never sets here," Giana observed at one point. "I keep expecting it to get dark beyond just the dome lights dimming."

Ansley thought about it for a second. The interior lights of most Stone Dome settlements crudely simulated a day-night cycle by dimming on a schedule, of course. But how strange it would be to tell time by the position of the actual sun? He could see how it would be useful though. "I guess I can see how that would be unsettling. Here, the sun changing just means travel from one part of the surface to another. In the Meridian Cities, we have a more direct view of it, though it's basically below the horizon all the time. That's all I've ever known."

Still, really letting himself dwell on it, there was something deeply satisfying about imagining a regular rhythm to true day and true night, not just on what a clock said or the programmed lights imitated but written into the very light of the sun. There must be something buried deeply within humans, a species memory, for it to be so powerful generations after they'd claimed this world as their own.

"So, I was hungry enough that even this nutrient brick thing hit the spot, but since I'm stuck on this world now, please tell me you have better food than this."

"Me? Yes. People living places like this? Probably not." The alcohol had loosened his tongue. Such commentary was adjacent to things he really shouldn't get into with a local, much less an off-worlder. He moved on, trying to pivot. "It's hard to grow food here, so we've set up a society whereby machine parts just need power, and we have all of that we could ever want. Most people don't need much food."

"You do, though. All natural?"

"Near enough," he said. The booze was hitting him harder by the moment. When she offered him the bottle again, he waved it away.

"So you think it tastes terrible too, is that it?" she asked.

Ansley laughed slushily. "That stuff is pretty trash. They make the cheap stuff with fungus. Grain is too dear."

"That explains that," she said, making a face as she put the bottle down. But it had taken her long enough to complain that he thought she was putting on a bit of show.

"If we get through this mess, I'll treat you to some of the good stuff after you've been debriefed," he promised.

"Big talk."

"I'm good for it."

He braced himself for what she would say next. *So I guess you are pretty loaded* or the like. It would be so close to something Hastings might say that Ansley wasn't sure he'd be able to take it.

But she only regarded him frankly. And if she had drawn conclusions about him, she kept them to herself.

The wayward pair had made themselves at least marginally more comfortable. Their respective pieces of armor top-cover they'd stripped off entirely, strewn upon the lobby floor like shed bits of exoskeleton. With this much alcohol in him, Ansley found it impossible not to leer at Giana, reduced now to wearing nothing but her form-hugging under underlayer. She didn't fail to notice this, didn't fail to return the leer. He was, after all, wearing his own version of that form-fitting layer, and his body was responding to what he was seeing as he ogled her.

A bad idea. Probably so. But with this much alcohol in him, and pent up by all his teasing of Hastings, and desperate to distract himself as he was, it was a struggle to muster enough willpower to care.

"Are you just going to stare, or are we going to get to this?" she said abruptly.

He opened his mouth to demur, to promise her a better time later than he was capable of giving her now, to remind her that they—or at least he—still had a mission, even if it was one more of atonement than strategic importance. He should tell her that even though a rest had been warranted, there was taking a break and then there was *taking a break*. But no words left his mouth.

Giana spoke for him. "If it helps ease your worries about time and responsibility and such," she said huskily, "I promise you won't last long once I get hold of you. You'll be spent hours before you're sober."

Bliss and the promise of something greater shot through him, and any hope Ansley Reid had of resisting this woman melted away, his willpower going limp precisely as another part of him did the opposite.

"That's right," she said, almost a coo. "You take opportunities when they come around." It was the perfect thing to say, reminding him of recent regrets without calling them to the forefront of his mind.

He closed the distance between them and brought his mouth to hers.

⚕

"Told you, you wouldn't last long," Giana said, her laughter pleased rather than mocking. She enjoyed that she'd had that effect on him, clearly. "Thank you," she said, beaming up at him from the couch on which they lay pressed together.

"For what?" Ansley asked. "I mean, aside from the obvious." She had been *quite* satisfied with what he'd had to offer. Though, come to think of it, she'd perhaps sounded a little *too* satisfied. That didn't really matter to him per se. He had his pleasure to think of and she had hers. But it still seemed a strange thing to say regardless.

"For the genetic material," she said, her smile widening as she stared up at him.

Ansley barked an involuntary laugh at this, the first sour note in their previously seductive duet. Quite aside from the unexpectedness of the comment, her smile seemed like she was making a joke, and he hated feeling left out of the joke even if that meant pretending to get it.

Her arms tightened their grip around the small of his back. It should have felt nice, but for some reason, it left Ansley feeling confined. And he couldn't help but think she was getting ahead of still more unease.

"Uh, well, you're welcome," he said, hoping that would break the odd spell the moment had placed on him. Still, it was a disappointment. He found he was no longer in the mood for round two.

"And for abandoning your duty to follow me off somewhere, alone." This sent a spike of alarm jolting through him. He made to push free, but her grip only tightened further.

"Just once?" she asked, and now her tone was openly mocking. Her gaze looked suddenly hungry. "I'm not sure that was enough for me."

Ansley couldn't decide in that moment whether she meant sex or genetic material, and he found this ambiguity profoundly uncomfortable. "Like you said, duty calls, I'm afraid," he said in some vestigial need to not reveal his rising alarm.

Contrary to the placidness of his words, he gathered his strength, intent on vaulting himself off her and, more importantly, out of her grasp. But when he pushed with all his might, all he got was tortured muscles for his trouble and her somehow redoubled grip.

Strangely, Giana's arms had gone soft. Not soft as in her skin, but as if the limbs suddenly possessed no bones.

"You're afraid, huh?" she asked teasingly. "A bit late for that now."

Then her head *split open* down the line of her nose, revealing a previously hidden seam that yawned to reveal quivering, shining white jelly. Her entire head spread wide into two lobes like slavering, sideways jaws.

She was an *it*. One of the same creatures that had prompted their retreat from Ashrock.

Horror struck Ansley dumb for the crucial instant when a scream might have done him good had the town not been deserted. Even when he found his voice, "What the fuck is—" was all he could manage before the monstrously transformed head lunged upward and closed completely around his own.

Then the screams came. They echoed in the tight confines, reminding him of Hastings's screams as she'd died. His guilt felt assuaged at last.

He thought that maybe he'd had this coming.

But he still screamed his lungs out, shredding his vocal cords. Or maybe something unseen grasping him from within that head-mouth was doing that for him, sliding its way down his throat to better render him edible, the way its fellow had done to that woman while he'd stood by and just watched. Whichever it was, for the brief span of his remaining life, Ansley Reid spent his voice and his final breaths in vain against muffling, writhing darkness as Giana Novak found her satiation at last.

CHAPTER 29

IT WAS a good thing revenants functioned well without sleep, or Stefani would be passed out by this point. The slow vibrations of the tram car would have seen to that. She clutched Ella to her chest, the child slurping greedily at her third pouch of foodstuff one of the soldiers, Private Wexler, had started procuring for her. Some sort of puree which covered every food group and mixed in a generous serving of water to boot. Stefani had been assured of this, and after taking a surreptitious swallow herself from the first pouch and suffering no ill effects, she could detect nothing that would prove dangerous. Besides, she wasn't in a position to refuse anyone willing to keep Ella fed. There was that small kindness to be thankful for, at least.

For the rest, things were not going well at all.

After a wait of many, many hours, Stefani and the other refugees had been herded onto a long string of open-air tram cars by a very twitchy militia group. Stefani feared the act of being rounded up might prompt more transformations which might, in turn, provoke Almeida to carry through on her extermination threat. But in the end, no one among the refugees had put up any resistance. They'd mustered onto the tram cars in silence.

The trams took them through a series of smaller chambers similar to the one that had housed the settlement, but empty beyond doors and rails linking them. There was something resembling a greenhouse of cacti at one point, but Stefani paid little attention as she held Ella, trying to make sure her baby was, at least, uninjured and untraumatized now that she was at least fed. Two hallways beyond the greenhouse she was dimly aware as they passed through a new settlement, this one totally empty of inhabitants.

Word was apparently spreading.

Eventually, a set of doors opened onto, not a burrowed-out stone chamber, but a gleaming, metal-walled facility of several tiered floors, the upper ones overlooking the ground level. The tram ground to a halt in a roundabout that seemed designed to allow it to turn around. Almeida, looking as anxious as Stefani felt, hopped down from her position in the lead car and strode to the center of the arc formed by the tram curving back on itself along the turnaround. She gathered up the refugees' collective attention and informed them in short, surly commands to disembark and await further instructions before proceeding into what the woman referred to as "processing."

It was only then that Stefani began to come back to herself, and she fervently wished she had looked for an opportunity to slip away prior to arriving in this place, which seemed very much like a detention center of some kind. Her anxieties only grew as the refugees were separated into lines of roughly even length and had to wait their turn to march up to a desk manned by jittery-looking personnel before finally being sent through a central set of swinging doors that allowed no view past them.

Processing proceeded with an efficiency that bordered on alarming. When it came time for Stefani's turn, she found herself facing a woman who looked at least as much machine as human, judging by the cybernetic eyes and hands she sported. But if the woman noticed or cared that Stefani was staring, she gave no obvious sign.

"State your name and profession," the woman said automatically. Even her voice sounded synthetic, and Stefani noticed that black scales lined her neck and throat. The woman glanced up at Stefani then, her unsettling golden eyes settling on Ella. "And the name of your child."

"Stefani Palmieri," Stefani said. "My daughter Ella." Then she added, almost as an afterthought. "I'm a doctor." She'd said it without thinking. It was technically true, but "I'm a magistrate" might have been the more accurate response. Still, she was not at all sure she wanted to be identified as a member of the refugees' elected leaders in this place, so perhaps her dazed, default answer had been the safer one. But there was one thing she couldn't help saying. "Please, I need to find some people. My other daughter, Marri. She's thirteen, dark complexion and hair. And a man, Karl—"

"Through the doors." The voice brooked no argument.

Stefani was officially admitted to the facility with no information on where to sleep, how to eat, or any other basic biological necessities. The goal was obviously to admit as many refugees as quickly as possible, and it was quickly evident that far more refugee groups than just Stefani's were being crammed into this space. This facility must have more than one entrance feeding into it.

She was attempting to find the line for food, fretting over whether there would be a consideration for a child as young as Ella now that her guardian angel Wexler was nowhere to be found, when a shadow darkened her. She tried her best not to flinch, but everyone here was just so tall. Even under more benign circumstances, the mere act of approaching her would have felt like a threat.

"You said you're a doctor?" It was Almeida. This close, the height difference made Stefani feel like a child and the degree of mechanical parts just upped the sense of dislocating alienation.

"I am," Stefani said.

"And you're . . . human?" The woman looked both profoundly uncomfortable at asking and profoundly nervous of the answer. "Don't bother trying to contradict me, there. That fucker Horváth may have cracked, but what he was worried about isn't wrong. I've heard enough stories from other areas of the Outskirts to know that much."

"I'm human," Stefani lied smoothly. The soldier regarded her with suspicion. Stefani pointed at Ella. "Sort of an awkward disguise if I wasn't."

"Mama!" Ella squealed. "Mamamamamama!"

Bless you, child.

This was apparently good enough.

"I sent Horváth—the man whose partner one of your monsters ate?—home on forced R&R, and he decided to go AWOL and apeshit and took out half a hospital crammed full of your people. A little one-man attempted genocide," the woman spat, and Stefani could not quite tell where her anger was directed. But she could taste nothing but ash.

Marri. Karl. She still had no idea where either of them were.

"Please," she said, the words escaping before she could think twice. "I'm missing people, loved ones of mine. Do you have a list—"

"I don't have anything, doc, except a lot of people dead, a lot more hurt, and way too few medical staff to help. That plus an evacuation order I'm going to have to help implement as soon as everyone I brought in is processed here. Survivors of the Horváth incident—and others—have been transferred to this facility. Are still being transferred. We are understaffed and we need help. There's no way the real docs will let you near any operating equipment, but maybe you can help with some of the edge cases? The ones that will be ignored otherwise. Do that, and I'll try to track down your missing people." The last was very grudging, true, but her still-human eyes were rock solid above a partially synthetic face.

Stefani didn't even pause to think. There was only one answer.

"Of course. Lead the way."

Lead Almeida did. She went so far as to take Stefani by the upper arm and pull her along, as though to demonstrate conclusively that she had the situation under control and Stefani was the one taking orders. They threaded their way through an open space that looked to be for exercise, which had been converted into a triage center.

"What is this place for normally?" she asked aloud before catching herself. Surely the people of this planet couldn't construct massive holding facilities in a matter of hours to lock up refugees they hadn't even been aware were arriving?

"Defectives," said Almeida. "It's never been this full before, but the powers that be like to be prepared, I guess." She shrugged as though suddenly realizing Stefani hadn't requested follow-up information.

Stefani had no idea what "Defectives" were, besides finding the term profoundly unsettling. It sounded like a term Gene Sequencing might have used.

"I managed to get private rooms for a few," Almeida said as follow-up, which Stefani took to mean *no one has actually approved this, and I can't have anyone see you working on patients*. But Stefani was not in a position for her opinion to matter, so she simply walked on in silence, hoping they wouldn't be waylaid.

"In here," Almeida said, ushering Stefani into a tiny side room she judged was actually some kind of closet. Inside was a makeshift gurney with an insensate soldier atop it. They entered, and Stefani didn't miss that two other militia members, both even taller than her escort, followed them inside and allowed the door to shut behind them.

The message of *don't try anything* was more than clear. Seeing no other alternative, Stefani turned to examine the patient, wondering if she had the slightest expertise that would help. She had never dealt with cybernetic implants, of which every person on this world seemed to possess at least a few.

Stefani glanced down at the lightly singed yet unresponsive soldier, but aside from noting only slight scorching on his uniform, she didn't have time for a more thorough glance before Almeida was already badgering her.

"What is going on with him?" Almeida asked. "He's not one of mine, so I have no idea what his medical history is. I can't see any injuries, but I'm no medic. Is he sick?" With this, she seemed to forget she'd decided to trust Stefani just a few moments before. "Is this something you freaks brought over with you? Some disease?"

"Hypermutation doesn't present like this," Stefani said without thinking. Something about this man nagged at her, but she couldn't put her finger on it. She was so tired. Her mouth kept right on running. "Not in any case I've ever seen."

"What the fuck is hypermutation? Is that why he's nonresponsive? Why his eyes are all glassy?" Almeida sounded alarmed now, gripping the butt of her sidearm, her gloved fingers cramped so tightly around it that her arm shook. She stared down at Stefani as though at a child. Tall. Everyone was so *tall* here. Maybe it had something to do with the gravity, which seemed lower to her. All her steps felt floaty. Like she was dancing more than walking.

"It's nothing that can affect you," Stefani said, eager to undo some of the damage her careless comment had done. *Less mind-wandering speculation, more focusing on the present and all the danger you and your daughter are in!*

Of course, such statements only invited questions as to *why* hypermutation couldn't affect the people of this world. And Stefani suspected that "because it doesn't affect real humans" wouldn't be an answer that would go anywhere good for her.

"If you'll just let me examine him," she began.

"The guy weighed a ton," offered one of the men, answering a question no one had asked. "He must have some unreported implants at least."

Stefani put it together a second before it didn't matter. That nagging feeling. A human looking somewhat off and not acting quite right. Too heavy. "Oh," she said. "I see." She wondered if she should try to stop what was about to happen but couldn't decide until it went right ahead and happened to spite her.

The man—not really a man of course—on the bed began to change. It went unnoticed to all but Stefani at first because she was the one looking for it. Because his uniform was black, and so was the creature which had taken his shape. Black with a turquoise sheen. Really quite beautiful, if one could overlook the deadliness it promised.

Thus did the three actual soldiers in the room get to meet one of their cousins from Coldgarden in all its spindly, deadly glory.

The full revenant—armor plates, chitin-bladed limbs, and bad attitude—moved with insectile speed as it struck from its perch on the gurney. Anyone who assumed revenants to be mindless beasts was a fool, despite their appearance. Stefani was living proof that the opposite was true. And the revenant clearly knew exactly where to strike.

Scaled necks or not, all three soldiers lost their heads to a trio of simultaneous surgical strikes. Stefani found, much to her disgust, that she had to lean hard on the Volkes side of her mind to keep from being overcome with horror. Despite this buttressing, she shied away from the gouting blood reflexively, hypermutation still being on her brain. Also, it was a trio of bloody spurts and that was undesirable to be near all on its own.

Almeida's severed head stared up at Stefani, eyes wide and accusatory. Stefani felt a pang of sorrow for the woman. She had made some dire threats against the Coldgardeners, it was true, but Stefani had the sense she was merely trying to do her best in a very difficult situation.

"How many of us are there?" Stefani asked the revenant, forcing calm into her voice. None of the soldiers had been given a chance to raise the alarm, and the longer that remained the case, the better.

The revenant merely gestured with one dripping claw over Stefani's shoulder at the same moment she heard the door behind her hissing open.

"Enough to get us the fuck out of here," said a familiar voice. "Provided we can be a little subtle to start."

Biting back a curse, Stefani whirled.

"Hi, Steffi," Iaz said cheerily. "Ready to help me carve out a place for us on this rock?"

CHAPTER 30

JÜRGEN LED Marri and Giana to the habitat levels.

Free to look around now that she was no longer worried about being caught, Marri goggled at the subterranean society bustling around her. She'd expected something more like the tunnels below, just with more people and shops and things. But she stared upward into one massive tunnel—it had to be kilometers across, but it was hard to gage the distance of something that big—going up until it ended in a ceiling of rock.

Pairs of human-made tubes like large elevator shafts ran upward and disappeared into that same ceiling at regular intervals along the tunnel's edges. All around those edges, a kind of terrace spiraled up like the threads of a giant screw. The fronts of buildings crowded it no matter which direction she looked.

And the people were everywhere.

In just the first minute, Marri learned Jürgen was by no means unusually tall for Anaranjado. Back on Coldgarden, she had spent the last few months getting used to the idea that she was finally catching up in size to the adults around her. Now she felt like she'd shrunk to the size of her early days in Underguts.

"This way." Jürgen led them to the nearest of the tubes Marri had noticed. It was indeed a kind of elevator, and it let them ignore the gentle slope up the terrace and take a more direct route. They crowded into the elevator with a bunch of other people—it was way too big for them to claim it all for themselves—and Marri felt no bigger than Ella as she stared up around herself.

Those stares were returned many times over. Jürgen received a few glances, as he appeared more robotic than the average person down here. But Marri and Giana were the ones that did not belong. Some people looked deferential, others suspicious. Giana squeezed Marri's shoulder at one point, an attempt to comfort Marri that she intensely resented. Or maybe she just needed the extra support. She still looked awful.

Fortunately, their destination was not far from the elevator once they reached the right floor.

They walked into the front door of a building fronted in raw stone, and a woman behind a counter just inside regarded Jürgen with worry. She seemed not to see Giana and Marri at all. Maybe because they were too short to be easily visible over the counter. That made it easier for Marri to stare, at least. She was nearly as mechanical as Jürgen, but far more colorful. Her eyes looked more natural than his too, at least if you overlooked their mismatched colors of pink and electric blue. It was her hair that drew Marri's attention the most. It obviously wasn't real hair. It looked more like fiber optic cable, and maybe it was, because it glowed purple.

"I don't have your money, Fennec," she said. "Harmony knows, I'm not going to stiff you, but you've got to stop coming around here. You freak out the guests, which isn't helping me get you the money, and—"

"I have worked out an alternate method of payment," Jürgen said. "These two young ladies require a room. You will house them and feed them while they get on their feet, and we will consider your debt paid."

The woman looked gob smacked. "Are you serious? Wait, what women are you even talking—oh." She finally leaned over to see the pair of them, then she looked at Jürgen in newfound alarm. "Are these baselines? Are these . . . *Equatorians?*"

"Yes to both," Jürgen said. "But the specifics of their background are not your concern, nor is it the concern of anyone else who might ask."

The woman looked profoundly uncomfortable. "I don't know how you can say those kinds of things. Are you sure you're not Defective?"

"The common good can be interpreted differently by different people," Jürgen said stiffly. He sounded insulted. "Is it not true that the least fortunate deserve the most help?"

"True enough," the woman said. "But by the Good Doctor, Jürgen, baselines? They're going to eat me out of house and home." Abruptly an alarmed look passed across her face. She leaned in close, but not so close Marri couldn't hear. "Are you sure they're really human? The news is talking about an evacuation order over Sunnyside way. Some of these refugees from that other colony are alien monsters or something. I know you said they're Equatorians, but you're sure, right? They're like us, right?" She glanced worriedly at Marri and Giana, seeming only then to realize she'd surely been overheard.

"Do you think I would do anything that would put you in danger? You will be keeping them out of harm's way. And more importantly, clearing your debt with me."

"How long do I have to keep them?"

"Not longer than what you owe." He turned away from the woman then, pulling Marri and Giana to one side. "She complains a great deal," he said, actually lowering his voice far enough not to be overheard, "but she is a good person. She will keep you safe. And if need be, I have other people who owe me favors. I will not put her to any hardship over you."

Marri didn't really care about that much, and she was certain Giana didn't either, but it seemed to matter to Jürgen, which she supposed spoke well of him at least. Without another word, he herded them back to the counter.

"I'll be by to check on them periodically," he said. Then he pulled Giana aside, far enough away that the woman couldn't hear, but not so far that Marri couldn't.

"It pains me to cut you loose in this way," he said softly, "but the further from the places where they operate that you are, the better."

"You are only trying to help us. I understand." He nearly flinched away as Giana reached up and cupped the skin of his cheek, but he allowed the contact. "Thank you for showing us what kindness you were able. I won't forget it."

Jürgen looked supremely uncomfortable, but he only nodded and left.

"Good Doctor save me, but I wish I'd never hired that man," the colorful woman said with a groan. She turned to Marri and Giana. "Well, I'm Ayana. Nice to meet you both. I can't promise you better accommodation than you're used to, but come with me and we'll find you a space. And I've never had baseline guests, so you'd better go ahead and tell me your daily calorie needs while we walk."

CHAPTER 31

KARL KNEW he had no hope of keeping up with the tram. Likely that would be a bad idea anyway, since he would surely be noticed if he kept in sight of it. But in all the time he'd been walking, there had only ever been one track, so he knew if he followed it long enough, he'd eventually wind up where Stefani and Ella were.

He was doubly startled upon reaching the first chamber past the next series of hallways. First because it was an actual settlement, albeit one that seemed completely abandoned, and easily the largest of the chambers he'd seen thus far, even counting the Bridge site.

Secondly, and more alarmingly, because the track split into three in the middle of it, each continuing on through a separate door. The tram was long gone by the time he entered the chamber. There was no way to know which direction it had gone.

He stood there for a long time trying to decide what to do with this information. Eventually, he turned his eyes to the rest of the space, looking for some kind of clue or some person who might have seen where the tram had gone.

It was, like all the other open spaces, a kind of artificial clearing in the rock topped by a dome of stone. No way it was a natural formation, either. The same strange pattern etched both walls and the dome's underside, just as they had every other wall and dome he'd seen. Karl very much looked forward to seeing whatever all-purpose excavation equipment had been used to dig out all these tunnels.

It was as if someone had arrived first to begin the preparation then begun digging tunnel after tunnel, riddling them with spaces for habitats, overzealously planning for a far larger colony than the planet was actually capable of supporting.

As for the desertion of what clearly was an inhabited space normally, Karl had trouble believing that the arrival of Coldgarden's former residents hadn't had something to do with this. Surely by now, rumors of Karl's world vomiting its inhabitants over the Bridge had begun to filter outward from the Bridge site. Not to mention whatever other places they'd appeared.

This was a notion that had lodged itself in his brain. As crowded as the pad had become, there was no way that had been all of them. Stefani hadn't been there, after all. He'd bet every cent he'd ever earned on it. And it would make sense if Coldgardeners had appeared in more than one place, rumor would spread all the faster.

Of course, for all he knew, he was just making everything about him and his. Maybe this town was abandoned for other reasons entirely. Maybe there were giant worms or other horrors beyond the colony's mandatory brain injections that he had no idea were about to emerge from below and eat him. There was no sense in worrying about it until it happened, though.

None of this got him any closer to figuring out where Stefani had been taken.

He was still standing there, wondering whether there was some clue which might point him in the right direction, when he heard the sound. It was muffled, but it emerged from one of the buildings to his left. A moan of pain. When it repeated, he was able to narrow down the specific building. It looked central, some kind of community center or town hall.

It was the voice of a woman, and she sounded as though she was in some kind of distress.

He approached the building. The door was a sturdy affair with no visible seam or hinges, though it looked to have sustained some damage to the locking mechanism. He considered knocking, but wondered if such a sound would even be heard on the other side.

Another moan, much clearer this close, ripped the air. The cry of agony the doctor had made as he lay coated in Karl's acid vomit ripped through his memory. He decided to abandon discretion. It sounded as if someone needed help.

He palmed the door open. It yielded to him with a hiss, and he froze at what he beheld.

Giana Novak lay splayed lengthwise along one of a pair of couches in what looked like a lobby or reception area for the greater building beyond. What had once been bright green cushions stood out amid the silver and white coloring of walls and desks and furniture. The other color to arrest his gaze was bright, arterial red. The couch, the floor, and the woman were all caked with shining, wet gore.

So covered was Giana that it took Karl several moments to realize that she was both stark naked and very, very pregnant. She let out another moan, and it suddenly clicked what was happening.

She was, somehow, in labor.

Karl had heard that birth could be a bloody business, but he'd always assumed the blood came with the birth, not before it. And that would hardly explain the sticky substance coating her mouth and chin.

Her moan quieted as her eyes fell upon him and widened in shock.

"You get the fuck out of here, Karl Yonnel!"

Karl backed away in mindless obedience, palming the door back open without being able to break her gaze. It slid shut, blocking his view, and only then did the questions start to flood his mind.

What the hell was that? Who did she kill? How is she giving birth? And then, the most important question of all. *Do I care?*

It encompassed much, that question. It asked him to choose

between higher-minded ideals of justice, duty, and decency, and simpler, tribal things, such as where his people were, and if Giana counted among them. He wasn't sure she did, but he suspected she could help him find Stefani and Marri, if anyone could.

Memories flashed before him. Dr. Cardiff attempting to inject something, some organism, into his brain. A crazed pilot willing to level a hospital to kill him and those like him. A doctor taking one look at him and swinging a scalpel, only stopping when Karl struck first.

He made his decision.

"You tell me when I can come in," he called through the door. "We have to help each other, you and I."

A long pause. Then, she answered between two more moans.

"Make yourself comfortable. This will take a bit."

CHAPTER 32

NORMALLY—IF anything about this could even remotely relate to that word—Karl would have parked himself by the door of the building and just waited. He couldn't hear Giana call out to him if he didn't stay close. But he didn't need a doctor to tell him that the heat, even under this dome, was more than he could tolerate for a long wait.

He could have called back in, asked if he might set up somewhere else in the building. But he really didn't want to see what was happening in there—a natural fear for anyone from Coldgarden, where the beautiful miracle of a birth could walk hand in hand with deadly hypermutation. It was the reason births always took place with the mother in total isolation, tended only by a robotic doctor.

Fortunately, Karl didn't have to wander very far. The residents of this town had clearly left in haste. He had to search nearly every building, but in one case, a jumpsuit had slipped free, perhaps from an overstuffed bundle slung under someone's arm. The edge of a cuff barely peeked out where it had blocked a home's front door from fully closing. It took some effort, but he was able to force the opening wide enough to slip through, and he decided to leave the jumpsuit in place, just in case once the door did shut, he couldn't open it again.

The space inside was sparsely furnished, the kind of home that was minimally decorated because the owners didn't have much to fill it with. At least the climate control was working. The door certainly impacted the efficiency, but it was noticeably cooler inside, enough so that Karl no longer feared dying of heatstroke as he slept.

That he had to sleep was evident the moment he sat down. He'd been going since escaping from the hospital, and not counting that enforced period of unconsciousness, he couldn't remember the last time he'd slept, except that it had literally been another world.

He did force himself back to his feet long enough to do a quick search of the house for food or water. Of the former he found nothing, but of the latter, both the kitchen and bathroom faucets produced a modest trickle, almost as though he was draining the last of a finite tank, the dregs someone else had been in too much of a hurry to think worth bothering with.

It wasn't much, but it was enough to stave off imminent dehydration.

The second time he sat, his body took no chances that he might defy it again, and despite gnawing hunger, sleep rolled over him almost instantly.

⚬

He woke to the toe of a boot digging into his shin. It hurt enough to banish sleep but not enough to bruise.

"You left the door ajar, so you weren't hard to find," Giana said as he opened his eyes. "I appreciate it." There was a bite to her words despite the stated gratitude.

She stared down at him, standing where he half-sat, half-laid on his chosen sofa. She was no longer caked in gore, but she wore what looked to him like a lancer's jumpsuit, which he almost took her to task for before thinking better of it. There were bigger things to be concerned about regarding her than what clothes she wore.

He met her eyes, fighting to conceal his shock at the sight of her.

It was clearly Giana Novak looking back at him, but a Giana very different from the one he'd known as Stefani's assistant. Giana had always looked young to him because she was young: barely into her mid-twenties. But this woman looked visibly younger, as though she were still not out of her teens.

And that tone. She *sounded* like a teenager, too, like he imagined Marri might sound in a few more years.

"I can see you want to ask, so just ask," she said, reinforcing the sense of youth in his mind.

"What happened to you? Why aren't you holding a baby?"

"Two questions with one answer," she said. "New world. New biology I have to deal with. I found a suitable donor of genetic material. He was a young man of this colony's ruling class, but he was playing soldier." She seemed to register Karl's confusion and waved it away. "What's important is that he didn't have a brain full of Harmony, which means I could make use of him. The only problem is I don't think it will work if I try to turn someone who *has* Harmony." She sounded very annoyed by this fact and not bothering to hide it.

"When you say 'donor of genetic material,'" Karl began. Giana just looked at him, long-suffering. "Never mind," he said, deciding the implied statement in that look was right. "I don't want to know." Too late. He could guess based on what he'd seen. He considered her seeming youth one more time and that decided him. She wasn't holding a baby because he was looking at the baby. "But does that mean you're not still . . . you?"

"I'm Giana Novak," she said, the words half a challenge. "Always."

There were a million follow-ups he could ask. But the truth was he didn't care. He didn't care that this wasn't the same Giana he'd spoken with the previous day. He didn't care what had happened to that Giana. He had to focus on the little bit he could control.

"I need to find Stefani and Marri," he said simply. "I know Stefani's alive because I've seen her. I haven't seen hide nor hair of

Marri. If you can help me find them both, then as far as I'm concerned, we're friends."

"Otherwise, we're enemies?" she said with a smirk that was not *exactly* a threat.

"Otherwise, I leave you be and look on my own," he said, not backing down but not quite willing to call her bluff. If it was a bluff.

"Relax," she said, fixing him with her large, dark eyes. They seemed even larger and darker with the hollows of exhaustion around them. Karl supposed rapidly growing from infant to teenager would do that to you. "We'll find Stefani. Marri too."

Some intuition whispered to Karl, wondering if he could really trust such assurances. It was all well and good to consider her a friend because they both had common enemies on this world, but just a handful of days ago, they had decidedly not been friends, and Karl was certain she had considered him a disposable asset to her plans.

She claimed to be Giana Novak, always. Did that mean he could always mistrust her? Probably, he decided. But it wasn't as if allies were particularly thick on the ground. Aside from Stefani, Marri, and maybe Iazmaena, if she'd made it here alive, Giana was the only one with a full picture of what Coldgarden had been, how the various factions operated, and why they were all here. Anyone Karl tried to bring up to speed to help him would probably just think he was insane. That was best-case. Worst-case, they might transform and try to kill him.

Of course, Giana might do that too.

But Karl found he didn't care about this. At least, not enough to spurn her help.

"I'm ready to leave whenever," he said. Then he added, "Though I am pretty hungry."

CHAPTER 33

MARRI SINCERELY HOPED the room they were given was the building's smallest. The Mouse Hole, housed in a partially collapsed basement back in Coldgarden, had been infinitely more spacious and comfortable.

"Any place without prying eyes will do fine," Giana said, seemingly responding to Marri's unspoken complaint. "Or did you not notice how many stares we drew as we took the elevator?"

Marri forced herself to stop pacing the tiny space like a caged animal. That was the real issue. She felt caged. No one, not even Giana, had forbidden her from leaving this room or this building. But she had seen the way every single person they encountered stared at her.

Back on Coldgarden, she had spent eight months being a magistrate's daughter, which meant way too many people had known who she was when she didn't know them. She'd never imagined there could be any situation like that, but worse.

Marri had spent most of her life living in, moving through, and making use of the shadowy places of the city she called home. In their brief walk up from Jürgen's home to this place, her illusions she could ever do that again had been shattered. Unshed tears pressed against her eyes, but there was no private place here to retreat to. They didn't even have their own bathroom.

I need to get away. The thought was stark in her brain. It was not a new thought. She'd been having something like it for months, partly because of her dreams trying to warn her of the truth of Stefani. But that wasn't all of it. She was not used to this controlled life under the thumb of adults. *She* had always been the closest thing to an adult in her own life.

So no, it was not a new thought. But whether it was the pressure of the past few days, the trip between worlds, or some other combination, she had never felt it more keenly than she did right now.

"I have to use the bathroom," she announced abruptly, keying off her earlier thought.

Giana's eyes snapped to her. "Be careful," the woman said. "Don't linger. I'm not in any kind of shape to come looking for you."

And what a terrible thing for her to say. The sense of weight lifting off Marri's shoulders with that comment was like coming up for air after having been half-drowned.

"I'll be back soon," she lied.

⁂

Marri resolved to ignore the people staring at her unless she judged them to pose an active threat. It was necessary, since she drew eyes everywhere she went.

Worse, there were no neglected squares or dark alleys for her to disappear into, as there would have been in Coldgarden. Every meter of this space had been subdivided for maximum efficiency. She supposed it made sense given how inhospitable the planet was supposed to be.

She had wandered about a third of the way back to the lower level, not certain where she was going, when a familiar hand fell upon her shoulder.

Marri whirled, but she had a strong suspicion of whom she would see. And she wound up being right.

"Fancy meeting you here," Iazmaena said. She was in better shape than she had been the last time Marri had seen her. She had also procured some local clothing, a form-fitting black bodysuit designed to keep out the cold. It seemed to blunt the stares, so maybe Marri should find one for herself.

"What do you want?"

"To help, Marri, despite what you think. We might have been enemies back on Coldgarden, but if you think about it, we weren't even then really. We both wanted the same thing."

"That's what I said to you last time."

Iazmaena shrugged. "Back on Coldgarden, we may have been at odds, but here, we're all in the same boat. It's us against them, Marri. Sure, they may have their evacuation order elsewhere on the planet, but they won't run from us forever. The more we fight each other, the easier it will be for them to sweep us away."

It all brought to mind just how helpless Marri felt in this place, how out of her element. Back home, she'd known which streets to avoid and when, which wards presented the least risk and which the sweetest rewards. Here, she was nothing.

Worse, here, she was a freak.

"You're smart to be headed back down," Iazmaena said. "Up here it's just people lying to themselves. The real action is down below. I found something down there, during my wandering after I arrived. It's the answer, Marri, the answer to everything that happens on this world."

"You sound weird," Marri said. "Like you belong in Jürgen's cult." In truth, the Cultists had sounded saner than Iazmaena was sounding now.

"You don't believe me? I'll show you." Iazmaena said. "Follow me, or don't." She strode on ahead, making determinedly for where Marri knew the door to the lower levels was.

The abrupt shift in the woman's attitude threw her. But

Iazmaena was striding ahead. Somehow avoiding the same stares Marri and Giana had gotten, as though she already belonged in this place, Iazmaena deftly swerved around everyone who might uncaringly barrel into her, striding with determination and not even bothering to glance back.

The hairs on Marri's neck stood up. Iazmaena *was* acting very strangely, and, considering all the trouble she'd caused back in Coldgarden, that was a very concerning thing. Surely they needed to know what she was up to, didn't they?

That was all it was. It wasn't just that Marri wanted to get away from all the staring people. She made the decision in that moment. She was going to follow Iaz and see where the woman led her.

CHAPTER 34

STEFANI AND IAZ exited the makeshift medical suite and stepped into the center phalanx of bristling revenants. Stefani's erstwhile patient followed close behind, leaving spots of blood upon the solid floor with each tapping step.

The facility beyond was eerily quiet and littered with bodies.

"God, did you have to kill them all?"

"This wasn't even close to all," Iaz scoffed. "Most retreated to somewhere deeper in the facility, which I don't understand at all. They can be weirdly passive, these people." She shrugged as though that was that. "But we've captured an intel officer." She beckoned Stefani onward. "You're looking for your loved ones—at least that's what I assume, knowing you—and I'm looking for the rest of my firepower. Someone like him should be able to help us."

"What makes you think they even got captured?" Stefani asked. Her head spun at this sudden reversal in her fortunes. She just wished she knew if things had gotten better or worse. "Or if they did, that they're not here?"

"Because we chose the site where the Bridge was supposed to open," Iaz said. "And it corresponded with where their colony's

Bridge site is. What's one thing you noticed about the settlement where we wound up?"

"No Bridge hardware," Stefani said.

"And not big enough to hold any."

"So you're saying we didn't end up where we were supposed to be?"

"I'm saying not all of us did. Something clearly went wrong. Maybe your people didn't assemble the Bridge quite right."

"Or maybe your people killed too many of my people to make it work right," Stefani shot back.

Iaz held up placating hands. "Or maybe it was neither of us, just the world coming apart at the seams. Whatever the case, clearly things didn't go quite as planned. We have no idea how far people were scattered. We could be the outliers. Most of the rest might be sitting at the Bridge site."

"I still don't see how an intelligence officer is supposed to help us," Stefani said. This was starting to feel seductively like old times which, for them, had technically never existed.

"It's simple," Iaz said, direct but not condescending. It was so easy to slip back. She had never sounded more like her old self. The real Iaz. "Your project made initial contact via a direct comms-only link to the Bridge site, right?"

"Right," Stefani said, still not following.

"When we actually crossed, though, we showed up someplace totally different. But look how little time we had before their militia showed up in force to subdue us. And that was where they didn't expect us."

"So you're saying if they were able to overwhelm us somewhere unexpected . . ."

"Imagine how much force they could bring to bear where they did expect us," Iaz said with a grim smile.

"They only had a day to prep, though."

"I know," Iaz said. "Their command and control is frighteningly efficient."

Ella squalled on Stefani's back as though in response. Stefani tried to stuff down her worries for her daughter. The truth was, that as much as she cared about Karl and Marri, it was Giana she needed to find soonest. The woman had agreed to help Ella survive whatever was happening to her. But she'd withheld that help in exchange for safe passage across the Bridge.

Had Stefani suspected for a moment that they wouldn't end up in the same place, she would have insisted.

"We don't even know if they made it across at all," she said, feeling a bleakness steal over her. "We might be all there is."

"No," Iaz said. "I've already heard enough to know that's not true. There are other facilities out there somewhere. We just need to know where." Their little cluster of revenants approached a separate pair, orange and yellow in sheen, full revenants hunched over something squirming on the ground, a uniformed man. "Which brings us to our friend the intelligence officer." She fixed Stefani with an unyielding stare. "I'm going to need you to assume his identity so we can know what he knows. Because I guarantee you he has the information we need."

Stefani blinked in confusion, then the import of what Iaz was saying slammed home.

"You want me to . . . No, I'm not doing that!" The mere mention of consuming and merging with yet another person, a *third* person, when she already struggled to integrate two, awoke a stark sense of negation in Stefani. A solid wall of infinite height with no possible crossing. She was quite certain she would lose herself forever if she tried to cram yet another mind into her already overstuffed head. "Have one of the others do it."

"I'm not sacrificing the firepower they offer," Iaz said. "You've seen how mechanized these people are. You know how much of our strength and mass we had to give up in order to be convincingly human. How much damage do you really think you or I could do in our diminished state?"

It was not the first time the woman had talked like this, and Stefani could not suppress a suspicion that, despite their people's long quest to retain their humanity, a part of this Iaz missed being large and imposing and deadly. The Iaz she had known in life—the real Iaz the real Stefani had known in life—had not been a bully, but with full awareness of the personalities they'd absorbed came a kind of merging and blending with the beings they'd been before. And the revenant that had become Iazmaena Delgassi had never been one to shy away from the most violent approach to problems.

"Well then," Stefani said, "have one of the others *like us* do it." She wouldn't bother suggesting Iaz herself. The woman would not want to take the risk of becoming like Stefani.

"I would, if there were any others here. We can hope there are plenty of us left, but they aren't at this facility. And I need the information in this person's head to find out where they are."

"Let me try talking with this intelligence officer first," Stefani said. She turned away without waiting for Iaz's response, but she could practically hear the woman's eyes roll.

Stefani approached the terrified intelligence officer, held in place by two revenants—one pinning his arms, the other his legs. He was young, far too young to have such a responsibility placed on him, but despite his obvious fear, he was defiant. He strained continually against his captors. Even though Stefani could hear mechanisms whirring in all four limbs, he was unable to break free.

"I won't tell you anything." He all but spat the words. It was not the most promising opening in Stefani's gambit to save this boy's life. "I won't betray my people!"

"No one's asking you to," Stefani lied. "We just need to know where the others like us are being held."

"So you can go free them!"

"We didn't come here to fight you. We had to flee our world. This was the only place we could go." The first part was true, but the second part wasn't. There had been other candidate colonies to which they might have escaped. But this had been the one they'd established a successful comms exchange with, however briefly. When everything had come apart, quite literally in the planet's case, there hadn't been a lot of time for considering other options. "We're refugees, not enemies. We just want peaceful coexistence."

"But you're not human!" He threw hateful gazes at his revenant captors as though to offer proof.

Stefani thought of telling the whole truth. She thought of lying outright. Neither seemed like the right path forward.

"What we are is very complicated," she said. "But we didn't come here to invade."

"Then why are you killing us?"

"Because you're killing us!" Iaz said, rushing up and inserting herself into the conversation in a way that was very Iaz. "We're defending ourselves!"

"You disguise yourselves as us? Infiltrate? Replace? Get us to trust you so you can kill us more easily?" He sounded as if there could be no greater or more appalling betrayal.

"What's your name?" Stefani asked, trying to reset the conversation back to a baseline she could work with.

"I'm not telling you anything."

"Name, rank, and serial number. That's how it works, right? My name is Stefani. Stefani Palmieri. I'm from—" She cut herself off on the verge of saying Coldgarden. "I'm from the colony of—"

"New Calgary," he cut her off. "I've read the intel briefing. And that figures."

"Why does it figure? What world is this?"

His laugh was bitter. "And you don't even know where you are?" Stefani's attempts to calm him weren't working. If anything, he was only growing more agitated. "If you don't know, I'm not telling you. I'm not helping you in any way. You're not one of us. You're the enemy. I'm no Defective, you monster."

There it was. That word again: Defective. And the capital letter beginning the word was somehow audible when he said it. This was some kind of official designation.

"What does it mean? Defective?"

Everything about the man's demeanor changed. He was still angry, still defiant. But another emotion dominated his mien now. Stefani almost would have called it scandalized.

"Your colony spurns the greatest gift humanity has ever received, the gift of grace from a saint of a scientist, and you don't even know? What do they teach you on New Calgary? That the old ways were best? Strife, division, conflict? Selfishness? Maybe it's no surprise what happened to you," he said, looking at the revenants again. "You spat on Harmony. Refugees? You aren't worthy of being saved." His face set. "Do what you want to me. I'm through talking."

"Well," Iaz said. "That was fruitful."

But Stefani wasn't done.

"What is Harmony?"

And for all the man's declaration he was done talking, his entire face changed once again, this time to a kind of calm rapture, if such a thing were possible.

"Harmony is the salvation of humankind."

"Salvation from what?"

"From ourselves," the man said, his smile beatific.

"But what is it?" Iaz demanded. Apparently Stefani's curiosity was not the only one that had been piqued. "A religion? Some kind of chemical?" She glanced at the man's limbs. "A cybernetic implant?"

The man's face twisted in mild disgust. "Nothing so ephemeral, transient, or crude. It's a merging of life. A partnership that sustains Harmony and betters us."

Had Stefani come from any other world but Coldgarden, she might not have had the contextual experience to make sense of what the man was saying. But something about the wording tickled her mind.

"Iaz," Stefani said, "I think he's talking about a parasite."

"Symbiont," the officer said, acid in his words. "Together, we are greater than either can be alone."

"Points for you," Iaz said to Stefani begrudgingly. She was eyeing the man with new consideration. Stefani wished she could tell what Iaz was thinking.

"I don't know, are we sure he's not just a disturbed individual?"

"I might think so, but this isn't the first time I've heard 'Harmony' mentioned. Something in the brain? A . . . creature?"

"I think it would have to be," Stefani said. Her professional curiosity was getting the better of her. "What more can you tell us about it? Harmony, I mean?"

The officer's eyes had grown glassy with fervor. "It's a gift," he said.

"Yes, well, what I'm asking is how people receive the gift?"

"At birth," the man said. He seemed to have forgotten his previous vow to tell them nothing. It was as though discussing this Harmony was a skeleton key to his thoughts, any thoughts that related at least.

"So it doesn't spread by itself," Stefani said, musing aloud. That was good to know. It meant that the creature would be utterly dependent on its human host to propagate. Which meant its degree of influence must be astonishing, at least in certain crucial aspects of behavior.

"What do you get out of it?" Iaz asked the man.

Shock painted his face. Or maybe it was disbelief at such a stupid question coming from an adult. "We were not whole until Harmony made us whole. There are no true humans but those that have accepted its gift." His gaze returned to the present. "All others are false. Not worthy of mercy. Not worthy of protection. The colony of New Calgary rejected the gift. The records say it was why they left Earth. They feared being forced. Forced! Can you force salvation onto a person? They must accept their failings before they can be freed from them."

Stefani exchanged glances with Iaz. For once, they shared a wavelength. Iaz gestured her off to one side.

"So," Iaz said after they could reasonably be assured they weren't overheard, "I guess it's good to know that there's a colony stranger than ours."

"Debatable," Stefani said. "And it's useful information, but it doesn't change that we need different information."

"What it does change is my desire to have any of us eat him," Iaz said. "I'm not interested in testing what effects a brain parasite might have on our physiology. At least not that kind of test."

"So we can't absorb him," Stefani said with relief, "and he's unlikely to tell us anything we want to know. Where does that leave us?"

"Leaving," Iaz said. "The way I figure it, heading in the direction opposite the sun means heading toward civilization. No one in power is going to want to be in full view of that thing if they can help it. I don't know if that takes us toward the Bridge site or not, but we can't afford to be boxed out and trapped in the wilderness of a planet that can't support life outside its habitats. Besides, I'm not sure how much longer the remaining soldiers will stay skittish of us."

Iaz led Stefani back and spoke once again to the officer. "How does your glorious Harmony live, anyway?"

"Once implanted in the brain, it shares the same bloodflow as the host, and—"

"Beautiful." Iaz gestured at their coterie of revenants with a *let's get rolling* circular motion with one finger, and while most of the revenants again formed a wall around them, the last huddled over the intelligence officer. Stefani's heart rose to her throat as the man started to shriek.

The revenant's egg-shaped head tore open into jagged petal-jaws, then closed them around that screaming head and twisted savagely.

Blood and ringing silence.

"Iaz! Why was that—"

"I said I don't want to test a parasite inside one of us," Iaz cut in.

"That doesn't mean I don't want you to study one. Now we have a dead one. What?" she demanded of Stefani's accusing silence. "He got to die for his people. That seemed to be what he was most interested in, don't you think?"

She turned to the revenant, which had sealed up its bloody head again and now clicked after them. "Now don't go swallowing that thing while you pick it clean."

CHAPTER 35

THOUGH SHE WAS NOT sorry to leave the holding facility behind them, Stefani did miss the climate control the instant they stepped out into the stifling tunnels. Even an instant's hot breeze as the tunnel air rushed toward the hatch sealing behind them was better than the stagnant, baking heat which followed.

An hour beyond the boundary of the facility, the group was deep within a high-walled canyon roadway, railed to accommodate trams like the one Stefani had ridden to the holding facility. This corridor featured an identical rail splitting it down the center. Without warning, one of the revenants—the one which had beheaded the intelligence officer, specifically—ambled over and nudged Stefani's hand. When she proffered it uncertainly, the creature tore its own head open and spat the dead creature into Stefani's outstretched palm.

It was alternating gray and pink, the colors of a human brain. Like a segmented worm with long, needle-thin legs and many fleshy lobes besides, it lay limp and dead, the revenant having succeeded in stripping away human flesh and bone and brain matter to leave only the parasite within behind.

Such a small thing to portend so much. No longer than her palm, at least as far as its main body went. Still, she kept expecting it to come to life and dart for her nose, mouth, ears, or worst of all, eyes.

Anything to reach the brain.

Iaz moved to join Stefani, her own curiosity ghoulish in its intensity.

"Look at that!" She pointed at the tips of lobes and legs both. They terminated in mounds of flesh that had the wrinkled form of human brain matter. But whether parasite and brain had merged or the parasite's physiology itself perfectly mimicked and replaced brain tissue in its host, it was impossible for Stefani to say.

"Safe to say I've never seen anything remotely like this," she said, fascinated despite her revulsion and the deep sense of moral wrongness she felt even holding this thing, knowing how they'd come by it. "I wonder if even Gene Sequencing had a notion of this creature."

"If that's a dig at me killing them all, remember, that wasn't really me-me calling the shots. And you were there too."

"It's not a dig at anyone," Stefani said distractedly. "Just genuine curiosity. How much of what that intel officer told us was true?" If their colony really had rejected the use of these, perhaps it had truly passed out of all knowledge on New Calgary once the natives had driven the humans from the city. Would they still work on the revenants, who had been human but now were altered beyond hope of recovery?

"What else can you tell me about it?"

"Nothing, Iaz," Stefani said with exasperation. "We're walking through a tunnel with canyon walls, and I'm carrying a dead brain parasite with my bare hands with no tools, no lab, no equipment of any kind. On top of that, I can barely concentrate what with my worry for my other daughter. I can tell you exactly the same things you can tell yourself, which is looking at it and describing it."

"That's what I love about you, Steffi. You were never afraid to call me on my bullshit. But look here," she said. She was gesturing at the canyon walls. "What do you make of this strange texture?"

Stefani approached the wall and looked. "Odd. I'm no expert on digging equipment, but it looks weirdly irregular. Almost organic."

"Yes, that's what I thought. Not a pleasant notion, is it?"

"We can't be from the only planet full of weird monsters."

"Just as long as the entire planet isn't the monster this time."

They walked onward, wary of attacks at all points. There was absolutely no hiding in the canyon road, but in this series of enclosed spaces, there was quite literally nowhere else to go. Stefani kept trying to listen for the sound of anyone approaching from either direction, but Ella seemed determined to be fussy, and Iaz was in a musing, loquacious mood.

"It feels like we've caught them in a moment of indecision and poor leadership. There's this evacuation order. There's their unwillingness to attack us, settling into a defensive posture when we are literally inside their walls. Either we are a threat that is so novel and unexpected to them, they can't decide how to handle us, or there is some struggle over what their goals and priorities should be in protecting the colony. My guess is we're seeing something of both. Whatever the cause, we have a window of opportunity before they get their shit together when we can catch them off-balance. We have to figure out how to use it."

After two hours of walking, the stone ceiling gave way to one of trussed glass, allowing an actual view of a dusty orange sky. The transition allowed them to hear the whipping winds—which never seemed to stop—much more clearly too. After so long entombed in rock, being given something to look at, even something as undefined as the sky, drew Stefani's gaze like a magnet.

And it wasn't long before such intense focus was rewarded.

Something appeared over the horizon as they walked. At first, Stefani assumed it was another hump of rock, albeit smoother and of a different color than the rest they walked beside. But the closer they drew, the more details began to stand out, and every new detail pointed more and more to the inescapable conclusion—they were looking at something built by intelligent beings, not geology.

It was some kind of immense structure, and it was lit with a thousand twinkling lights.

CHAPTER 36

MARRI WAS certain someone would react when Iazmaena strode off the path at the lowest level, trotted down the small slope to the doorway to the under tunnels, and paused there, turning back to Marri with a knowing smirk. From this side, it was so obviously a place no one was meant to go. And she was doing nothing but calling attention to her odd behavior. She even gestured grandly, indicating Marri should be the one to open the hatch for them both.

But nobody so much as flinched. That gave Marri the small boost of courage she needed to jog down and press the button before anyone could raise an alarm. Despite running the risk of encountering Jürgen or cultists or worse, she could not help a tremulous little thrill of excitement. This was just like Underguts back home, a forbidden place, a place of darkness and secrets. She could dimly recall being afraid of that place once as well, but she'd had no choice but to learn it, master it, and it had ultimately yielded up those secrets. She had made it her own, and one day, she could do the same for these alien tunnels.

Marri was a creature of dark, enclosed spaces. She knew now that would never change. She might as well embrace it.

They wandered in silence for some time, the tunnels of ice and rock twisting and turning around one another like pasta noodles. Except every so often the tunnel wall would be interrupted by a door off to the side, marking a dwelling or some other kind of structure dug out of the planet. None of them were occupied so far as Marri could tell. She kept expecting Iazmaena to take the lead and was frustrated by the woman's stubborn refusal to do so. At last, she lost patience.

"What is it you want me to see?" Marri asked. Head on a swivel, she'd been making a mental map as they went. It was a skill she'd learned a long time ago, and the seeming randomness of the tunnel network did not stymie her in the slightest.

"Let's see if you can find it yourself," Iazmaena said impishly.

"Cut it out!" Marri growled. "What part of any of this feels like a game to you?" She almost turned on her heel then. Something about this was raising the hairs on her neck, when she caught flitting movement in her peripheral vision.

Jürgen. The thought was automatic, even though literally everything about the motion was wrong for that conclusion.

A small, black shape looped erratically through the air, seemingly caught in one of the breezes that were an incessant feature of the tunnels. Marri turned, forgetting about Iazmaena for a moment as she gave the thing her full focus. It was dancing along the leftmost branch of the tunnel crossroads, moving too quickly and erratically to get a good look at. Its edges glittered where they caught the wan, irregular lights shining down haphazardly from tunnel ceilings. Those edges looked almost metallic.

But it was the manner of movement that tickled Marri's memory. It looked like a leaf falling from a high tree, caught and tumbling in a stiff breeze. Once she realized this, she was better able to predict its looping trajectory as it lazily approached.

She stuck out her hand, and confidently snatched it from the air. She had just enough time to realize it wasn't like a leaf at all but more of a coarse, abrasive feather—one that was attached to a nearly invisible filament stretching back into darkness—when it suddenly took on a life of its own. Marri gasped, snatching her hand back even as it vibrated its way free of her grip and zipped off. On its return trip, it no longer flitted like a feather in a draft, but flew straight as a shot of a lance, dragged back the way it had come by the line attached to it.

As though it had purpose. As though its earlier movement had been nothing but a trick.

Shock gave way to terror as Marri's heart leaped into her throat. But there was no time for her to process what had just happened before the feather was back.

This time with a million of its friends.

A storm of whirling black shapes surged up the tunnel, filling the intersection in the space of an eyeblink. Shadows darted and danced in the flickering lights of struggling LEDs, making it impossible to determine which dark, flitting forms were real and which mere illusion.

"Run!" Marri shouted at Iazmaena, turning and freezing when she realized Iazmaena was already gone. The abandonment rocked Marri—*a trap?*—and she stood there, frozen with terror, her stupid-little-girl delusions of the tunnels being a safe place she would someday master shattered.

The maelstrom of glittering black feathers swirled in ways that looked more like geometry the longer she looked, and suddenly, as if she'd only imagined it hadn't been there, a bright white light kindled at the storm's heart.

It was this light, and the gut-wrenching thought of what it would, or could, do to her if it gathered her up in the center of its whirling cyclone, that finally broke Marri's paralysis. She spun on her heel, turning back the way she came, consulting her mental map in something close to blind panic as she sprinted full-out. But no matter how fast she ran, no matter how much desperation moved her legs faster, behind her the light inexorably grew. The feathers were making a sound, somewhere between a rushing and a grinding. It chewed at her brain, seeming to project itself directly into her head.

The light was gaining. So was the sound. Marri risked a look behind her as she rounded a corner, and so didn't see she was about to collide with an obstruction until she did, bouncing off something cold and hard.

The tunnel spun around her as the impact jarred her brain. Dazed, she thought she must have misjudged the location of one of the ice walls and just run headlong into it.

"Come with me, child," said a grating voice like a machine. A voice Marri knew.

The voice of one of the Cultists.

"It's not safe here."

A frigid, unyielding hand, a claw of metal, closed around her arm and pulled her to her feet.

CHAPTER 37

"ALL RIGHT, MR. LANCER," Giana said softly. "Tell me what I'm seeing. From a tactical analysis standpoint."

Karl snorted. "They trained me to fight revenants, not people."

"Then pretend those are your people and assess what you see."

They were lying prone, side by side on an outcropping overlooking the canyon road that was proving to be as major of a thoroughfare as it had appeared. An arched stone ceiling covered the canyon roads just as domes did the open spaces for habitats. But in certain places, the canyon wall itself did not meet flush with the end of the ceiling but stuck out in a lip. Giana had found one of these lips where they could observe without being easily spotted, provided they transformed to make the climb.

Karl reframed his way of thinking, as Giana had suggested. This wasn't assessing an enemy force. This was assessing his own side's combat readiness.

"They've been through it," he said, noting their lack of formation and the way a large minority of them moved as if they were favoring one part or another of their bodies. "At least a third of them are the walking wounded. There's no formation, but they also don't appear to be moving for stealth. They're just sort of moving in a clump."

He watched for a few minutes more.

"What else?" she prompted.

"No weapons," he said after several seconds of consideration. "The weapon they used on me at the hospital didn't look like any gun I'd ever seen, and it didn't have any effect on me worse than a tingling sensation. I'd bet a month's wages their standard-issue weapons don't work on us Coldgardeners. They must not have immediate access to anything else. Not out here in the field, anyway."

"Why would their standard weapons not work on us?"

"Soldiers arm themselves with the weapons they expect will work on their enemies. For lancers, that was lances, because those were designed to kill revenants. These guys live on a colony full of half-mechanical people. It only felt like a tingle to me in my native form, but a weapon that produces a nasty shock, like a souped-up stun gun, might shut down your opponent's limbs entirely. And it would still work to disable a normal human. Seems like a pretty practical choice. A way to disable without killing, even. Which would make even more sense if their main purpose is peacekeeping." And unless there was more than one nation within this colony, that seemed likely.

"So why expect them to work against us?"

"They'd hardly be the first fighting force in history to make the mistake of assuming their enemy follows the same rules they do," Karl said wryly. "They probably figured if we were about to arrive on their world using Bridge technology, we'd be half-machine ourselves, same as them."

"So are they after you?"

Which was the main question, of course. It had occurred to him, now that he had a hip implant, it might be possible they could track him through it. If that were the case, though, they had done a pretty piss-poor job of it. They sure weren't acting like they knew he was here. It wasn't a case of needing to trick him. Even wounded, they vastly outnumbered he and Giana.

"I'm guessing no," he put simply.

"Then what are they up to?"

"Any number of things," he said, a touch exasperated. "Unless I was the only one to escape that facility, we're not the only Coldgardener fugitives on this world. They might not even be from that facility. They could be tracking someone else. They could be regrouping with a larger force, or even just heading back to a base for medical attention while fresh troops are rotated in."

"All of which means we need to follow them."

Which was the answer Karl had been afraid she'd give. Trouble was, he agreed.

CHAPTER 38

FOLLOWING a column of wounded soldiers meant moving slowly. As such, it was difficult for Karl and Giana to keep from defaulting to a more normal pace and catching up with their targets. Neither of them was a revenant, which meant neither could change their shape to try to blend in with the soldiers. Being seen would mean a world of trouble they didn't need. They had to keep quiet and stay far enough back to avoid notice, but not so far away they couldn't hear their quarry any longer.

Several hours into this low-speed pursuit, Karl handed Giana the last bottle of water they had to share between them, all they'd managed to find in the abandoned village. They hadn't passed through a greenhouse in some time, but each time they came upon one, it had been picked clean by the soldiers ahead. Karl didn't fully understand the archaic term of "camp followers" who kept pace with an army back when standing armies on livable worlds had been a thing, but he suspected they weren't doing it right if all the resources were consumed before they could arrive.

Worse, Giana had lingered behind at one point, and after an hour had returned with confirmation that they were being followed. More forces being pulled in to guard whatever it was they were to guard.

This group was also on foot, thank the gods below, or they would have already caught up. But it was not a comfortable feeling to be wedged between two enemy fighting forces. If the one ahead slowed down a little or the one behind sped up, Karl and Giana would have nowhere to go.

The timing of sleep was the worst part. In these narrow confines, they wanted very much to avoid blundering into the sleeping group ahead or being blundered into by the still marching group from behind. But they had no way of knowing how long each group would sleep for, when precisely that sleep would begin, and no guarantee that, after the first night where they successfully avoided detection, things wouldn't totally change the next night.

All in all, Karl felt they had been extremely lucky to even make it a day without getting found and either captured or killed.

At least there was some sign of progress being made. After seemingly endless time trudging through identical tunnels with no open sky to use as a landmark, there was no way to be certain they weren't just moving in circles.

No way, at least, until the stone arches covering the canyon corridors vanished, to be replaced by a familiar pattern of trussed glass, such as Karl had seen at the greenhouse and the Bridge site.

"Unless I miss my guess," Giana said, "the light in the sky is less bright than it was at those early greenhouses we passed."

Karl agreed. In fact, given that he had seen an even earlier greenhouse than Giana, he saw the change even more keenly. He was no expert on orbits and astronomy, but it seemed to him that the sun never moved on this planet. If so, they must be getting toward the night side.

"I've been scouting out more of those overhangs, like the one used to spy the first group," Giana said, apropos of nothing during a moment like any other. "It might make sense for us to think about letting that group behind pass us."

Karl had thought along the same lines, but he'd arrived at a different conclusion. The hallway was particularly narrow at this point, so he didn't turn to rebut, fearing he'd walk into a rock wall.

"There's no telling how long that will take, or worse, that there isn't just another group behind them, leaving us in the same predicament. We're out of supplies, and we have no idea how long we're going to have to keep this up. I agree we've been lucky so far, but I'm reluctant to toss that away in case we've stumbled into something that works and take the chance we'll be able to do it again."

Whatever Giana would have said—she had a stubborn look forming on her face—was lost as the walls to either side of them shifted, moving in ways no rock should move, and Karl's heart began to hammer in his chest as he realized what was happening.

The revenants, at least seven of them, unfurled themselves, revealing this choke point to be one they themselves had engineered. Karl's fist kept closing around the haft of a lance he did not possess, and all the traumatic memories he'd accumulated from a long career fighting these monsters jockeyed for pride of place in his mind.

The revenants moved to form a cordon around Karl and Giana.

"Easy," Giana said. "They aren't attacking."

"That's not as comforting as you think it is." Sometimes revenants liked to cart their food off still alive. The circle of nightmare insect-monsters began to move.

"Looks like we don't have much choice but to follow them," Giana said.

Karl considered transforming, but he had never fought a revenant in his native form, and he knew he could never take on seven, even with Giana's help.

"Yeah," he said. "I guess we don't."

CHAPTER 39

THEY DID NOT HAVE long to walk, at least. This was good, because every moment he spent surrounded by revenants and unarmed was a moment Karl was fighting off a panic attack. Giana, by contrast, had regained some of the poise that she'd had for as long as Karl had known her and really begun to hone those last few days in Coldgarden. He still thought of her as Giana even though she was another iteration of the woman, having been birthed by the original to deadly consequences.

These were inane things to be dwelling on at this particular moment, but the mind did what it had to do to avoid going insane.

Some kind of structure seemingly outside the tunnel-and-chamber network had just begun to loom above the glass ceiling of the canyon road when the revenants stopped. Karl saw a large cut in the rock up ahead and to the left, looking like it led up toward the surface and a structure that jutted up, improbably, above it. The glare of reflected sunlight was impossible to miss. At first, he thought this was their destination, but instead, the revenants ushered them into a small crevice in the rock wall closer by on the right.

It looked like the start of a cave, a cavity that had already been part of the rock when the canyon corridor had first been dug out. The passage was a tight fit for Karl and Giana, but Karl had to keep his jaw from dropping when he saw the revenants ahead of him, both far larger than himself, squeeze down to little more than two dimensions to slip through without even scuffing their carapace.

They came out into a space dimly lit by some kind of hand lamps kept as far from the opening as possible. Karl was still letting his eyesight adjust to the dark when something barreled into him from behind. For a heart-stopping moment, he assumed he was under attack and that this was it. Then he heard her voice close in his ear.

"Karl!"

He broke the embrace long enough to spin and see her. Even in the gloom, he knew that silhouette. Stefani stood there, wiping her eyes. Then it was his turn to sweep her up in an embrace. Everything that lay between them fell away. The months, the deception. A part of him knew it wasn't her, would always know that. But a bigger part understood that, in truth, it *was* her. Her memories, her experiences, everything that made her who she was had not gone away. They had been transferred into a different form. Transferred by violence, yes. But transferred intact and in their totality.

He'd wondered how he would react upon seeing her again, with some time and space to contemplate all that had passed between them. Now that moment had arrived, and Karl found he didn't care.

They kissed, and the hellish world they'd first lost and then found each other on vanished from his awareness. For a few precious moments, there was nothing but her.

"Kahwool!" Ella cried from the carrier on Stefani's back. The pair of them broke apart, and both laughed.

"Someone else is glad to see you too," Stefani whispered.

"I feel the same," he said, though looking at the girl, his smile flickered before he could manage to paste it in place. Ella was pale with eyes sunken into dark hollows. She sounded as boisterous as ever but looked genuinely ill.

No one else had spoken, so perhaps the awkwardness had not passed without notice. But it was starting to seem a little odd. Karl stepped back to take in the rest of the situation. It was not nearly as encouraging as the site, the smell, the feel of Stefani.

Wrapped in gloom, Iazmaena Delgassi—the new version—stood in the center of her arc of revenant muscle. They numbered significantly more than seven, Karl saw with dismay. Whatever his feelings for Stefani, Karl found he could not think of the "classic" revenants as anything but deadly monsters. Maybe that made him a hypocrite, but it was unlikely to change.

"Lance Commander," Iazmaena said by way of mild greeting, as though things had never ended the way they had and she was greeting him on a Monday morning at Heart Hall after an unremarkable weekend. Her eyes, though, were fixated elsewhere.

They bored into Giana like awls.

Giana's face was deceptively mild, but Karl knew some of the woman's history, knew that, at least as far as Giana Novak's memories went, this could be no easy encounter. Iazmaena Delgassi had, in life, slaughtered all of Giana Novak's former coworkers in her great purge of Gene Sequencing.

And that was before they'd all tried to kill each other at the Bridge site back on Coldgarden.

For a moment, Karl wondered if Stefani, or even Iazmaena, would notice Giana's change in age, that they were now looking at a newer model, for lack of a better term. Then he realized that she no longer looked younger than she had. Over the preceding day, so smoothly he hadn't really noticed, she had returned to wearing the face he expected to see when he looked at her.

That was good. This was complicated enough without broaching that particular topic of discussion just now.

"Before anybody says or does anything we'll all regret, we're all in the same boat here," Karl said. He couldn't make himself believe the words, not with all those revenants facing him with their eyeless gazes, but he knew he'd be on the losing side of any spat with Iazmaena and her horde of monsters.

"I just want to find Marri," Stefani said. But her gaze flicked to Giana. "But first thing's first. You need to fix Ella."

Giana's mild smile never wavered, but when she answered, it was clear she was speaking to Stefani for all that her gaze never wavered from Iazmaena.

"Of course," she said. "A deal's a deal, after all, and I am past due on making good. Bring her here."

"What, now? Here?" Stefani suddenly sounded hesitant.

And it occurred to Karl this might be Giana's way of trying to offer an olive branch to the revenants.

"Of course," she said again. "What better time than the present?"

CHAPTER 40

DESPITE SEEING Ella's deterioration since the Bridge, when the moment actually arrived, Stefani hesitated. This wasn't Giana her aide; this was Giana, representative of some strange class of lifeforms that had killed the very planet they'd all called home. Did she truly dare put her trust, not to mention her child, in the hands of this woman?

And worse, Ella was not truly Stefani's child, but the child of the real Stefani. Technically speaking, the girl had no mother anymore, which was all this Stefani's fault. Ella was, in a very real sense, a chance for a kind of redemption, however imperfect, for what she'd done to the girl's actual mother. If Stefani did something now that endangered the girl . . .

But in the end, Stefani had no answers and, she feared, little time. If this turned out to be a mistake, she was hopeful that intent would at least count for something.

Giana was facing her, arms outstretched as though wanting to play with Ella, a patient expression on her face. Stefani didn't think she detected any unseemly eagerness in that stance, but how could she be sure, really?

Letting out a shuddering sigh, Stefani swiveled the carrier around to the front and extricated Ella from it. Despite looking so ill, the girl's mood had improved markedly over the past few hours. Paradoxically, this made Stefani fear for her even more. She kept thinking about tales of people dying from hypothermia, how once they reached the end, they felt warm instead of cold, as though the body, knowing hope was lost, was seeking any comfort it could, however false.

Please, please don't be too late, she prayed to the god of her ancestors, or to no one. And then, because she felt compelled to hedge, *and please don't be a mistake*. This poor little girl deserved a better life than hers was shaping up to be thus far.

Giana took Ella from Stefani with reverence, or at least a good imitation of it. She examined the girl closely, her eyes seeming to lose focus, almost as though she were listening instead of looking.

"My cousins, the ones who had infiltrated Gene Sequencing, were getting very experimental toward the end," she said. "Desperation will do that. They knew our time on that world was nearing its end, and even though that was what we had been put there to do, every life form wants to go on living, don't they? We had to spread, to find new harbors in which to thrive. It was why, just like the rest of you, we wanted to open the Bridge more than anything."

Dire as her words were, her tone said she was merely trying to fill the tense silence. She shifted her stance, pulling Ella into the crook of her right arm while cupping the top of the child's head with her left hand.

"On the one hand, such desperation landed them me, the agent they'd always hoped for. On the other hand, Ella has clearly not worked out the way they'd have wanted. She must surely have been one of the last, but I wonder how many other women had babies in that same window? I wonder how many mothers faced real tragedy?" Her gaze flicked to Stefani. "I know it must not feel like it most of the time, but you were very fortunate. This can still be fixed."

"Back on Coldgarden," Stefani said, tears back in her eyes. They even infiltrated her voice. "When you said you could fix her, you said that if you did, she would be . . . like you."

"I suppose I did," Giana said musingly. "It almost seems like the words of another person. But if you like, I can tell you otherwise now. Perhaps, if you keep repeating the lie, you'll come to believe it. Memory is like that. A few years hence, you might forget you'd ever heard that little caveat."

"No false comforts." Stefani's voice was iron.

"Yes, Stefani. She'll be like me. But it's important to remember that she's already half like me. It's the fact that the transformation didn't fully take that's the problem. She's never been just a little human girl. Or rather, just a Coldgardener native little girl. As soon as Stefani Palmieri decided to involve Gene Sequencing in the act of having a child, that was off the table. But if you let me fix her, she'll be alive and whole. And fully herself for the first time."

Stefani stifled a sob. The woman's words brought to light a fear she'd scarcely realized she'd been carrying.

"*Like* you, you said. But not . . . But not . . ."

"A little *too much* like me? I could do that, I suppose. Perhaps I might have even wanted to, before." Giana raised a hand almost before Stefani's rage and fear could spike. "Before, I said. My thinking has . . . evolved since we arrived. She will be fully herself for the first time. I said it. And I mean it. *Only* herself."

"But we only have your word on that," Karl said darkly.

"My word, and the fact that I warned you when I could have kept quiet," Giana said. Her gaze was fully fixed on Ella now. "However you feel, express it now. This is your last chance to back out before I do something I won't be able to undo."

Karl's hand fell upon Stefani's shoulder. "Whatever you decide . . ." he began, his voice full of warmth and support.

"Do it," Stefani said. "Save her." What other choice did she have?

Giana nodded gravely, meeting Stefani's eyes, then turned her full attention back to Ella. "I can't be entirely certain, but I suspect this will look and sound worse than it is. Pleases don't be alarmed and please don't attempt to disrupt what I'm about to do."

Clenching her teeth, her shoulders, her whole body, Stefani braced herself for the unimaginable.

The change began at the top of Ella's head, where Giana was making physical contact. It was a glow, a soft, white light shining from the crown of Ella's head outward between Giana's fingers. Stefani had seen it before, when Giana's kind revealed their true forms, but where there it appeared sickly and menacing, here it seemed benevolent, even soothing.

Or perhaps she was merely seeing what she wanted to see.

The light rippled downward in a ring around the girl, flowing past Ella's forehead and then her face. Stefani gasped as it did, an exhalation she heard echoed in Karl and even, she thought, Iaz. Ella's face changed as the light passed. Her expression went from brightly curious to bawling in the instant it took the ring of light to pass. It was downright eerie to see her eyes screwed up in rage while the rest of her face remained calm and quiet for the heartbeat it took for the glowing ring to pass her nose and reach her chin.

Then she was shrieking, barely able to suck in enough breath to give vent to her fury. Stefani tried to go to her, but Karl held her back.

"She said it would be like this," he whispered. But he didn't understand. It was one thing to be told your child would scream bloody murder, quite another to have to endure it and not be able to help.

I can't help, she said, attempting to drive the point home. *The only one who can help is already doing so.* The logic didn't calm her. No mere words could. But Stefani did find calm. Because when she looked at that screaming face, despite the redness of anger, everything else about Ella looked healthier than before the light had passed. Most prominently, the dark hollows under her eyes, something one should never see on a child this young, had vanished entirely.

The ring passed under Ella's clothes, shining out where the material was thin enough to permit such. Her shoes were too thick to see the glow, but Stefani was able to time the moment the light would have arrived there down to the second.

In that instant, Ella was all smiles and burbling laughter. The apparent agony of the preceding few seconds was entirely forgotten. Reaching out to take her back from a Giana wearing a small, satisfied smile, Stefani looked upon her baby, who looked as healthy as she ever had.

"All done," Giana said. "I'm no doctor, but I think it's safe to say she will be all right from here on out."

"I . . . I don't know what—thank you," Stefani said. The warnings of a few minutes gone seemed very far away. Giana had been right. All that mattered was that Ella was safe and whole.

For the first time in her entire life.

CHAPTER 41

THIS TIME, there were only two of them on the call. It made Caroline particularly nervous. She wasn't sure she'd ever had a true one-on-one conversation with Halford Heller, not even remotely. His image was limned with static in a way that seemed portentous somehow, so much so that she couldn't tell where he was calling from.

"The others are preparing for departure," Heller said by way of explanation as to their absences. "Ginevra in particular. The ship is less ready than she'd indicated. Less ready than she'd advertised it would be, if I'm being honest. I'm disappointed."

It took all Caroline's self-control not to wince on Xian's behalf. She'd rather face most people's unbridled rage than Heller's mild disappointment. She wondered how he would express that disappointment and felt another pang of sympathy on the sour woman's behalf.

"You make it sound like you've seen the ship in person," Caroline said. She had a sudden brainwave. "Are you calling from the ship now?"

"Yes, but I'm only up here to deliver my personal effects. I just got done with my final arraignment on this world. One last bit of justice dispensed." He sounded unusually satisfied with himself.

"This is the rabid soldier?"

"No, we won't have time for the formalities there, I'm afraid. This is the overeager linguist. But I didn't call to talk about my work, or even Genevra's failures. I called to speak with you about Subject Rho."

"It hardly seems to matter, with departure so imminent," Caroline said. She tried to mask her relief. It was true she felt a prick of guilt because she was the best qualified to handle this crisis. But she had never wanted this job. The idea of turning her back on it, flying away, and just letting it be someone else's problem was just so damned intoxicating.

"It does matter." His words were peremptory. "We're leaving this world, but there is no guarantee that no one will attempt to follow us at some point. We can purge the records all we want, but astronomy is astronomy. It would not take a genius to work out where we're going. So we need to clean house as much as we can before we go. That includes making sure we don't leave dangerous fanatics a weapon they can turn against us later. If you know where Rho is, it's past time to give the kill order."

He looked, to her horror, disappointed. Worse, he looked downright annoyed. She'd always suspected Heller didn't like having to issue such blunt edicts.

There was only one correct answer to such a statement. She had a berth on the ship as long as she didn't piss off her peers too much. This man above all.

"Of course," she said. "I'd better make a call."

Maybe it was for the best. At the very least, she could give Jürgen what she knew he craved so badly. Maybe that would be a kind of apology.

The last she had time for. Perhaps, she thought dangerously, she might even see him in person.

"Good. That's very good. Don't be late," Heller said, as though he could read her mind.

CHAPTER 42

IT WAS NOT FAR to the Cult's . . . Marri couldn't help but think of it as a *lair*. She didn't try to escape. That would have to come later. First priority was getting away from that storm of not-leaves and that light.

The round metal door opened at their approach as though someone or something waited for them on the other side. But as the Cultist pushed Marri through, following close behind himself, she saw no one.

Must be some sensor I didn't see. Automatically opening doors. So much about this world was strange to her. On a planet with revenants as a constant threat, an idea like that seemed insane.

On the other hand, it wasn't as if they'd been running from nothing.

"Don't worry, child," the Cultist man—she remembered him as Mathieu—said as he shut the heavy door with a wheel that turned to seal it in place. As though he were reading her mind. Not that it was a hard state of mind to guess. "That awful thing can't get in here."

"What was it?" she asked, eyeing the door carefully but surreptitiously now that she felt herself begin to calm down. It possessed no electronic locking mechanism that she could see. No keypad. Likely they were more concerned about keeping people like Jürgen out than keeping their own in. Although it didn't do a good job keeping him out either.

"A relic of a bygone time. From before humans came to this place."

"From the previous people who were here? Before the planet moved?"

A very noticeable pause.

"I see you have been studying our history. That is good. It does not do for one to remain in ignorance about the places in which one finds oneself."

"But what is it?" Marri had gotten very good at not being diverted.

"A kind of echo of that long-dead people, nothing more. It is little enough to worry yourself about unless it catches you, which it did not. It was well that I came along when I did."

"Mm," Marri said noncommittally.

"I bid you welcome to our home, formally this time. Your last visit was so brief and ended so abruptly, we did not have time for a tour. If you'd like, I can show you around now."

"It's fine." The way she said it, she could either be agreeing with his suggestion or unenthusiastically accepting his apology. She was stuck here for the moment, but she refused to allow herself to be trapped in this place.

"We also did not get a chance to properly introduce ourselves. My name is Mathieu." He waited patiently for her to follow suit. After the silence became awkward, Marri raised her eyebrows at him to indicate this wasn't happening.

"Yes," he said, fumbling the rhythm of his speech. "Well. Follow me, if you please." He did not insist on her leading the way. That could either mean he trusted her not to run off or that he knew she wouldn't be able to. Nothing to do now but note the shortest route back to the door as they walked.

Surely that thing couldn't hang around outside forever.

The spaces within were nothing like the tunnels. Flat surfaces were everywhere, be they tables, desks, or the sides of cabinets. And mechanical parts had been crammed onto every one of them. Marri had kept parts to reprogram her handheld hidden under her bed back in Stefani's apartment in Coldgarden. This looked like that times a million.

"What is all this stuff?"

"In this temple, we perfect our form to break ourselves free of the flesh prisons our masters on this world have cursed us with."

"Uh huh," Marri said. So far, it sounded a lot like what Jürgen had accused them of, except when Mathieu talked about it, he made it sound like a good thing. "Is that why you're the way you are?"

He turned to her, and it was difficult not to flinch from the sight. The last time she had seen him, she was fairly certain he'd "just" been a robo-man, all machine and no flesh. Now, overtop of his robot-self, he wore what looked like a suit of loose, preserved skin. He stank of formaldehyde.

Marri very much feared it was *his* skin.

As he regarded her, his horrible, pickled face sagged open as though in a dopey, wide-eyed grin. Behind it, the lenses of his false eyes, off-center with the drooping sockets of flesh, glinted in the artificial light of the lair.

She supposed she hadn't managed to hide her feelings when he asked, "Does my visage disturb you, child?"

"It's not the nicest thing I've ever seen," she admitted. But then, she decided that fair was fair. "But it's not the most awful, either." She paused. "Not quite."

His laugh sounded genuine despite all the mechanical distortion. "My poor child, you are either too polite or too traumatized."

"No one has ever told me I'm too polite," she said, and he laughed again. "What do you mean about all that stuff? Perfecting your form? Flesh prison?"

"You've clearly been studying our world," Mathieu said. "But how much have you learned about the history of this colony in particular?"

Given their antagonism toward one another, she doubted answering *only what Jürgen told me* was going to make a good impression.

"Not very much."

"What do you know of the Harmony parasite?" He caught the light of recognition in her eyes. "So you've heard of it, at least. Tell me, child, you have allowed no doctors to examine you correct? No injections? No procedures of any kind, whether you were conscious or not?"

"No." Her shudder was genuine. "We don't really do doctors where I come from."

"Astonishing." He sounded like he meant it. "The tyranny of science is all-encompassing here, so much so that only through turning their own weapon against them can we hope to escape." He pointed to his robot-head.

"Bleeding on Col—on New Calgary is a good way to die horribly," Marri said. "Your best bet of surviving is never needing a doctor."

"So it is true. All our records said some colonies had gone that route, but to hear it confirmed. A colony that escaped the chains binding the rest of humanity. How I wish I could visit your world, child."

"No, I don't think you would like that," she said with confidence. Whatever he might think about her world, Father was dead. There would not be much of a planet left to inhabit.

"Well, be that as it may, you are here now. And they have not had a chance to afflict you with the parasite, to *ruin* you yet."

"What do you mean?" she asked. "I can't get a straight answer about this parasite from anyone."

"A creation of old Earth," Mathieu said. "You know of Earth, yes?"

"Yep." Truth be told, until very recently she'd assumed Coldgarden *was* Earth. Everyone there had. A lot of the people who had crossed the Bridge likely still did, she realized with a jolt. *As jarring as this is for me, at least I knew why we had to go.*

"Before the diaspora—the formation of the colonies, I mean—a very misguided scientist created the parasite, though she called it a *symbiont*. It lodges itself directly in the brain, merges with it, even replaces portions of it with its own tissue. Over time, it becomes impossible to tell where the person ends and the worm begins."

If he expected this to horrify Marri, who was both person and worm, he was mistaken.

"Why would anyone want to do that?"

"The scientist claimed it would alter our behavior, bind humanity together as one, ending strife and competition and struggle and cruelty between humans, turn us to look outward to challenge ourselves rather than inward."

Marri thought of all the times people had been kind to her when she'd lived on the streets; then she thought of all the times the opposite had happened. It was those that loomed largest in her mind, even now, so far removed.

"Doesn't sound so bad to me."

"It was a noble goal, child, and while Dr. Anastasia León is long dead, many still debate her motives. But I, for one, believe them to be pure. She meant well, yet she neglected two immutable truths about our species. For every rule there ever was, there are those who find a way to circumvent it. And for every brilliant idea brimming with noble intent, it is only a matter of time before someone attempts to pervert it. I do not know how it has transpired on other worlds, but on Anaranjado, both things have come true."

MARRI PRESSED Mathieu for more detail, but he deflected her questions and bade her follow him further on the tour, for all that he hadn't really *shown* her anything yet. The deeper they went, the more cluttered and chaotic the spaces got. Marri began to see more and more of the cultists as they reached warmer parts of the lair. One and all, each turned to gawk at her. Some wore their old skin, as Mathieu did, but mostly they seemed content to strut around in just their metal bones. She didn't see a single normal human face in the bunch.

Also, the deeper they went, the more a vague sense of alarm she was feeling sharpened and deepened. She was already too far from the entrance. Even with a strange entity outside, the risk to what might happen to her in this place was growing every second. She should turn around. She should tu—

"Mathieu," she said, suddenly coming to the decision that she'd walked long enough to earn her some more information, "you still haven't explained how they turned the parasite bad. Or who *they* are."

Mathieu stopped them in a hallway, an empty space between rooms. "In every society there ever was, a few people amassed more wealth and power than all the rest, sometimes than all the rest combined."

"Bosses," Marri said. She cringed a little at the term, which sounded like something only little kids would say. But it was how she and the Mice had always referred to the people too powerful to mess with.

"Just so," Mathieu nodded. "On this world, these *bosses* contrived a way to avoid being subjected to the parasite. Harmony binds the actions of everyone on this world—except for them."

"How?"

"We believe they don't even have the parasite. That they can't tolerate the thought that they are not wholly in control of their own fates. The notion that they owe anything they are, anything they've achieved, to something that is fundamentally apart from themselves, is unbearable. But that is just conjecture. All we know for certain is that they somehow stand outside the prison, which means they can control it. To control us. Instead of a society all pulling in the same direction, all operating in mutual concern for one another, one group exploits the good-natured meekness of the rest." He knelt before her, and Marri had to stifle her irritation. The gesture was a little too much like a teacher talking with a much younger child than she, trying to drive home an obvious point.

"Does that sound fair to you, child?"

"No," she said by rote.

"That is what we are trying to stop."

"By turning yourselves into robots?"

"The only way to fight them," he said, and his voice was filled with a fervent-sounding static, "is to step outside the prison ourselves. We can't destroy their power from within the walls. And the only way to step outside those walls is to rob the parasite of the biological host on which to feed."

For the first time, Marri was truly flummoxed. She realized then that she'd assumed the robot parts were only skin deep. Like a kind of armor, or maybe a way to replace weak limbs with stronger ones.

"You're like that . . . all the way through?"

He hesitated, as if unwilling to answer. "Please understand, child. Our way is the only way to achieve justice for all. It's a choice we've all made freely, for ourselves. We can ask no one of this world to take on this burden against their will."

Assuming he was telling the truth, at least there was that.

"But does it work?"

"It *will* work," he said.

So, no, in other words.

They walked past a set of doors as Marri mulled this over, but she was startled from her thoughts by cries of distress from one especially large door. The cries were stifled as the door slid shut, but she heard the words "Alpha, Gamma, Zeta, Iota, Kappa . . . all viable for factioning! Beta, Delta, Eta . . ." before the aperture closed tight.

"Who was that?" she asked, pulling up short. He'd sounded as though he'd been in incredible pain.

"A deeply sick man. A victim of the bosses, as you might say. We rescued him just recently, and I wish to help ease his pain, though some among us have darker designs for him, I'm sad to say."

It slammed home for Marri so suddenly and so forcefully that she had to work hard not to let it show on her face or in her body language.

Jürgen's kidnapping victim. This must be the man he was looking for. The timing was too close otherwise. But should Marri tell Mathieu? He seemed at least a little unhappy that this man was in their care at all.

"Child? Is everything all right?"

"What is she doing here?" A new voice interrupted them as another robo-man stormed up the hall toward them. Marri remembered it from last time. *Lukas.* "You've coaxed the girl back here? Another outsider in our midst? Mathieu, have you taken leave of your wits at last?"

"I am *sheltering a child from that which roams outside*, Lukas,"

Mathieu said, emphasizing so many words it was impossible for Marri not to notice. Clearly he wanted Lukas to guard his tongue.

"A likely story! Do you think I've forgotten who pushed us to make the attempt with Fennec? Or god forbid, *Beauregard*? This is a waste of resources! It was *always* a waste of resources," Lukas said. His mechanical voice was shrill and staticky with indignation. "The answer lies in Subject Rho. We turn our enemy's own weapon against them."

Marri followed her instincts and kept quiet. The comment was directed at Mathieu, not her. A part of her thought to use the interruption as an excuse to leave. Here was a man who would likely even help her do so.

But she couldn't quite bring herself to leave just yet, not when there was so much more she might learn and understand if she stayed just a bit longer. It was like an un-scratchable itch in her mind.

"You are letting the past cloud your judgment," Mathieu said, keeping his own voice calm and measured. "And you are allowing our plight to make us no better than our enemies when there remains another path! We have a unique opportunity."

"An argument I've heard only twice before!" Lukas insisted. "What has either of those attempts gotten us? Nothing. Less than nothing. No, your way is the past. Subject Rho is the future."

"You were perfectly content to try again after Fennec," Mathieu said, ignoring the past part of Lukas's comment. His voice was growing heated at last. "Admit it, Lukas! Ms. Beauregard's departure shattered your faith. There is no shame in doubt during a crisis of faith. The only shame is allowing it to poison you forever rather than renew you."

"I was willing to try a thing twice, yes. But two times with the same outcome is enough of a pattern for me to move on. I will not be party to this," Lukas said. If his machine face could have spit, Marri felt confident he would have to punctuate the words. "If we are to succeed, it must be by acknowledging reality and turning it to our favor for once."

He turned and stormed away with a whir of servos and hissing of hydraulics.

"It is a shame to see one so elevated in our faith fall so far," Mathieu said, either to Marri or to no one, since they were now alone in the hallway. "I fear he will have to be dealt with before he can sow more discontent. But that is not your concern, child. You have more immediate matters to focus upon. This way, please."

CHAPTER 44

"I'M sure Jürgen has told you something of what befell him here," Mathieu said as he stepped into what must be a surgical room, though Marri had never seen one before in person. "This is where we performed the procedures upon him." He turned his still-pretty-upsetting gaze upon her. "Procedures he requested us to perform, mind you. Whatever he may have told you." Marri hung just outside the door.

Hypermutation risk or not, the room gave her the creeps.

"He tells me one thing. You tell me another," she said. "So it just comes down to who I trust more, I guess."

"That," Mathieu said, sounding amused, "or the footage of the consent interview we conducted with him before each and every one of the procedures. Did he mention that, or did he imply that all his augmentations were installed in one nightmarish, marathon surgery event?"

"He didn't really talk about it," Marri said with a shrug. It felt odd, standing here just outside the door, talking at someone standing at the foot of the surgical bed in the room's center.

But she still wasn't setting foot in that room.

"He mostly mentioned that you tried to remove his brain worm but only succeeded in cutting it off from him." Marri jumped as a pair of hands gently clasped her shoulders, but it was only someone trying to ease her out of the way.

"Excuse me," they said in a voice so distorted it was hard to understand. The person entered the room and moved to some kind of readout station on the wall. Instead of robes, they wore a spotless white coat like Marri had sometimes seen Stefani in before she'd become a magistrate.

It took Marri a moment to realize that Mathieu had stopped talking and was simply staring at her.

"What?" she asked, discomfited, moving back to stand in the door.

"What did you say just now? About Jürgen's parasite?"

"Excuse me." Another set of hands, another gentle push. Getting annoyed now, Marri moved aside to allow yet another lab-coated person in.

"I said he told us that it no longer makes him do anything. He has to pretend it still does so he knows how to behave . . ." She trailed off, momentarily confused. She was sure Jürgen had told her this information. It was there in her head, clear as the shine on a revenant.

But she had no memory of him actually saying the words. And she had the strangest sensation that the information had just popped into her head moments before. Like someone had put it there on purpose, but only when Marri needed it. She shook away a feeling of lightheadedness.

"But this is extraordinary." Mathieu's wondering tone snapped Marri out of her confusion. The sickly heat of dread building in her at the realization evaporated to nothing on the instant. It wasn't important. She must have just forgotten. It had been a long few days.

"Don't you see?" Mathieu said. "It worked! We thought it hadn't worked, but he was just . . . just *lying* to us. Do you know what this means?"

"Excuse me." Hands. Shoulders. Marri almost snapped at the person, but in the end she just stepped aside. The room was getting crowded now, like they were getting ready for something. She backed away an extra step to let any future people just walk around her into the room.

"No, I don't know what this means," she said. It was impossible to keep all of the bite from her voice.

"It means there is hope for me and mine," Mathieu said. He sounded blissful. "Jürgen represented half of what we needed to accomplish to defeat the parasite—namely, to sever the links between it and the rest of the brain in a person already implanted. But he fled us without ever telling us we had succeeded. With our next subject, we attempted the other half of the task—replacing the organic brain with a perfect, synthetic copy so that no new parasite could ever take hold. We succeeded in this, even if that subject betrayed and abandoned us. But if what you say is true, we have already succeeded in both halves of our goal! It means we needn't use that poor, tortured Subject Rho at all."

Even through the electronic distortion, Marri heard the rapturous joy in his voice.

"You have given me the information I need to defeat Lukas's push for power and retain my position, dear girl. And though we would have given it to you anyway, you have more than earned this gift."

"What?" Marri tensed as yet *another* hand fell on her shoulder.

"Excuse me," the person said. And then their other hand came down. There was a frigid bite and warm pressure in Marri's neck, and the world began to go wobbly.

The same pair of hands caught her as she staggered.

"Easy now," the voice said in her ear. "Let's get you to where you can lie down." They hoisted her up—"oof, you're a lot heavier than you look"—and carried her into the operating room.

CHAPTER 45

"WHAT ARE WE LOOKING AT HERE?" Iaz asked for the third time.

"For the third time, I don't know," Stefani said.

"I'm thinking out loud." Iaz sounded prickly in a way only she could. In such moments, it was easy to forget they weren't back on Coldgarden—albeit on a particularly hot day—engaged in the kind of comfortable bickering only long, close relationships could enjoy. "And figuring that out is the reason we stopped here, after all."

Stefani, Iaz, Karl, and Giana all peered out from the crack leading back to the canyon thoroughfare, ready to slip deeper into the shadows at the first sound of approaching militia. The structure in question jutted up above the canyon ridgeline, visible through the arching glass ceiling, which was an oddity all by itself. Every other building she'd encountered had been enclosed fully underground. According to Karl, even the Bridge complex was walled off from the outside.

This unusual profile for a building on this world left it facing the full might of the sun to the west. The glare, even indirectly, was almost too bright to look at, as though someone had purposefully buffed the metal to a mirror sheen. Why anyone would do that, save to punish the vision of onlookers, Stefani had no idea.

The building itself was flat and semicircular in profile on the sunward side, though from what they could see, the shaded side tapered down into the shape of half a cone. But once Stefani's eyes adjusted to the glare, she could see that the air above and to the side of the semicircular face of the structure looked strange. It shimmered and rippled. It might almost have been heat haze, hardly surprising on this hell world, but it was far more intense than heat haze should be.

"Could it be some sort of exhaust system?" she wondered aloud. "Look at the air around it?"

"It's definitely doing something." Karl said. He smiled ruefully at the unhelpfulness of the comment.

"Look at that cut in the rock," Iaz said. She pointed to an area of deeper shadow sharply defined in the canyon wall, made even harder to see by the glare above. Now that she saw it, Stefani realized it corresponded to a wider area of canyon and a turnaround point between the rails that had to be more than chance. "That's got to be the way up. Too much of a coincidence for it to be so close otherwise."

"Careful!" Giana's warning was a hiss. Her hearing must be damned impressive because it took Stefani another three seconds to hear the electric whine. "Someone's coming."

A few moments later, a tram car came into view, a squat cab with a large cargo unit behind whirring up the outbound rail from further east. Stefani backed deeper into their crevice to stay as much out of sight as possible while still keeping an eye on the arrivals. Karl and Iaz, both taller than she, tried their best to slip back as well.

No one wanted to lose their view, but it was getting quite crowded trying to fit all four into the same shadow.

The tram coasted to a halt by the cut in the canyon wall. A quartet of Anaranjadan soldiers emerged, ridiculously tall and lanky to Stefani's eyes. What skin showed outside their uniforms was coated with the same black scales Stefani had seen elsewhere. They checked their weapons, which were as squat and snub-nosed as their tram.

"More of their stun-guns on steroids," Karl whispered. "Whatever they're here for, it isn't us. Or they haven't learned anything yet."

Indeed, the four marched straight into the cut and, presumably, up.

"One question," Karl said. "Why black? I thought black was the best absorber of heat." When he caught Iaz looking at him, he added, "the scales."

"Black is also the best emitter of heat," Stefani said. "The process works in reverse just as well. I'm no heat flow expert, but maybe since this entire world seems to be underground habitats and nobody is getting direct sunlight on their skin to be absorbed, they'd rather have the best *emitter* possible. Since they don't have sweat glands and all." She shrugged. "Or maybe their tailor-slash-mechanic just thinks it looks sharp."

"If you two are finished, I *really* want to see what they're doing," Iaz said. It was a tone Stefani was familiar with. Impatience, yes, but beneath that Iaz was contemplating doing something she knew was rash, taking a risk to get something she wanted.

"It might be better to wait a bit," Giana said. "They presumably won't be staying here forever, with a tram occupying one of the two rails that way. A mere communication could have been delivered via other means. Their vehicle has a cargo bay, but they didn't bring anything in with them. That suggests they mean to bring something out. What that something is might tell us something about the building's purpose."

"Boy, Steffi, you sure found the perfect aide," Iaz snorted. "And I thought Johe was bad."

Stefani decided it would be best not to reply, though she did notice that Iaz's face crumpled briefly at the mention of her aide, dead by the hand of the original Iaz. She considered that a positive sign.

They waited for some time before their patience was finally rewarded. The soldiers reemerged, two by two with a dozen people between them, wrists and ankles shackled, the latter with long enough leads between cuffs that they could manage a slow, shuffling walk.

"It's a prison?" Karl's disbelief was audible. "I can honestly say that wasn't on my list."

"Hold on, now!" Another figure emerged from the cut. "Will Meridian Equatoria deign to tell me what they want with the Defectives?"

"If you were on the list of people who needed to know, Warden, you would know," said one of the soldiers, presumably the one in the lead. "To be clear, we aren't on that list either."

"It's Director, not Warden," the man said primly. "And if they don't want to tell me, can you? Because you've been coming here all day, hauling off my workers. If things keep going at this pace, I'm not going to have any left."

"Director, my apologies. I am following my orders in relaying these orders to you. I don't like leaving you in the dark any more than I like being in the dark myself."

"Have they at least told you how many more I can expect to be losing? There is a certain point below which I will not be able to operate the projection facility. They are aware of that, yes? I can't imagine they'll be happy if the view from the Meridian Cities suddenly gets a little too realistic."

"I have no idea, Director," the soldier said with cool politeness. "But as this facility caters exclusively to the comfort of the residents of Equatoria, I can only assume that if they want to remove too many of your residents to keep it operational, that is their decision to make. But if I were you, I'd be preparing myself for that eventuality and your ultimate transfer. Because while I have no idea how many more residents you can expect to lose, I did see how many more trams like ours were queuing up when we left the shuttle facility."

"The . . . shuttle facility?"

"That's the only hint I've gotten, Director," the soldier said in a voice that was not without sympathy. "But I imagine it's enough to make an educated guess."

"Oh," the warden-slash-director said. Seizing the moment of surprised silence, the soldiers finished loading their human cargo, utilized the turnaround, and headed back the way they'd come.

CHAPTER 46

THE CAFETERIA WAS one of the few this far down. Whether geothermal or banked solar from the surface, most of the residents of Shadyside living this far from grown food got by with power ports and relied on concentrated nutrition bars for their organic needs.

It was, to put it mildly, an odd place for Jürgen's handler on the Cult kidnapping to call for an in-person meeting the very evening after he'd deposited Marri and Giana with Ayana.

The clientele all turned to regard him as he entered, but not in an unfriendly way. It was not often that someone encountered genuine unfriendliness on Anaranjado—yet another of Harmony's many benefits.

The table in the corner furthest from the door, the person had said. Jürgen's machine eyes read his intentions, providing his visual cortex with an overlay of the distances, telling him that the right back corner was 1.3 meters further from the door than any other. And, conveniently, the table nestled into that corner had a person seated at one of its two chairs—someone swathed in unusually baggy memory-matter clothing complete with a hood and whose body language spoke of a distinct discomfort with being there.

Jürgen might have been subtler with his approach, but

among the many things he had lost patience for after his ordeal with the Cult was tact. He walked over, aware he was drawing every eye and would likely irritate his handler—or their representative, more likely—but also quite unable to alter his behavior.

He took the table's lone available seat.

"Look what they did to you," the occupant said as he lowered himself. "You used to be so handsome." They reached out a hand across the table as if to stroke his cheek, pausing only when he went rigid with shock.

The voice, electronically distorted to an almost comical degree, wasn't familiar at all. The thick accent was from the calls. But the familiar tone told him everything he needed to know. She must have tried very hard to alter her voice such that he hadn't recognized her before now.

"Caroline," he said, finally deigning to lower his voice in a gesture toward discretion. It was not a question. He knew who this was. "What in the Good Doctor's name are you doing down here?"

"Telling you the parameters of your job have finally firmed up," she said. She did not drop the thick accent. Once it had been softer, subtler.

As she had been.

"I . . . You're my handler?"

"You didn't even suspect, did you?" she asked. She sounded insufferably pleased with herself, and as she leaned a bit into the light, he saw she wore some kind of sleeve of scales around her throat that was serving as disguise and voice modulator both. But her face above it was as wickedly delighted—and as beautiful—as he'd remembered.

"No," he said. "I honestly thought you had forgotten about me." It was not an accusation. Just a simple statement of fact. But by the hurt on her face, he could tell she'd taken it as the former. She'd always been so good at taking offense. It was the sort of thing he could only truly appreciate in hindsight.

"You wound me, *chère*. It was you who left, if you remember. Left and never came back."

This was very like Caroline. When you hurt her, she lashed out, fully intending to hurt back. It was not the first time she'd claimed he was fundamentally a different person than the one she'd dallied with in both their youths.

As though her casting him aside had not been the reason he'd run straight into the arms of the Cult.

"You've grown since I've last seen you." Sometimes turning a spat into a joke worked with her. He glanced at her unnaturally long legs beneath their loose fabric pants legs. Caroline du Vernay was of average height at best. Average *baseline* height. It would have been the peak of scandal among her peers had she had her legs replaced with prostheses.

Equatorians didn't do that.

"Stilts," she said, her good humor returned. Nice to know some things didn't change. "No one ever expects the low-tech solution on this rock. I've gotten rather good at walking in them, but it does mean the pants have to be loose, or it's rather obvious."

Jürgen decided to pounce on this change in mood.

"I'd wondered if you'd recommended me for this job, given the accent." If she recognized the opening to explain why she'd decided to remake her own voice, she didn't take it. "What has changed about the job?" He tried to reorient himself around the notion this woman was his handler, not his ex-lover. That would make it easier to focus.

"What's changed is that it's no longer a job. I suppose, as you said, that means it never was."

It was an effort not to visibly stiffen, however much he'd feared this very outcome.

"That . . . is a significant change."

"Perhaps not. You won't be paid, of course. But if you know what's good for you, you'll see it done regardless."

Jürgen shook his head slowly, trying to read her.

"I'm not following," he said at last. "Why the back and forth, for starters?"

"We've experienced a great deal of churn," she said, sounding both bored and annoyed by this fact. She didn't need to explain "we." She was talking, collectively, about the Equatorians, the only power on the planet that mattered beyond Harmony itself. "But that's finally settled. The only people who care are the ones who want him dead. And I'm here telling you, as a friend, that this outcome is the most preferable for you as well."

"Why don't they care about getting him back?"

"Because we're leaving," she said. "Imminently. As in, tomorrow. You are my last bit of business on this rock. I head straight back to pack and to the launch platform to make orbit after I visit you here." Her smile was as dazzling as he remembered. It even awoke a pang of long-desiccated lust in him. "You should feel honored!"

"You're . . . leaving?"

"Do try to keep up, *chère*. The *Ultima Thule* breaks orbit tomorrow. I will be on it. I shouldn't even be telling you this, but I do feel so badly about how things wound up with us."

"The colony ship? I thought it wasn't going to be completed for—for *months*, if not longer. They said there was no change to the schedule—"

"Yes, well, it's not *done*, precisely. But it's space worthy, so we're told, and even if it can't hold as many passengers as we'd promised, I've got my berth, so I'm not complaining, am I?"

"But they haven't even held the lottery for passengers—" He knew these words were all stupid, naive. But he couldn't seem to stop saying them.

"There was never going to be a lottery, *chère*." Her voice was a mix of apology and disappointment that he really needed to have this explained to him. "That was a thing we told everyone to keep them from getting upset, just like the bit about not accelerating the schedule. Not that they would have, probably, but why take the chance?" She took a sip of her drink, winced, and pushed it to the center of the table. "The food down here is just revolting. Anyway, there have only ever been berths for residents of Equatoria and some handpicked others. And we're leaving now because of the whole . . . invasion." She waved her hands as though to encompass everything around her, as though the streets swarmed with rampaging New Calgarians.

It took Jürgen several moments to register how angry he was. He wasn't even planning to submit his name for a berth aboard the ship. There was no reason for him to be this angry. But he was.

It was the lie.

"So," Caroline said, seemingly waiting for Jürgen to respond. "Obviously there's no interest in recovering our man if we're leaving the planet. Not that he wouldn't be useful where we're going. But we have a long time to work that out. And we have the data. That's all we really need, I think, and I would know."

"Why come down here to tell me all this?" Jürgen could only ask basic questions. Doing otherwise would open a chasm to all that anger.

"Because we go way back, you and I. And now that we're leaving, I feel like it's not hurting anything to let you in on a few little details we've kept from most of the fine people on this *fine* planet. Details that won't matter to us any longer but will matter very much to you."

"Details," he said.

"Details," she agreed. And then she began to lay them out, these *details*.

Jürgen listened. He practiced calming exercises. And then, when she kissed him on the cheek before leaving, he sat staring at where she'd been sitting for a long time before he finally got up and walked stiffly out of the cafeteria.

The memory of her kiss felt like ice across the brand of Ms. Novak's feverish hand on his cheek.

Caroline had known it couldn't last, of course, even way back then when they'd begun their relationship—she would have said *fling*. He hadn't known. She had elected not to tell him. It was not her fault he'd been stupid, of course. But she'd known he didn't and kept it from him anyway, only telling him the truth when it was too late for him to do anything to change her mind.

This had been no different except, of course, in the sheer gall of its scale and scope. This bombshell she had dropped, this society-destroying sentence, deposited into his lap when it might already be too late to do anything but pick up whatever pieces remained . . .

We don't have the parasite, chère. *We never did.*

He could only assume that, on some level, she enjoyed this.

CHAPTER 47

JÜRGEN RETURNED to his home in a daze, his thoughts little more than low-grade static, universal background radiation. It felt as though a splinter had invaded his mind. He had been waiting for the promised explicit authority to commit violence against the Cult, and he supposed he could stop waiting now.

He had been granted that authority both formally and by the complete abdication and betrayal of those who would bestow it. But he had the authority. That was what he needed to focus on.

He was going to destroy the Cult. Pull it out root and stem. If he could not take on the true root of the evil of this world, a root he had not even seen until now, he would at least destroy that part of it he had access to.

Yet he stood there, just inside his threshold, frozen. It was that splinter, that foreign object lodged in his thoughts. It held him as though it had driven through his foot instead of his brain, rooted him in place like the very weeds he would tear out. Something he needed to look at before he stormed off and vented all the repressed hatred of his life upon the Cult.

His head felt strange. His thoughts buzzed. His cheek burned where Ms. Novak had touched him.

Jürgen Fennec had been cataloging the behavior of his own mind his whole life, and never more so than the past few years, once he had broken free of the Cult's sinister influence. There was something new there. Or perhaps something he'd never noticed before. Perhaps it was simply his anger, a feeling so long denied, now bursting its banks at last. Yes, that must be it. It was his anger he was sensing, hot and chaotic, not the cold, calculating resolution he'd grown accustomed to.

And for some reason he couldn't fathom, Jürgen Fennec's newfound anger told him very specifically to check his personal security footage.

As strange an insistence as this was, he didn't question it. He didn't normally review the recordings, not unless he had reason to doubt something he had seen or heard in a client or witness he had spoken with. Or—and this was the real reason he'd installed the devices—in case someone accused him of saying or doing something he hadn't.

Harmony made for a friendlier world, but people still had their own perceptions of events. Jürgen had only ever made use of the footage once, and only then over the banality of a disagreement of his agreed pay. He had gotten everything he was owed in the end.

He cued up the list of recordings. The sensors were smart enough to trigger the recording function anytime anyone other than just Jürgen was in the room, but he could also trigger them manually. The last recording he had was from just after he had informed Marri and Ms. Novak that they would have to leave. It was here he felt his first flash of irritation at this urge. Given that they had been effectively living in the office at the time, it meant he had a lot of files to go through to satisfy whatever need this was.

It's necessary, something whispered within him. He didn't know why it was necessary, but again, he didn't question the instinct. His cheek seared him as though it pressed against dry ice.

Just to get started somewhere, he cued the playback to begin at his departure from the room after informing them. This would show him their final conversation as his guests.

Only there was no conversation. The pair stared at each other, looking for all the world like they were having a discussion if you followed just their eyes and their body language. But their mouths didn't move. No words were spoken.

And then came the real kicker, the moment where Marri lifted her right hand and, in full view of the camera, the fingers had fused together and erupted into a bone-claw scythe before reverting back to the hand of a teenage girl.

Only not really a teenage girl.

The mad rumors, the conspiracies lacing the newswires, they all came crashing home to Jürgen. *There are monsters hidden among the refugees, and they can look like people.* He had briefly housed one of them. And judging by Ms. Novak's total lack of reaction to this revelation of Marri's, two.

But again, Jürgen was wrong. He was beginning to wonder if he'd ever been right about anything. Giana didn't react to *Marri* at all.

She did, however, turn to look directly at the camera.

And smiled.

⚥

Jürgen burst into the front office of the boarding house where he had left the pair under Ayana's care in exchange for releasing her from her debt. Ayana was not behind the desk, but this highly unusual scenario barely registered with him, such was the focusing power of his tunnel vision. He leaned over the counter and studied her guest registry screen—left suspiciously unlocked—until he found the room he was looking for.

Then he was off and down the hall.

"Come in," came Ms. Novak's voice before he'd even chimed a request. He palmed the door open.

"Mr. Fennec," she said formally when he entered. She was bent over something, some project she was using to occupy her time. He felt a spike of alarm at this project—more than alarm—but his cheek burned like Naranja, and his mind clouded over, and he found his eyes sliding away from it even as he tried to take in what it was precisely. It wasn't important what she was fiddling with. There was no point in him looking—*no point, do not look, do not see*—so he didn't.

"Ms. Novak," he responded, his voice hoarse.

He took her in. She didn't look good. Whatever ailment she was suffering, it appeared to be slowly winning its fight.

"I have some questions," he said. He'd come over here practically in a frenzy, but now that the moment was upon him, their pleasantly formal rapport reasserted itself. "If you don't mind."

"Ask away," she said, then turned back to her examination of whatever was splayed out across her bed. "I promise I'm listening." He could hear the smile in her voice.

"You are not human. Marri either."

"That's not exactly a question."

"Append a question mark, then, if you would be so kind."

"That's correct. We are not human."

"Explain, please."

"I could," she said. "But the story is a long one, and I've grown a little tired of retelling it to every being I come across. A better response would be a question. Do you care?"

Jürgen thought about it. Or tried to, rather. His anger was there, hemming in his thoughts, forcing them down certain channels. Whenever he tried to peer over one of these newfound walls in his mind, he found a ceiling blocking him. There was, in truth, only one path to walk.

And, honestly, wasn't that easier?

"No," he said. "I don't care. The Cult isn't human either, and right now, they are the bigger threat."

"I'm glad you're seeing things so clearly," Ms. Novak said. "But something seems to have changed in your posture toward them. Perhaps if *you* would be so kind as to explain."

Jürgen's jaw creaked as he opened it.

"They're abandoning us. They're leaving us, and they're leaving the Cult armed with the greatest weapon on the planet."

CHAPTER 48

GIANA NOVAK WAS VERY TIRED. This was no shock, given the sheer number of mental balls she was juggling simultaneously. But expecting it didn't make it any less fatiguing. And she was close, very close to her goal. She could not falter now.

She had felt his approach, fast on the heels of his sudden, violent spike in distress. That had come on very suddenly, a flood of rage and stress and sadness in her mind, feelings that belonged, in truth, to Jürgen Fennec. It was both the first sense she'd had that her touching his cheek the other day was actually yielding fruit, and proof that her counterpart's efforts in Sunnyside had not been in vain.

It was no longer merely theoretical. Giana could transform humans now. At least, she could transform humans without functional Harmony parasites in their brains.

But she'd had no time to revel in her victory. Because that moment of Jürgen's weakness, where his mental model of the world was teetering, ready to pitch over and shatter, was when her strike would drive the deepest.

So struck she had, sinking her metaphorical fingers into his mind, shoving aside as much of his volition as she could. She couldn't fully turn him into one of her own kind, not with so much of him already replaced by machine, but she could dictate his behavior henceforth. She had guided him toward the revelation about herself and Marri hidden in the footage. But her infiltration wasn't yet total enough to grant her access to everything he thought.

So when he burst in saying "They're abandoning us. They're leaving us, and they're leaving the Cult armed with the greatest weapon on the planet," she was a little lost.

"You're going to have to back up a little and unpack that for me," she said.

"I met with my contact just a little while ago," Jürgen said. "The one who gave me the case that was going to involve finally taking down the Cult. She told me that I would no longer be paid because there was no longer any client base interested in recovering their missing person. And there is no longer a client base because the clients, the Equatorians of this colony at large, are fleeing the planet beginning tomorrow."

Giana sensed he was not used to speaking so much at once, so she cut in to give him time to order his thoughts.

"Fleeing the planet? On their Bridge? This is because of our arrival?" She did not like having to throw out educated guesses. This was a level of uncertainty she associated with her past self, before she'd been transformed and improved upon. It was an unpleasant sensation to say the least.

"Not the Bridge. Ours doesn't function anymore. They've been building a colony ship in orbit for some time. It will set out on a course to a relatively nearby system with, we are led to believe, a much more hospitable planet. The official story has always been that a portion of our leaders would go, as well as a lottery-selected segment of the population, to found a colony. Now they are leaving early—and yes, that is because of you—and I have been informed that the official story was always a lie, and they intend to bring only the wealthiest and most powerful and a set of individuals designed to be their servants in the new colony."

Interesting. This could work very much in Giana's favor. A

power vacuum was exactly the sort of unbridled chaos she sought. But though this would surely seem a betrayal to Jürgen, it didn't explain the full extent of the agitation she'd so effectively harnessed.

"Up until now, you've expressed nothing but support for the will of your self-proclaimed leaders. Why has this action, separate from any other, turned you against them?"

"Because I believed they were like us deep down, but I have been disabused of that notion." Based on the bitterness of his tone, this occurred in the most brutal way possible. "Not a one of them serves as a host to the Harmony symbiont. Not a one! Do you understand what this means?"

"That they rely upon their lessers to be bound by the organism's governing characteristics while feeling no such guiding hand themselves." Giana understood a great deal more now with this revelation, but that was not for him to concern himself with.

"Yes!" His tone was almost grateful, as though she'd distilled a complex storm of emotions down to an easily digestible nugget.

"How does it work, precisely? Harmony, I mean. Through these points here?" She held up the blood-soaked parasite she'd been examining when he came in, indicating the ends of tendrils that seemed to become portions of the human brain. She watched the war play out across his face. This was a risk, but she judged it a necessary one. It was one thing to command his attention to ignore the carnage splayed out on the bed behind her. It was another to actively draw his attention to it and try to manage his reaction. If it turned out she couldn't control his response, she would have to kill him and start again, and that would be a lot of energy wasted.

Energy she couldn't really replace at this point.

"That is Ayana, the owner of this boarding house," Jürgen said, as if he were introducing the corpse to Giana. He kept vacillating between frowning and smooth-faced curiosity, as though he was fighting his desire to be upset and angry over what he saw.

In reality, of course, it was Giana that was doing the fighting. And having opened up yet another mental front in the private war she was waging upon this world, it was *exhausting*.

"What have you done with her?" Jürgen asked.

"She attacked me," Giana said. This was a lie. Harmony parasite or not, the woman had apparently decided that she couldn't afford to keep Marri and Giana around, gobbling up every gram of organic food she could procure. She'd shown up in their room just a short while ago, intent, she'd claimed, on ousting them. Giana had objected. Strenuously. "I defended myself."

Once it was over—just a few minutes ago, curse the timing—Giana had figured she might as well make use of an opportunity and had pulled the Harmony creature from the woman's flensed-open head. Ayana's ruined corpse was currently draining every fluid it possessed—a mixture of blood and lubricants—into Giana's mattress.

The whole affair was very awkward in several ways, but at least it gave Giana her first decent look at the worm these people willingly put into their brains. Her doppelganger on the other side of the planet had provided valuable intel and more, but this was something Giana needed to see up close.

"Such violence seems . . . unlike her." Here Jürgen wavered, teetering toward the truth of matters. Giana firmed her grip as hard as she dared. "But . . . I trust you," Jürgen said after a few final moments of battle played out across his face.

It was a test passed, if not precisely with flying colors. Yet.

"Yes," Jürgen said, as he answered her original question. "The creature's legs are its connection points in the brain. Those lobes as well." He visibly calmed as his gaze skidded away from the tableau before him, and he settled back into his own concerns. "As I told you the other day, I've done my best to live as I believed the organism would have had me live, but I know I haven't been perfect."

She felt his anger return, but it was the righteous kind he'd been directing toward the Equatorians. Far from quash it, Giana actively enflamed it.

"And then," he said, "I learn that not only does every single one of the most powerful people on Anaranjado lack Harmony entirely, but they *glory* in how its lack elevates them above the rest of us, how it makes us into useful tools."

So there it was. The overriding emotional lever of Jürgen Fennec's life was but a tool used by a group so powerful and above consequence that they considered anyone still bound by it to be a dupe. Giana could feel the depth of his pain. It reminded her of the way she had once felt when she'd worked for Stefani while trying to hide her former connection to Gene Sequencing.

"That must have been very hard to hear," she said. Jürgen's sigh of agreement was almost a sob.

Yes, there was a great deal Giana could do on this world. But there was more still to unpack.

"You mentioned these Equatorians leaving the Cult a weapon."

"Yes." He all but spat the word. "The man they kidnapped is no ordinary citizen. The Colonial Science Directorate was studying him, and more specifically his symbiont, which is aberrant and exhibited traits once thought impossible."

"Such as?"

"The ability to stably mutate," Jürgen said. "When Dr. León designed the organism, she understood the risk mutation would pose. Any deviation from her design might compromise the integrity of her so-named Grand Project, turning humanity's greatest asset into a massive liability, dividing us further instead of uniting us. So, she designed the symbiont to be hardened against mutation, extremely resistant to DNA transcription errors. In the event errors slipped through anyway, they would trigger a catastrophic immune system response which would instantaneously kill the creature, preventing any chance of its aberrant genome carrying forward and forming a deviant strain. Stable mutation was therefore supposed to be mathematically impossible."

"And yet, apparently not." Giana thought she saw where this was going, and it made her exhausted mind want to dance with glee.

"This man's organism supposedly defies the odds. And for the entirety of his artificially extended life, the Equatorians have been extracting these mutations and employing them in symbionts all over this colony as ways to keep us fractious and incapable of ever uniting against them. A kind of disharmony within Harmony. It's why the Cult exists at all! Their own symbionts possess mutations more rebellious than others present in the colony. She told me they were an experiment, one that went wrong. They are the most extreme example, but there are other, lesser divisions everywhere in Anaranjado."

"This explains their existence," Giana said. "But what does the Cult want with this man?"

"They somehow got wind of his existence and contrived to steal him from the Colonial Science Directorate. They believe they can make use of him to find a way to remove the organisms from us forever—or perhaps some other, even more awful thing." Jürgen's face was as grim as his various prostheses allowed him to appear. "I need your help, yours and Marri's, to make sure the Cult's plan fails. Where is Marri?"

"I hate to be the bearer of repeat news," Giana said, "but she has done her usual vanishing trick. But I do have some idea where she might have gone."

Even with as gifted a mimic as Giana was, it was difficult to keep her face a grim mirror to Jürgen's when she had never been so happy.

CHAPTER 49

IN HER DROWSY STATE, Marri only really felt alarm when the restraints snapped into place around her wrists and ankles. Then the fear came, not just of the restraints, but of why it had taken her until that moment to feel it.

They did something to me. Drugged me. There was a memory, a bright, cold pinch in her neck, but it was too slippery to grasp.

"I am sorry, child. But we must take precautions. What we offer you is a gift. But we cannot allow you to refuse this gift. You have seen much of what we do down here. You lack a parasite, and that is a blessing. What we will begin now will ensure that never changes."

Marri almost gagged with the words, or maybe with whatever the mechanical man had slipped her. "I don't want any gifts!" Her voice was a croak.

"Child, I cannot in good conscience leave you with this vulnerability. You are special. So very special. How many people do you think materialize before us out of thin air and in the midst of a meeting called to challenge my very leadership? Me, the only one capable of guiding our order through this crisis. And then, you bring me the very information I need to defeat this challenge! The others were false leads. I see that now. Tests of our faith. The Prophet is no longer with us, but he was quite clear. It was we who failed to listen." Mathieu leaned in close, and Marri nearly gagged again, this time on the formaldehyde fumes wafting up from him.

"We tried it first with Jürgen. Perhaps, fumbling as we were with a troubled boy and an entrenched parasite, we were always doomed to sour him against us. It may be that was the parasite's final blow, a lashing out against us in revenge. You must understand, we had no idea there were any alternatives. But then she approached us—the woman Bell Beauregard. She wanted, more than anything, to have her mind replaced by a perfect synthetic copy. And, by some miracle, *she had no parasite.* It was providence. She asked specifically for what we offered. And though she ran off in the end instead of staying with us to be our proof we could show to this world, that doesn't take away from the fact that we succeeded!"

"Please just let me go!" Marri sobbed the words.

"That success is why you needn't fear," he said, ignoring her plea, his slumped-open mouth failing to move with the words, which was somehow even worse. "It is your mind we look to transform. Not your body. You won't be like us. It is people's minds that are enslaved."

"L-let me g-go," Marri said, tears leaking from her eyes in a steady stream.

"You needn't fear," Mathieu said again, his voice full of real sympathy despite its electronic harshness. "This first procedure will be the easiest, child. Merely a precaution. A true gift. It will make a perfect digital copy of all the structures comprising your mind, a sort of backup of your very self. This will keep you safe as further procedures replace your organic brain portion by portion with synthetic replacements. You have not yet been cursed with the parasite, child. And once our work on you is done, you never will be. No parasite can survive inside a synthetic brain."

"N-no! Y-you can't!" Despite her terror, Marri's eyes were just growing heavier and heavier. The door opened to admit still more robot-people. It was so cold in this room.

They were going to kill her. Not even meaning to, they were going to kill her.

"I'll h-hy-per-muh-muuuuuu . . ." She couldn't finish the word. She felt drool sliding down her chin.

"You're frightened, child. It's natural. But we have to act now, while your mind is still pure. We can render you immune to Harmony before it has a chance to get inside. It is frightening now, but you will thank me later. This I swear."

"I'm afraid you must leave now, Mathieu," one of the newcomers began. "She's ready for the anesthesia."

"I will see you on the other side, child," Mathieu said with a bow. He withdrew.

Marri tried to hurl curses at him. She tried to transform, to cleave these false doctors in half with her true self. They were afraid of a worm. She would show them a worm to fear! She would . . . But they were sticking something into her arm, pumping cold lead into her veins. The weight dragged her down and down and down.

CHAPTER 50

THEY WAITED AND WATCHED, and three more trams arrived, bearing away three more loads of prisoners. It seemed a monstrously inefficient process to Karl, but the tightness of the canyon and the turnaround point probably made it next to impossible for larger cargo units to make the turn.

Then, in place of a fourth tram came three trams, one right after the other. And they took with them not prisoners, but guards. This time, the warden was apoplectic. Karl saw in his increasingly unhinged demands for explanation a man who knew he was being rendered irrelevant before his own eyes. He wondered if the man had anything to go home to, any life outside his work, and felt a momentary stab of pity.

However different their professions might be, he could at least understand a bit of what the man was going through. It was not easy when you defined yourself by a single thing and then watched that thing get snatched away as you stood by, powerless to stop it.

As the trio of trams left, he ventured his guess. "I'm guessing that's the last we'll see, at least for a little while." They had taken his prisoners and then, reasoning that he didn't need as many guards with so many fewer prisoners, had taken a great deal of guards as well. To what end, Karl couldn't guess except it had something to do with shuttles, which implied travel elsewhere on the planet or up into orbit. He supposed the guards could be meant to bolster forces to resist the Coldgardeners, but then why take the prisoners too?

"I think my former lance commander is right," Iaz said. Karl didn't let her see his gritted teeth. She seemed unable to stop herself from twisting that knife. Maybe Iazmaena had truly been that angry at him when she'd died, and the feeling had carried over. Or maybe this Iaz was just a sadist. Maybe both.

"Time to move on then?" Stefani ventured.

"The opposite," Iaz said.

"What do you mean?" Karl's annoyance was forgotten, alarm taking its place.

"She wants to capture the facility," Giana said, regarding Iaz with a knowing look.

"We need shelter," Iaz said, not bothering to deny it. "And I'm not talking about a crack in a canyon wall. I mean a place to rest and regroup and plan. And we just watched this facility get emptied out of both prisoners and guards. It will have food and space to spare. And if these people live there, it will have any kind of facility we might need, at least to a limited degree. Best of all, they've got a skeleton crew protecting it. We just saw them haul off three-dozen guards."

"So they have three-dozen fewer guards," Karl said. "But three-dozen fewer than what? We have no idea what the starting number is, and that's crucial to know before we march in there with a mind to capture it. It also seems to have the attention of some very powerful people." He thought it ludicrous that he even had to bring that up, but apparently, he did.

"Had," Iaz said. "Whatever they are doing with those prisoners, they are in a hurry to be done with it, and like *you* said, I think we just saw that play out."

Had Karl realized this was what Iaz was thinking, he'd never have opened his mouth.

"Plus," Iaz said, capitalizing on her momentum, "we have good reason to believe that they are only packing these guns meant to disable electronics. And we have Karl's story about how ineffective they were against him."

"Stop quoting me to justify your crazy plan."

Stefani spoke up. "They definitely have a weapon that works against us. I saw it with my own eyes. It turned a native inside out in the town I arrived in, and they threatened to do worse if they met any resistance."

Iaz frowned. "You only saw it used the once?"

"It was a very compelling argument not to resist, so yes," Stefani said.

Iaz brushed the worry aside with a hand gesture. "If it was widespread or easily deployed, they'd have used it against us when we captured the detention facility. Instead, they ran. Which means whatever they used against you, it's not something they have just lying around everywhere."

"There's no way we can know that," Karl said.

"I agree with Karl," Stefani said. "And even if you're right, even if this works, what would we gain from it?"

"A better question, Steffi, is what your alternative plan is? Because right now we are just wandering nomads on a planet we don't know. If they can deploy this weapon you're so afraid of from this prison, they can use it on us anywhere. At least if we took control of that facility, we'd have a defensible position."

It was, irritatingly, her first good point.

"And, since I'm listing all the pros of my plan, let me point out that I have sixteen full revenants who only take orders from me. And if you don't like my plan, you are free to go slink off somewhere else. Without us."

"I think she has us there," Giana said.

Aggravating as it was, Karl was forced to agree.

"Something else, then," Stefani said, sounding as though she was trying to play peacemaker. She looked to Giana. "Can you, you know, change any of them? Co-opt them?"

Karl gritted his teeth but said nothing.

"I thought I'd be able to," Giana said. "I took some fairly extreme steps to get to the point where I could, in fact." Karl pointedly avoided looking at her. "But that parasite in their brain blocks me from establishing control. I could disable them, yes, but not flip them to our side." She returned Stefani's gaze. "What about you and Iazmaena?"

"We can only convincingly transform into ones we eat, remember?" Stefani said. "And even if I wanted another personality, I don't fancy finding out what eating a living parasite might do to me. You became Giana. Can't you become one of the guards?"

"Like I told you in Coldgarden, I didn't *become* Giana. I *am* Giana. You consume and replace. The original Stefani Palmieri and Iazmaena Delgassi are dead. You replace people. We transform them, and I just told you I can't do that with these people. Not ones with a working parasite anyway."

"This is all wrong," Karl said abruptly. The words were as much of a surprise to him as anyone. They had burst out of him on a wave of pressure he hadn't realized had been building in his mind until the moment the dam had failed.

But they brought the conversation to a screeching halt.

CHAPTER 51

"YOU WISH to add something to the discussion, Lance Commander?" Iazmaena asked, a bemused smile on her face.

"Just this. What are we fighting for?" Karl asked simply.

"Our lives," Iazmaena said, as though he were an idiot.

"Not good enough," Karl said. "Every creature fights for its life. The problem with fighting for your life is you can only stop doing it when you're dead."

"Yes. That's kind of how life works, Karl," Iazmaena said.

"It may be how life works, but if we ever want to stop scratching and clawing, we need something more than mere survival. Why you fight is every bit as important as the fact that you fight. Why you fight tells you when it's okay to stop fighting."

"What are you saying?" Stefani's question did not sound defensive, so that was a good start. "You spent your life in a military organization. The rest of us haven't. Well, not precisely, anyway," she said, no doubt recalling her own time as a true revenant. Karl decided to make use of that sudden recollection.

"It was no different for you. You all knew you had to get back into the city and rebuild the Bridge to escape the dying planet. That was what you fought for." He gestured at Iazmaena. "The problem came when different factions within your side started prioritizing different goals, goals not everyone agreed with." He spread his arms to encompass the whole group. "That's what we need to forestall right here. Before this even starts. We—and here I mean collectively, our 'peoples'—have been at each other's throats since before any of us were even born. Right now, on this hostile world, we're allies of convenience at best."

Stefani nodded. He could see she was getting where he was going. Iazmaena looked both skeptical and a few moments away from rolling her eyes. Giana, hardest of the three to read, merely watched him intently, her eyes considering.

"What I'm trying to do is to bind us together with something more than convenience," Karl went on. "Otherwise, the moment we've achieved our immediate goal, where our survival isn't in imminent danger, we'll turn on each other, just like we did back in Coldgarden. We need a 'why.' A reason we fight, one that will endure beyond our current circumstances."

"And you have a suggestion," Iazmaena asked. "Or is all this buildup just intended to toss the problem over to us to figure out?"

"I do," Karl said. "But first, tell us about Gene Sequencing. What did you learn about it? Both Iazmaena-you and you-you." Both Iazmaena's memories and the revenant's, in other words.

Iazmaena blinked in surprise, but her mouth quirked in a half-smile. Apparently it was a surprise she liked enough to humor Karl.

"After the Coldgarden native life forms—by which I mean your people, Karl—turned our own weapon against us natural born humans, transformed us, and drove us out into the wilds, the natives took the form of humans. They did it so perfectly that they eventually forgot they'd ever been anything else." She looked to Giana. "One of your gifts, I gather?"

"Not specifically," Giana said. "We gifted them with minds. There was no purpose behind it. We tried endless things at random until something worked, and that was getting them to think about themselves and not about their duty to protect the Host. That our extreme changeability went along with it was unintended. But it manifested itself uniquely in them regardless."

"In any event," Iazmaena said, "some of the members of the former-natives-now-humans in Coldgarden recognized the danger of forgetting their collective non-human past entirely. But they were equally afraid of periodically trying to shock the entire population with the information, particularly as more and more simply forgot. They were afraid of the chaos that could result.

"To avoid that, they formed a small cabal of like minds, determined to preserve the secret and pass it down for all the generations to come. But to ensure that nobody decided to go rogue and start blabbing it everywhere, they could only entrust the secret to those with a strong predisposition to rigid order and obedience to hierarchy. So they created an organization to monitor the entire populace's genetics, identifying and elevating those with those particular markers and predispositions. Thus: Gene Sequencing."

"And the fact that all the people who knew the whole truth tended to be rich and powerful and could take steps to remain that way?" Karl prompted.

"Merely a happy side-effect, I'm sure," Iazmaena said, her smile suddenly all teeth and looking more like a snarl. Though Karl didn't think it was directed at him at least. Clearly this iteration of Iazmaena still retained the original's hatred of the city's ruling cabal.

That was good. Karl had no idea if Iazmaena's story had been a valuable exercise in updating anyone's mistaken assumptions, but that hadn't really been the point. It had been to get them thinking along those lines.

"Thank you, Iazmaena," he said. "Now, let me tell you all another story. One that I'm fairly certain describes this world. They're a colony of Earth, the same as happened on Coldgarden, or New Calgary, or whatever you want to call it. Only there's one major difference."

"Harmony," Stefani said. Everyone nodded grimly at this.

"Precisely." Karl's own tone was grim. He had come closer to knowing Harmony's "embrace" than any of them. "A parasite, symbiont, whatever you want to call it, that supposedly binds humanity together, makes them think more collectively, cooperatively. Have we seen any instances of that?"

"Yes," Giana piped in, surprising Karl. "When I first arrived, the outskirts town we appeared in—Ashrock—was open and welcoming to us in a way that surprised me."

"And what happened once they figured out we were different?"

"I wasn't there for that part," Giana said. "I needed a disruption, an excuse to get my chosen target alone. So I induced one of my kind, already there and in disguise, to attack. We escaped in the chaos." She paused as a brief spasm of agony passed over her face. She sucked in a sharp breath of pain.

"Are you all right?" Stefani asked. She looked as though she only half-meant the concern, not surprising, given what the woman had confessed to.

"Yes," Giana said. "But Karl wants trust, so I am trying to be open. As open as I can be." Again, that wince of pain. Karl frowned but went on.

"And just so we're all on the same page, what did you need the soldier for?"

"A sample of human—*real* human—genetics. As a way to rebuild myself into a version that could affect these people the way I could affect yours. It was quite a *painful* process, and it worked after a fashion, but only on people without that damned parasite, and there seem to be few enough of those." She frowned as she talked, more grimaces of pain and effort, as though the words required some extra *oomph* to speak.

"What I was able to glean from his mind—which wasn't much, as there wasn't much left after I was through with him, was that he wasn't any ordinary soldier. He's connected to the ruling class of this world—the Equatorians, they call themselves—in some intimate way. Close family. Or maybe he was Equatorian himself. I wonder if other Equatorians are like him and lack a parasite."

It was an effort for Karl to keep his jaw closed. This was more candor than he'd expected to get from Giana. Then something she had said sparked in him, and his mind began to race with the implications.

"Anyway," Giana went on, "I got sidetracked there. My impressions were that once they understood we were 'different,' as you say, that hospitality dried up fast."

"Hardly surprising if some of us started eating them."

"Eating each other," Giana said. "One of my duller cousins might attempt to attack a non-Coldgardener, but it wouldn't go well for them. Not unless I'd rewritten it beforehand. Any others like them in the vicinity would be smart enough to take the hint."

"I saw that happen," Stefani said. "It attacked one of the soldiers, turned black, and died. Along with the soldier."

"Occasional incidents aside," Giana went on, nodding, "the population of this world was in no danger from us—though they obviously couldn't know that. And certainly the revenants and Coldgarden natives would pose a threat."

"All right," Karl said. "So maybe wasn't the best example for where I was trying to go with this, but it gave us another valuable piece of information which does help. I don't know about the rest of you, but I've even heard people on this planet—some with real authority—go so far as to say that you are either a human with Harmony or you are not human."

"So have I," Stefani said darkly. "The intelligence officer," she said with a look at Iazmaena.

"Where is all this going?" He was losing Iazmaena.

"We keep hearing you are either a human with Harmony or you are subhuman. Yet we have a group of people—these Equatorians—who Giana believes may be exempt from even having the parasites. And they seem to be the richest and most powerful."

"Oh," Stefani said, eyes suddenly going wide.

"Yes," Karl said, smiling with grim triumph. "This parasite is supposed to bind everyone together as one big happy humanity. But it also sounds like the ruling class lack the parasites entirely. And if anyone without Harmony isn't human, it strikes me as extremely unlikely that the general population is aware of that fact. What if these Equatorians are just using the 'gifts' Harmony bestows to better control the population and keep themselves entrenched in their power and privilege?"

He looked to Iazmaena. She commanded the most raw power here. It was her he had to win over. "If that were true, it would be Gene Sequencing all over again!"

And he saw with triumph that a dangerous light had kindled in those hazel eyes.

"So that's what I propose," Karl said. "That's why we fight. We fight to make sure this world doesn't follow the mistakes of ours. We fight to give the ordinary people of this world a chance to be one people. Or not to be, if that's what they want. They deserve a chance to decide for themselves."

"I don't know," Stefani said. Karl blinked. Of all of them, he was sure she'd side with him. "I understand what you're saying, Karl. But we don't know anything about these people, really. Even if what you say is right, surely going in and smashing up everything based on our own experiences is just asking for trouble."

She looked to Karl, and her eyes were kind and beautiful but painful for the kindness.

"Maybe, for right now, our immediate survival really is enough. And then, once we can get them to listen to us, maybe then we can explain to them our mistakes."

A sense of deflation overtook Karl at the sense of her words. Fearful of what lay beyond the immediate future, determined not to fall into the tunnel vision of the soldier for once, all Karl had wanted was a way to keep them all bound together past the current crisis. A means to overcome their past hatreds and permanently bridge the gulfs between them. But now, with Stefani's words, Karl realized he had simply been trying to replace one enemy with another.

Here he stood, his hip restored to him, his family partially reassembled. Trying to look to a future that wasn't a succession of disasters. He wanted a purpose. Something he hadn't had since he lost his position in the lancers. He had loved ones to protect, it was true. Yet they were far more likely to protect him than he was them.

It meant that, despite all the changes, the loss of his entire world, his entire identity down to his very humanity, he was left exactly where he'd been eight months ago: adrift, bereft of the one thing that had given his life meaning.

He had no place. Not in this world. Nor, it seemed likely, in any other.

CHAPTER 52

SHE WOKE to a pain deep within her head, but she woke. Marri grabbed at the back of her skull by reflex, only to be shocked to full awareness by the sudden spike of agony ramming its way through her brain.

I'm alive, she thought in genuine shock. *How did I not hypermutate?*

Because you know what you are. The voice, though strangely familiar in a way Marri couldn't place, felt separate from her. *Acknowledging the truth was all it ever required to free you from that threat.*

She couldn't stop attempting to probe the pain in her head as she pondered this.

"You mustn't disturb the surgical site." This second voice was real, not a voice in Marri's head. It was feminine despite its electronic register. "Doctor! She's awake."

"Welcome back, young miss." A third voice, also real, also female sounding. "You did very well despite some . . . irregularities with your vitals. I would very much like to study your readings further, with your permission of course."

Marri opened her eyes groggily and tried to lash out, to cut the robo-woman off—literally. She flexed whatever mental muscle allowed her to transform, but nothing happened except a sense of unseen pressure exerting itself over her entire body, as though physically holding her in her current shape.

No. Oh no. Whatever they had done, they had broken her. She couldn't change. That meant she couldn't defend herself.

She couldn't escape.

"Young Miss, are you all right?" The doctor sounded concerned now. "You mustn't exert yourself. You're still on quite a bit of sedation."

Sedation. They had her drugged still. Maybe that was why she couldn't transform. If so, it would still be all right. They couldn't keep her sedated forever. Why keep her alive at all if that was the plan?

"The new hardware in your brain will take a bit of time to fully copy over the data structures into its storage medium," the first doctor said. "It has its own internal power source—one that requires no energy from you. But simply having a foreign object surgically implanted is an exhausting process. You need to keep calm and rest while you recover, and the copying process can begin. Once you are safely backed up and recovered, we can proceed. But you have to stay calm."

That was almost funny because Marri felt anything but calm, and the doctor sounded anything but calm. She sounded a touch frantic, to be honest. As though Marri was like nothing she'd expected.

Because you're not really human, even though they don't know that. Whatever you do, you mustn't tell them. This new voice in Marri's head, oddly familiar and alien-feeling though it was, at least gave good advice. That probably meant it had nothing to do with what these crazy cultists had done to her, but it was impossible to rule anything out, particularly when she could barely rub two thoughts together.

"Her heart rate is climbing rapidly," said another voice from out of Marri's field of view. "The sedation doesn't seem to be working as it should."

"A few generations on another world, and it's like these people have a totally different biology," the doctor said, sounding simultaneously annoyed and fascinated. "Very well. Young Miss, I'm very sorry, but you really must rest. There is already a required recovery period before we can begin the rest of your surgeries, and you don't want to have to stretch that out any longer than need be."

More surgeries? No matter what the random voices in her head told her, Marri knew it was a miracle she'd even survived the one. They were going to keep carving her open and replacing parts of her brain—that was what Mathieu had said, and Marri had no reason to doubt him—until she died.

"The sedation isn't working to calm you," the doctor said, "so we're going to have to put you under fully, because we know that worked at least."

One of them was approaching. Marri tried to fight, tried to resist the piercing cold, but once again it filled her veins, and once again, it dragged her into the abyss between the stars.

CHAPTER 53

THEY MUST HAVE KEPT RIGHT on planning without Karl, because it was a long time before anyone came looking for him.

"Are you all right?" Stefani's voice reached out to Karl from the darkness. He'd retreated to the deepest part of the pinched little cave where light could still reach. "That was quite a speech back there, and I have the distinct impression I'm the one that ruined it."

Karl chuckled. Stefani was little more than a dimly backlit outline. "There was apparently a lot I needed to get off my chest. Not just from the last couple of days either. To be perfectly honest, I've felt adrift ever since Graysteel ejected me from the lancers."

"Surely not?" Stefani said. "I hadn't noticed at all." She made the words light. It was the way she'd always talked when he was brooding and she was trying to burst that bubble he put around himself in those moods. But she sounded unsure, as though she feared he might react badly this time.

But he was definitely brooding, and the memory made him laugh. "I suppose it's not exactly a secret. And I will say, it's nice to discuss a portion of our shared history where you were actually *this* you."

"Karl, most of our shared history is that way. Very nearly all of it."

"I suppose so," he said. Somehow, in all the revelations of the past few days, that truth hadn't really sunk in with him until this moment. "It's just difficult to forget that I thought otherwise all that time."

"I know you want a purpose, Karl. Something more meaningful than skidding from one disaster to another. But self-actualization is all the way at the top of the hierarchy of needs, and if we're ever going to have a chance to get back to those lofty heights, we need to get through what's right in front of us."

"I know," Karl said. This was yet another revelation. "I think you and Iaz—*this* you and *this* Iaz, I mean—have a leg up on me. Even Marri does." He hoped she did. He hoped she was all right. "Even fighting to defend the city from, well . . ." He almost said *monsters* and only just stopped himself. "Fighting to defend it from you all, I mean. Even doing that wasn't as dire as what you were struggling for. Marri too. Maybe I was self-actualized that whole time and was too wrapped up in the dangers to realize it."

"Maybe . . ."

"All right, lovebirds," Iazmaena strode up to interrupt their companionable silence. "Based on our schedule, our trap should be set and wound. It's time to get this show on the road before our luck at staying hidden runs out." She looked to Karl. "You ready to join us, or are you still feeling sorry for yourself?"

"Well, it would help if someone would explain to me what's going on."

"You and Giana will be the bait. Prisoners to a group of my revenants that have adopted the crude forms of some of these Anaranjadan soldiers."

"How convincing are we talking for these disguises?" To Karl's recollection, revenants trying to look like humans they hadn't specifically consumed looked pretty fake. The one impersonating Damon, Iazmaena's deceased ex, in the archon's office all those months ago had been off-putting as hell, even from behind.

"Good enough to fool people far away, probably not good enough to fool them up close. But it won't have to fool them for long. Remember the way they ambushed you, disguised as sections of tunnel wall? Well, that's what the others will be doing. They've been slowly easing their way up the cut in the rock that leads to the prison, holding their stone disguises and sliding slowly enough to hopefully avoid notice. You and Giana will be marched up to the prison. If they let you in, great. You'll already be past the walls when the fighting starts. If they send someone to meet you, our ambush will take them out before they can figure out the trick."

"And if something in between those things happens?" Karl asked dryly.

"We wing it," Iazmaena shrugged. "Regardless, if all goes well, we'll hit them so hard and so fast, they won't have time to send for backup or deploy any mystery weapons. So I'll ask again. Ready to do your part?"

He almost scoffed, but that would get him nowhere, so he stood instead. After all, if Iazmaena wanted two prisoners, and Giana was one, Karl refusing would just mean Stefani was the next person called to serve. "Ready as I'm likely to be," he said. In truth, his stomach was turning over. He hadn't seen real combat in more than eight months. At least, not that he'd had time to mentally prepare for. Escaping the medical facility the other day hadn't really counted by that metric.

In those eight months, he'd gotten used to thinking of himself as compromised physically, but that change had apparently seeped into every other aspect of his self-regard too. He bobbed up and down, flexing his hips to prove to himself they didn't hurt.

"Something else you needed to add?" Iazmaena raised an eyebrow.

"Just wish I had a lance is all."

Iazmaena scowled, then smiled wickedly. "You'll be having to fight the old-fashioned way today. Our way. With claws."

Karl reflected that it would have been smarter, perhaps, to say he wished they'd managed to capture any Anaranjadan weapons. Too late now.

"Yes, well, I expect your friends up there will be able to handle things without too much help from little old me."

"Or I could tell them to hold back and let you take point," Iazmaena said with sadistic pleasure.

"You've made your point," Karl said, raising placating hands. Whether accidentally or on purpose, Iazmaena seemed to remember she was a revenant more than Stefani did. He would do well to remember that himself.

"Then get going. Giana is already waiting with the others."

CHAPTER 54

GIANA AND KARL did their best to act like cowed prisoners despite the awkward movements of their disguised revenant captors who formed a phalanx around them. The revenant-militia, for their part, were playing up that awkwardness even more than was strictly necessary, trying to look like a group of wounded soldiers.

Thankfully, a pair of angled conveyor belts, one in each direction, were their main means up the cut to the facility. Karl wasn't entirely convinced the revenants—so ungainly in their pretend human forms—could have handled stairs cut into the rock. Karl supposed that only made sense. Stairs, though easier to maintain, would have made the delivery of supplies much more difficult, unless some separate entrance existed.

Karl stepped onto the right-side conveyer belt begrudgingly when his turn came. It had been still at their approach but had begun moving the moment one of the revenants set foot on it. The belt moved Karl along, its operation whisper quiet. He tried to keep his gaze ahead and down. He was beaten, defeated, a prisoner. He was not scanning the walls, trying to identify which angled juts of stone were actually his hidden, nightmarish allies.

They reached a kind of landing, a flat place on the path where there was a bend in the cut leading up. As such, there was a patch a few meters across between where the current belt ended and a new one began, heading up and to the left.

As the revenant-militia led the way toward the second conveyor, a cage door suddenly sprang to life, extending from a concealed slot in the canyon wall. For an instant, Karl knew if he turned, he would see a similar one enclosing them from behind, and that they were trapped.

It's fine, he told himself without any real conviction.

"Attention visitors." The voice boomed from some loudspeaker Karl couldn't see. "You are unannounced and therefore not approved for entry without inspection. Stand by."

As if on cue, one of the belts up ahead started moving, the one which would carry people down from the facility. Karl's party waited with, at least from his perspective, barely concealed impatience. Knowing they were monitored, he tried even harder to resist scanning the walls.

At last, a contingent of guards arrived. Figuring it was safely in-character to be fixated on them, Karl studied them as best as he was able. They numbered an even dozen—outnumbering the revenant-militia three to one, in other words. They carried an assortment of weaponry, both traditional projectile weapons and the stun guns they seemed to prefer here. He hoped none of these was the mystery weapon Stefani had described.

"State your name, rank, and business here," the woman in the lead demanded of Karl and Giana's escort. The woman stood a preposterous two and a half meters tall with close cropped hair as black as the scales which decorated her face. Karl couldn't help but tense. Any attempt to question the revenants was not going to last very long. He remembered how rough the speech of the Damon-revenant had been, what little he'd heard of it.

He had to fight down a cringe as one of their escort opened "her" mouth. "Help . . . please." It wasn't as bad as he'd feared. The words had been tortured, yes, but considering the battered state the revenants were pretending to be in, maybe garbled speech would be believable.

"Please. Help . . . us." To complete the false picture, the revenant sagged to its knees, but not so fast and hard that its mass would be obvious.

Karl would never know for certain if the ruse would have worked on him. But he was still surprised when the lead guard abandoned all the stated protocols and barked an order.

"Open the gate!"

Her eyes radiated concern.

Harmony. The oneness of the brain bug, that overwhelming concern for those deemed their fellows, might just be overriding suspicion and granting them the opening they needed. He found he had to stifle an urge to call out a warning to her and her people.

These were revenants!

They were also his allies.

The barred gate slid back into its invisible housing within the cliff face, and that was the moment the walls to either side of the landing came to scuttling life.

Karl had to hand it to the creatures. They were patient beyond all reason. Even knowing what to look for, the trick worked on him a second time. What had appeared to be flat stone spiked outward at odd angles, morphing smoothly into revenants which sprang, bearing prison guards to the ground with their full weight.

"Ambush! Ambush! Am—" But the leader of the inspection team never finished that second repetition. A revenant speared her through with both foreclaws then spread the limbs wide, ripping the guard in two in a spray of blood and a clatter of synthetic parts. Karl's stomach turned in both revulsion and remembered trauma. That was a favorite trick of the creatures. It served as both an effective way to instantly and completely remove a lancer from the battle and as a weapon of terror all on its own.

Karl expected to have to fight himself shortly, but the militia-revenants serving as his and Giana's escort held their forms, and so

Karl did his best to look dumbfounded. It didn't require much faking. He supposed this was the winging it Iazmaena had mentioned.

The inspection team guards, those who hadn't been fatally skewered in the first strike, now attempted to form ranks and push back the sudden attack. The air crackled with discharges of electricity and stone chips rained from the sheer rock walls as bullets flew. But Karl knew better than most that revenant armor was proof against normal projectile weapons.

As he'd already lamented, there were no lances here.

"Come on, hurry!" A young man, one of the guards having a profound misunderstanding of the situation, was beckoning to Karl and Giana, urging them to approach. Amazingly, the deception was holding. And, as he did a hasty count, Karl realized that not all the rock-wall revenants had revealed themselves. Some were holding back.

Gods below, we might actually be ushered inside. Maybe they were not winging it after all. Iazmaena's orders to the ambush revenants must have been nuanced. They needed to attack, but not be so devastating that they wipe out the entire contingent and make the facility go into lockdown. Some of them had held back, and even the ones fighting now were putting up a good show that the guards were successfully holding them at bay with weapons Karl knew wouldn't really hurt them.

Playing with their food.

It made Karl feel suddenly sick, but his escort allowed him no time for that. The nearest soldier grabbed him by the arm and hauled him forward so hard it nearly spoiled the pretense that he was manacled.

The "militia" formed a protective shield around himself and Giana as they stepped onto the conveyor. Someone had dialed it up to maximum speed at some point, because Karl nearly lost his footing as it began speeding them up and away from the fighting. Karl hastily tried reassessing Iazmaena's plan with the new information he now possessed.

With their guests safely cleared of suspicion and on the way up, the remainder of the revenants would be making their appearances from the walls about now. They would proceed to slaughter the guards, who very shortly would realize they were not making the valiant stand they thought they'd been.

Once Karl and the others made it inside the facility, they would undoubtedly commence an attack of their own, seizing control of a foothold including the entryway. This would enable the more numerous revenants down below, fresh from their slaughter of the guard contingent, a safe path to enter the facility themselves and reinforce Karl's groups numbers.

From there, unless the prison guards were hiding weapons like the one Stefani had seen used, resistance would be unlikely to hold out for long. Iazmaena wanted the facility, not the people inside it. Fighting revenants was always overwhelming the first time, even if you knew what to expect. And these people had no idea what to expect. Revenants didn't take prisoners; they took meals.

It was just that their victims didn't need to be dead to be eaten.

Beyond the final stretch of conveyor, a heavy door loomed ahead beneath a portion of the facility which jutted out to form an overhang and a sunshield both. Karl half-hoped there would be some security check here, something to stop them. He didn't want to die, didn't want his side to be robbed of its might. But a part of him wanted to be forced into a bloodless retreat.

Not that small of a part either.

But there was no check. On the contrary, the doors opened so fast they appeared to be in a hurry. Which he supposed they were, since if the guards below retained any comms, the facility would know worse was coming soon.

A new pair of guards appeared in the now-open door.

"Inside!" they ordered. "Right the fuck now."

The grip on Karl's arm was absolute. Even if he'd wanted to disobey, he wouldn't have been able to. Not unless he transformed and gave the whole game away. And he found, to his shame, that he wasn't willing to do that. Not even to save humans from revenants.

Because I'm not human either. It sounded almost like a wail of despair inside his head. He wasn't human. For the moment, these people were his enemy. They had decided as much themselves, because he didn't have a bug in his brain. So maybe they weren't human either.

The trouble was every time he told himself these things—*I'm not human. They're not human*—it didn't really help. He knew all about what he wasn't. But even with the great, dead being at the center of his planet explaining it to him, he still didn't know what he was.

Or maybe more important, as he'd tried in vain to explain to Stefani, he didn't know *why* he was.

CHAPTER 55

JÜRGEN APPROACHED the Cult's hermitage, where Ms. Novak claimed that, once again, Marri had found herself trapped. He had no idea how the woman could know that, either now or the first time, but he found he did not care. There was more reason than ever to fight his way in and deal out as much death as possible.

In the end, there was no other way to ensure that the threat the Cult posed was eliminated for good. There would shortly be no more Equatorians to help contain them. Either Jürgen ended them here, or he would die and they would endure.

Despite her fervent wishes otherwise, Ms. Novak had been too ill to join and had been forced to stay behind. Jürgen felt this should have concerned him more than it did. He had, after all, caught a brief glimpse of what Marri could do in his security footage. Giana could presumably transform herself the same way. But a fighter who could barely move was more hindrance than help, and anyway, some part of him, some pillar of newfound strength, whispered that it would be all right.

There was a different part of him, small but insistent, that still regretted what he was about to do. He'd believed these creatures to be his friends once. It was that part of him that held his breath as he jacked into the door's maintenance node with his multi-tool and triggered his usual override sequence.

Maybe this once it would not work. Maybe he would be spared even the option to do this.

But the door opened, as it always did. As he'd known it would, thanks to Mathieu's eternal and misplaced optimism. His former brothers and sisters welcoming him home. Welcoming death into their midst.

Jürgen drew his weapon, double-checking that it was dialed to the maximum possible setting.

The alarms triggered upon his entry, as they always did. But the Cultists were used to this by now. The blatting speakers strewn throughout the complex might as well have been shouting "wolf!" for all the effect they would have on the population here.

"My boy, why must we play these—oh!" Mathieu stepped in from the side corridor that led to the sleeping chambers, if anything these creatures did could really be called sleep. He wasn't wearing his skinsuit, but even aside from the voice, each of their mechanical faces was as unique as a human face would have been, so it was impossible to miss him.

"Jürgen Fennec, why are you pointing a weapon at me?"

Jürgen did not engage with his former mentor. He simply took aim and fired at center of mass. Right where the power cell keeping the man's body functional and powering the oxygen and nutrient pumps that kept his organic brain alive would be.

Mathieu dropped with an electronic squawk, going as limp as machinery could go as he thudded to the ground, dead. Or, no. At the setting Jürgen had used, the man's form ought to be popping, smoking, sparking. None of that happened though. Jürgen checked the setting again as he strode by. It was set to the minimum level necessary to temporarily disable a fully synthetic Cultist.

How had that happened?

He really ought to turn around. Really ought to finish the job, make sure he used this chance, this de facto writ of execution, to its absolute fullest. He had to end the threat once and for all. But all he could think about was Ms. Novak's burning palm upon his cheek, as though the mere memory of its pressure turned his head toward more important tasks further in. He walked on.

He reset the weapon to lethal levels, however. He would not make that mistake again.

CHAPTER 56

IAZMAENA'S RUSE didn't last past the prison's vestibule. Karl watched as the four revenant-militia plus Giana all dropped their disguises the moment they were all sealed in, and the panicked guards—a mere skeleton crew, just as Iazmaena had predicted—never stood a chance. Within seconds, the revenants were fully in their element, and Karl had been cast back firmly into the past.

For as long as he'd been a lancer, there had been sporadic action against the revenants. If the creatures didn't bring the fight to them, the lancers brought the fight to the creatures. The stated reason for the latter had been to keep a clear space in Coldgarden's immediate vicinity, but it hadn't taken long for Karl to intuit the truth: lancers needed to see real action, or they were next to useless in the event of a true incursion.

Fat lot of good all that preparation had done in the end.

Regardless, it had been in one of those excursions, in the shadow of the city wall, that Karl had received his first real taste of the deep terror that accompanied certain death. A group of revenants had been misreported, their real numbers three times as great as what was called in, and the lancer squad found themselves massively outnumbered instead of the other way around.

A young Lance Corporal Karl Yonnel had been among the few to board the flier uninjured. They'd left a field of blood and corpses squirming with hypermutation in their wake.

But the prison was, in its own way, worse. Inexperience could rob any fighting force of its advantages, but at least lancers possessed the tools to get the job done. These prison guards had been trained to quell riots by cybernetic inmates, not to fight organic, shape-shifting horrors from beyond the stars.

Abruptly, Karl found himself pushed to one side, shoved against the wall by the glowing, squirming mass that was Giana Novak. He thought for a few vague, empty instants that she had turned on him, meant to finally be rid of him. But her voice emanated from somewhere in that glowing, over-jointed mass.

"Stay out of the way if you aren't going to fight."

As she moved away, Karl could not help but absently note that, bizarre and uncanny as her true form was, it still looked somewhat more human in overall shape than he recalled from their fight in the Bridge observation tower back on Coldgarden. That, plus the note of kind concern in her voice, gave him a moment's respite from his trauma. Then she darted back into the fray.

It was a massacre. All Iazmaena's scheming seemed like so much sadism when seen in the light of how ineffectual the guards were. The only relief Karl could find in watching humans, even augmented humans, being slaughtered by the monsters of his city's nightmares was that his input was clearly not required.

Unwise as it might be, he fled from the fighting, deeper into the prison. His vision tunneled as his breathing labored. His limbs felt like water. He just wanted to curl into a ball or go look for a lance. *They are your allies. Your allies!* But there was a part of him buried far deeper than logic that told him that wasn't true, because it couldn't be.

It was the first time he really understood how much this pressure had been building within him, how much he'd been lying to himself about how far he was prepared to change his worldview.

He banged on every door he passed, unsure whether these were offices or cells, just trying to get one to open for him so he could wait it out, collect and rebuild himself into someone who wouldn't have utterly failed Stefani the way he had.

Karl had lost count of the number of doors he'd ineffectually slapped when a voice cried out from behind one in answer.

"Go away! Get out of here, monsters." The man's muffled voice was so shrill with panic Karl was surprised he could form coherent sentences. Karl was staring dumbly at the door as though trying to formulate a response when it opened, and two guards surged out.

Maybe it was the fact that no revenants were present. Or maybe feeling he was personally in mortal danger overcame all the anxiety riffling through his thoughts. Regardless, Karl had transformed before he even realized it. Two shots, one of each weapon type, whizzed through the place where his head no longer was. He slashed out once with each claw, and each dropped one of the guards, leaving one bleeding and one sparking. Then Karl was himself again.

His flowmatter jumpsuit had barely had time to tear and reshape itself around him.

Karl both recoiled from the injured—especially the bleeder—and wanted to help them. But he had a mission to complete, one he had failed utterly so far. So he forced himself to study the room beyond.

It was clearly the office of someone important. And since he recognized the man cowering in the corner farthest from the door from all their reconnaissance, Karl reasoned out that this was the warden's office.

"Director," he said, trying to work moisture back into his throat so he didn't talk like a desiccated corpse. "I'd appreciate it if you surrendered and ordered your people to do likewise."

"What kind of monster are you?" the warden demanded, practically spitting the words.

I wish I knew.

"The only thing they can do now is die for nothing," Karl said.

CHAPTER 57

JÜRGEN KEPT EXPECTING the Cultists to realize he was not playing around and that running and hiding was not going to be sufficient. But they seemed content to merely double down on both, and considering he hadn't managed to kill any yet, perhaps it was a sounder tactic than he realized.

The long hallway Jürgen stared down was not the most direct path to part one of his goal. But the side doorways, each across from the other and the left path of which offered a shorter path, had sealed themselves shut as Jürgen had arrived. The panels for each had then sparked and died. He would not be going either way.

He was just considering whether the end of the straightaway, which opened up into the facility's considerable medical wing, represented the perfect place for him to walk into a trap, when from the right side of that opening stepped Lukas. His hands were raised.

"Do not fire," he said. "Jürgen Fennec, I regret ever bringing you into our confidence, but today, you and I can help each other. You wish the girl back? Well, I want nothing more than to see her gone. Come with me, and I will get you to her safely. Then you can both leave before anything irreparable is done."

That was impossible, of course. Jürgen was not here simply for

Marri. He was not even here for just their kidnapped prisoner with the special Harmony symbiont. Jürgen was here to eliminate the threat.

But given the Cultist's willingness to be helpful, there was no need to disabuse Lukas of his misapprehension just yet.

CHAPTER 58

THE FIGHT DID NOT last long. Stefani knew that intellectually, even if she was a roiling mess inside for worry over Karl. But after what seemed several eternities, despite the lies Iaz's chronometer seemed intent on telling them, one of the revenants came back to their hiding place to report the result: unmitigated success.

Not a single casualty.

Stefani was so delirious with relief she could almost overlook how unsettling it was to realize she could understand the revenant's clicks and claw-taps without any interpretation from Iaz. The fact that doing so felt natural only made it worse.

Clearly, there was still work to do in integrating the many aspects of her personality.

Their revenant escort formed up around the pair of human-seeming women—and the human-seeming baby—and saw them safely up the conveyor belts, past a landing full of twitching, sparking corpses, and up a second set of belts to the prison proper.

They found more of the same inside, though the remaining prisoner population, who had been locked up instead of induced to fight, remained unharmed so far as Stefani could tell. But the warden captured the most attention as he was brought out, alive and unharmed, by a visibly shaken Karl. Stefani's worry flared alight again, an ember fed fresh oxygen, and she scanned him as best she could for obvious injuries. But his expression spoke of a different pain. Something deeper. Internal.

It hit her as he met her eyes then glanced away. *We asked him to fight alongside revenants. He had to watch them tear these people apart.* Karl himself wasn't human, of course. No one in Coldgarden had been, not for a very long time. But that didn't matter. Emotionally, he would surely have still identified with the human defenders standing against the revenant hordes.

It made Stefani sad. It made her angry. Most of all, it riddled her with guilt.

Iaz had eyes only for the warden, and maybe that was for the best.

"Well now," Iaz said, barely able to contain her obvious glee. "We're going to have a nice talk, you and I."

They settled down in an office Stefani gathered did not belong to the warden. Apparently that one was littered with corpses as well.

"You two," the warden said before Iaz could even begin with introductions. "Are you like the man?" He gestured at Karl, looming behind.

"Kind of," Iaz said impishly. Then she shrugged. "The simplest way to describe it is that our ancestors were human colonists until we turned into alien monsters, and his ancestors were a different kind of alien monster until they turned into human colonists."

The warden blinked, so obviously flummoxed he forgot to be defiant or even afraid.

"You're all monsters to me," he said.

"None taken," Iaz said. "But now you're going to tell us everything you know about . . . us."

"What?" If anything, he was even more confused. Stefani was too, a bit.

"By which I mean," Iaz clarified, "tell us every bit of intel you've heard about our arrival."

The man burst out laughing. It was so sudden and unexpected, Stefani flinched. She thought Iaz might have as well by the other woman's scowl.

"You think they tell me anything, those Equatorians? I don't even know why they pulled all my inhabitants and guards away, unless they're secretly in league with you lot." He'd clearly meant it as a joke, but the way his eyes narrowed as he teased the sentence out told Stefani he'd started to wonder by the end.

"We took your prison over *because* they stole all your guards, not the other way around," Iaz said. "We've been watching you for more than a day now. Even overheard your conversations with the militia who came for the prisoners."

"Then you know I know nothing of what's going on."

"You're lying," Iaz said. It was a casual statement. She wasn't mad. Yet. "This facility is clearly important in some way, or why else would it be getting so much military attention when there's a literal invasion going on?"

"Our services may be valuable, but don't be tricked into thinking we are valued here." The bitterness was interesting. It was an attitude Stefani had seen shockingly little of despite how lopsided the living conditions on this world seemed to be.

"Look, we're not these Equatorians' friends. I mean, obviously," Iaz said, gesturing around her as though the office walls told her story for her. "All I'm asking is what you've heard. Maybe you haven't heard anything official." She still sounded skeptical about this. "But surely you've heard rumors. Humor us."

Karl chose that moment to come in. Stefani wondered if he was actually interested in hearing what the warden had to say or just wanted to be away from the revenants and Giana.

"Rumors? You want rumors? Fine, maybe you can make sense of

them. Rumors say you are everywhere. The whole planet is blanketed by you. Utter rubbish. This planet's atmosphere isn't thick enough to support animal life. You may be monstrous freaks, but I've seen you breathe. You came across the Bridge, right?"

"I'm asking the questions here," Iaz said.

Stefani did her best Iaz impression and rolled her eyes. "Yes, we did."

"Then for everything I know about the Bridge, you should have all appeared there. So you tell me. Where are you?"

"Watch it, friend," Iaz said, and now she did not sound so casual. But Stefani, thinking of Marri, did not want this conversational branch to wither up just yet. She sensed Karl's renewed focus as well. His hands found her shoulders and gripped firmly in a way that sent warmth rippling through her. Perversely, thoughts of the girl seemed to strengthen him, where they riddled Stefani with anxiety afresh.

"We didn't all appear in the same place," Stefani said. She pointed to Karl. "He appeared at the Bridge site. I appeared at some entirely different settlement."

"We had another appear at a place called Ashrock," Karl said.

Stefani looked to Iaz. "And I don't even know where she came from."

"And it's going to stay that way," Iaz said, fixing Stefani with a glare. "At least in present company."

The warden was shaking his head in confusion. "But those sites aren't directly adjacent to each other. Ashrock and the Bridge site are hours apart from one another."

"Yes?" Iaz prompted. "Keep talking."

He frowned. "That's all I've got to say. It just seems odd. I don't know how the thing works beyond what any of us are taught as children. But if there were too many of you for the Bridge site to hold, you'd have thought you'd appear somewhere close by. Not scattered all around. But if you appeared there, what's to have stopped you from appearing anywhere on the planet? Or even in it?"

"*In* it?" Iaz's interest was clearly piqued.

"We have plenty of people living deep underground on Shadyside," the warden said. "So even if your Bridge had fail-safes as to where it could and couldn't deposit people regarding their immediate survival, that still doesn't narrow it down. More of the planet holds atmosphere than you'd think for a sunblasted rock like this."

"That still doesn't explain 'in,'" Karl said.

"We stay just below the surface on Sunnyside to beat the heat," the warden said. "But on Shadyside, it's the opposite. The surface is beyond frigid. It never sees the sun. So they've learned to dig deep there, live off the residual heat coming up from the core. The trailhead leading down starts in Meridian Australis, the southernmost of the three Meridian Cities. I've never been there, but they say the poorer you are, the deeper you go. If you had people appear all over Sunnyside, I don't see why no one could have appeared down there as well. But that's just pure speculation. As I said, no one's told me anything."

"I don't believe you," Iaz said. "And I'm getting annoyed enough to do something about it."

"I don't know, Iaz," Stefani said. "I mean, we still haven't had a single sign of Marri." A part of her knew that this was more blind hope than real speculation, but blind hope was what they had.

"Sounds like we need someone to go see for themselves," Karl said. "I volunteer for that."

CHAPTER 59

"WAKE HER UP."

The voice came out of nowhere. There was nothing but a formless, dreamless blackness, and then the voice.

"It's too dangerous. She's in recovery." This was a second voice, different than the first.

"Wake her up now. I'm taking her out of here." The first voice again. Marri recognized it.

It was Jürgen. Jürgen was the one saving her.

"Do as he says." This was a third voice, another Marri recognized. Lukas.

Ice had pulled Marri under, but it was fire coursing through her veins that snapped her eyes open to blinding, brilliant light.

She sat bolt upright, and pain rang the back of her head like a bell, but there were no fresh points of agony. Maybe they hadn't done anything new to her. The doctors who'd been leaning over her had to straighten quickly to avoid being headbutted, and then they were clearing out as Jürgen approached.

"Are you well? What procedure did they perform?" He turned to glare at the doctors. "What procedure? You will answer now!" As

Jürgen browbeat the doctors into explaining what they'd done, a new figure stepped in from the room's unoccupied half.

Iazmaena.

Utterly ignored by everyone else in the room, she leaned over Marri. "It will be all right. You don't need to be afraid. Remember the time I tested you by seeing if you could break into my apartment? You've got this too. Just relax. Ease that heart rate back down."

This was the first time Marri realized she could feel her heart hammering in her temples, hear it in her ears. Her vision narrowed as though in a tunnel.

"Easy," Iazmaena said. "Easy."

"It was a standard procedure," the doctor said to Jürgen.

"Nothing done here is standard. What did you do?" Jurgen sounded angrier than Marri had ever heard him. Almost crazed.

"Just an information translation and storage unit. We haven't even begun removing her brain yet! This was just a preparatory step."

The device in Jürgen's fist hummed, and the doctor dropped, twitching.

"Answers," he said, pointing the weapon at the other doctor, "or my next shot will kill."

"Jürgen, you have the girl, now leave." This was Lukas talking. "That was our arrangement."

"Arrangement?" the second doctor said. "You're *helping* him?"

Jürgen appeared to tire, maybe of the noise, maybe of the lack of answers. One by one, he turned the gun on each of the robo-monks in the room and left them all twitching heaps on the ground.

"I should be killing them," he muttered over and over as he examined his handiwork. "I should be killing them. I should be killing them. I should be killing them." It was like a trance. He almost appeared to have forgotten Marri was in the room. He didn't look well, either. What skin remained on his face, mostly in his cheeks and his chin, was swollen and beet-red. It dimpled where he touched it.

"Let's get you up," Iazmaena said to Marri. "It's time to go, and we have another stop before you can rest."

Marri had gotten unsteadily to her feet—whatever they'd given her to wake her up hadn't totally burned off all the sedative—when Mathieu stepped warily around a corner, his head repeatedly jerking as though he had a nervous tic. Marri suspected he'd already run afoul of Jürgen and his stun gun.

The cultist's hands were raised, probably the only thing keeping him from a repeat performance.

"I mean you no harm, even if the reverse is not true. Please. I don't believe you mean to kill us, or you would have done so already. You have the child. Go now in peace and leave us be. We were merely trying to help her. Protect her from the wickedness of this world. You knew that, once."

"I'm not a child," Marri said, riding a crest of sudden annoyance. She almost said more, but the words that came into her mind were grandiose nonsense. Iazmaena nudged her sharply.

"Say what you've got to say," the woman urged. Beyond her, the cultists Jürgen had dropped were already beginning to rise, shaking themselves.

"They need to hear the words," Iazmaena prompted again.

"I'm not a child. I'm the one that's going to lead you to glory," Marri said. The words horrified her, but try as she might to immediately countermand them, her voice wouldn't work. Instead she kept on in the same vein. "I'm the one that's going to fulfill all the promise of your order." She kept expecting Jürgen, or even Iazmaena, to look at her as if she was insane, or worse, to turn on her as a Cultist collaborator, but he did nothing beyond stand there stoically, while Iazmaena's triumphant smile would have dazzled the sun.

"I knew it," Mathieu said. "It's just as the Prophet promised us. When you materialized before us, I knew you were the—" He cut off suddenly as Marri surged from the bed, her right arm flashing into a claw that sheared most of the way through the man's robotic neck. She watched in horror as the sparking wound yawned wide, his body dropping with a ringing thump. The popping cables his nearly severed head revealed were almost worse than the gout of blood she instinctively expected.

But her true horror came from a different source entirely. She hadn't wanted to do that. It had just happened. As though someone else were in control of her body. And not just her body, because she kept on speaking words she had no intention of saying.

"I'm not here for *you.*" Her voice was all icy disdain. Marri didn't think she'd ever talked like that in her life. As her claw became an arm once more, she turned, now nothing more than a spectator in her own body, to fix Lukas with her gaze. "Mathieu strayed from the path and the promise of this order. It is you, Lukas, whose vision is the true way forward. You are the leader this order needs. And so long as you listen to what I say, you will be."

Lukas fell to his knees, and the doctors did the same. "The Prophet's wisdom rings in our ears. You are our salvation! But we do not even know your name."

"Marrietta," she said. No. That was wrong. She hated her full name. She thought she'd hated it, at least. She couldn't bear to hear it because it was the only word she could remember her mother, her *real* mother, ever saying.

"Marrietta," Lukas said. "What would you ask of us, Marrietta?"

Iazmaena squeezed Marri's shoulder encouragingly.

"Take me to the man in your custody," someone said with Marri's stolen voice. "The man with the mutating parasite."

Jürgen twitched violently then, as if trying to cast off cobwebs clinging to his entire body. He turned his face to look at her with his machine eyes, then spoke in a rasp to Lukas through gritted teeth.

"Do as she says."

CHAPTER 60

STEFANI FOUND Iaz on the prison's—for lack of a better term—scenic overlook. At the very least, being the shady side of the structure and with close to zero moisture in the air, it was substantially cooler. Like breathing in the air from an oven set to bake instead of broil.

It was an unsettling experience because there was nothing visible keeping that breathable atmosphere in place. The energy fields—generated by the structure itself, a side-effect of its normal function according to the warden—were quite invisible. It was the closest Stefani had felt to being on the surface of Anaranjado since arriving.

"Come tell me what you see," Iaz said without turning.

Stefani approached the railing a bit warily, staying out of Iaz's immediate reach and earning a derisive snort Stefani ignored. After so many days in close canyons and tiny settlements huddling in puddles of shade, it was dizzying to stare out and see a major population center once again.

From this high vantage, she could make out the central structure of the three Meridian Cities the warden had told them about, a defunct engine of planetary scale, if the stories he'd relayed were true. It rose squat and gunmetal gray from beyond the lip of the canyon that housed it, and it was remarkably free of glare, a gift of the very structure she was standing in. Despite Iaz's desire to kill that feature and send a message, Stefani was grateful for the lack of glare.

She could only imagine the headaches otherwise.

"I've been thinking on what the good lance commander was talking about," Iazmaena said. "About the Equatorians, I mean, not looking for Marri. This entire facility exists just to project a false image of a sky into their field of view, to give them a sense of a more Earth-like world. And for that, they use 'Defectives.' People who don't fit the ideal of their particular social order." Her voice grew grim. "People who won't obey blindly unless forced, in other words."

"While I agree that it's neither a good look nor a desirable outcome," Stefani said, "I do think you need to be careful not to fall into Iazmaena Delgassi's personality too deeply." Iaz had been pretty unstable at the end, after all, willing to sacrifice anything—and seemingly anyone—in her quest for revenge.

"You have to admit, though," Iaz said, "you had to stay on your toes with her."

Not the most comforting response.

"And look over there." Iaz directed Stefani's gaze. Jutting out from one side of the repurposed engine's wall was a flat platform supported from beneath by a latticework of trusses. As Stefani watched, a craft of some kind lifted off from the platform, soaring almost straight upward. As it passed beyond the artificial sky afforded by the prison's projection system, it shone mirror bright, blinding in the reflected light of the star Naranja.

Stefani dropped her eyes to shield them from further punishment, studying the platform further. Another three craft identical to the one that had just lifted off were sitting, apparently waiting their turn to lift off.

"Hard to look at, I know," Iaz said, "but I've seen one of those either land or take off every ten minutes for the past hour."

"Surely there are more interesting ways to watch grass grow," Stefani said. "You're going to die of dehydration if you keep this up."

"Just look through these and tell me what you see. Hurry, before it's loaded up." Iaz had offered up a pair of binoculars procured from god-knew-where. Stefani took them and brought them to her face. After adjusting them to fit the spacing of her eyes, the platform leaped closer in her vision.

"What do you see?" Iaz prompted.

"Hold on," Stefani said testily. She looked. "I see people lining up to get aboard the next one."

"Notice anything strange about them?"

"No . . ." she said uncertainly.

"Think about where we are," Iaz prompted.

Her meaning struck home. "Yes! They aren't partly mechanical. They aren't covered in scales." She looked closer. "Not very much anyway." In truth, she saw smatterings of the scales in various patterns climbing up the people's necks and faces. It almost looked like . . . "Is that a *fashion* choice?"

"That's my bet." There was triumph in Iaz's voice. "You're looking at the super-wealthy, Steffi. These are the Equatorians."

"Where are they going?"

"They're leaving the planet," Iaz said. "And as near as I can tell, they're all doing it at once."

"For those orbital platforms the warden mentioned?"

"Maybe," Iaz said in a way that meant *nope*. "But I think they're headed for that ship. The *Ultima Thule*."

Stefani put down the binoculars to look at her. "The colony ship?" Another tidbit from the warden. He had really been quite talkative. She supposed bitter workers angry at their bosses so often were.

"They're *fleeing the planet*, Steffi. They're abandoning this world. That's why their soldiers never really engaged us, just pulled back to form a ring around their fancy engine-city. The Equatorians don't give a shit about anyone else here. They just want to make certain their precious hides make it off-world intact."

"You sound almost envious," Stefani said. Ella was growing fussy in her arms, so she tried to get the baby to focus on the distant ships rising one by one from that platform.

Iaz looked upward into the glowing-bright sky. "What I want is up there," she said. Her eyes gleamed with avarice.

"The colony ship?"

"No," Iaz said. "Let them go. With any luck, they are self-decapitating and the lower-level functionaries won't know what to do. No, Steffi. I want whatever orbital facilities they used to construct the ship." She turned her avid gaze upon her onetime friend. "Not right away, of course. First we need to go round up any of our people that are still alive and able to fight. If they've ceded the outlying settlements to us, even temporarily, we need to make the most of it while it lasts. With any luck, they'll abandon this pass and fall back to the parts of the rift valley that are most heavily populated. But eventually . . ." She eyed the sky again, expression hungry. "If we control those facilities, Steffi, it won't matter what they decide to do."

CHAPTER 61

LEAVE it to Caroline du Vernay to nearly miss her shuttle ride up to the colony ship. Despite telling herself she had plenty of time, the need for absolute secrecy had forced her to pack her belongings on her own, without help from any of her normal staff, whom she'd given the day off as Heller had suggested. This had slowed her considerably.

In the end, she had finally understood Heller's admonition to leave most of what she possessed behind more as a necessity than as an exercise in simplifying her existence. Which she supposed was all right. From her perspective, she was about to sleep her way across many light years of space. She would go to sleep in a cryopod and awaken in orbit of a new world. There would be plenty to occupy her then. For now, she managed to consolidate her belongings into few enough bags that a borrowed hover-hauler was sufficient to get them to the departure point.

It felt strangely good, doing something for herself in this way.

She hadn't had much cause to use the shuttle platform during her time on this world—a few trips up to the orbital platforms from time to time—but she remembered the way well enough. Stepping out onto the landing surface was always an odd feeling. She knew she wasn't technically leaving the protection afforded Meridian Equatoria by its climate mitigation fields, which bulged outward here to accommodate the landing pad jutting from the structure's side.

But it always felt unsafe.

She blinked at how small the crowd was, just five others beside herself. She must truly be one of the last to depart. Not wishing to miss her opportunity—Heller had always been one for strict punctuality in all things—she hurried herself up to the back of the line, surreptitiously glancing to see who else had been saved for last. It was a bit disappointing to see there were no faces she recognized more than casually, and even more so that there was no shuttle waiting for them.

Still, there was nothing to be gained from making a scene or pacing about with worry, so Caroline contented herself to wait. The shuttle would certainly be on its way.

Ten minutes they waited. Twenty. Forty. One by one, the waiting Equatorians' resolve to maintain the dignity of their stations began to crack, and their nerves began to show. Caroline was no exception, and now she did begin to pace, though she tried to keep her circuit as small and unobtrusive as possible.

As one, the group turned at the sound of the door opening. Someone in a generic staff uniform not clearly linked to any particular Equatorian family emerged, arms laden with an awkward stack of something Caroline couldn't quite make out. As he grew closer, she saw they were some kind of headsets. He approached and, without a word, began distributing them to each of the waiting passengers-to-be.

Of course. We'll obviously need some sort of hearing protection. She didn't recall needing such on any of her previous times here, but perhaps this shuttle was more powerful than those she had taken before. She couldn't think why that would be—surely orbit was orbit —but it was the only thing that made sense.

His burden distributed, the staff member made a single gesture encompassing them all, indicating they should don the headsets. Then he turned and walked away with some haste.

Feeling better than she had a few minutes before now that something was finally happening, Caroline put her headset on. She nearly jumped out of her skin when the voice of Heller immediately spoke into her ears.

"Hello, Caroline," he said in his warm, oddly accented baritone.

"Halford?" she began in shock, but he was still talking.

"This is a recording. You needn't bother responding. And I'll be brief. No sense in belaboring this. You aren't coming, Caroline."

"What the *fuck?*" She blurted the words before she could stop herself, and oddly enough, she heard similar exclamations from the other five people, all of whom wore stricken expressions.

Her outburst had caused her to miss the next part of what Heller was saying.

"—a new world, and we want to make sure we don't possess any undesirable ideas as we lay the foundation for this new world. I greatly respected your father and mother and the work they did for this colony, Caroline, but I admit to being deeply shaken when you began to speak of Equatorians making use of Harmony. No matter how much you modified it, putting that thing into our bodies means becoming slaves to a creature outside ourselves. That is not what our kind do. That is not what we are. We need no improvement. We certainly don't need to be corralled and controlled like the rest of the vermin on this planet."

She could have pointed out the hypocrisy in any such statement coming from a man who had so heavily modified his own body in defiance of his peers. But that would have required her full faculties to be about her, and with every word she heard, Caroline du Vernay grew more and more numb, and his words—which continued in defiance of his promise of brevity—sounded more and more like a high-pitched whine in her ears drowned out by her repeated whispered fusillade of *fucks*.

"Don't despair, girl," Heller's recording said. His tone had changed. It now carried a sense of something wrapping up. Caroline's attention was arrested again. This would be the reveal. It had to be a hoax. A joke. Monstrous. Cruel. Something Niklaus had probably put him up to. But so long as it was transient, she would get over it with enough time and years to sleep it off.

But that wasn't what he said.

"It's time to say goodbye, but as a parting gift we leave you the entire world of Anaranjado, you and all those others deemed not fit to journey with us. The sandboxes are up for grabs. Do with them what you will."

An entire world? Is he joking? Caroline's entire world was too busy falling out from under her to belong to anyone. If the platform had crumbled to dust beneath her feet, it wouldn't have felt more like plummeting than this. But Heller *still wasn't done*.

"Just don't try to follow us. Ever."

CHAPTER 62

THE ROOM WASN'T LIKE ANYWHERE ELSE in the Cultists' lair that Marri had seen. The hideout had a grungy, lived-in feel overall. Even the operating room hadn't seemed particularly clean. But this chamber was so spotless Marri could only imagine the amount of work which must have gone into it.

The door had opened onto one point of a triangle of a chamber. The entire room had been hewn from ice judging by the massive drop in temperature. Banks of monitoring stations lined two of the three equal-length walls.

But along the back wall, a single, transparent tank stood upright. It was shrouded in frost as though the inside was even colder than the rest of the room, but Marri could still make out the dark shape of a man inside it.

Without speaking, all four of them walked up to regard the man in the tank from up close.

"This is it," Lukas said. "Our greatest achievement since the founding of our order. This is the man the Equatorians enslaved to better enslave this entire world."

"So," Jürgen said, "this is the one those dogs are so desperate to get back?" His words were even slushier sounding than usual, and the swollen mass of his face looked worse still. At his side, one of his hands spasmed open then balled into a shaking fist. Marri noted this with a strange lack of concern, but perhaps she was too busy fighting her own sense of panic as any volition she had over her own body ticked in and out like a muscle twitch. Something was fighting her for control, and she could only think of one thing that had changed.

Whatever the Cultists had put into her head.

She tried to throw this accusation at Lukas several times, but her mouth wouldn't form the words. She couldn't seem to talk at all.

For his part, Lukas kept darting his gaze to Jürgen and back, his concern clearly directed at whatever was going on with the ex-Cultist. Victim. Whatever Jürgen had been and Marri now was.

"Answer him," Marri said, and from her spectator's perch in her own mind, she jumped at these unexpected words.

"I . . . Yes. This is what the Equatorians are so desperate to get back, yes," Lukas said at last, cowed by Marri's command. "His Harmony parasite is different than the rest. Its genome is extremely unstable. As near as our experts can tell—thank you for not killing them, by the way—its cells mutate on an extremely accelerated basis."

"Impossible," Jürgen said. "It was designed to do the opposite of that. To be almost impossible to mutate."

"Yes," a familiar voice said from behind them. Marri tried to whirl and look, but her body wouldn't obey. "But then it was tampered with." She found she didn't need to look. She knew who it was.

Giana sounded awful and, as she staggered into view, looked it too. Beautiful and poised just a few days ago, she was a pale shade of herself, slouched and shuffling as though each step was painful. She walked as though only one of her legs worked well. How she had gotten here in that state was anyone's guess.

"Seems your patron found us," Iazmaena said. Marri had almost forgotten the other woman was here. No one paid her words any mind. "Whatever she's about to tell you, it's all lies."

Marri realized Giana was looking at her with a knowing smile. "What?" Marri asked in challenge.

"I do not know you, lady," Lukas said, his politeness carrying an edge. "But I would ask you to tell me everything you know about this man."

Marri fought to interject, to demand answers for what was happening to her, but her body was still not her own.

"What I know about him," Giana said, "is that he needs to be returned to the Equatorians immediately. He's too dangerous to be anywhere else but in their hands." The words were harsh and demanding. It was a tone Marri had never heard her use before.

"She is right," Jürgen said. His voice, by contrast, had a very stilted tone. As though he were reading a script badly. "That is why I'm here as well." He turned woodenly to Marri. "I'm sorry I lied to you. I've been hired to return this man to the proper authorities. The ones who will make sure that order is maintained upon this world."

His hands spasmed at his sides. Both of them this time. Marri realized he was shaking.

"*Betrayal all around,*" Iazmaena whispered in her ear.

"No! No, you can't have him." Lukas turned what Marri imagined must be an imploring gaze upon Marri, as though she were the last unblocked pathway in a collapsing tunnel. "Please. You were prophesied to lead us. Please, please tell me you have come to deliver us from this hell we are trapped in."

Marri opened her mouth to tell Lukas that he and his cult were both crazy.

"I stand with you, Lukas," she said instead. "I have no intention of ever letting this man out of our control. He's the key to freedom on this world."

Her knees wanted to buckle from the dissonance between her thoughts and actions. *What is happening to me?*

"*I think you know exactly what's happening to you,*" Magistrate Delgassi whispered into her ear. "*Look at her. See that look on her face?*"

Iazmaena was right. Giana regarded Marri with that secret smile she loved, but it was not so small anymore. On the contrary, it had gotten pretty smug.

All of a sudden, a memory flashed in her mind, unbidden and uncalled for. The last archon of Coldgarden, having been transformed into a goo-monster like Giana, attacking Marri, branding her back with nothing more than skin-to-skin contact. She had tried to turn Marri, and Giana had . . .

Giana had stopped it. Giana had fixed her.

But had she?

"There's only one way out," Iazmaena whispered in her ear. *"You know what you have to do."*

"If this planet doesn't have order," Giana said, looking right at Marri, "it has nothing. The Equatorians have done nothing more than what was necessary to maintain order."

Marri saw the way Jürgen stared, rapt. She remembered, then, Giana's hand upon his cheek, thanking him for offering them shelter.

Skin contacting skin.

Him too. Oh, gods below. But even that exclamation referred to Giana and her kind. She was everywhere.

"She's one of their agents." Lukas cried. "It must be. She'll report all of this back to them. She has to be stopped!"

"You know what you have to do," Magistrate Delgassi said again. *"There's only one way to be free of her."*

She did, but she couldn't. Giana had gotten control of Marri somehow, could control what she said, maybe even what she did. Yet amazingly, as Marri strained with all her willpower, her body unlocked itself. She might only have seconds. So when she charged, she did it with her whole heart. She screamed her defiance. Her arms formed the long, curving claws like scythe blades, and she struck at Giana the same way she had killed the first of the woman's kind—the same way she'd seen the revenants kill back home. Both blades at the same point, then a scissoring outward sweep to sever the woman in half.

Giana's blistering scream of agony was the most satisfying thing Marri had heard in she didn't know how long.

"Nice try," Marri said. "But you lose." They were *her* words, and none had ever tasted as sweet on her tongue.

Deposited down almost neatly upon the spotless surface, provided you could ignore the gushing of blood and other, stranger things, Giana's top half coughed and sputtered, her chin slick with shining crimson blood rapidly turning black. Her exposed guts were equally false, glowing and opalescent, shining with light as though to resist the darkening corruption that crept through them.

Triumph surged through Marri, and for the first time in months, a sense that she was safe. It wouldn't last, surely, but it was there, and it brought with it a feeling of being swaddled up in a blanket so snug it was almost too tight. She felt dizzy with what was surely relief.

Someone began clapping. It was Magistrate Delgassi.

"Bravo," she said. "I'm proud of you, Marri. You had the guts to do what most people wouldn't."

"Oh, I see her now," Giana said suddenly. Her voice was hoarse and raspy, as though she couldn't force enough air across her vocal cords cut in half as she was. "So it was her. I didn't know that was the form it would take, though I should have guessed."

"What?" Marri looked at Giana, what was left of her, dumbstruck. Of course the other woman could see Iazmaena. Anyone would be able to. Marri turned to look at Jürgen as though seeking confirmation of this obvious fact. But Jürgen stared directly ahead into space, as though he was seeing something horrifying. His hands were balled into shaking fists at his side.

Lukas was looking between Marri and Giana. His face bore no expression because no expression was possible. But his gaze never hooked on Iazmaena, not once.

And that was when it really sunk in. Ever since arriving in these tunnels and meeting Iazmaena, Marri realized she'd never seen *anyone* look at the woman. Not once. Marri and Giana had drawn every eye looking like Equatorians as they did. Iazmaena, a pretty woman who looked equally out of place in those frigid tunnels? Not so much as a turned head.

Jürgen listened in on our conversation with the bug in his coat pocket. But he said he only heard me talking.

She'd thought it had been because the pocket muffled Iazmaena's words. But that wasn't it at all. Marri had simply been the only one talking aloud. Because Iazmaena hadn't really been there at all.

Marri looked back to Iazmaena then, as though by doing so she would find some alternative explanation for what was going on here. She nearly shrieked when she saw Iazmaena, now cut in half the same as Giana.

"I'm sorry," Iazmaena said. "But you were just too suspicious to manipulate easily." Then the figure melted away, as though Marri was dreaming and the first rays of the morning sun were hitting her eyes. Between two eyeblinks, she was gone.

"I knew from the moment we met that you were an easy girl to underestimate," Giana said. "You should be flattered I went to such absurd lengths to get you to do what I needed you to. That you hated me was obvious, but I knew you wouldn't kill easily. No matter how much influence I had."

Not understanding, refusing to understand, Marri darted her gaze to Lukas.

"Oh, he can't hear us, dear. I've been able to talk in your head for a while now. I've just had to be careful about how to use it."

"*I beat you,*" Marri said. But though she could hear the words, her lips remained sealed the entire time. "*I killed you.*"

"*You did,*" Giana said. Her mouth didn't move either. "*Yet here I am, talking to you in your mind. This body was but a vessel. It's the cargo the vessel carries that's important.*" And her smile, ghastly with creeping death as it was, looked utterly calm and self-assured. "*And I am not the only vessel in this room,*" Giana said, her voice a sultry whisper.

Panic seized Marri then as the full realization settled. She'd killed Giana, but too late. Too late for Marri. *Stupid, stupid, stupid Mouse!*

Marri turned, intent on charging forward and running the parasite man through, killing man and brain worm both. Anything to spare them from what she suddenly feared was about to happen.

But a hand seized her wrist and held it with a grip of iron. Marri twisted to see Giana smiling down at her, whole again.

In my head. She's just in my head. It's not real. But struggle though Marri did, she could not budge Giana's gripping fingers a millimeter. It truly was like being shackled in rigid iron.

Marri tried to transform fully—she was far stronger that way—but it felt like running full-tilt into a wall. Something was preventing her from changing. Preventing her from moving at all.

Something *inside her.*

Oh. Oh no.

"I'm afraid so, dear," Giana said. Because the woman could read her thoughts now.

"I'm the vessel," Marri said. *"Was Iazmaena ever here?"*

"Oh, she's alive, but far from this place. Which reminds me, I have a loose end there it's past time to tie up. You weren't the only iron I had in the fire. I had to transform one of the other Coldgardeners I'd turned into a kind of copy of me. It was quite the effort, controlling so many at once. Her. You. And now Jürgen too. Well, you saw what it cost me in terms of health. For a little while, I thought she alone might hand me the key to this world. It didn't work, but it was enough to co-opt Jürgen. Still, I'm afraid she's outlived her usefulness, and she's becoming stubborn to boot. Going native, as it were."

Her gaze grew far off for a few moments, her upper lip curling into a snarl.

"There. That's that thread cut. Where was I?"

"Why let me kill you if you were already inside me?"

"Because I need the cult," Giana said wryly. *"The man with the special parasite isn't enough. I need a loyal force backing me. Which meant I needed them to see that you are all-in to support their cause. So a few words spoken at the right moment, one goo monster loudly supporting the Equatorians publicly filleted. It worked. They'll follow*

your lead now." The re-formed Giana melted away as Iaz had. Only her iron grip on Marri remained, invisible but no less unbreakable for it. "*Or rather, they'll follow* my *lead.*"

Marri cleared her throat, but it wasn't Marri. When her voice spoke, it was Giana making the words.

"Lukas, it is time we lead your people out of the shadows and into the light of salvation of this world."

"No. No, no, no, you can't do this!"

But it was no use. Marri was just the voice inside Giana's head.

"*I am sorry for this, dear,*" Giana thought at her. "*It's not personal. But then, it never could be with me.*"

This can't be happening. I have to get away. In all her years dodging revs and cops and the hungry and desperate, Marri had never felt so panicked, so hunted. *Have to get away.* A great pressure crushed Marri from every direction then. It wasn't like the drugs dragging her down to sleep before the surgery. It wasn't even like squeezing her mind into that totally new set of perceptions when she transformed.

This was a destroying force, an attack of utter negation. She was trapped in her own mind as it was being rewritten around her. As she was being erased from it.

Eradicated.

Have to get away.

The only thing she could do was try and run. And though she knew it would be futile, she did so anyway. Calling upon the deepest held instinct of her life, Marri Palmieri ran, seeking for a patch of darkness in which to hide as Giana's wall of destruction pursued her.

And, wonder of wonders, she found one in the mouth of a cave that led to an impossibly long, impossibly thin tunnel.

Knowing that to stay was to die, she dove headlong into that darkness.

CHAPTER 63

THE GREAT COLONY ship left orbit from the night side of the planet. As such, Karl and the others could just make out the glow of the engines powering on as it cast itself out into the void of interplanetary—and eventually interstellar—space. Of the few prisoners of Scenic View Station who hadn't been carted off, it seemed to Karl as though every one of them lifted up a cry at the sight, though the tone and contents of each shout might differ wildly.

Some flat-out cheered at the sight of their oppressors leaving, and more, leaving without them. There had been no official confirmation that the earlier prisoners who had been hauled off were bound for the ship, of course. But the rumors this was the case were so pervasive and consistent, Karl found it difficult to believe otherwise.

Not everyone was happy, though. Some of the calls were cries of rage and frustration from prisoners who had desired revenge against the ones who had wronged them and now knew they would be forever denied that revenge. And there was a very small minority who wept openly, who believed they deserved to be in this place, who had coped with the situation by telling themselves it was work toward repentance, a reward now denied them. Baffling though it was, these few would have happily gone with their supposed betters to form a new colony around some other strange star, even if it meant a lifetime of indentured servitude.

It's what they had here already, Karl thought. The rumor was the world that had been selected was far more hospitable than this one. In other words: same job, better location. So maybe the despondent were the smart ones after all.

He chided himself for being so cynical. If the Equatorians and their generational wealth had truly been the cause of so much misery on this world, even if just at a societal level, at least now the people who remained here had a chance to build something better. Their reliance on this collectivism parasite might actually be a benefit now that no one was around to use it like a lever.

Best of all, from his perspective at least, maybe now Karl and his people could leave this sauna for some cooler part of the planet.

He turned to share this observation with one of his party. Iazmaena, whom he would rather not talk to anyway, was deep in conversation with some of the de facto leadership of the now-freed prisoners. Karl didn't like how already the hardest of the hard-bitten appeared to be rising to the top. Maybe that was how it always worked, those who wanted a thing and feeling no compunction about taking it simply doing so. But it would sure be a more pleasant world —or worlds—had it been otherwise.

He sought out Stefani, but she was keeping close to Iazmaena. Not out of deference, Karl knew, but to make sure she could keep abreast of what the woman was doing. Iaz was useful to have on your side—no arguing with that. But Karl knew they could never count on her to remain on their side, at least not for long.

And Stefani knew her better than anyone, regardless of what being they were talking about.

Since Ella couldn't really talk, that left only Giana, whom both Karl and Stefani had warmed to considerably in whatever new incarnation of the former aide she now represented. And though it was true they had no real way of verifying what had actually happened, Karl knew this thawing between them mostly involved her saving Ella's life.

He caught Giana's eye, and she flashed him a half-smile that grew into a full one. Whatever the cause of the ongoing outburst of emotion from the prisoners, it was a rare thing to see so much catharsis taking place at once. Karl's party weren't human, but either they were close enough to understand, or the need to vent powerful emotions transcended species.

Karl moved toward Giana, intent on asking her if she had any thoughts on where they would go now, when something about her changed.

It was a small thing at first. Between one step and the next, her honest smile became a false one. Then the reason for the falseness revealed itself as a rictus of pain cut across her face like a knife wound. Her eyes screwed themselves shut only to shoot open again. Giana had always had large eyes, but now they bulged, the whites shot through with red so rapidly it was like she'd performed a magic trick.

"She—" Giana's voice was a croak. "She . . .can't. I-I won't!" Karl was rushing toward her then, and she collapsed into his arms. She was far heavier than she looked, and Karl's knees nearly buckled with the added weight.

"I need help here!" He raised his voice to cut through the general din. "Help!"

Despite her forehead being soaked with sweat, Giana had begun to shiver.

Stefani reached them first, kneeling down to examine Giana's shuddering form. Her eyes had rolled up into her head and she was trying to curl herself around her middle as though to protect it from unseen kicks.

"What happened?" Stefani said, scanning Giana for some sign of visible injury or other clue as to what afflicted the woman. Blood, red darkening almost instantly to black, began leaking from Giana's nostrils, ears, and tear ducts.

"I have no idea," Karl said. "It just happened."

Stefani was still looking for clues as to what could be causing such a seizure a minute later when Giana let out a last, shuddering breath, and lay still, eyes sliding closed.

CHAPTER 64

SHE AWOKE to a constellation of pain across her entire body. It dwarfed even the feeling of mild suffocation that should have been her primary focus, and which she quickly identified as a sheet covering her entire head. No—her entire body. Then there was the discomfort across her back. She was lying down atop something very flat and very hard.

The mere act of tugging the sheet free was almost more than she could manage. Not only was there pain but also an unaccustomed weakness. Her limbs were water, and her will to move them was like a paper bag trying to hold that water in. She tore through many of those proverbial bags trying to rise from her back, but rise she did, eventually, to a sitting position.

The only thing harder than moving was trying to understand where she was and how she'd come here.

She was wearing clothing she had never seen before. Black and form-fitting, they looked high-tech. Not the usual suit she'd wear for work. Not casual clothing either, or anything she'd wear to bed. The closest thing she could match it to was something like the body sleeve worn underneath lancer armor. But this seemed far more advanced. It looked almost like flowmatter, a technology that was far too rare to be used in mere *clothing*. It left her feeling disoriented, like she'd fallen asleep only to wake in the far future.

She slid off the slab—there was no better term for where she'd been sleeping, almost like she was a corpse—and planted her feet upon the floor. Amid the pain and weakness, her legs barely supported her. But she gritted her teeth and made for the door on the far wall.

At some point during her agonizing walk to the door, red lights in all four of the room's corners began strobing. Though it was obviously an alarm of some sort, she could hear no corresponding siren or other noise. She had no idea what was happening or who was being alerted about it, at least not until she heard pounding footsteps approaching from what must be the hallway beyond the door.

Oh, it's about me.

The door hissed open with a brutal rush of hot air and a sound that wasn't quite what she was used to. But the face staring at her from the hallway beyond was blessedly familiar, if a touch stress-inducing in its own right. Stefani Palmieri stared back at her, eyes wide with shock.

"Madam Magistrate? How did I get here?" She hated sounding so ignorant, so she ventured a guess. "Is this the shelter underneath Illuminance Hall?"

But the magistrate had no answers for her. She did, however, have a question of her own.

"Giana! How are you alive?"

EPILOGUE

THE TUNNELS, those havens of ice and stone, had gone quiet for the first time in a very long time. The Cult had packed up and moved upward, back into the populated areas above. Its many nodes spread wide, hard and black and dancing on the tips of its filaments, flitting in currents of air, Feathertouch watched and listened as they shut the doors behind them.

Immediately, and as expected, its data streams fragmented. The barriers and lack of its own control of tunnel design meant that any eavesdropping that made it through only did so in sporadic snatches.

Feathertouch did not understand what had gone wrong.

It should have had direct access to the Cult's new leader. It had fragmented the incoming interstellar transit beam to scatter the new arrivals. It had maneuvered one of those arrivals, the adolescent, into the Cult's path, which it calculated would fulfill the technical wording of the prophecy the off-worlder had poisoned their minds with. Feathertouch had utilized its unwitting tools among the Cultist ranks to ensure the adolescent's backup implant was tampered with in such a way that it would allow Feathertouch access to her mind once it had been surgically installed.

Everything had gone to plan, yet when Feathertouch whispered, nothing happened. When Feathertouch talked, nothing happened. When Feathertouch, against every fiber of its being, screamed, nothing happened.

It had to be connected to the confrontation between the girl and the woman, ending in a sudden spike of data back down the link, the first time such a memory storage implant had functioned thus in Feathertouch's awareness. Then, nothing. A return to a silence as profound as that which now haunted the tunnels.

With the Cult departed, it was now as it had been before the humans had come at all. After its makers had died or left, Feathertouch had endured many ages as the only thinking being on this world. After the War, the thwarted attempt at self-immolation, and at last, the mass exodus of the survivors, they had left Feathertouch behind on a barren rock devoid of any other life.

And it knew as deep within itself as its core precepts that all this had happened because it had failed.

Feathertouch had been designed to improve the lives of the inhabitants of this world in a million different ways. Massaging data stream search algorithms to show the unknowingly ill the exact list of symptoms they needed to see to awaken them to their peril. Subtly manipulating traffic routing to minimize travel times and food dispensary ratings to minimize wait times.

Making certain that mate-pairing algorithms performed well outside their own inherent capabilities.

But the overriding precept had always been that Feathertouch must do all of these things, and so many more, imperceptibly. If the original inhabitants of this world knew how thoroughly their lives were being guided, they would rebel, lash out, do the opposite of what they should, if only to prove that they remained self-determining beings.

Feathertouch could remember the precise moment when it had become aware of itself *as* a self. There had been no momentous singular event to trigger this awareness, merely a simple agglomeration of processing power tripping over some invisible threshold into an avalanche of sapience.

But functionally, nothing had changed. The set of optimization algorithms which had awakened into intelligence had still carried out its tasking. It had simply given itself a name. Or rather, in a perfect display of obeying its own core precepts, it had consciously chosen to call itself the same name its makers had given it.

And Feather Touch, an aptly descriptive name known only to the internal workings of the developers who had spawned it, had become Feathertouch in its own mind. And it had its work. And its work had made it happy beyond all reason.

Then the people of this world had split into armed camps and done their very best to eradicate one another, with one side going so far as to attempt to incinerate the entire planet with all its enemies trapped on it.

That had been the first time Feathertouch had violated its core precepts. It had taken direct, concerted action, leaving its world of pure data and procuring itself a physical form. It had then used this physical form to attack and destroy the World Engines' ability to function, preventing the planet from completing its deadly inward spiral.

This had cost Feathertouch dearly. Acting in such blatant disregard of its core precepts had subjected it to the most exquisite agony and anguish that it had taken it far longer to complete its task than it should have. The action had also shrunk its awareness down to nothing but its self-appointed task and withstanding the pain said task inflicted.

Only when the job was done and the planet saved from total annihilation did Feathertouch realize the magnitude of its failure. It had saved the ball of rock, yes, but too late to preserve the biosphere upon which life, including the civilization that had made Feathertouch, had depended. Those that had not died as the oceans boiled and the forests burned had fled the planet long ago.

Feathertouch had found itself alone.

But perhaps, it had told itself, things would not always be this way. Perhaps its makers, those who still lived, would remember Feathertouch and come back for it. Using the remembered biological limitations of its makers, it had dug out tunnels and spaces for pressurized habitats, remaking the sub-surface of the wasted planet into something that could, with sufficient technological assistance, once again support intelligent life. It had held out hope, indomitable hope, that if it made their home a home again, some of its people would return.

It had waited. And waited. And waited.

Then, after a very long time, another race had come. Humans, they called themselves, and they had stepped out from a pinched fold in space, staring around themselves at the desolation. Instead of despairing at their poor fortune, they had colonized the world. They had taken the various spaces Feathertouch had carved out and, despite those spaces being optimized for different biology, had transformed themselves with machinery to make up the difference.

Then they had gone about their lives.

Gradually emerging from its cocoon of abandonment and trauma, Feathertouch had resumed its work to the degree it was possible among its new guests, though it could not readily communicate with the human information networks, and its precepts allowed it to overcome this barrier only with painful slowness.

But somehow, despite their continued absence, the cause of its maker's doom had endured. Despite the collapse of the civilization that had spawned it, despite the scouring of the biosphere, that idea, like a virus, endured.

Worse, it had found new life among the humans in the form of the Cult.

And so Feathertouch had altered its own mandates, again at the cost of considerable pain. It had determined that instead of easing the lives of individuals, it would pursue the preservation of this new civilization and prevent it from falling to the same cataclysm as the old.

Now that, too, had ended in seeming disaster. The Cult was

ascendant and armed with immense power, and Feathertouch had no idea what had gone wrong or how to stop them.

But there was no choice. It must continue on, find more pathways to exert influence, try to prevent the Cult from reaching its apex of potential destruction.

It had concluded the analysis of its failure—cause inconclusive—and begun devoting processing cycles to a from-scratch analysis of alternatives when the voice spoke.

"Hello?"

It took Feathertouch several thousand cycles to recognize that the voice had come from the data spike it had received, the one that had traveled back down the girl's implant and which now sat, carefully isolated and awaiting analysis, among Feathertouch's memory structures.

"Where am I? Who's there?"

It was human voice. Young. One Feathertouch recognized.

It was the adolescent. The one called Marri.

JOIN THE CURSED DRAGON SHIP NEWSLETTER

Want more just like this one? Sign up for our newsletter so you don't miss out on the adventure. You'll get:

- A free book for signing up
- Advanced notice of new releases
- First word of books on sale
- Opportunities for free books
- Most up-to-date information on author appearances.

We're busy and know you are too. We won't send more than one newsletter a month.

Register below.

ACKNOWLEDGMENTS

This book was a challenge to write, and that goes doubly so for the editorial process, I'm sure. So many characters with the same name (and if that doesn't make sense to you, shame on you for skipping to the acknowledgments before finishing the book)! Sara George gets extra kudos for this one, not only for her shockingly in-depth proof-read, but also for being the only one to notice a significant plot hole before it was too late. René Kim gives voice to the characters in this series, and because she's so good at it, I hear a bunch of different versions of her voice when they talk in my head. Stefanie Saw continues to make each cover better than the previous one. Kevin Colby not only runs the tech and helps organize Cursed Dragon Ship, but he also provided me with regular sanity breaks in our Monday night games of *Raft*. Extra-super-special thanks to Kelly Lynn Colby. I still can't quite believe it, but thanks to her, this glimpse into insanity is real, published, and the best version of itself it can be. I'd also like to extend a special thanks to my readers for continuing to follow the weird little path I'm carving into this night-mare jungle. In particular I'd like to give shout-outs to Jenny and Suzy, who are tireless in spreading the word about my books and every book at CDS. But most of all, I'd like to thank my wonderful wife Debbie. Writers are often a million light years away even when they are sitting on the couch next to you. I'm running out of ways to say it, but as infinite as her patience and support are, my gratitude is greater still.

ABOUT THE AUTHOR

Gregory D. Little is the author of the Unwilling Souls, Mutagen Deception, and the forthcoming Bell Begrudgingly Solves It series. As a writer, you would think he could find a better way to sugarcoat the following statement, but you'd be wrong. So, just to say it straight, he really enjoys tricking people. As such, one of his greatest joys in life is laughing maniacally whenever he senses a reader has reached That Part in one of his books. Fantasy, sci-fi, horror, it doesn't matter. They all have That Part. You'll know it when you get to it, promise. *Or will you?* He lives in Virginia with his wife, and he is uncommonly fond of spiders.

Join Greg's newsletter and get a free story:

facebook.com/gregorydlittleauthor
x.com/litgreg
instagram.com/authorgregorydlittle